THE THIRD WOMAN
MARK BURNELL

HarperCollins*Publishers*

HarperCollins*Publishers*
1 London Bridge Street,
London, SE1 9GF

www.harpercollins.co.uk

This paperback edition 2019
1

First published in Great Britain by HarperCollins*Publishers* 2005

A catalogue record for this book
is available from the British Library

ISBN: 978-0-00-833920-3

Set in Meridien by Palimpsest Book Production Limited,
Falkirk, Stirlingshire

Printed and bound in Great Britain by
CPI Group (UK) Ltd, Croydon, CR0 4YY

MIX
Paper from
responsible sources
FSC™ C007454

For Greta with love

The true religion of America
has always been America.

NORMAN MAILER

Most people are other people. Their thoughts
are someone else's opinions, their lives a
mimicry, their passions a quotation.

OSCAR WILDE

Early October

He loved the ritual. It was as essential to his enjoyment of the countryside as the open space or clean air. A final stroll around the property before bed, the last of a cigar to smoke, the glowing embers of a good cognac warming his stomach. His only regret was that he didn't come here often enough. Otto Heilmann stepped out of his dacha onto brittle grass; five below zero, he estimated, perhaps even ten.

His guests had gone to bed. Their cars were parked beside the boat-shed; a black Mercedes 4x4 with dark glass, and an Audi A8 with an auxiliary engine and armour-plating. Frost had turned both windscreens opaque.

Heilmann wandered to the edge of the lake, trailing clouds of breath and smoke. The silvery light of a three-quarter moon shone on the ice. He saw buttery pinpricks in the blackness of the far shore; two dachas, one belonging to a senior prosecutor from St Petersburg, the other to a Finnish architect.

There was no cloud and only the faintest whisper of a breeze. Heilmann smoked for a while. As Bruno Manz, a Swiss travel consultant based in St Petersburg, he felt a very long way from the grim years of the German Democratic Republic. A long way from Erich Mielke, his Stasi boss during those years, and a long way from Wolfasep, the ubiquitous industrial-strength detergent that was the defining odour of the Honecker regime for millions of East Germans. Once smelled, never forgotten, a scar of memory.

He tossed his soggy cigar stump onto the ice and continued his circuit. Along the lake shore, past the creaking jetty, up towards the wood-shed.

'Hello, Otto.'

A female voice. He thought he recognized it. Except she was supposed to be in Copenhagen. But it was her face that emerged from the darkness of the birch forest.

Heilmann clutched the coat over his chest. 'I hope you know what to do if I have a heart attack.'

Krista Jaspersen stared deep into his eyes and smiled. 'Don't worry, Otto. I'll know exactly what to do.'

He wasn't reassured.

She was wearing thick felt boots, a great overcoat and the sable hat he'd given her two nights ago at the Landskrona restaurant on top of the Nevskij Palace Hotel in St Petersburg.

He tried to recapture his breath. 'What are you *doing*, Krista?'

'Waiting for you.'

'Out here?'

'I remembered your routine.'

An answer of sorts, Heilmann conceded, yet hardly adequate. 'You could have phoned to say you were coming. Like normal people do.' He glanced over one shoulder, then the other. 'How did you get here?'

'By car.'

'I mean . . . *here*.'

'The men at the gate let me through.'

'Just like that?'

'Just like that.'

She looked the same – long fair hair, dark green eyes, a mouth of invitation – but she was radiating a difference that Heilmann couldn't quite identify.

'It's freezing,' he said. 'Let's go inside.'

'You have guests.'

'They're asleep.'

'I'm not staying, Otto.'

'The mystery is why you're here at all. You should be in Copenhagen.'

Krista reached inside her coat and pulled out a gun. A SIG-Sauer P226. Moonlight glittered on a silencer.

There was no outrage. That surprised her; Heilmann had a notoriously fragile temper. Instead, after a digestive pause, he simply nodded glumly and said, 'Let me take a guess: you're not even Danish.'

She shook her head. 'Not really, no.'

'Who are you?'

The seconds stretched as they stared at each other, eyes watering in the cold, neither prepared to look away.

'The stupid thing is, I knew it,' he murmured. 'In my head, I knew it. But I let my heart over-rule and . . .'

'More likely it was another part of your anatomy.'

'You were too good to be true. That was my initial reaction to you.'

'I've been accused of many things but never that.'

A deep breath deflated slowly. 'So . . . what is it?'

'You'll never guess.'

'The ghosts of the past?'

'That doesn't narrow the field much, does it? Not after your glittering career with the Stasi. But no, it's not that.'

His surprise seemed genuine. He considered another option. 'The S-75s?'

Krista smiled. 'I knew you'd say that.'

The S-75 air defence missile was a relic of the Soviet era, prominent in conflicts from Vietnam to the Balkans. Hundreds of them had been trans-ported from the nations of the Warsaw Pact to the Ukraine for decommissioning and dismantling. Many had vanished into thin air, leaving no trace, a feat made possible by the astonishing elasticity of the accounting practices at the Ukrainian Defence Ministry.

'Scrapyard junk,' Heilmann declared.

'Maybe. But you know what they say about muck and brass. How much time have you spent in Kiev over the last decade?'

'I don't know. Plenty. What is your point, Krista?'

'Otto Heilmann, store manager at the Ukraine Hypermarket, flogging the decrepit remains of the Soviet arsenal to Third-World psychopaths. A lucrative business judging by the way you live, Otto. And better than pulling fingernails out of old ladies in the damp cellars of Leipzig, I imagine. The gap in the military inventory from the Soviet era – how much would you say it's worth today?'

'I have no idea.'

'The figure I hear most often is $180 billion. But I've heard higher. Last year, the Ukraine's spending budget was $10 billion. In terms of a trading environment I'd say that left plenty of room for manoeuvre. What do you think?'

'Is that what this is about? Missing missiles?'

'Two hundred of them.'

'They're museum pieces.'

'There's value in antiquity, Otto. Even in yours,' Krista smiled coldly. 'Actually, that's not what this is about. But it's nice to know I was right about you. No, this is a private matter.'

'Between you and me?'

'Between you and your bank.'

'My *bank*?'

'You've over-extended yourself, Otto.'

'So here you are? With a gun?'

'That's right.'

'That's *shit*. I have business with a lot of banks. Which one?'

'Guderian Maier.'

Heilmann looked incredulous. 'You work for *them*? I don't believe you.'

'You made a mistake in Zurich.'

'And you're making one here.'

'Your money's no longer any good.'

'What are you talking about?'

'Most bank managers send you a letter. Yours has sent me.'

Heilmann snorted dismissively. 'Very funny. But banks don't shoot people. So no more games, okay? Just tell me. Why are you here?'

Krista Jaspersen raised the SIG-Sauer P226. 'I've come to close your account, Otto. Permanently.'

Day One

When she opened her eyes, the face beside her was a surprise. She'd expected to be alone in the bedroom of her crumbling apartment off boulevard Anspach. Instead, she found herself in a room with curtains, not shutters, a room overlooking avenue Louise, not rue Saint-Géry.

Brussels, twenty-to-seven on a bitter January morning. Outside, a tram grumbled on the street below. She'd always liked the sound of trams. Next to her, Roland was still asleep, half his head lost in the quicksand of a pillow. Stephanie pulled on his blue silk dressing-gown, which was too big for her, and rolled up the sleeves. In the kitchen, she poured water into the kettle and switched it on.

Gradually, she recalled a day that had started in Asia. She'd called Roland from the airport at Frankfurt while waiting for her connection to Brussels and again when she'd touched down at Zaventem. Earlier, in Turkmenbashi and then on the Lufthansa flight back from Ashgabat, she'd been aware of the familiar sensation; the seep of corruption that always followed the adrenaline rush. She'd needed Roland because she couldn't be alone.

His bathroom belonged in a hotel; heated marble floor, marble sink, fluffy white towels folded over a ladder of hot chrome rails, a soap dish full of Molton Brown miniatures. Typical, really; a bathroom at home to remind him of the hotels he used abroad. Still, lack of imagination in a man was not always a disadvantage.

She showered for five minutes. Stepping on to the white bath-mat in front of the mirror, Stephanie saw Petra Reuter looking back at her. Her other self, the differences between them at that moment counting for nothing, though the body they shared now belonged more to Petra than Stephanie. In that sense, it was a barometer of identity. Where Petra favoured muscular defi-nition, Stephanie slipped happily into softness.

She ran a hand over the stone ripple of her abdomen and looked into a pair of hard, dark eyes. Only her mouth appeared warm and inviting; there was nothing she could do about those generous lips. The rest of her looked cold and mean. When she was in this mood, even the slight bump on her nose – courtesy of two separ-ate breaks – looked large and ugly. Worse was the cosmetic bullet-wound through her left shoulder. In forty-eight hours, beneath an Indian Ocean sun, Stephanie knew she'd despise it; Petra's badge of honour was a reminder of the life she couldn't escape.

She dressed in the crumpled clothes she'd scooped off Roland's sitting-room floor; dark grey combat trousers with a neon-pink stripe down each leg, two T-shirts beneath a Donna Karan jersey and a pair of Caterpillar boots.

Towelling long, dark hair she returned to the kitchen, made coffee, then took two mugs to the bedroom, setting one on Roland's bedside table. He began to stir. She drew the curtains. On avenue Louise, the first hint of rush-hour, head-lights slicing through drizzle.

From behind her came a muffled murmur. 'Marianne.'

Stephanie turned round. 'You look a little . . . crumpled.'

Roland grinned, pleased at the description, then propped himself up on an elbow and patted the mattress. 'Come back to bed.'

'I've got to go.'

'So have I. Now come back to bed.'

'Exactly what kind of investment bank do you work for?'

'The kind that understands a good worker is a happy worker.'

The candle of temptation flickered briefly. Generally, the more attractive the man the more cautious Stephanie was. In her experience, good-looking men tended to make lazy lovers. Not Roland, though.

'Last night,' he said, reaching for the mug, 'that was really something.'

If only you knew.

A surgical procedure to cut away tension. That was what it had been. There, on the floor of the entrance hall, tenderness cast aside as roughly as their clothes. Around nine, they'd gone out to eat at Mont Liban, a Lebanese place on rue Blanche, a couple of minutes' walk away. By the time they'd returned to his apartment, her desire had been back, less frantic but just as insistent. Which was how her clothes had ended up on his sitting-room floor.

Strange to think of it now, like an out-of-body experience. Roland was staring at her through the steam rising from his coffee, his disappointment evident.

'What are you thinking?' she asked.

'That I went to bed with one person and woke up with another.'

Stephanie said, 'I know the feeling.'

It's no longer raining when I step on to avenue Louise. Winter blows shivers through the puddles and snaps twigs from the naked plane trees. Ahead, the rooftop Nikon and Maxell signs are backlit by a cavalry charge of dark cloud.

Brussels; bitter, grey, wet. And perfect.

This city at the heart of the European Union is an ideal home for me. It's a city of bureaucrats. In other words, a city of transient people who shy from the spot-

light and never have to account for their actions. People like me.

In some respects, the city is an airport hub. When I'm here, there's always the feeling that I'm passing through. That I'm a stranger in transit, even in my own bed.

I had a proper home once. It didn't belong to me – it belonged to the man I loved – but it was mine nevertheless. It was the only place I've ever been able to be myself. And yet he never knew my name or what I did.

With hindsight, civilian domesticity – Petra's professional life running in parallel to Stephanie's private life – was an experiment that failed. I took every precaution to keep the two separate, to protect one from the other. But that's the truth about lies: you start with a small one, then need a larger one to conceal it. In the end, they swamp you. Which is exactly what happened. One life infected the other and was then itself contaminated. The consequences were predictable: I hurt the ones I loved the most.

These days I no longer delude myself. That's why I live in Brussels but spend so little time here. It's why I was in Turkmenistan the day before yesterday and why Eddie Sullivan's obituary is in the papers today. It's why I see Roland in the way that I do and it's why he calls me Marianne.

He became my lover in the same way that Brussels became my home; by chance and as a matter of temporary convenience. Random seat assignments put us together. We met on a train, which seems appropriate; sensory dislocation at two hundred miles an hour. All *very contemporary, all very efficient. There is no possibility that I will ever give anything of my soul to him. For the moment, however, like the city itself, he serves a transitory purpose.*

Rue Saint-Géry, the walls smeared with graffiti, the pavements with dog-shit. Home was a filthy five-storey wedge-shaped building with rotten French windows that opened onto balconies sprouting weeds. The bulb had gone in the entrance hall. From her mail-box she retrieved an electricity bill and a mail-shot printed in Arabic. The aroma of frying onions clung to the staircase's peeling wallpaper.

Stephanie's apartment was on the third floor; a cramped bedroom and bathroom at the back with a large room at the front, one quarter partitioned to form a basic kitchenette. There were hints of original elegance – tall ceilings, plaster mouldings, wall panels – but they were damaged, mostly through neglect.

Her leather bag was where she'd left it late yesterday afternoon, at the centre of a threadbare rug laid over uneven stained floorboards. The luggage tag was still wrapped around a handle. So often it was the smallest detail that betrayed you. In the past she'd been supported by an infrastructure that ensured there were no oversights, no matter how trivial. These days, as an independent, there was no one.

On the floor by the fireplace a cheap stereo

stood next to a wicker basket containing the few CDs she'd collected over ten months. They were the only personal items in the apartment. She slipped one into the machine. *Foreign Affairs* by Tom Waits; more than any photograph album could, it mainlined into the memory.

The first albums she'd listened to were the ones she'd borrowed from her brother: Bob Dylan, *Bringing It All Back Home*; David Bowie, *Heroes*; The Smiths, *The World Won't Listen*. She remembered being given something by Van Morrison by a boy who wanted to date her. Not a good choice. She'd disliked Van Morrison then and still did.

Elton John's 'Saturday Night' had been the song playing on the radio the first time she sold herself in the back seat of a stranger's car. Every time she heard the song now, that same meaty hand grasped her neck, jamming her face against the car door. The same fingernails drew bloody scratches across her buttocks. Later, she'd been routinely brutalized and humiliated but nothing had ever matched the emotional impact of that initiation. She felt she'd been hung, drawn and quartered. And that the music coming from the tinny radio in the front had somehow been an accomplice.

Sometimes mainlining into the memory was as risky as mainlining into a vein; you didn't necessarily get the rush you were depending on. So she changed the CD to *Absolute Torch & Twang*, a k.d.lang album she'd discovered as Petra.

Petra meant no bad memories. In fact, no memories at all.

She emptied the leather bag. Dirty clothes, a roll of dollars, a wash-bag containing strengthened cat-gut in a plastic dental-floss dispenser, an Australian passport in the name of Michelle Davis, a ragged copy of Iain Pears's *An Instance of the Fingerpost* and a guide to Turkmenistan featuring out-of-date maps of Ashgabat and Turkmenbashi.

In the bathroom, beneath the basin, she kept a battered aluminium wash-bowl. She shredded the passport, luggage tag, receipts and ticket-stubs, then dropped them into the bowl, which she placed on the crumbling balcony. She squirted lighter fuel over the remains and set light to them. A small funeral pyre for another version of her.

There were four messages on the answer-phone including one from Tourisme Albert on boulevard Anspach. *Your tickets are ready for collection. Shall we courier them to you or would you like to collect them from our office?* She looked at her watch. In thirty-six hours, she would be gone; a fortnight in Mauritius, intended as a buffer between Turkmenistan and the next place. Yet again, a woman in transit.

In her bedroom, she shunted the single bed to one side, rolled back the reed mat and lifted two loose floorboards. From the space below she recovered a small Sony Vaio laptop in a sealed plastic pouch.

Back in the living-room, she switched on the

computer and accessed Petra's e-mails. Spread over six addresses, split between AOL and Hotmail, Petra hid behind four men and two women. She checked Marianne Bernard's mail at AOL; one new message. Roland, predictably. Gratitude for the best night of the year. Not the greatest compliment, Stephanie felt, in early January.

She sent one new message. To Stern, the information broker who also acted as her agent and confidant. It had to be significant that almost the only person she truly trusted was someone she had never met. She didn't even know whether Stern was a man or a woman, even though she called him Oscar.

> Back from the Soviet past. With love, P.

She left the laptop connected, then took her dirty clothes to Wash Club on place Saint-Géry. She bought milk and a carton of apple juice from the LIDL supermarket on the other side of the square, then returned home to find two messages waiting for her. One was from Stern. He directed her to somewhere electronically discreet and asked:

> How was it?

> Turkmenistan? Or Sullivan?

> Both.

> Depressing, dirty and backward. But Turkmenistan was fine.

Eddie Sullivan was a former Green Jacket who'd established a company named ProActive

Solutions. An arms-dealer with a flourishing reputation, he'd been in Turkmenistan to negotiate the sale of a consignment of weapons to the IMU, the Islamic Movement of Uzbekistan. The hardware, stolen from the British Army during the run-up to the invasion of Iraq, was already in Azerbaijan, awaiting transport across the Caspian Sea from Baku to the coastal city of Turkmenbashi.

Petra's contract had been paid for by Vyukneft, a Russian oil company with business in Azerbaijan. But Stern had told her that the decision to use her had been political. Made in Moscow, he'd said. Hiring Petra meant no awkward fingerprints. It wasn't the first time she'd worked by proxy for the Russian government.

The final negotiation between Sullivan and the IMU had been scheduled for the Hotel Turkmenbashi, a monstrous hangover from the Soviet era. Hideous on the outside, no better on the inside, she'd eliminated Sullivan in his room, while the Uzbek end-users gathered two floors below. She'd masqueraded as a member of hotel staff, delivering a message with as much surliness as she could muster.

Distracted by the imminent deal, Sullivan had been sloppy. He'd never looked at her, even as she loitered in the doorway waiting for a tip. When he'd turned his back to look for loose change, she'd pulled out a Ruger with a silencer and had kicked the door shut with her heel. The gun-shot and the slam had merged to form one hearty thump. Two minutes later she was heading away from the hotel on the long drive back to Ashgabat and the Lufthansa flight for Frankfurt.

> Are you available?

> Not until further notice.

> Taking a vacation?

> Something like that. Anything on the radar?

> Only from clients who can't afford you.

> Then your commission must be fatter than I thought.

> Petra! Please. Don't be cruel.

The second message, at one of the Hotmail addresses, was a real surprise. No names, just a single sentence.

> I see you chose not to take the advice I gave you in Munich.

Petra Reuter was sipping a cappuccino at a table close to the entrance of Café Roma on Maximilianstrasse. It was late September but winter had already made its presence felt; two days earlier there had been snow flurries in Munich.

The man rising from the opposite side of the table was Otto Heilmann. A short man, no more than five-foot-six, with narrow sloping shoulders, he wore a loden hunting jacket with onyx buttons over a fawn polo-neck.

'We will meet again, Fräulein Jaspersen?'

'I expect so, if you wish.'

'Perhaps you would consider coming to St Petersburg?'

Petra wondered where this stiff courtesy came from. Probably not from two decades with the Stasi. Nor from the last fifteen years of arms-dealing. She didn't imagine there was much call for Heilmann's brand of politeness in Tbilisi or Kiev. Or even in St Petersburg. Yet here he was, dressed like a benevolent Bavarian uncle, hitting on her with a formal invitation that fell only fractionally short of stiff card and embossed script.

She gave him her best smile. 'I'd certainly consider it, Herr Heilmann.'

'Please. Otto.'

'Only if you promise to call me Krista.'

A small inclination of the head was followed by a reciprocated smile that revealed a set of perfectly calibrated teeth. 'This could be the beginning of something very good for us, Krista.'

She watched him leave, a navy cashmere overcoat folded over his right arm. Outside, a Mercedes was waiting, black body, black windows, a black suit to hold open the door for him. Perhaps that was why he'd chosen Café Roma; black wooden tables, black banquettes, black chairs. Crimson walls, though. Like blood. A more likely reason for Heilmann to choose the place. Her eyes followed the car until it faded from view.

The remains of the day stretched before her. Nothing to do but wait for the call. More than anything, Petra's was a life of waiting. Like a movie actor; long periods of inactivity were intercut with short bursts of action.

She drained her cappuccino and decided to order another. Twenty minutes drifted by. It grew busier as afternoon matured into evening; shoppers, businessmen and women, mostly affluent, mostly elegant.

'Jesus Christ, I don't believe it. Petra, Petra, Petra . . .'

She looked up and took a moment to staple a name to the face. Not because she didn't recognize him but because he was out of context.

He misunderstood her silence. 'Or are we not Petra today?'

John Peltor. A former US Marine. Still looking every inch of his six-foot-five.

'Is this bad timing?' he asked.

'That depends.'

He glanced left and right. 'Am I intruding?'

'No.'

Clearly not the answer he was expecting. 'You're alone?'

'Aren't we all?'

'Always the smart-ass, Petra.'

'Always.'

'I wasn't sure at first. The hair, you know.'

It was the longest she'd ever worn it. Halfway down her back and dark blonde.

'Kinda suits you,' he said.

'Do you think so?'

She didn't like it: although it went well with her eyes, which were now green. She wasn't sure Peltor had noticed that change.

He looked into her cup, which was two-thirds empty. 'Want another?'

'I've got to go,' she lied.

'You sure? It would be good to catch up again.'

Perversely, that was true. Social opportunities in their solitary profession were rare although it wasn't the first time they'd run into each other by chance. Peltor wasn't her type but that hardly mattered. How many of them were there in the world? Not the cheap battery-operated types, but those rare hand-crafted precision instruments. Less than a hundred? Certainly. Whatever their respective backgrounds they were bound by the quality of their manufacture and they both knew it.

'How long are you in Munich?' she asked.

'Leaving tomorrow, around midday. How about tonight?'

'Busy.'

Another lie.

'Can you make breakfast? At my hotel. Say nine?'

Petra tilted her head to one side and allowed herself a smile. 'You won't be sharing it with some lucky lady?'

Peltor feigned wounded pride. 'Not unless you say yes.'

Petra arrived at the Mandarin Oriental on Neuturmstrasse at nine. When she asked for Peltor at the front desk – '*Herr* Stonehouse, *bitte*'

– her instructions were specific: he was running a little late so could she take the lift to the sixth floor, the stairs to the seventh and then proceed up to the roof terrace.

It was a freezing morning, no hint of cloud in the sky. The sun sparkled like the Millennium Star over a roof terrace that offered an unobstructed view of all Munich.

'Not bad, huh? It's why I always stay here when I'm in town.'

Peltor was floating at one end of a miniature swimming pool. Petra had seen baths that weren't much smaller.

'I hope that's heated.'

'A little too much for my taste.'

'Always the Marine, right?'

Petra looked at the board by the pool. Next to the date was the air temperature taken at seven-thirty. One degree centigrade.

'Love to swim first thing in the morning,' Peltor declared loudly.

'I thought you people loved the smell of napalm in the morning.'

'Not these days. How long's it been, Petra?'

'I don't know. Eighteen months?'

'More like two years. Maybe longer.'

'The British Airways lounge at JFK? You said you were going to Bratislava. Two weeks later I was stuck in Oslo airport flicking through a copy of the *Herald Tribune* and there it was. Prince Mustafa, the Mogadishu warlord, hit through the heart by a long-range sniper. A Sako rifle . . .'

'A TRG-S,' Peltor added. 'Won't use any other kind . . .'

'A 338 Lapua Mag from seventeen hundred metres, wasn't it?'

'Seventeen-fifty. What were you doing in Oslo?'

'Nothing. I told you. I was stuck.'

'Cute, Petra. Real cute.'

Peltor climbed out of the pool. Massive shoulders tapered to a waist so narrow it was almost feminine, a feature that reminded her of Salman Rifat, the Turkish arms-dealer. But where Rifat's extraordinary physique was steroid-assisted, Peltor's was natural. He exuded power as tangibly as the steam coming off his skin.

Oblivious to the cold, he dried himself in front of her, neither of them saying anything. It was an extravagant performance. A muscled peacock, Petra thought, as he reached for a dressing-gown. She wondered whether he was really running late or whether he'd orchestrated the display deliberately.

His suite was on the seventh floor. He emerged from the bathroom in a navy suit without a tie. Stephanie caught a trace of sandalwood in his cologne. Peltor wore a trim goatee beard at the same thickness as the hair on his head, somewhere between crop and stubble. He stepped into a pair of black Sebago loafers and they went down to Mark's, the hotel restaurant.

Orange juice and coffee arrived. Peltor ordered scrambled eggs and bacon, Petra stuck with fruit and croissants. She said, 'You running into me at Café Roma yesterday . . .'

He took his time, sipping coffee, playing with the teaspoon on the saucer. 'Yeah. I know.'

'And?'

He struggled for an answer, then looked almost apologetic. 'All my adult life, I've had my finger on a trigger, Petra. First for my country, then for my bank balance. In that time, I've been the best there is. We both have. Different specialities, same environment. But nobody knows what we do. We have to lie to everyone. We can't relax. That time at JFK – we were just a couple of business colleagues shooting the breeze in an airport lounge. A few stories, a few drinks. It was nice. But I didn't think I'd get the chance to do it again. Then yesterday . . . there you were.'

'A coincidence?'

'I hope so.'

'Someone I used to know said that a coincidence was an oversight.'

He sat back in his chair and held open his hands. 'Shit, it happens, you know? You're walking down a street somewhere – Osaka, Toronto, Berlin – and some guy calls out your name. When you turn round there's a face you haven't seen since the fourth grade back in Austin, Texas.'

'Is that where you grew up?'

'Never let your defences down, do you?'

'Never.'

Peltor held up his hands in mock surrender. 'Look, I saw you in Café Roma. I could've walked away but I didn't. That's all there is to it. I just thought we could talk again like we did in New York. You know, take a time-out. If you're uneasy with that . . . well, then I guess you'll leave.'

But she didn't. Perhaps because she'd enjoyed JFK too. Taking a time-out, talking shop. Relaxing.

Peltor's eggs and bacon arrived. The waitress poured Petra more coffee. The restaurant was mostly empty, the businessmen long gone, just four other tables occupied, none of them too close.

Gradually, they drifted into conversation. Nothing personal, not at first. They talked about Juha Suomalainen, a Finnish marksman whom Peltor had always regarded as a rival rather than a kindred spirit. Petra asked whether he was still active.

'I doubt it. He's been dead for six months.'

'Who got him?'

'Husqvarna.'

'I don't know the name. Sounds Nordic.'

'Husqvarna make chainsaws.'

'I'm not with you.'

'Juha was at his home in Espoo. Up a ladder, cutting branches off a tree. Somehow he fell and the chainsaw got him. And before you ask, I was in Hawaii with a drink in my hand.'

Petra pulled apart a croissant. 'Well, statistically

speaking, this is a risky business. You just don't expect any of us to go like that.'

'Right. Like Vincent Soares. Cancer. Wasn't even forty-five.'

When Peltor talked about his time as a Marine, Petra was surprised to learn that he wasn't the rabid jock-patriot she'd suspected he might be, although he admitted to missing the comradeship. But not much.

'This is a lot better. Like owning your own business, know what I mean? You work hard but you got no boss busting your ass.'

As far as Peltor was concerned, she'd always been Petra Reuter, the anarchist who turned assassin. Originally, however, Petra had been created by an organization. And controlled by that organization. Petra was an identity handed to Stephanie. A shell to inhabit. And in those days there *had* been a boss. A man who had regulated every aspect of her life. But as time passed, flesh and fabric had merged and Stephanie had *become* Petra. Or was it the other way round? In any case, Petra had outgrown her fictional self. Now, both the organization and the boss were consigned to her past while Petra Reuter was more of a reality than she had ever been.

Peltor ate a piece of bread roll smeared with butter and marmalade. Petra waited for the predictable reaction: the grimace. He picked up the small marmalade jar.

'Look at this, will you? Look at the colour. Way

too light. Like dirty water. Too much sugar, not enough orange. And no bitterness. Marmalade doesn't work unless there's a trace of bitterness.'

When he wasn't killing people Peltor liked to make marmalade. The first time she'd discovered this she'd laughed out loud. Later, when she thought about it, it simply reinforced a truth: you can never really know someone.

'You still getting the same kick out of it?' she asked.

When they'd last met, Peltor had explained what drove him on: the quest for perfect performance. *It all comes down to the shot, Petra. Last contract I took was nine months from start to finish. All of it distilled into half a second.*

There was no longer any trace of that enthusiasm. 'To be honest, I'm not sure I'll take another contract.'

'That surprises me.'

'I'm kinda drifting into something new right now.' He tugged the lapel of his jacket. 'Something . . . *corporate*.'

'That surprises me more.'

'It shouldn't. You know the way the math works. I've had my time at the plate, Petra. And if you don't mind me saying so, so have you.'

'If you don't mind *me* saying so, I'd guess you're a decade older than me.'

It was more like fifteen years, but technically Petra was older than Stephanie.

'It's not about age. It's about time served.'

She reduced her indifference to a shrug. 'I'm touched by your concern.'

'Don't outstay your welcome, Petra. Most of the assholes out there – I couldn't give a rat's ass if they get wasted. But I like you. You got class. Don't be the champ who doesn't know when to quit.'

'When it's time, I'll know.'

'Bullshit. The people who say that never know. Know why? Because the second before they realize it, they find their brains in their lap.'

'I'll try to remember that.'

'Just do it. Retire. Or shift sideways like I have.'

'What is this venture, then?'

'Consultancy I'd guess you call it. First-class travel, expense accounts, places like this. I swear, there are corporate clients out there – the biggest names – ready to pay a fortune for what we have up here.'

Petra watched him drum a finger against the side of his head and said, 'Not quite the double-tap I've come to associate with you.'

'Funny girl. Seriously, though, you can name your price. They pay off-shore, share options, anything you want.'

'Now I've heard it all.'

'You're not too young to think about it, Petra.'

'It's not that.'

'No?'

'No.'

'So what is it?'

'You know perfectly well. It's obviously already

happened to you. But it hasn't happened to me. Not yet.'

'What are you talking about?'

'The moment.'

Peltor's evangelism sobered into silence and she knew she was right.

She said, 'The moment you know. But before that moment . . . well, you don't just retire from this life, John. You know that as well as I do. *It* retires you. Sometimes after just one job.'

Beyond the recognition, she thought she detected a hint of regret in his voice when, eventually, he said, 'Damned if you're not right, Petra. Damned if you're not right.'

Stephanie was still thinking about Peltor's e-mail and the meeting that had prompted it back in September when her taxi pulled up beside the church of Notre Dame du Sablon. When Albert Eichner had told her that he was coming to Brussels to take her to lunch, she'd been faintly amused by his choice of restaurant. The exterior of L'Écailler du Palais Royal was the essence of discretion; premises that were easy to miss, the name lightly engraved on a small stone tablet beside the door, net curtains to prevent inquisitive glances from the street. As the chairman of Guderian Maier Bank in Zurich, these were qualities that Eichner appreciated more than most.

He was at a table towards the rear of the restaurant, a solid man with a physique that had defeated his tailor. When she'd first met him his thick head of hair had been gun-metal grey. Now it was almost as white as his crisp cotton shirt. Each cuff was secured by a thick oval of gold. On his left wrist was an understated IWC watch with a leather strap.

Stephanie was wearing the only smart outfit she now possessed, a black Joseph suit with a plain, cream silk blouse. Chic and conservative, just the way she suspected she existed in Eichner's imagination. As she approached the table he rose from his chair.

'Stephanie, as beautiful as ever.'

Eichner was one of the few men Stephanie had entrusted with her original given name. As for the surname with which he was familiar – Schneider – that had been her mother's.

A waiter in a blue tunic poured her a glass of champagne.

She said, 'How long are you in Brussels, Albert?'

'A friend of mine lent me his Bombardier. I flew here from Zurich this morning. I have to get back for a family engagement this evening.'

'I'm flattered.'

'Don't be. You've earned it.' He raised his glass. 'To you, Stephanie. With our sincerest gratitude.'

It was three months since Otto Heilmann's death. She smiled but said nothing. Eichner was right to be grateful. In the past, she'd saved him from personal disgrace and in return he'd consented to become her banker. This time, however, the entire institution had been under threat. In the first week of September, Eichner had implored her to come to Zurich. An emergency, he'd said. An emergency that threatened Guderian Maier. He'd let her fill in the blank spaces.

An emergency that threatens your arrangement with us.

Otto Heilmann. One of the very few to have become rich during the era of the GDR. Heilmann had links with Guderian Maier going back to the Seventies. When Stephanie had asked what kind of links, Eichner had reddened.

'In those days, my uncle ran this bank. In the same way that he did when he first ran it back in the Forties.' He'd paused to let her dwell on this, the gravity in his voice suggesting the subtext. 'We do things differently these days. Heilmann doesn't understand that. He's of the opinion that a bank like ours will accept anyone's money providing there is enough of it.'

'I assume you've explained that this isn't the case.'

'As politely and as firmly as possible.'

'But he's not dissuaded?'

'Unfortunately, no.'

'Distressing.'

'We can't possibly be associated with an arms-dealer.' When Stephanie had raised an eyebrow at him, Eichner had qualified himself. 'Not like Heilmann. It's simply out of the question. You

30

know the kind of clients we have. The very idea of it is just too . . . *appalling.*'

'I'd have thought your stand might have worked in your favour.'

'On one level, possibly. But there's something else. When the Stasi disintegrated, Heilmann headed to Russia and took what he needed with him. Information for his own protection, information for profit.'

'Let me guess. You refuse him and he'll find a way to incriminate the bank, tying it to the crimes of the Stasi.'

'He won't find a way. He *has* a way.'

'The sins of the past . . .'

The traffic on Bahnhofstrasse and the ticking of the carriage-clock on the marble mantelpiece had provided the soundtrack to a moment of awkward truth.

Eventually, Eichner had said, 'As I have already explained to you, Stephanie, we don't behave that way any more.'

'Yet you have me as a client.'

He'd smiled lamely. 'The point is, my generation and the next generation have gone to great lengths to restore some honour to a very noble heritage. Despite that, if we had to, we *would* be prepared to face the potential humiliation he's threatening. But it's gone beyond that now.'

He'd slid a photograph across his desk. Stephanie had recognized Eichner at the heart of the gathering, his wife sitting to his right. A family portrait, the faces of their seven grandchildren scratched out by a sharp point.

'Hand-delivered to this office last week. Six people in the bank have received similar material. Including my secretary.'

She'd told him not to worry. And when he'd raised the subject of her fee, she'd refused to discuss it. *Consider it a gift*, she'd said. *From one friend to another*.

Now, four months after that conversation, Eichner looked five years younger. 'Shall we share a bottle of something good? The seafood here is fantastic but I hope you won't be offended if we drink red wine. From memory, they have a very fine Figéac 93 but I think we'll go for something a little better.'

He ordered for both of them, Iranian caviar with another glass of champagne, followed by grilled turbot and a bottle of Cheval Blanc 88. When they were alone again, he said, 'That place you used to live – that farm in the south of France – remind me where it was.'

Her heart tripped. 'Between Entrecasteaux and Salernes.'

'Were you aware that it's for sale?'

How many years was it since she'd been there? Four, perhaps? It felt longer. She'd rented it. The owner had been a German investment banker stationed in Tokyo. It was a beautiful place, a little run-down, terraces rising behind the house, olives, lemons, a vineyard falling away to the valley below, the house itself afloat on clouds of lavender bushes. She'd picked it as somewhere to hide from the world and had never wanted to leave.

'The directors and I have discussed this and – with your permission, naturally – we have decided to acquire the property.'

Stephanie frowned. 'I don't understand.'

'For you. As a token of our gratitude.'

'I told you in Zurich that I would deal with Heilmann for free.'

'Exactly so. And we would like you to view this gesture in the same spirit. Consider it a gift. From one friend to another.'

She reached across the table and took his hand. 'Thank you, Albert. That's so sweet of you. But I'll need to think about it.'

'Is that you, Petra?'

Ten-to-eleven. When the call came, she was sitting on the living-room floor, sorting through Marianne's domestic bills, listening to *Bright Red* by Laurie Anderson. The track 'Tightrope' was on repeat.

Roland doesn't know me as Petra. That was her first thought, quickly followed by another: *it's not his voice.*

'Who is this?'

'Jacob Furst.'

Out of the blue. Or, to be accurate, out of the past.

Furst took her silence incorrectly. 'You don't remember me?'

'Of course I remember you.'

Furst was an old man – in his late eighties now, she guessed – with each year etched into the timbre of his voice. Not surprising, given the life he'd led. And now she recognized the strangely distinct sound of that voice too; high and quavering, almost feminine.

'I apologize for calling you like this but I need to see you. It's urgent.'

Another thought was forming; this was Marianne's mobile phone. How had Furst obtained the number? Through Cyril Bradfield, perhaps, a mutual friend. Stephanie felt Petra taking over, concern making way for pragmatism. 'Where are you?'

'Paris.'

Where Furst lived, so far as she knew. 'I'm going away tomorrow but I'll be back . . .'

'Where are *you*?'

She felt Petra's reflex, her mobile had a German number. Did Furst imagine she was in Germany, or did he know that she was in Belgium?

'I'm right . . . *here*.'

He seemed to understand. 'Could you be in Paris tomorrow?'

'I could be just about anywhere tomorrow.'

'I would never have called you if I'd thought there was an alternative but . . .'

From what she remembered of Furst, that much was true. 'What is it?'

'I can't say,' he whispered. 'Not over the phone.'

'Can it wait?'

The pause undermined the lie that followed. 'For two or three days, maybe.'

Stephanie pictured Furst; a small man with a crooked frame and surprisingly large hands. Miriam, his wife, was taller and broader.

'Tell me this: is it the same as last time?'

His reply was barely audible: 'Almost.'

Almost?

She said, 'I can't promise you anything.'

'Will you try?'

No. Instinctively, that was what she felt. Petra hated situations like this. Unsolicited, unprepared. But there would be no easy escape here. There was a barrier in the way constructed of obligation and sentimentality.

'One o'clock. If I'm not there by half-past, I'm not coming. Shall I come to your home?'

'No.'

'Where?'

'The place we first met. Do you remember it?'

Day Two

My carriage is almost empty on the Thalys train
service from Brussels-Midi to Gare du Nord in Paris.
Belgian countryside scrolls smoothly across my window
at high speed, flat and brown beneath a grey sky,
ploughed fields speckled with small woods and copses.
The tops of the electricity pylons are lost in low, rolling
cloud.

A woman in a dark red uniform pours me more
coffee. In an hour I'll be in Paris. In four, I'll be hurtling
through this same stretch of countryside in the opposite
direction. In twelve, I'll be at thirty-five thousand feet,
heading for the Indian Ocean.

I'm not sure what I can achieve while I'm with Jacob
Furst but I'll manage something. Furst is a man with
a fierce sense of honour; the kind of man to squirm
under obligation. And he will feel obligated towards me,
no matter how hard I try to persuade him not to be.
The truth is, my debt of obligation is greater.

For almost sixty years Furst was one of the great
document forgers. A gifted painter from childhood, he

was faking masterpieces for wealthy clients by the time he was twenty. At the outbreak of the Second World War, he turned his talents to a more practical purpose, forging documents to help Jews fleeing Nazi persecution. Later, he joined the Resistance, creating papers for SOE agents dropped into France between 1942 and 1943, before his eventual capture. He survived for two years at Auschwitz. After the war, he developed the trade in forged documents for profit, protected by the legitimate screen of the family garment business.

He retired from his art – art being exactly what he considers it – in 1995 when the arthritis in his fingers began to affect the quality of his work. Over the years, Furst passed on his expertise to a small handful of apprentices. One of them was an Irish art student who was studying in Paris during the 1960s. His name was Cyril Bradfield.

Cyril has been creating independent identities for me as long as I've been Petra Reuter. In that sense he knows me better than any person alive. In the perverse way that logic works in my world, it seems appropriate that he's the closest thing I have to a parent; after all, he's fathered so many of me.

Cyril feels for Jacob Furst the way I feel for him. Which is why the only time he's ever asked me for help was when it was on Furst's behalf. It wasn't a complicated situation, just undignified; an elderly man and his wife threatened by a crooked landlord and his troop of Neanderthal thugs.

That was four years ago and it was the only time I spent with Jacob and Miriam Furst. But we formed a *bond. A bond that feels as strong today as it did then. It's no exaggeration to say this: without Furst, there would have been no Cyril Bradfield for me, and without some of his documents, I'd probably be dead. But the reason I'm going to Paris is that I liked Furst. If I think of Cyril as a surrogate father it's easy to think of Jacob and Miriam as surrogate grandparents. With some people, you don't need time to make the connection; it just happens. Often, when you least expect it.*

Twelve-fifty, boulevard de Sébastopol in Sentier. Stephanie dropped euro coins into the driver's palm and climbed out of the taxi. Despite the hard rain, she wanted to walk the last bit. She entered rue Saint Denis from rue Réaumur and it was how she remembered it; clothes shops and garment wholesalers along either pavement, the road itself a narrow artery clogged by double-parked vans, their back doors open, rolls of fabric stacked for delivery. And noise everywhere; bleating horns, music, the rain, half a dozen shouted languages. At the intersection with rue du Caire a dozen Indian and Bangladeshi porters were loitering with trolleys, waiting to be summoned. In the doorways and alleys were the whores; oblivious to the weather, the wrong side of forty, sagging breasts and bloody make-up done no favours by the dismal daylight.

Stephanie entered Passage du Caire, an arcade of cramped passages with filthy glass overhead, and came to the place where the Fursts' family business had once been. Part of the sign still hung above the door, the red plastic letters faded to dirty pink. The window was crammed with mannequins; beige females with no heads or arms. A piece of paper pasted to the glass offered fifty percent discounts for bulk orders.

Four doors down was La Béatrice, the kosher café where Cyril Bradfield had introduced Stephanie to Jacob Furst. Seven tables with magnolia Formica tops, a selection of snacks laid out behind a glass counter, fluorescent tubes taped to sagging ceiling panels, one of them hanging loose. On the wall beside the espresso machine was a large wooden framed photograph of George Clooney next to a smaller frame containing a certificate bearing the words 'Shin Beth de Paris'.

There were half a dozen people in the place. Mostly from the arcade, she guessed; none of them were wet. Stephanie recognized Béatrice, a haughty-looking woman with dyed black hair. She ordered a cappuccino and took it to a vacant table by the small circular staircase leading to the upper floor. Béatrice fiddled with the portable radio on the counter until Liane Foly was singing 'Doucement'. In the café's wet warmth, Stephanie caught a whiff of cinnamon.

One o'clock came and went. So did Béatrice's customers. Stephanie noticed a man who seemed vaguely familiar; slim, tall, well dressed, in his fifties with the same dark blonde hair she'd had as Krista Jaspersen. He was sitting at a table near the staircase. She couldn't pin a name to the face but wondered whether she might have seen him on TV.

At one-fifteen her mobile rang.

'Petra?'

'Jacob?'

'Where are you?'

The high-pitched voice sounded more tremulous than usual.

'I'm where you should be. Unless my memory's going.'

He didn't reply straight away and she regretted her sarcasm.

'I apologize, Petra.'

'Where are *you*? I don't have long, Jacob.'

'Fifteen minutes, okay?'

'Okay.'

'You'll stay?'

'Of course.'

'Good. Two minutes, then . . .'

He finished the call and Stephanie sat there for a moment trying to remember something she'd forgotten. Something she'd intended to ask him. Something that had come back to her on the train.

The phone. The number. How had Furst got Marianne's number? And now that she thought about that, there was something else. Fifteen minutes? Or two?

She found she was reaching into her coat pocket for loose change; as usual, Petra was ahead of Stephanie, her instinct taking over. There were no coins left. The last of them had gone to the taxi driver. She put a ten-euro note beneath the saucer and stood up.

Out in the passage she looked both ways. Nothing. She decided to wait for his call somewhere nearby. When he arrived and discovered that she'd left, he'd phone again. She was certain of it.

She turned back towards the rue Saint Denis entrance.

And was airborne.

The shockwave *was* the sound somehow. A flash. Light, heat, no air in her lungs. She was aloft in a hurricane of debris. Then gravity reclaimed her and she was smeared across . . . *what, exactly*?

Darkness followed. Unconsciousness? Or *just* darkness?

The screams began. Cutting through the hum in her head. When she opened her eyes she couldn't see. A cloud of dust enveloped her, as impenetrable as highland mist. She didn't know if she was injured because she was numb. But she was aware of wetness down her back. And dirt in her mouth. There was a smell too; something cloying. Burning plastic, perhaps?

Her foot was trapped, wedged between two solid shapes.

She closed her eyes. Time to sleep.

No.

* * *

41

Petra twisted her body so that she could see her right foot. A grey filing cabinet was on top of it, two of its three drawers blown out. Beneath it was half a beige mannequin. She used her left foot against the filing cabinet, creating a gap for the right, then rolled off her mattress of fractured dummies.

Water droplets splashed on her face. A burst pipe. Or rain. She looked up but saw only smoke and dust.

The right ankle was tender. She hauled herself to her feet. Nausea rose up inside her. One step, then another. For now, that was enough. Adrenaline, her most faithful servant, would see her through.

In the remains of the passage fires sprouted in the gloom, deep orange and gold. A severed cable spat white hot sparks over a soggy roll of material with a floral print. Except it wasn't a roll. It was a body in a dress. Petra made out an arm, filthy black, the hand crushed to pulp.

The passage had a lawn of broken glass. Not just from store windows but from the canopy overhead; metres and metres of it reduced to splinters.

La Béatrice was burning rubble. How many people had been inside? Half a dozen? Maybe. The upper floor had collapsed into the café. She didn't know whether there had been anyone up there. Scorched body parts hung from the fractured iron staircase. At the foot of the stairs,

Béatrice's head and upper torso were on fire. Petra couldn't see the rest of the corpse but could smell her burning hair. Closer to the entrance, a single boot and shin protruded from beneath a concrete slab. Less than a metre away, blood was oozing through cracked brick.

There was music. Weak, muffled, rising up from beneath the debris; Béatrice's portable radio, still working, no matter how improbably. Petra looked to her right. Rue Saint Denis had gone, concealed by the cloak of smoke.

She began to cough, lining her nostrils and mouth with dust. Stunned, all her training suspended, she staggered away, each step as uncertain as the one before. A few metres on, a pretty blonde woman in a lilac cardigan and brown tweed skirt lay on the ground, twitching, flayed by glass.

Under the screams she heard distant shouts; people making their way *towards* the carnage. Boots scrambled over loose brick, muttered curses followed falls.

To her left, a large fire was taking hold, glass cracking in the heat. She came to a fork in the passage. Over the ringing in her head an orchestra of alarms grew louder. She veered right, then stopped.

'. . . to be careful, okay?'

A snatch of conversation coming her way. Then another voice: 'Check everywhere.'

'. . . watch overhead for collapsing . . .'

Shapes were forming in the murk.

'. . . somewhere in here . . . keep looking . . .'

'. . . extremely dangerous . . . and armed . . .'

Two figures, certainly, perhaps three.

'. . . take any chances . . .'

Petra coughed again, spitting out brown saliva.

The first figure emerged from the dust, a light grey raincoat billowing around him. The next was in uniform. An armed police officer with a full moustache. Other silhouettes took shape behind them.

The first man saw her, halted abruptly, then pointed directly at her. '*Shit!* It's her! There she is!'

There who is?

Who was he looking at? Why was he pointing at her?

A third figure was forming, another armed officer in uniform, then a fourth man in a tan leather coat.

'Shoot her.'

A mistake, clearly. Except Petra knew that it wasn't.

The first armed officer looked unsure.

'It's her,' barked the man in the grey raincoat. 'I tell you, it's her!'

'I don't see the . . .'

'She's *armed*! Now shoot her!'

The man in the leather coat was already raising his right hand. The second officer was pushing past the first. And Petra was moving, taking the passage directly ahead, already aware of the fact that it was too straight. In a matter of seconds, before she could melt into the smoke, they would have a clear view of her back.

Behind her now, the same voice again. 'Henri! Watch out! She's coming your way! She's got a gun . . .'

What gun?

Movement grew in the dimness ahead. Petra entered the smoking remains of a boutique; retro-punk T-shirts, studded leather mini-skirts, frayed tartan hot-pants, a severed hand with a silver thumb-ring. She dragged a sloping chunk of partition wall from across the doorway at the back.

'*Shit* – Didi, you asshole! I nearly shot you! Where is she?'

More coughing. 'I don't know. Maybe you passed her . . .'

'In there!' cried a third voice. '*Look!*'

There was a single shot as Petra plunged into more darkness. She felt the thud of a bullet hitting a panel of MDF to her left. She came to a shoulder-wide passage with stairs to her right. Up to the first floor, a cramped storage area, the ceiling less than a foot taller than she was. The blast had blown the glass from the internal window overlooking the passage. She could hear them arguing below.

No weapon. No way out.

Except for the window. She approached the

45

hole cautiously. Just above her was a web of iron struts, pipes and rubber cable, all of it ancient. Through the dust-haze she watched the four men beneath her. They were looking into the blackened shell of the boutique, shouting at those who'd followed her inside.

No choice, so no need to think about it. Up on to the sill and out on to the ledge, the remaining fragments of glass in the window-frame nibbling the palms of her right hand. There was a rusting water-pipe above her head. She gave it a quick tug; it seemed secure. She held on to it and swung, her toes catching the corner of a sturdy junction box, one of six bolted to a panel, cables spewing from them like black spaghetti.

'Up there!' bellowed a man below. *'Quick!'*

But not quick enough. She was already over the ledge above, propelling her body through a mesh of twisted metal ribs. On the roof, she gauged the way the passages worked, the ridges, the intersections. Most of the glass had gone. To her left, thick black smoke was curling skywards, the flames beneath undeterred by the rain.

It was slippery underfoot, years of grime given gloss by the downpour. She tried to work out where rue Saint Denis was so that she could head in the opposite direction. It wasn't obvious from the backs of the surrounding buildings but there was a gap so she headed for that. The roof tapered to a short stretch of crumbling wall that abutted a taller building; apartments from the first floor up, a business at street level, the shutters pulled down over the windows.

She took the drainpipe to the first floor, swiping three potted plants from a window-ledge, then lowered herself on to the roof of a white Renault Mégane that was parked on the pavement.

Now she was in a small triangular square: rue Saint Spire, rue Alexandrie, rue Sainte Foy. She took Sainte Foy.

Five-past-two, the sirens now a long way behind her. She was still walking, the rain still falling. And helping. Under the circumstances, better to be drenched than dirty. Which was all the logic she could handle.

Head for Gare du Nord. Use the return ticket. Go home, have a shower, catch the plane. Worry about it over a cocktail on the beach.

She was sorely tempted yet knew she couldn't. Stations were out. So was home. Which meant Marianne Bernard's integrity was suspended. And it was Marianne's name on the air ticket.

How had the police got there so quickly? How had they identified *her* so quickly? And the order to shoot – because she was *armed* – what did that mean?

One part of her wanted to stop and think. To collate. But another part of her wouldn't let her. She had to keep moving. That was the priority.

Never stop. The moment you do . . .

* * *

Three-thirty-five. The cinema provided a temporary sanctuary of darkness. The film was a Hollywood romantic comedy, predictably short on romance, utterly devoid of comedy. Stephanie waited until the main feature had started before going to the washroom. She peeled off her denim jacket and the black polo-neck. Both were soaked. The long-sleeved strawberry T-shirt beneath was stuck to her skin. She filled a basin with warm soapy water, rolled up the sleeves to the elbow, scrubbed her face, hands and arms, rinsed, refilled the basin with clean warm water and dipped her head into it, before trying to claw some order through her hair.

A little cleaner but still dripping, she locked herself into one of the stalls, hanging the jersey and jacket on the door-peg. She lifted the T-shirt, examined her torso and ran her fingertips over as much of her back as she could. Nothing but a few cuts and grazes. She pulled down the toilet lid, sat on it, pulled off a dark grey Merrell shoe and checked the right ankle; swollen, tender to the touch, but no significant damage. When she envisaged Béatrice it seemed little short of a miracle. And all because of Petra; Stephanie would have stayed at the table for Jacob Furst.

She pulled on her wet clothes and checked her possessions; the return portion of her train ticket, Marianne's credit-cards, a Belgian driving licence, flat keys, six hundred and seventeen euros in cash, mobile phone, cinema ticket.

Stephanie returned to the comforting dark of the auditorium, taking a seat near the back, and was grateful for the stuffy warmth. First things first, a plan of action. The primary urge was to run. And she *would* run. As she had in the past. That was the easy part. Nobody ran as effortlessly as Petra. But she couldn't allow fear to be the fuel. Before that, however, there were questions.

She rose into the ethnic melting-pot of Belleville. The pavement along the eastern flank of the broad boulevard de Belleville was busy. Stephanie weaved through Afghans, Turks, Iranians, Georgians, Chinese. A group of five tall Sudanese were arguing on the corner of rue Ramponeau. A Vietnamese woman barged past her dragging a bulging laundry bag. Traffic was stationary in both directions, frustrated drivers leaning on their horns.

Stephanie switched on her mobile. No messages and no missed calls since she'd turned it off twenty minutes after clearing Passage du Caire. She return-dialled Jacob Furst's number. No answer. She switched the phone off again and walked up rue Lémon to rue Dénoyez. The five-storey building was on the other side of the road. At street level, the Boucherie Shalom was closed. The restaurant next to it was open but Stephanie couldn't see any diners through the window.

The Fursts' apartment was on the third floor. No lights on, the curtains open. There were weeds sprouting from the plaster close to a fracture in the drainpipe. There was no building to the right. It had been demolished, the waste ground screened from the street by a barricade of blue and green corrugated iron.

She ventured left, away from the building, heading up the cobbled street past graffiti and peeling bill posters, past the entrance to the seedy Hotel Dénoyez – *rooms by the hour* – until she came to rue Belleville. Then she made a circle and approached rue Dénoyez from the other end at rue Ramponeau.

The Furst family had a Parisian lineage stretching back two centuries. In that time, there had been two constants: a family business centred on the garment industry and active participation within the Jewish community. Which included living among that community. And here was the proof. On rue Ramponeau, Stephanie stood with her back to La Maison du Taleth, a shop selling Jewish religious artefacts. Restaurants and sandwich shops all displayed with prominence the Star of David.

She returned to boulevard de Belleville. From the France Télécom phonebooth by the Métro exit she rang the police. An incident to report, some kind of break-in, she told them. She'd heard noises – screams for help, breaking glass, a loud bang – and now nothing. *Please hurry – they're an old couple. Vulnerable . . .*

When they'd asked for her name, she put down the phone.

50

She watched from the bright blue entrance to Hotel Dénoyez. When the patrol car pulled up a pair of officers emerged and she noticed two things. First, they looked casual; from the way they moved she guessed they were expecting an exaggerated domestic disturbance. Or a hoax. The second thing was the dark blue BMW 5-series halfway between her and the patrol car.

It had been there as long as she'd been loitering by the hotel entrance. She'd assumed there was no one in it. But when the patrol car pulled up, the BMW's engine coughed, ejecting a squirt of oily smoke from the exhaust. She peered more carefully through the back window and now saw that there were two people inside. The car didn't move until the police officers had entered the building. Then it pulled away from the kerb, tyres squeaking on the cobbles, turning right at rue Ramponcau.

She continued to wait. A third-floor light came on. Stephanie pictured Miriam Furst in the kitchen at the rear of the flat. Making coffee for the policemen, taking mugs from the wooden rack above the sink. That was how she remembered it. Beside the rack, a cheap watercolour of place des Vosges hung next to a cork noticeboard with family photographs pinned to it: three children, all girls, and nine grandchildren, none of whom had been inclined to steer the Furst textile business into its third century.

Fifteen minutes after the arrival of the first

51

police car, a second arrived. Followed within forty-five seconds by an ambulance, then a third police car and, finally, a second ambulance. Three policemen began to cordon off the street.

Now it was no longer just Stephanie's fingers that were going numb.

We pull into Tuileries, in the direction of La Défense. I'll probably change at Franklin D. Roosevelt and head for Mairie de Montreuil, then change again after a dozen stations or so. It's five-to-eleven and I've been riding the Métro for more than two hours. There's no better way to make yourself invisible for a short while than to ride public transport in a major city late at night. Later, they'll see me on CCTV recordings, drifting back and forth. But by then I'll be somewhere else. And someone *else.*

Above ground, in the bars and restaurants, in private homes, there is only one topic of discussion tonight. The bomb blast in Sentier. Many dead, many wounded, many theories. There'll be grief and outrage on the news, and plenty of inaccurate in-depth analysis from the experts.

I know that Jacob and Miriam Furst are dead. Nobody will read about them tomorrow. They will have died largely as they lived; unnoticed. I also know that I should be dead too.

The men who chased me through the smoking wreckage in Passage du Caire were there to make sure. They were there so quickly. And they weren't looking for anyone else; they recognized me.

I try to fix a version of events in my head. Furst is held against his will until he's made the call to establish that I'm in place. He's surprised that I'm there. Did he think I wouldn't come? He tells me he'll be with me in fifteen minutes, then two. Why the difference? To arouse my suspicion? To warn me?

How did he get the number? And why wasn't I more vigilant? Perhaps, mentally, I was already halfway to Mauritius.

After our conversation is over, the explosion occurs within a minute. But the more I consider it, the more perplexing it becomes. They – whoever 'they' are – needed to be sure that I'd be in Paris today. That I'd be in La Béatrice at one o'clock. How could they be confident that I'd make the trip from Brussels? And if I'm to assume that they knew I was in Brussels, which as a matter of security I must, shouldn't I also assume that they know I'm Marianne Bernard? And if they know that, where does the line of enquiry stop? Whether they knew about Marianne Bernard or not, it's obvious who they really wanted. Petra Reuter. She's the one with the reputation.

So why the elaborate deceit? Nobody who knew anything about her would risk that. They'd take her down the moment they found her. At home, for instance, in a run-down apartment in Brussels. They'd catch her with her guard down. Simpler, safer, better.

There can be only one answer: they needed me to be at La Béatrice.

Day Three

The Marais, quarter-past-five in the morning, the streetlamps reflected in puddles not quite frozen. Rue des Rosiers was almost empty; one or two on the way home, one or two on the way to work, hands in pockets, chins tucked into scarves.

It had been after midnight when she abandoned the Métro. Since then, she'd stopped only once, when the rain had returned just before three. She'd found an all-night café not far from where she was now; candlelight and neon over concrete walls, leather booths in dark corners, Ute Lemper playing softly over the sound system.

Stephanie stretched a cup of black coffee over an hour before anyone approached her. A tall, angular woman with deathly pale skin and dark red shoulder-length hair, wearing a purple silk shirt beneath a black leather overcoat. She smiled through a slash of magenta lipstick and sat down opposite Stephanie.

'Hello. I'm Véronique.'

Véronique from Lyon. She'd been awkwardly beautiful once – perhaps not too long ago – but thinness had aged her. And so had unhappiness. Stephanie warmed to her because she understood the chilly solitude of being alone in a city of millions.

They talked for a while before Véronique reached for Stephanie's hand. 'I live close. Do you want to come? We could have a drink?'

Petra considered the offer clinically: Véronique was an ideal way to vanish from the street. No security cameras, no registration, no witnesses. Inside her home, Petra would have options; some brutal, some less so. But it was after four; there was no longer any pressing need for a Véronique.

Stephanie let her down gently with a version of the truth. 'It's too late for me. If only we'd met earlier.'

She turned left into rue Vieille du Temple. The shop was a little way down, the red and gold sign over the property picked out by three small lamps: Adler. And beneath that: *boulangerie – patisserie.*

Stephanie knocked on the door. Behind the glass a full-length blind had been lowered, *fermé* painted across it. A minute passed. Nothing. She tried again – still nothing – and was preparing for a third rap when she heard the approach of footsteps and a stream of invective.

The same height as Stephanie, he wore a

creased pistachio shirt rolled up at the sleeves and a black waistcoat, unfastened. A crooked nose, a mash of scar around the left eye, thick black hair everywhere, except on his head. The last time, he'd had a ponytail. Not any more, the close crop a better cut to partner his encroaching baldness. There was a lot of gold; identity bracelets, a watch, chains with charms, a thick ring through the left ear-lobe. As Cyril Bradfield had once said to her, 'He looks like the hardest man you've ever seen. And dresses like a tart.'

'Hello, Claude.'

Claude Adler was too startled to reply.

'I knew you'd be up,' Stephanie said. 'Four-thirty, every day. Right?'

'Petra . . .'

'I would've called, of course . . .'

'Of course.'

'But I couldn't.'

'This is . . . well . . . *unexpected*?'

'For both of us. We need to talk.'

It was delightfully warm inside. Adler locked the door behind them and they walked through the shop, the shelves and wicker baskets still empty. The cramped bakery was at the back. Stephanie smelt it before she saw it; baguettes, sesame seed bagels, apple strudel, all freshly prepared, all of it reminding her that she hadn't eaten anything since Brussels.

Adler took her upstairs to the apartment over the shop where he and his wife had lived for almost twenty years. He lit a gas ring for a pan of water and scooped ground coffee into a cafetière. There was a soft pack of Gauloises on the window-ledge. He tapped one out of the tear, offered it to her, then slipped it between his lips when she declined.

'Is Sylvie here?'

'Still asleep.' He bent down to the ring of blue flame, nudging the cigarette tip into it, shreds of loose tobacco flaring bright orange. 'She'll be happy to see you when she gets up.'

'I doubt it. That's the reason I'm here, Claude. I've got bad news.'

Adler took his time standing. 'Have you seen the TV? It seems to be the day for bad news.'

'It is. Jacob and Miriam are dead.'

He froze. *Both?*

Stephanie nodded.

At their age, one was to be expected. Followed soon after, perhaps, by the other. But both together?

'When?'

'Last night.'

'How?'

'Violently.'

He began to shake his head gently. 'It can't be true.'

'It *is* true.'

'How do you know?'

'I saw the police. The ambulances . . .'

'You were there?'

'Afterwards, yes.'

'Did you see *them*?'

Stephanie shook her head.

'Then perhaps . . .'

'Trust me, Claude. They're dead.'

He wanted to protest but couldn't because he believed her. Even though she hadn't seen the bodies. Even though he didn't know her well enough to know what she did. Not exactly, anyway.

'Who did it?'

'I don't know.'

He thought about that for a while. 'So why are you here?'

'Because I'm supposed to be dead too.'

Adler refilled their cups; hot milk first, then coffee like crude oil, introduced over the back of a spoon, a ritual repeated many times daily. Like lighting a cigarette. Which he now did for the fourth time since her arrival, the crushed stubs gathering on a pale yellow saucer.

Now that he'd absorbed the initial shock, Adler was reminiscing. Secondhand history, as related to him by Furst: the pipeline pumping Jewish refugees to safety; the false document factory he'd established in Montmartre; 14 June 1940, the day the Nazis occupied Paris; smuggling Miriam to Lisbon via Spain in the autumn of 1941; forging documents for the Resistance and then SOE. And finally, betrayal, interrogation, Auschwitz.

Adler scratched a jaw of stubble, some black, some silver. 'He always said he was lucky to live. Listening to him tell it, I was never so sure.' He stirred sugar into his coffee. 'You survive something like that, the least you expect is to be left alone to die of natural causes. Fuck it, he was nearly ninety.'

'You're right.'

'You know what I admired most about him?'

'What?'

He drew on his cigarette and then exhaled over the tip. 'That it never occurred to him to leave. From 1939 on, he could've run. But he didn't. He chose to stay behind, to create false documents to help others escape. He knew the risks better than most. Yet even when they got Miriam out, it never crossed his mind to go with her.'

'That was the kind of man he was. Silently courageous. Understated.'

'True. He was a man who believed in community. *His* community.'

'Talking of which, did Jacob ever go back to Sentier?'

Adler stared at her. 'That's a blunt question on a morning like this.'

'That's why I'm asking it, Claude.'

He shrugged. 'Not so much, I don't think. Not since he sold the shop.'

'I saw it yesterday.'

'What?'

'The shop. In Passage du Caire. Part of the sign

is still above the entrance. At least, it was. It's not any more.'

Adler's jaw dropped. 'You were *there*?'

'Moments before the explosion, yes.'

'My God . . . *why*?'

'To see Jacob. He called me the night before last and asked me to come to Paris. He said it was important. He wanted to meet at La Béatrice. I turned up. He didn't.'

'At La Béatrice? That used to be his favourite place.'

'I know.'

'A coincidence?'

'Your guess is as good as mine.'

Adler's gaze drifted out of the window. 'We were up all night watching the news. Twelve dead, fifty injured. We were wondering who we'd know.' He looked her up and down. 'Are you okay?'

'I'm fine.'

'You'd already left?'

'No. I was just lucky. Everyone around me was dead or injured. I hardly got a scratch.'

'What about Jacob?'

'I told you. He never turned up. He died later. At their apartment.'

'With Miriam.'

'Yes.'

'You think there's a connection?'

'I don't want to. But it's hard not to. When did you last see him?'

'Thursday. Sylvie and I went over to their place and we went to the street market on boulevard de Belleville. Lately, it's something we've been doing almost every week. The market is on Thursday and Friday mornings. After it, we have lunch. Usually at old Goldenberg's place – you know it? He and Jacob were friends.'

She shook her head.

'On rue de Tourtille. Great service, shit food. Jacob and Miriam have been going there since it opened, back in the Seventies. Jacob always used to say he only started enjoying it about five years ago when his taste buds went. He used to lean across the table when Goldenberg was hovering and he'd say to me, "Claude, there are two things that give me pleasure when I'm here. Not tasting the food and watching your face. Every mouthful is a masterpiece." That was his big joke. Goldenberg has a sign in the front window: *every mouthful is a masterpiece.*'

Stephanie tried to muster a smile. 'Did you always go over to see him? Or did he come here?'

'Usually, we went there. When he sold the business he began to slow down. Recently, he'd become . . . *fragile.*'

'At his age, he was entitled to.'

'I agree with you. But *he* wouldn't have.'

'You didn't notice anything on Thursday? He didn't seem upset or preoccupied?'

'Nothing like that, no.'

'What about the last few weeks?'

'No.'

'Does it surprise you that he would have arranged a meeting with me at La Béatrice?'

'Frankly, yes. He was fond of you. They both were. I would have expected him to invite you to their home. That was their way.'

'That's what I thought.'

'How could he be connected to what happened in Sentier?'

'I don't know.'

'What are you going to do?'

'I can't tell yet. I guess I'll take a look at his place. After that . . . who knows?'

'How will you get in?'

'I'll find a way.'

Adler stood up and shuffled past her into the hall. She heard the scrape of a drawer. When he returned he was holding a set of keys.

'The one with the plastic clip is the top lock, the other one does the main lock. The number for the building is 1845.'

'Thank you.'

'It was Miriam's idea. In case they needed help.'

Stephanie took the keys and put them into the pocket of her denim jacket.

Adler said, 'Is there something I can do, Petra? I'd like to help.'

'Then forget this conversation. In fact, forget I was even here.'

I'm sitting at a small circular table beside the window. Outside, the traffic thickens along rue de Rivoli. The street shimmers in the wintry light of early morning. Silver rain streaks the glass. I order some breakfast from the waiter and then spread the newspapers across the table; Le Monde, Libération, International Herald Tribune. *The bomb dominates the front pages of the two French papers and shares the lead in the* Tribune.

According to the French reports, there are twelve dead and forty-five injured. The Tribune *has thirteen dead and forty-nine injured. A spokesman for the Préfet de Police concludes: 'It's a tragedy. And a grotesque act of cowardice.'*

Much of the coverage is analysis. Since Sentier has a strong Jewish presence, the focus inevitably falls upon anti-Semitic extremists. With all the awkward questions that poses for a country like France. Or even a city like Paris. Libération *reports that the Gendarmerie Nationale have two suspects, both men, both seen entering La Béatrice two or three minutes before the explosion. The shorter of the pair is about one-metre-sixty and is twenty to twenty-five years old. He was wearing a Nike tracksuit – dark blue with white flashes. The older one is probably in his mid-thirties, around one-metre-eighty, and was wearing denim jeans, black running shoes and a khaki jacket with a zip. They are Algerians but might be travelling on Moroccan passports. No names are suggested.*

I read the descriptions several times. The detail is convincing but false. No such men entered La Béatrice while I was there, which was over a period of about twenty minutes. And if they'd gone in after I'd left, they'd almost certainly be dead.

The name of al-Qaeda is tossed over the coverage as casually as confetti at a wedding. The French papers, in particular, concern themselves with the possibility of an anti-Muslim backlash. Nothing I read is new.

The café is quiet. A crumpled, middle-aged man beneath the menu blackboard nurses a glass of red wine. I can't decide whether it's the last of the night or the first of the morning. Three tables away from me, a plump dark-haired woman is smoking a filterless cigarette. Smudged eye-liner draws attention to bloodshot pupils.

The waiter brings me bread, butter and hot chocolate. He stoops to lay them on the table, a lock of greasy grey hair falling from his forehead. He sees the newspapers, shakes his head and clucks his disapproval.

There's no mention of me anywhere. No female suspect. No chase through the ruins. No gun-shot. I've been air-brushed from the picture.

Number 16, place Vendôme. Just inside the entrance, on the wall to the left, was a mirror with the names of the resident institutions picked out in gold letters; R.T. Vanderbilt Company Inc., Lazard Construction, Laboratoires Garnier. Under *Escalier B*, Stephanie found the name, once familiar, now largely ignored: Banque Damiani, Genève. This was only her second visit in seven years.

Escalier B was at the back of the paved courtyard, past the offices of Comme des Garçons, through a set of black double-doors. Inside, Stephanie took the stairs.

The reception room had been redecorated; a large Chinese carpet laid over a polished parquet floor, heavy curtains of plum brocade, a pair of Louis XIV armchairs either side of a table. There was a collection of oil portraits set in large oval gilt frames, each hung within a wall panel. Stephanie knew that the faces belonged to the original Damiani brothers and their sons.

The receptionist was about the same age as her. But standing in front of her desk, Stephanie felt like a gauche teenager. She wore a beautifully cut suit; navy-blue, simple, elegant. She was sitting in a throne chair, her spine nowhere near the back of it. On her wrist was a gold Piaget watch.

She greeted Stephanie with a warm smile. Elsewhere, that might have been a surprise considering Stephanie's appearance – *perhaps you are looking for some other place?* – but not here. The few who made it to the receptionist's desk at Banque Damiani usually did so intentionally. Regardless of appearance.

'I have a box.'

'Of course. One moment, please.'

The receptionist directed her towards the Louis XIV armchairs, then disappeared through the door to the right, the panels inlaid with antique mirror glass. Alone, Stephanie hoped she'd remember the process accurately; two number sequences and a one-time password to allow her access to the strongroom. She would be accompanied by a senior member of the bank and one security guard. In a private cubicle, her box would be brought to her. Once the door was closed, she would open the box using a six-digit code on the keypad. There were no keys in the process, which was one of the reasons she'd chosen Banque Damiani. Under the circumstances in which she might want access to the box, carrying a key – or even collecting a key – might not be possible.

Inside the box was Helen Graham; a thirty-one-year-old Canadian, born in Vancouver, now living in Chicago. Passport, identity card, driving licence, credit-cards, euros, dollars, a pair of glasses, a small case with two sets of coloured contact lenses (grey), a cheap plastic wallet containing thirteen family snapshots, and an insulin pen. Containing, instead of insulin, a strain of engineered tetrodotoxin, a substance found naturally in puffer fish, designed to act instantly by closing down the sodium channels in the nerves, thus rendering them useless, leading to death by paralysis of the breathing muscles.

Helen Graham was a member of the Magnificent Seven. She was one of five exit identities Stephanie had spread across Europe. The others were in Frankfurt, Valencia, Bratislava and Trondheim. Each was held in a safe-deposit box in an institution where the means of access was carried solely in the memory. Beyond Europe, there were versions of her in Baltimore and Osaka.

Over the years, these identities had been rotated. New ones were established, old ones destroyed, nearly always intact. This was only the third time she'd had to activate one. The last time had been in Helsinki and that had been almost four years ago. Since then, she'd only interfered with the identities once. Two months after the introduction of the euro, she'd visited all the European safe-deposit boxes to swap bundles of condemned deutschmarks and francs for pristine euro notes.

The Magnificent Seven had been established as an insurance policy. Created by Jacob Furst's protégé, Cyril Bradfield, without the knowledge of her former masters, their existence had, until now, been more of an expensive comfort than a practical necessity.

The door opened and a man in a dark grey double-breasted suit entered, holding in his left hand a leather clipboard. Olive-skinned, black hair flecked with silver at the temples, he stood an inch shorter than Stephanie.

In clipped German, clearly not his first language, he said, 'Welcome. A pleasure to see you again.'

Stephanie had never seen him before. He was speaking German because she was Stephanie Schneider, although no one at the bank was likely to mention the name in conversation with her.

'I'm Pierre Damiani. Sadly, my uncle is abroad this week. He will be upset to have missed you.'

She doubted that. She hadn't met him, either.

'I hope I can be of some assistance to you. Sophie told me why you are here. Before we proceed, I would just like to take this opportunity to say that this bank and my family regard the interests of our esteemed customers as absolutely sacrosanct.'

Said with conviction, nothing obsequious about it.

'I don't doubt that,' she replied.

He nodded curtly, then gave her the leather clipboard. On it was a cream-coloured card with the bank's name and crest embossed across the top. Beneath, there were three boxes for the numbers and password.

'You are familiar with the procedure?'

'I am.'

'Please read the sheet below.'

Stephanie lifted the card. The message was handwritten in blue ink: *Your safe-deposit box has been contaminated. The front of this building is being monitored. Your appearance here has already been reported. In a moment, I will leave the room. Please do not go until then. Take the door on the opposite side of the room to the one I use. At the far end of the passage, there is a fire-exit. It's unlocked. Our cameras are recording us –* I hope you understand *– so could you sign the bottom of the declaration form then fill out the card, as normal. Please understand that it is not safe for us to talk. With our sincerest apologies, your faithful servants, Banque Damiani & the Damiani family.*

Ten-forty. The easyInternetCafé on boulevard de Sébastopol was busy. Stephanie settled herself at her terminal and sent the same message to three different addresses.

> Oscar. Need to speak. CRV/13. P.

She'd followed Pierre Damiani's escape route without a problem. What more could they have done for her? *Our cameras are recording us – I hope you understand.* A plea more than anything else, meaning perhaps: *our cameras are recording us . . . and who can say who will see this?* Some entity with powers to sequestrate such recordings?

Yesterday she'd had security in numbers: Stephanie, Petra, Marianne, the Magnificent Seven. Now she was down to one. But which one? Or was it worse than that? Perhaps she was no one at all.

Generally, the deeper the crisis, the deeper she withdrew into Petra. Which fuelled the contradiction at the heart of her; Stephanie was only ever extraordinary as Petra and the more extraordinary Petra was, the more Stephanie resented it. Now, however, Petra seemed marginalized, her confidence faltering.

Helen Graham was useless to her now. That meant the rest of her Magnificent Seven were contaminated by association. Which prompted an unpleasant thought: Cyril Bradfield was the only other person who'd been aware of their existence. She tried to think who might have penetrated their secret. And, more worryingly, how. Through Bradfield himself? What other way could there be? The possibility made her nauseous. Magenta

House had to be the prime candidate. Which was faintly ironic, since the identities were designed to protect her from them.

Magenta House was the organization for whom she'd once worked. Based in London, if an entity that doesn't exist can be based anywhere, it had no official title; Magenta House was the nickname used by those on the inside. Created to operate beyond the law, it had never bothered to recognize the law. In that sense, it was a logical concept, especially if one accepted that there were some threats that could not be countered legally. *Somebody has to work in the sewers, Stephanie. That's why people like you exist.*

They'd created her, they'd tried to control her and, in the end, they'd tried to kill her. Which, paradoxically, made them unlikely candidates now. They'd let her go. There had been a change. One era had ended, another had begun, and Petra had been consigned to history.

Nothing that had happened in the last twenty-four hours bore any trace of Magenta House. They shied away from spectaculars. They didn't plant bombs in public places. Instead, they liquidated the kind of people who did. Quietly, clinically, leaving no trace, and sometimes no body. They deleted people from existence. If they'd wanted to kill her and they'd discovered where she was, they wouldn't have bothered luring her to Paris.

On the screen, a reply directed her to a quiet confessional in the ether.

> Hello Oscar.
> Petra. Bored already?
The cursor was winking at her, teasing her.
> I'm in Paris.
> Not a good choice for a vacation at the moment.
> Especially not in Sentier.
> You were there?
> Yes. Has anybody been looking for me?
> You're always in demand.
> I need help, Oscar. I'm running blind.

There was a long pause and Stephanie knew why. This was the first time Stern had encountered Petra in trouble.
> What do you need?
> Something. *Anything*.
> Give me two hours. We can meet here again.

She terminated the connection. Out on the street she buttoned her denim jacket to the throat and pressed her hands into the pockets. Which was where her fingers came into contact with the keys that Adler had given her. In the other pocket was Marianne Bernard's mobile phone. She cursed herself for not dumping it earlier; when a mobile phone was switched on, it was a moving beacon. But she'd heard a rumour that it was now possible to track a mobile phone when it was switched off. She dropped the handset into the first bin she passed.

Five-to-one. Stephanie was back with Stern through a terminal at Web 46 on rue du Roi du Sicilie.

> I have a name for you, Petra.

> How much?

> This is for free.

> You must be going soft in your old age.

> Has it ever occurred to you that I might be younger than you?

> Only in my more humorous moments.

>This isn't sentimentality. This is business. If anything happens to you, I'll lose money.

> That's more like it. Who is it?

> Leonid Golitsyn.

> Don't know him.

> An art-dealer. Very rich. Very well connected.

> What's his story?

> He has a gallery in Paris on avenue Matignon but he's based in New York. He goes to Paris three or four times a year, usually on his way back to Moscow. Golitsyn is old school. Chernenko, Gromyko, even Brezhnev – he was cosy with all of them. In those days he was a virtual commuter between the United States and the Soviet Union. He's always been close to the Kremlin. Even now.

> Putin doesn't strike me as an art collector.

> I think it's safe to say that Golitsyn's been carrying more than canvas over the years. He's one of those strange creatures who knows everybody but who nobody knows. A friend of mine once described him – rather memorably – as a diplomatic bag. An insult and a truth rolled into one.

> Why is he relevant?

> Anders Brand.

> What's he got to do with this?

> He was one of the thirteen who were killed yesterday.

Stephanie was amazed. Anders Brand, the former Swedish diplomat, fondly known as The Whisperer. A man who spoke so softly you began to wonder if your hearing was impaired. A peerless mediator during his time at the United Nations. Stephanie remembered seeing him on BBC World's *Hard Talk*. He'd only been half-joking when he'd said that being softly-spoken was one of the keys to his success at mediation: 'It forces people to listen more carefully to me.'

She pictured Brand as he was usually seen – on a conference podium, in a TV studio, disembarking from an aircraft – and realized that his face matched a face she'd seen at La Béatrice. The face she thought she'd recognized but hadn't been able to name.

> How come this isn't headline news?

> It will be this evening. As I understand it, his death won't be officially confirmed until later this afternoon.

> After more than twenty-four hours?

> I wasn't there, Petra. But I've seen the pictures.

The photo-flash memory of Béatrice Klug's flaming head gave the concept of delayed identification unpleasant credibility.

> What's the connection with Golitsyn?

> I don't know that there necessarily is one. What I do know is this: the day before yesterday, they had dinner together at the Meurice. Golitsyn arrived earlier in the day from New York. Brand was due to fly to

73

Baghdad today. Golitsyn heads to Moscow tomorrow. Golitsyn and Brand go back a long way. Brand is another of Golitsyn's twenty-four-carat connections. Maybe they discussed something that is germane to your current situation.

He's not telling me everything.

Typical of Stern. Their relationship had lasted longer than any of Stephanie's romantic relationships. Even the good ones. Both of them had secrets yet both of them had entrusted part of themselves to the other. That wasn't something she could verify, it was something she felt.

> How do I meet Golitsyn?

> Tonight Golitsyn will be at the Lancaster. Do you know it?

She did. But only because the name of the hotel prompted another name: Konstantin Komarov. One of only two men to have found a way past all her defences. Even now, the mere mention of him was enough to send a jolt through her.

There was an image engraved on her memory; Komarov in front of the Lancaster with a woman on his arm. Not Stephanie but a tall Russian. Ludmilla. The woman who'd taken Stephanie's place in his bed. A woman who, it transpired, was as intelligent as she was beautiful. In other words, a woman who hadn't even allowed Stephanie hope.

> I know it.

> He has a series of business meetings there. I've arranged for you to see him at eight.

> And that's it?

> Not quite. You will have to be Claudia Calderon.

> Who's she?

Hector Reggiano's brand-new art consultant. Reggiano was a name Stephanie recognized. An Argentine billionaire. Technically, a financier, whatever that meant in Argentina. In the real world, a common thief. But a cultured thief; an art collector with an appetite.

> Golitsyn has been courting Reggiano for years. From your perspective, Claudia Calderon offers two distinct advantages. One: she's currently in Patagonia. Two: Golitsyn's never met her. And he won't turn down a last-minute opportunity to see if he can seduce the woman who controls Reggiano's purse-strings.

> Is all this really necessary?

> To get you to see Golitsyn? Absolutely. Claudia Calderon gets you past Medvedev. Once you're with Golitsyn – then it's up to you.

> And who's Medvedev?

> Golitsyn's personal assistant. Ex-Spetsnaz. These days, everywhere Golitsyn goes, Medvedev goes too. He takes care of everything. Hotels, flights, meetings, money, girls.

> Perhaps I'll suggest to Golitsyn he gets himself a female assistant so he can save himself some cash.

> Hardly a pressing consideration.

> Too rich to care?

> He's more than rich, Petra.

> Meaning?

> Golitsyn floats above the world.

*   *   *

As Petra, there aren't many situations I find intimidating. Composure is part of her make-up and when I wear it, it's a genuine reflection of who I am at that moment. But everyone has an Achilles heel. And this is both hers and mine.

I'm on avenue Montaigne. So far I've been into Gucci, Jil Sander and Calvin Klein, looking for something that Claudia Calderon might wear. I don't think Hector Reggiano's art consultant would turn up for a meeting with Leonid Golitsyn wearing a grubby denim jacket and scuffed Merrell shoes. I have an image of her in my mind; tall, slender, sophisticated. All I can do is pretend in fancy dress. Escada and Christian Lacroix come and go.

It's the fascism of fashion that annoys me. The eugenics of beauty. The people in these shops always seem to know that I don't belong. Eventually, however, salvation presents itself in the form of MaxMara, on the junction with rue Clément Marot, opposite the jeweller Harry Winston. Whatever the city, this is the one place that doesn't make me feel like a leper.

I drift through the store and end up with a figure-hugging dress, somewhere between dark grey and brown, with sleeves to the knuckle. To go with it I pick out a very soft dark brown, knee-length suede coat with a black leather belt, a pair of shoes and a black bag.

I take the deliberate decision to use Marianne Bernard's American Express card. The transaction will be traced. But I'm banking on a delay. It doesn't need to be a long one. Sixty seconds will do.

The purchase is processed without a problem and I

leave with Claudia Calderon in a bag. Later, I wrap all Marianne's cards in a paper napkin and toss them away. I'll miss the life we shared. Marianne was good to me; a sure sign that our relationship wasn't destined to last.

Late afternoon. Stephanie pressed 1845 into the keypad and took the damp staircase to the third floor. Jacob and Miriam Furst's apartment was at the end of the corridor. The door was sealed with police tape. There was no noise from the other apartments on the floor. She hadn't seen light from any of them from rue Dénoyez. She slit the tape and let herself in with Claude Adler's keys, quietly closing the door behind her.

Inside, she stood perfectly still, adjusting to the gloom. The dull wash of streetlamps provided the only light. She smelt stale cigarette smoke. The Fursts hadn't been smokers; Miriam had been asthmatic.

The small living-room overlooked rue Dénoyez. As her eyes became accustomed to the light, Stephanie saw a delta of dark splatters over the oatmeal carpet at the centre of the room. The blood had dried to a black crust. There was broken glass in the cast-iron grate. On the mantelpiece above the fire there had once been a large collection of miniature figurines, she recalled; horses, the glass blown with curls of fiery orange and emerald green. Only two remained.

In the kitchen, she recognized the cheap watercolour of place des Vosges and the wooden mug rack. There were no mugs left. They were all broken. Cutlery and cracked china littered the linoleum floor.

She wondered what the official line was. A violent burglary perpetrated against an elderly, vulnerable couple, their murders little more than some kind of sporting bonus?

The bathroom was at the back of the apartment, overlooking waste ground. It didn't look as though regeneration was imminent. She lowered the blind and switched on the light. The wallpaper might have been cream once. Now it was pale rust, except for black patches of damp in the corner over the bath. By the sink was a shaving kit, the badger-hair brush and cut-throat razor laid upon an old flannel.

Stephanie washed herself thoroughly, then dressed in the underwear and stockings she'd bought from a depressing discount store on boulevard de Belleville, followed by the clothes she'd bought at MaxMara. She put her belongings into the black leather bag and put her dirty clothes into the MaxMara bags, which she placed beneath the basin.

Using Miriam's hairbrush made her faintly queasy. She tried to ignore the sensation and examined herself in the mirror. What she needed was twenty minutes in the shower with plenty of shampoo and soap. And then make-up to mask the fatigue. But she'd forgotten to buy make-up and was sure that Miriam had never worn any. Besides, that would certainly feel worse than using the hair-brush; who'd wear a dead woman's lipstick?

The Lancaster was small and discreet, a town-house hotel, the kind she liked. The bar was an open area leading through to the restaurant. A few sofas, some armchairs, a cluster of tables. It was busy at quarter to eight, the centre of the room taken by a loud group; four skeletal women, two of them in dark glasses, and three skeletal men with designer stubble, open-necked shirts, suits. One of them was fiddling with a miniature dachshund. They were all drinking champagne.

Stern had said that Medvedev would be waiting for her at the bar itself, which was at one end of the dining-room. He was easy to spot; alone, a chilled martini glass at his elbow, on the phone.

Medvedev was a Spetsnaz veteran – FSB Alpha – but there was no longer any hint of it. Golitsyn's influence, she supposed. A life of luxury to smooth away the rough edges. As she approached the bar, he finished his call, folded his phone shut and raised his glass to drink.

'Fyodor Medvedev?'

He set his glass down without taking the sip.

In Russian, she said, '*Dobryy vecher. Minya zavut* Claudia Calderon.'

He took his time replying. 'Sorry. Please say again. My name is . . . ?'

It wasn't worth the wait; his accent was atro-cious.

79

Now Stephanie was the one looking confused. 'Fyodor Medvedev?'

He switched to English; American, east coast but tempered. 'Is that who I am? Thanks. I was starting to wonder.'

'You're not Russian.'

He shook his head. 'Just like you.'

'And you don't work for Leonid Golitsyn?'

'Never heard of him.'

She looked around – *where was Medvedev?* – and shrugged. 'I'm sorry. I thought you were . . .'

'Have we met before?'

'That's original.'

'I know. But have we?'

It occurred to Stephanie that they'd both thought they'd recognized each other. She'd thought he was Medvedev. And he'd thought she was . . . *who?* The moment he first saw her, who had she been to him?

'I don't think so.'

He offered his hand. 'Well, I'm Robert. Robert Newman.'

'Hello, Robert. Claudia Calderon.'

'Calderon – you're from Spain?'

'Argentina.'

'Lucky you. One of my favourite countries.'

Stephanie swiftly changed direction. 'So . . . what do you do, Robert?'

'Depends who's asking.'

'That makes you sound like a gun for hire.'

'But in a suit.'

Which he wore well, she noticed. *He has them made.* Grey, double-breasted, over a pale blue shirt with a deep red, hand-woven silk tie.

'They're the ones you have to watch,' Stephanie said. 'Like the vicar's daughter.'

His laugh was soft and low. 'Then I guess I'm in . . . finance.'

'You don't sound very sure.'

'My background is oil.'

'But no dirty hands?'

'Not these days. When I was younger.'

She could believe it. He was perfectly at home in the Lancaster's bar, in his expensive suit, with the heavy stainless-steel TAG-Heuer on his wrist. Yet she could see the oil-fields. In his eyes, in the lines around them, across hands made for manual labour.

He summoned the bartender and said to Stephanie, 'Can I buy you a drink?'

A question she'd been asked too many times by too many men. But she didn't mind it coming from him. He hadn't made any assumptions about her. Not yet. Usually, the men who asked her that question were already deciding how much they were prepared to pay for her.

She had champagne because she felt that would be Claudia Calderon's drink. That or Diet Coke. Newman ordered another vodka martini.

'You live in Paris, Claudia?'

'I'm visiting.'

'Staying here, at the Lancaster?'

81

'A man who gets right to the point.'

'It's an innocent question.'

The bartender slid a glass towards her.

'No, I'm not staying here,' Stephanie said. 'What about you?'

'I live here.'

'In the hotel?'

'In the city.'

'How original. An American in Paris.'

'If you consider a New Yorker an American . . .'

'You don't?'

'Not really. I think of New York as a city-state. America's another country.'

Which was something she'd felt herself. In New York, she'd always been at home. In the rest of America, she was constantly reminded of how European she was.

She tried to push past the remark. 'How long have you lived here?'

'I've had a place here for ten years but I don't use it much. I travel a lot on business.'

'Where?'

'The Far East, the Middle East, the States. All over. What about you? What do you do?'

Now that the moment had come, she couldn't pass herself off as an art consultant. 'Take a guess.'

He gave it some thought, allowing her to look at him properly. He had short dark hair and attractive dark brown eyes. His tanned face looked pleasantly weather-beaten for a businessman. In his forties, or perhaps a young-looking fifty, he appeared fit for a man with the kind of life he'd described.

'Well?' she prompted.

'You know, looking at you, I really can't think of anything.'

'You're straying.'

'Straying?'

'This is supposed to be a polite conversation. There are rules. One of them is: don't even try to think. Thought breeds silence. That's not allowed. If you can't come up with anything decent to say, say something shallow.'

'Sorry. I didn't know.'

'I'm surprised. All that travel, all those hotels. This can't be your first time.'

'My first time?'

'Being approached. In a bar. By a woman.'

His smile was the wry badge of the world-weary. 'I guess that depends on where you're going with this.'

Stephanie smiled too. 'That's very neat.'

'You didn't answer the question.'

'Maybe this is what I do. Approach strange men in hotel bars.'

'I doubt it.'

'Why?'

'You don't have the look.'

'What look's that?'

He sipped some vodka. 'Desperate predatory allure.'

Stephanie arched an eyebrow. 'Desperate

predatory allure? I like that. But it puts you at risk of sounding like an expert.'

'Well, you're right, of course. I've been in many bars. There have been many . . . *situations*. And they never fail to disappoint.'

'No value for money?'

'I quit before it gets to that.'

'Naturally.'

'You don't believe me?'

'Well, I'm not sure. I wouldn't expect you to admit it.'

He took his time, sizing her up, *deciding* about her. 'You always this direct?'

'Only with complete strangers.'

'Because you can be, right?'

'Yes. Liberating, isn't it?'

He nodded, comfortable with her; neither threatened, nor encouraged. She hoped he wouldn't spoil it by saying something crass.

'I guess that's the game we're playing.' He rolled his glass a little, watching the oily liquid swirl. 'Strange how that works, though. That you can say anything to someone you've never met before. The kind of things you wouldn't say to someone you know.'

'It only works when you think you won't see them again.'

'Like now?'

'Yes. Like now.'

Newman said, 'Scheherazade.'

'What?'

'I'm sorry. You're going to have to excuse me.'

Stephanie turned round. A woman had appeared on the far side of the bar. She had beautiful thick black hair. A dark, liquid complexion set off the gold choker at her throat. Slender with curves, she wasn't tall, perhaps only five-four, but she had poise and presence. Heads were turning.

'Your date?' Stephanie asked.

How typical, she thought, that she should be the one to be crass. Newman seemed to find it amusing.

'It's been a pleasure, Claudia. A rare pleasure.'

And then he was gone. Stephanie looked at the woman again. She recognized the face but couldn't remember her name; high cheekbones, large dark eyes, a wide mouth, which now split into a smile, as Newman crossed the floor to meet her.

The phone behind the bar began to ring.

Scheherazade who?

They embraced, his hand staying on her arm. She glanced at Stephanie then whispered something to him. They laughed and then settled on the only spare sofa.

'*Excusez-moi* . . .'

She turned round. The bartender was holding the phone for her. She took it and pressed the receiver to her ear. Over the crackle of bad reception, she heard an engine. Car horns blared in the background. 'Yes?'

'This is Fyodor Medvedev.' His American accent

was clumsy, words shunting into one another like old rail wagons in a verbal siding. 'I'm sorry to be late. I'm in traffic. Not moving.'

'At least I know you're in Paris.'

He didn't get it. 'I will be at hotel in ten minutes. Mr Golitsyn wants to see you now. Is okay?'

'Sure.'

'Room 41. Emile Wolf suite. He waits for you.'

As she handed the phone back to the bartender, the name came to her. Scheherazade Zahani. A favourite of *Paris-Match* and the gossip columns. Usually seen at the opera, or stepping out of the latest restaurant, or on the deck of her one-hundred-metre yacht at Cap d'Antibes.

The daughter of a rich arms-dealer, she'd married a Saudi oil billionaire. Stephanie had forgotten his name but remembered that he'd been in his sixties. A student at Princeton, highly academic, very beautiful, Zahani had only been twenty-two or twenty-three. There had been a lot of carping comment. Fifteen years later, following her husband's death in Switzerland, Zahani had moved to Paris, several billion dollars richer. Since then, the French press had attempted to link the grieving widow with every eligible Frenchman over thirty-five. If she was bored by the facile coverage she received, she never let it show. She seemed content to be seen in public with potential suitors but they rarely lasted more than a couple of outings. There had been no affairs, no scandal.

It was only in the last five years that her business acumen had become widely acknowledged. Now she was regarded as one of the shrewdest investors in France. As Stephanie watched Scheherazade Zahani and Robert Newman, she wondered whether they were discussing the only thing she knew they had in common.

Oil.

I know something's wrong the moment I enter Leonid Golitsyn's suite on the fourth floor. I knocked on the door – there was no bell – but got no reply. There are no Ving cards here either, so I tried the handle and the door opened.

Golitsyn is in the bedroom, lying on the floor at the foot of the bed. A large Thomson TV throws flickering light over his body. A game show is on, the volume high, amplified laughter and applause. A large maroon flower has blossomed across his chest. Blood is seeping into the carpet beneath him. There are drops of it on his face, like some glossy pox.

He blinks.

I circle the room slowly and silently, then check the bathroom. The second body is in the bathtub, one trousered leg dangling over the lip. On the floor is a gun. I pick it up, a Smith & Wesson Sigma .40, a synthetics-only weapon, the frame constructed from a high-strength polymer. It hasn't been fired recently.

The man in the bath is wearing a crumpled suit and a bloodstained shower-curtain. Most of the hooks have been ripped from the rail. There's blood on the floor and wall. He's been shot at least three times. Using a

87

very efficient sound suppressor, I imagine, because being a converted townhouse the Lancaster's sound-proofing is not great.

I return to the bedroom. When I move into his line of sight Golitsyn blinks again and manages to send a tremor to his fingertips.

I crouch beside him. What an impressive man he must have been. Two metres tall, by the look of it, with fine patrician features down a long face, framed by longish snow-white hair and a carefully trimmed beard of the same colour.

I look at the chest wound and then the blood. He should be dead already. There's nothing I can do for him.

He tries to force a word through the gap in his lips. 'Ah . . . ams . . .'

'Anders?'

He'd frown if he could move the muscles in his fore-head.

I try again. 'Anders Brand?'

Nothing.

'You and Anders Brand?'

I kill the volume on the TV.

'. . . da . . . ah . . . ams . . .'

This is all very recent.

'Passage du Caire. Do you understand?'

'. . . ter . . . da . . . ahm . . .'

'Anders Brand. He was there. He was killed. After you saw him.'

In Golitsyn's eyes the flame of urgency struggles against death's chilly breeze. '. . . ams . . . ams . . .'

'Who did this? The same people who killed Brand?'

'. . . ter . . . da . . .'

'What about the bomb?'

'Ams . . . ter . . .'

'Amster?'

I see an emphatic 'yes' in his eyes.

'Amster,' I repeat.

'Dam.'

It's almost a cough.

'Amsterdam?'

He blinks his confirmation because he's fading fast.

'What about Amsterdam?'

He tries to summon one last phrase but can't; the eyes freeze, the focus fails, the fingers unfurl. On the TV screen, a contestant cries with joy as she takes possession of a shiny new Hyundai.

Somewhere out there, a distant siren moans. Not for me, I tell myself. But a part of me is less sure. I take the cash from the table – Petra the vulture, a natural scavenger – and scoop his correspondence and mobile phone into a slim, leather attaché case that has three Cyrillic letters embossed in gold beneath the handle; L.I.G.

I return to the bathroom where curiosity compels me to check the body. Trying my best to avoid the blood, I reach inside folds of shower-curtain and pale grey jacket to retrieve a wallet and passport. I flip open the passport; flat features, light brown hair cut short and parted on the right, small grey eyes.

Fyodor Medvedev.

The man I spoke to . . . how many minutes ago?

There isn't time for this. Not now. Get out.

I drop the gun into my black MaxMara bag. Dressed as I am, the attaché case doesn't look too incongruous. At least something is working out today.

Outside the suite, I close the door and walk calmly to the lift. I press the button. A woman from Housekeeping passes by carrying a tower of white towels.

'Bonsoir.'

'Bonsoir.'

I step into the tiny lift with its polished wood and burgundy leather. The unanswered questions are spinning inside my head. The Medvedev in the bath isn't the Medvedev I spoke to over the phone at the bar. I'm sure of that. Even if he'd been sitting in a car outside the hotel he would barely have had enough time to sprint upstairs and get shot before I found him. So if the corpse in the bath is Medvedev, who was I talking to before?

As for Golitsyn . . .

The doors open. I step out and head right. There are raised voices coming from reception, which is now just out of sight to my left. Some kind of commotion. I back-track and go through the bar. The skeletal group are too self-absorbed to have realized anything is wrong but others have noticed; their conversations halting, heads turning. The sofa where Robert Newman and Scheherazade Zahani were sitting is empty. Perhaps they've gone through to the restaurant.

I push through the large glass door and head down the short hall towards the exit, catching a glimpse of the reception area to my right; two men are arguing with the woman behind the desk. One of them is showing her something. A card of some sort. She's speaking into the phone, clearly anxious. Beside her, a man sorts through a collection of keys.

I step onto rue de Berri. To my left, a flustered doorman in a long overcoat is standing by a black Renault. There's no one in it. Both front doors are open, the front left wheel has mounted the kerb. A blue lamp sits on the dashboard.

Whatever you do, don't run.

I venture right. I'm a stylish businesswoman carrying an attaché case. In this part of town, that shouldn't raise an eyebrow. Except my own; above the noise of the city, the sirens are getting louder. Ahead of me, at the junction with Champs Élysées I see the first signs of stroboscopic blue light ricocheting off buildings.

I look over my shoulder. The doorman turns round. We're fifteen metres apart. He can't decide whether he's seen me before. Someone cries out from the hotel. I feel like a rabbit stranded in headlights. Where is Petra?

Next to the Lancaster is the Berri-Washington twenty-four-hour public car-park, a blue neon sign above a long, sloping concrete ramp. My right hand is inside the black leather bag, my fingertips touching the Sigma. The first patrol car enters rue de Berri. There's another behind it. And I'm going down the ramp.

A subterranean car-park should have a fire-exit that rises somewhere else. I try to ignore the sirens but I'm expecting the shout. The order to halt, to remove my hand from the bag, to drop everything and turn round.

I'm halfway down the ramp when a car comes into view. The engine echoes off the concrete as it rises towards me. A silver Audi A6 Quattro.

Keep calm.

I'm just a woman going to collect her car. I move to one side to allow the Audi to pass. But it slows down . . .

Keep going.

. . . and then halts.

Please, no.

My right hand searches for the grip. A window lowers.

'Small world.'

For a moment I'm too dazed to say anything. It's Robert Newman.

Behind me, and above us, there are more sirens. Decision time. What if there is no other way out?

'Need a ride?'

This can't be right.

But I smile sweetly anyway. 'Sure. Thanks.'

I climb into the back of the Audi, which is not what he's expecting. He looks over his shoulder and says, 'You can sit up front if you like. I promise I won't . . .'

Which is when he sees the gun.

'Drive.'

'What the . . .'

'Trust me – you don't have time to think about it.'

He glances up the ramp.

I thrust the tip of the Sigma into his cheek and yell: 'Drive!'

He accelerates towards street level.

'Where to?'

'Right. Go right.'

'I can't.'

'What?'

'It's one-way.'

'Then go left!'

'And after that?'

'Just do it! And whatever happens, don't stop. If you do, I swear I'll kill you.'

We reach the ramp. He pulls out, past the black Renault, past two police cars, blue lights aflame. Officers hover on the street, a crowd gathers. I keep the gun out of sight. A young officer, eager to get us out of the way, waves us past. I peer through the rear window as the Lancaster recedes. At boulevard Haussmann we turn right.

How did they get there so quickly? Yesterday at Passage du Caire, it was the same; uniformed police officers only moments away. I close my eyes. When I open them, I see him in the rear-view mirror.

'Where are we going?' he asks.

'Nowhere. Just keep moving. And don't do anything stupid.'

'Looks like I already have.'

'Pull over.'

It was a quiet street off place de la porte de Champerret, just inside the *périphérique*. When Newman switched off the engine they could hear the rumble from the ring road. Almost an hour had passed, most of it in silence. Stephanie had tried to think but had found she couldn't. There were too many competing questions. She couldn't separate one from another, couldn't focus on a single coherent thought. Gradually, however, Petra had emerged and cold clarity had replaced panic.

'Put your hands on the steering wheel where I can see them. Don't take them off.'

The street was empty. She tightened her grip on the gun and shifted her position so that she had a less awkward angle.

'Okay. Who are you?'

'You know who I am. Robert Newman.'

'Believe me, your next cute answer's going to be your last.'

'I don't know what else to say.'

'Well you better think of something. And quick.'

'My name's Robert Newman. I'm a businessman.'

'We meet at the bar then you're driving up the ramp. Explain that.'

He shrugged. 'I can't.'

'Coincidence?'

'I guess.'

'I don't believe in coincidence. You and Scheherazade Zahani – that must have been the quickest date in history.'

Newman flinched at the mention of her name. 'I wasn't there to meet her. She just showed up. She was meeting a friend who's staying at the Lancaster.'

'Another coincidence?'

He couldn't bring himself to acknowledge it. Stephanie leaned forward and pressed the tip of the Smith & Wesson into the back of his neck, just above the collar.

She said, 'Let me explain something to you. Whoever you thought I was at the bar – she doesn't exist. She never did.'

'Look, I was due to meet someone. He called to cancel right after you left.'

'I'm going to give you one more chance.'

'See for yourself,' he snapped, reaching inside his jacket.

'*Stop!*'

Newman froze. And then clamped his right hand back on the wheel. 'Jesus Christ! Take it easy!'

'What did I tell you?'

'I know what you said. I was just going for my cell phone. So you could see. The number, the time.'

Stephanie focused on her breathing for a second. Anything to slow the pulse. A couple were walking towards them, arm in arm, heads shrouded in frozen breath, hard heels clicking on the pavement. Stephanie placed the gun in her lap and shielded it with the black leather bag.

'I need to disappear,' she said.

'Don't let me stop you.'

'Where do you live?'

'Île Saint-Louis.'

'Alone?'

He hesitated. 'Yeah.'

'I'm going to ask that again. If we get there and there's someone to meet us I'm going to kill them, no questions asked. So think before you speak. Do you live alone?'

'Yes.'

The couple strolled past the car.

'Give me your wallet.'

'It's in my jacket. Like my phone.'

Stephanie pressed the Smith & Wesson to the same patch of skin. 'Then be very careful.'

He retrieved it – Dunhill, black leather with gold corners – and passed it back. On his Platinum Amex the name read Robert R. Newman. He had two printed cards, one professional, one personal, which included an address on quai d'Orléans, Île Saint-Louis. The other card carried a name she didn't recognize with an address at La Défense.

'What's Solaris?'

'A company. I work for them.'

'An oil company?'

'Sometimes.'

'We're going to your place. I need somewhere to think.'

Quai d'Orléans, Île Saint-Louis, half-past-ten. They found a space close to his building. People passed by, heading home from the restaurants along rue Saint-Louis en Île.

Inside the Audi, Stephanie spoke softly. 'I don't want to have to do it. But if you make me, I will. Understand?'

Newman nodded.

'If we meet anybody you know, play it straight. I'm just a date.'

They got out. Newman carried Leonid Golitsyn's

attaché case and she clutched the Smith & Wesson which was in the pocket of her overcoat.

They reached the entrance to the building. He pressed the four-digit code – 2071 – and they stepped into a large hall, sparsely furnished. They took the cage-lift to the fifth floor. The entrance to Newman's apartment was a tall set of double-doors that opened into a hall with a smooth lime-stone floor. On the walls were gilt-framed canvases; flat Flemish landscapes beneath brooding pewter skies, moody portraits of pros-perous traders, pale aristocratic women. There were Casablanca lilies in a tall, tapering, octag-onal vase, their scent filling the hall.

Stephanie glanced at the flowers, then at Newman who understood. 'Yvette,' he said. 'She looks after the place. She's not a live-in. She comes daily during the week.'

'Does she have her own key?'

'Yes.'

'If you like her, remind me to get you to call her in the morning.'

At gun-point Newman led her through the apartment; two bedrooms, each with its own bath-room, a large sitting-room, a modest dining-room, a generous kitchen, a utility room and a study. The sitting-room and dining-room were at the front of the apartment, French windows opening on to a balcony that offered a truly spectacular view of Notre Dame on Île de la Cité.

'Nice place. Business must be good.'

They returned to the utility room. Stephanie made him open both cupboards; vacuum-cleaner, ironing board, a mop in a bucket, brooms, brushes, rags and cloths, cleaning products. She grabbed the coiled washing line from the worktop. On a shelf was a wooden box with household tools, including a roll of black tape, which she also took. Back in the sitting-room, she drew the curtains and dragged a chair to the centre of the floor.

'Take off your jacket and tie.'

He did, unfastening the top two buttons of his shirt and rolling up his sleeves.

'What happened to your wrists?'

Around each of them was a bracelet of livid purple scar tissue. She hadn't noticed them before. He didn't answer, glaring at her instead, his silence heavy with contempt.

'Do what I say and I won't hurt you. Now sit down.'

She bound his wrists with the washing line, securing them behind the back of the chair. Then she taped one ankle to a chair-leg.

'Don't make any noise.'

She left him and returned to the kitchen. It was a bachelor's kitchen, no question: a central island with a slate top; two chopping boards of seasoned wood, both barely scratched; a knife-block containing a set of pristine Sabatier blades. In the fridge were two bottles of Veuve Clicquot, some San Pellegrino, a bottle of Montagny, ground coffee and orange juice. No food.

His suits were hanging in a wardrobe in the bedroom, all tailored. But in another cupboard another Robert Newman existed; denim jeans, scuffed and frayed, T-shirts that had lost their shape and colour, exercise clothing, old trainers.

On the bedside table was a Bang & Olufsen phone, a bottle of Nurofen and a copy of *What Went Wrong?* by Bernard Lewis. On the other table was a single gold earring. Stephanie picked it up. It curled like a small shell.

In the bathroom, Newman's things were fanned out across more limestone. But in the cupboard behind the mirror Stephanie found eye-liner and a small bottle of Chanel No.5, half-empty. In the second bedroom, further evidence; a plum silk dress on a hanger, a couple of jerseys, a pair of black Calvin Klein jeans, some flimsy underwear, two shirts, a pair of silver Prada trainers.

She returned to the sitting-room. 'Who's the woman?'

'What woman?'

'The woman who leaves Chanel No.5 in your bathroom.' She showed him the earring. 'This woman.'

'That could be mine.'

'Trust me, I'm not in the mood.'

'It's none of your goddamn business.'

'Sure about that?'

'She's history.'

'If she shows up here, she will be.'

'It's been over for a while.'

'It was on your bedside table.'

'I'm the sentimental type.'

'Her stuff is still here.'

She saw that he was extremely nervous – the sweat, the shivers – but he was determined to maintain the façade. The pretence was all he had to cling to. 'You should see what I left at her place.'

There was no answer to that; Stephanie had left pieces of herself everywhere.

There was a large Loewe widescreen TV in the corner of the sitting-room. Stephanie sat on a sofa arm and flicked through channels; France 3, Canal+, France 2, pausing during a news bulletin on TF1. Continued analysis of the bomb in Sentier, riots in Caracas, an oil spill off the coast of Normandy. Then they were watching a female journalist with a red scarf around her throat. She was in rue de Berri, the Lancaster just discernible in the background, beyond the entrance to the Berri-Washington car-park.

The studio anchor was asking a question. The reporter nodded then said, 'The police will say only that Russian art-dealer Leonid Golitsyn and another unidentified man have been shot dead in what looks like a planned execution.'

'Have they suggested who might be responsible?'

'Not yet. All we know is that their bodies were discovered by a member of the hotel staff and that . . .'

Not true. By the time she'd left Golitsyn's suite, the police had arrived downstairs. She'd seen plain-clothed detectives at the front desk just seconds after stepping out of the lift. Yet seconds before, on the fourth floor, she'd exchanged a cordial *bonsoir* with the woman from Housekeeping.

Newman said, 'No wonder I couldn't guess what you do.'

'I didn't kill them.'

'This guy Golitsyn – when you thought I was someone else, you thought I worked for him.'

'When I got to the room, they were already dead.'

She couldn't believe how guilty she sounded.

Newman stared at the Smith & Wesson. 'That right?'

'It hasn't been fired. It's not mine. I picked it off the floor.'

'What are you saying – it was a suicide pact?'

She changed channels, choosing CNN's coverage of the Sentier bomb. There was footage of the wreckage in Passage du Caire, a reprise of the casualty statistics and still no mention of Anders Brand.

In the CNN studio two experts sat beside Becky Anderson. One was a spokesman for Le Conseil Représentatif des Institutions Juives de France (CRIF), the other was a terrorism expert from the London School of Economics. The CRIF spokesman insisted the bomb was part of a growing campaign of anti-Semitic activity in France and went on to castigate the government

101

and – by implication – the public for their lack of outrage.

The LSE analyst focused on the likely provenance of the two fake suspects. Snippets of information were threaded through the theory to lend it credibility; prescient rumours in recent days from sources at Le Blanc-Mesnil, a small town on the northern fringe of Paris with a largely immigrant population, formerly of Sephardic Jews from the north-African colonies, more recently of Muslims, many from the same countries.

The premise sounded convincing; racial hatred boiling over in an area known for it. Le Blanc-Mesnil fell under the scope of District 93, also known as the Red belt from an era when it was controlled by staunchly Communist mayors. Immigrants had always been a pressing problem. The man from the LSE managed deftly to link ill-feeling in Le Blanc-Mesnil to Jewish commercial interests in Sentier. Stephanie was almost persuaded by him until he mentioned the suspects again.

She turned off the television.

Two incidents in one city on consecutive days. Superficially independent of one another but linked by a third incident: the murder of Jacob and Miriam Furst. Not in itself significant enough to make the news – an old couple murdered in their home – but vital to Stephanie because she was the single factor common to all three.

Day Four

She woke with a start and checked her watch. Three-twenty-five. As a teenager, she'd been a hopeless sleeper. As Stephanie, she still was. But Petra had been trained to take sleep wherever she could, no matter how hostile the environment.

They were in the sitting-room. Newman was slumped in his chair, his head lolling to one side. Stephanie was on the sofa behind him. She'd chosen it deliberately for the small psychological advantage of being invisible to him.

Silently, she rose from the sofa and went to the bathroom. She showered then wrapped herself in one of his towels and sorted through his ex-lover's wardrobe. The black jeans were the right length but Stephanie's waist was slimmer. She pulled on a navy long-sleeved T-shirt, a chunky black jersey and the silver trainers.

She felt human again. As human as Petra could be.

In the kitchen she filled a kettle. While the

water heated she investigated Newman's study. On a large oak desk beside the window were two slim Sony monitors and a cordless keyboard. She looked in the drawers; stationery, bills and receipts, correspondence, cash – euros, dollars, Swiss francs – an Air France first-class boarding card from Singapore to Paris, and two American passports.

The first passport belonged to Robert Ridley Newman, aged forty-eight. It had been issued two years before but there were already dozens of stamps in it, some recurring frequently; Damascus, Riyadh, Beijing and Shanghai, Tehran, Jakarta. The second passport was seven years older. She flicked through the pages. There were only twelve stamps in it, nine of them issued at Ben-Gurion airport, Tel Aviv.

In the bottom drawer on the right she found a Vacheron watch with a leather strap. On the back was an inscription and a date: *Robert, with love, Carlotta, 10–11–2001*. A birthday? She checked the passports. Not his.

Back in the kitchen, she switched on the TV suspended over the slate worktop. Bloomberg was playing. She flicked through the channels until she came to BBC World, which was showing archive footage of Anders Brand. He was shaking hands with Kofi Annan, Bill Clinton to one side, the three of them sharing a joke. At the bottom of the screen the caption read: *Former Swedish diplomat named among Paris dead.*

104

A résumé unfolded; posts in Manila, Baghdad, Rome and Washington, as a junior diplomat, followed by two forays into business with Deutsche Bank in New York and Shell in London. Later, Brand had returned to the Swedish diplomatic service, serving in the Philippines, then Spain. After that, he'd joined the United Nations in New York, filling a series of increasingly undefined roles as his star rose. Divorced for almost twenty years, Brand was survived by his ex-wife, the former actress Lena Meslin, and their two adult sons.

A little late but just as Stern had predicted.

Stern.

Painfully, Stephanie surrendered to the one thought she'd been resisting since the Lancaster.

You set me up.

Now, more than ever, she needed information. For years, he'd been her preferred source. Information from Stern was bought at a premium but was cheap at the price. She'd never had reason to question its quality. He'd never sold her out. On the contrary. There had been occasions where he'd volunteered information to protect her. Or rather, as he usually put it, to protect his investment.

Safe from one another, their relationship had evolved into a form of sterile, electronic friendship, neither of them interested in finding out too much about the other because they both understood that security lay in anonymity. But in the beginning it had been strictly business; request, negotiation, payment, delivery. Cold and clinical.

Stern traded information, not affection. The *faux* relationship that Stephanie had allowed to develop between them had come to obfuscate that uneasy fact. Stern owed her nothing, nor she him. At the end of every transaction they were equal. It was true that he'd made money out of her. Just as she'd made money out of the information he'd sold her. She'd come to assume that he'd never trade *her* because she was valuable to him. But why not, if the money was right? She'd never guaranteed him anything. Each transaction ran the risk of being the last. Stern existed in a transitory environment; the currency of information tended to devalue with time. In both their worlds, it paid to seize the moment.

Ultimately, Stern's fidelity was always going to be a question of price.

At first, he thought he'd imagined it. The sound of running water. A shower. *His* shower. He tried to straighten himself. Had he fallen asleep? Perhaps, but not in the regenerative sense. Sleep was nothing more than a brief lapse between uncomfortable bouts of waking. He was slowly seizing; numb hands, stiff neck, sore spine, cramping muscles. His mouth felt dirty and dry.

He wondered how long he'd been alone. Not that it mattered. There was nothing he could do.

He and the chair had become a single entity, she'd made sure of that. An entity isolated at the centre of a Bokhara carpet, a castaway in his own apartment.

He couldn't reconcile the woman in his apartment with the woman who'd approached him at the bar in the Lancaster. Claudia Calderon had been confident, relaxed, playful. And sexy. He could admit that, even now. And then there was the creature with the gun. What had she done? What did she want?

He tried to convince himself that she wouldn't harm him. That she'd float away, like a bout of bad weather, leaving him as she'd found him. But Leonid Golitsyn and another man were dead. Newman had seen that on TV. She'd admitted to being in their room. And she had the gun. He'd barely heard her denial. Stranger still, she'd seemed more preoccupied with coverage of the Sentier bomb than events at the Lancaster. Were the two connected? Was *she* the connection? And if she was, what would that mean for him?

Stephanie said, 'I'm going to untie your hands. You need to get your blood moving.'

The purple scars around the wrists were shiny and ragged. There was no smoothness to them, nothing . . . *uniform*. The hands themselves were swollen. As they separated a shudder coursed through Newman. He brought his arms to the front of his body in a series of stiff jerks, catching his breath with each halt. Once his hands were in his lap he flexed his fingers. She saw the solid tension in his shoulders, knotted muscle crawling on itself.

'Who's Carlotta?'

He didn't answer.

'I usually like to know whose clothes I'm wearing.'

Still nothing.

'Was the earring hers?'

She could see no fear, no anger, no emotion at all.

She left him and took Golitsyn's attaché case to the sofa. Keys, pens, a leather-bound address book, lots of business documents. His letters were addressed to him at several locations: the head office of MosProm on ulitsa Tverskaya in central Moscow; Galerie Golitsyn on avenue Matignon, Paris; the Hotel Meurice, Paris; an apartment on East 62nd Street in New York City.

In a see-through foolscap plastic wallet was a set of architectural plans. Stephanie turned it over to see the address. Cork Street, London; another art gallery, she assumed. There was something inserted between the folds of the drawings. She unzipped the wallet and a sheet of paper slipped free.

It was an agreement with an *immobilier* named Guy Grangé on boulevard Magenta in the *10ème arrondissement*. A one-month rental, a one-room apartment in the Stalingrad district, cash paid in advance. Not the sort of area Stephanie would have expected Golitsyn to frequent. Or the sort of property, for that matter. There was no address, just a reference number. The printed key code corresponded to the number on the red plastic disk attached to the keys.

Why had Stern pointed her in the direction of this seventy-seven-year-old Russian?

There were some credit-card receipts in the attaché case, including one from the fabled jeweller Ginzburg, on place Vendôme. A small card was stapled to the receipt. On the back, written by a shaking hand, was a brief message:

Leonid, mon cher,
merci pour tout,
N x.

Beneath that, in Russian, was an addition:
Diamonds or bread? Only we know which.

Stephanie looked at the first part of the message. N for Natalya? Aleksandr Ginzburg's widow was Natalya. And alive, it seemed. Stephanie was a little surprised. Aleksandr Ginzburg had died a long time ago – a famous car crash outside Cannes sometime in the late Seventies or early Eighties – so Stephanie had just assumed that his wife had died since then. Apparently not. Which now made her a very old woman. Except that Aleksandr hadn't been so old when he'd died. Perhaps she was as young as eighty. In other words, of the same vintage as Golitsyn.

Stephanie stared at the message and felt the pull of its undercurrent.

Diamonds or bread? Only we know which.

London, 04:05

When the phone rang in Rosie Chaudhuri's small first-floor flat off Chichele Road in north London, she was already awake. She'd fallen into bed at one, exhausted, a little drunk, unhappy. The alcohol was supposed to have soothed the pain but hadn't. An inexperienced drinker, the very least she'd hoped for had been a deep sleep but she'd been awake by half-past-three.

Her first night out in a month, her first as a single woman in more than a year. Her friend Claire had insisted upon it. Time to move on. Time to consign him to history. Reluctantly, Rosie had capitulated. A poor decision, as it turned out. There had been no balm for the hurt, no boost for the self. Just a large bill and a hangover.

When her relationship failed, Rosie did what she always did: she buried herself in work. An easy solution which, for a week or two, seemed to deliver. Then came the familiar sensation; the weight in the chest, the suspicion of a greater malaise lurking at the heart of her. How could a smart, attractive woman continue to stumble from one third-rate relationship to another?

A second-generation Indian, Rosie ran an

110

organization at the cutting edge of global intelligence. From any point of view – race, gender, age – she was a success. But she didn't feel like one. Never had, if the truth be told, and now, at five-past-four on a dismal winter morning, she felt a total failure.

What good was her position – her *power* – if she couldn't hold down a relationship? Dumped by an out-of-work actor because he was intimidated by her professional success. He thought she worked for the Centre for Defence Studies at King's College, London. That was the lie by which she was universally known among her family and friends.

The actor was a lovely man; kind, funny, good-looking. But not much of an actor. When he'd complained about the hours she kept she'd seen straight through him; he'd resented her work because it fuelled his own sense of professional inadequacy. Which, in turn, she'd resented. It wasn't amusing to come home after a sixteen-hour shift to be criticized by a man who'd spent the day lying on a sofa watching *Countdown* and *Neighbours*, waiting for Steven Spielberg to call.

She picked up the phone. 'Yes?'

'This is Carter, S3.'

S3 was the intelligence section. 'What is it, John?'

'There's a car on its way. It'll be with you in eight minutes.'

'Give me the bare bones.'

'Last night, Paris. The Lancaster hotel. A shooting, two victims: Leonid Golitsyn and Fyodor Medvedev.'

The first name was vaguely resonant, the second meant nothing. 'Go on.'

'S9 has intercepted communication between DST and DGSE.'

Both agencies formed part of France's intelligence community. The DST, the Directorate for Surveillance of the Territory, was concerned primarily with counter-espionage, counter-intelligence and the protection of classified information, and was under the direct control of the Ministry of the Interior. The DGSE – Direction Générale de la Sécurité Extérieure – was responsible for terrorism, human intelligence and industrial-economic intelligence.

Rosie asked for a brief reminder of Golitsyn's significance and then said, 'So what's the problem?'

'Stephanie Patrick.'

A sequence of syllables to rob the breath.

Impossible, she thought. Well, no, not *impossible*. But as close to impossible as unlikely could ever be.

Carter said, 'They're looking for Petra Reuter. There's been positive identification.'

'Photographic?'

'We're not sure. There's something else, though. The two Algerians fingered by DGSE for the blast in Sentier – they're a smokescreen. She's the one they want.'

'A bomb?'

The closest Petra had come to using a bomb was an exploding mobile phone that had decapitated an American lawyer in Singapore. As glib as it sounded, bombs weren't her style.

'I know what you're thinking,' Carter said, 'but they seem very confident.'

'They usually do. Are we sure she's real?'

Like every star, Petra Reuter had her cheap imitators.

'As sure as we can be.'

Rosie put down the phone, hauled herself from the bed and entered the bathroom. She was still wearing most of her eye-liner, smudged like bruises. No time for fresh clothes, she dressed in yesterday's suit. In the sitting-room, she found her briefcase on a packing crate.

Six months on and she still hadn't settled into the apartment. She'd sold her place just off the Seven Sisters Road but had been part of a buying chain that had collapsed. This place, a short-term rental, had been a stop-gap. She'd been looking for something small and comfortable in the heart of the city. Now she wasn't sure what she wanted.

Her predecessor had installed a small bedroom at Magenta House. Towards the end, he'd never gone home. Rosie considered that symptomatic of much that had gone wrong within the organization; it had become too self-absorbed. Which, in turn, had led to levels of paranoia that had begun to affect its operational integrity.

In every walk of life, one needed interests outside of work in order to maintain a balance. Rosie believed that was especially true for the employees of an organization like Magenta House. Within a fortnight of replacing him, she'd had his bedroom dismantled to make way for a new debriefing suite.

The trouble was this: now that she was in his position, where would she find the time to achieve that balance herself?

She was outside her front door seven minutes after the call. The dark green BMW was already there. On the leather back seat was a slim briefing folder.

After Berlin, the future had assumed an obvious shape. Rosie would replace Alexander. His death had spared Magenta House's trustees an awkward dilemma: how to substitute a man who had become utterly synonymous with the organization to its ultimate detriment? As for Stephanie, she was to disappear for good, sending the legend of Petra Reuter into permanent retirement.

False reports of Petra's activities had always existed. Some were simply wrong, others were deliberate mischief. Several times she'd been accredited with assassinations that Magenta House knew to be the work of others. It didn't matter. Any rumour, true or false, added to the legend. So Rosie hadn't been surprised when new rumours began to circulate after Berlin; since nobody had ever suggested that Petra was dead there was no reason for stories about her to dry up.

Stephanie had spent most of her adult life seeking a divorce from Petra. Now that she'd got it, any form of reconciliation seemed inconceivable. Nobody at Magenta House knew Stephanie the way Rosie did. They'd been friends. They'd been the outsiders in an organization of outsiders.

Stephanie, can it really be you?

'I need to go to the bathroom.'

Stephanie knew the procedure. Let him urinate or defecate in the chair. Reduction was the road to compliance. Yet even as she thought it, she knew she wouldn't do it. She released his hands again and told him to tear the tape from his ankle.

He rose awkwardly. His thigh muscles and hip flexors were stiff, hamstrings tugging at his lower back. He had to place a hand on top of the chair to complete the movement. His first few steps were clumsy, as pins and needles began to work the nerves.

The bathroom door had a bolt instead of a key. Stephanie said, 'Don't shut it.'

'You're going to watch?'

She tossed a hardback on to the floor, steered it into the doorway with her foot, ushered him in, then pulled the handle, leaving a six-inch gap. At the flush she pushed the door open. Newman was fastening his trousers.

'Can I wash?'

'Get on with it.'

He cleaned his hands then filled the basin with cold water and pushed his face into it, holding it there. He straightened slowly, water dripping down the front of his shirt.

'How about a shave?'

'No.'

'I promise I won't attack you with my razor. It has a safety strip.'

'Let's go.'

Stephanie directed him back to the chair, waving the Smith & Wesson at him for emphasis. She gathered the washing line and crouched behind him. He offered his hands before she'd asked for them.

She tried again. 'How did you get your scars?'

'I told you. It's none of your goddamned business.'

She was tempted to pull the cord until the wounds reopened. But to hurt him would be to hand him a small victory. She wrapped the plastic-coated line around the wrists, securing them a little less firmly – something he would be sure to notice – before drawing the line down and fastening it to a strut beyond his reach. She was aware of him taking a deep breath and expanding his muscles as she bound him.

'What time does the maid come?'

'Seven-thirty.'

It was already after six-thirty.

'Do you let her in?'

'She has her own key.'

Stephanie picked up a phone. 'What's her number?'

'What do I tell her?'

'Anything you like as long as it sticks.'

'Is it just today?'

'Until further notice,' Stephanie said. 'Maybe a couple of days.'

She held the phone close to his ear but so that she could hear it too. When Yvette answered Newman said he had visitors and didn't want to be disturbed. He told her he'd phone her when he wanted her to resume her schedule.

Stephanie took the handset from him. 'She didn't sound surprised.'

'So?'

'Maybe she's used to such requests.'

'Her husband's serving twelve years for armed robbery. Two of her three sons are dead, the other's a drag queen. It's going to take more than a day off to surprise Yvette.'

'Maybe. But if she shows up unexpectedly, I think I'll manage it,' Stephanie said, as she noticed the keys to the apartment on the side-table. 'By the way, I may need to go out later. What's the number for the door downstairs?'

'9063.'

'Nine-zero-six-three?'

'That's right.'

'You sure about that? What about 2071? That was the number you used last night. Think about it. Take your time. Two-zero-seven-one.'

Newman bit his lip.

She shook her head. 'Disappointing. *And* stupid.'

'Why'd you kill them?'

'I didn't.'

'Then why are you running? Why are you *here*?'

'I don't know.'

Newman snorted.

And Stephanie reacted: 'What does that mean?'

'You don't seem like a novice.'

'How the hell would you know?'

He looked as though he had an answer but said nothing.

Annoyed with herself, Stephanie mumbled, 'Forget it.'

'Forget *what*? That you stuck a gun in my face?'

'Be quiet.'

'Maybe you *are* a novice.'

'Shut up.'

'What are you going to do? Shoot me?'

'You don't think I would?'

He wanted to press the challenge. She could see that. But he backed down. Just a fraction. He thought he was reading her correctly but what if he was wrong?

'Why were you at the Lancaster?' he asked.

'Are you deaf?'

'Tell me. I want to know.'

'I said . . . *shut up*.'

'Come on. You want me to believe you, don't you?'

'Just fuck off.'

I make myself coffee in the kitchen. I'm hungry but there's not even any bread. I expect the maid brings it. Still warm from the baker, I'll bet. With fresh Casablanca lilies to go in the octagonal vase in the hall. Nothing but the best for this one.

I'm angry with him, which is absurd. Only one of us has the right to be angry with the other. I should have let him piss himself. Just to establish my dominance over him. I hear echoes of a distant lecture: interaction with a hostage establishes a relationship, however unusual, which, in turn, humanizes the hostage in the eyes of the captor, making it harder for the captor to treat the hostage in the necessary fashion.

The necessary fashion. What is that in this situation? I have no idea. He was a matter of convenience. A spur-of-the-moment exit strategy in a crisis. He's of no value to me. Unlike his apartment, which is a haven.

Perhaps the 'necessary fashion' should come from the business end of the Smith & Wesson. Avoid complications, kill the hostage, occupy his apartment for as long as required. But I'm not going to do that. I may be Petra but I'm not that *Petra. Not any more.*

I stand by the window. Above the light pollution the sky is brightening to plum. I expect it's warm and sunny in Mauritius. I should be eating mangos to the sound of the surf.

119

I think about Stern, Amsterdam and Anders Brand. Most of all, though, Stern. My sense of betrayal extends beyond the professional to the personal. I feel like a rejected lover. I know that's ridiculous but there it is. It hurts. I thought we had something special.

I try to put my feelings to one side. Stern gave me Golitsyn for free. That, perhaps, should have been a warning.

> This isn't sentimentality. This is business. If anything happens to you, I'll lose money.

Only the first two sentences ring true. Stern was making money before I ever used him. And he'll still be making money long after I've gone.

Newman was angry. With her. With himself.

Now that he was alone again, he tried to impose some order on his scattered thoughts. It was an impossible situation to categorize. He'd been kidnapped. He was a hostage. But in his own home. These facts didn't fit the general profiles that he knew well after years in the oil business.

Ninety percent of kidnaps worldwide were for ransom and the vast majority went unreported. Official estimates put the annual number of ransom kidnaps between five thousand and twenty-five thousand. The discrepancy between the two tended to be a matter of definition. What was beyond dispute among the experts was the true number, which was over fifty thousand. In certain sectors of the oil industry this was common knowledge; in those areas of the world where kidnapping was a national sport, employees of oil companies were a preferred target. The remaining twenty percent of kidnaps were mostly political and were far less predictable.

Newman wasn't sure which kidnap category he'd fallen into. Most likely, something that accounted for a very small fraction of one percent of the total.

Once caught, there were certain rules for all hostages. Above all, that a hostage should do nothing to agitate a captor. Awkward hostages suffered. It was better to be cooperative. To try to establish a rapport. He knew this yet he'd still provoked her. And for what? Absolutely nothing.

His aggression had been fuelled by fatigue and anxiety but so long as she remained an unknown quantity he couldn't afford to make such elementary errors. A hostage's scope for influence was inevitably limited but the least one could do was not to make things worse.

He analysed what he thought he knew. His abduction wasn't about money. And it wasn't political. Or personal. Which probably made it criminal.

That was how it felt. A crime that had gone wrong. He was an accidental hostage. His had been a kidnap of chance, a kidnap of bad timing. Were the rules the same for such a thing? Until he knew better he chose to assume so.

Play the game.

These thoughts coalesced, gradually giving him

something to focus on – a lifeline to cling to – which was crucial.

He knew *that* beyond all doubt.

'I'll bring you something to eat when I get back.'

'You're going out?'

I pull some tape from the roll and bite through it, leaving me with a six-inch strip. 'For a while. Don't get over-excited. You'll still be here when I get back.'

'Wait. What are you going to do with that?'

'I told you. I have to go out.'

'Is it for my mouth?'

'Yes.'

'Please don't. I swear I won't make a sound.'

I raise an eyebrow. 'Do I have your word on that?'

He starts to fidget, snagging himself on his bindings.

'Relax,' I tell him. 'I won't be long.'

But he's not relaxing. His breathing quickens. The colour drains from his face. Being gagged is never pleasant but he seems to be over-reacting.

'Start breathing through your nose.'

He shakes his head.

'Calm down.'

He swallows. 'You don't understand . . .'

'Doesn't matter. The sooner we get this over with, the sooner I'll be back to take it off.'

'Please – don't do it.'

'Look, I'm not walking out of here so that you can shout the house down. Now stay still.'

His grey skin starts to glisten. I step forward and try

to place the tape over his mouth. He thrashes his head left and right.

'For God's sake, stop it!'

In his panic, he starts yelling. The chair rocks beneath him. I try to grab his hair but he ducks forward.

'Calm down! I'm not going to hurt you.'

'Get the fuck off me!'

My backhand swipe catches him on the cheek just below the right eye, snapping his head to the left. The contact feels like an electric pulse. It runs from the bones in my hand up to the shoulder socket.

For a moment, he's stunned into submission. So I move behind him, grab his head in a lock and smear the tape across his mouth.

'Now relax. And breathe through your nose.'

It was a beautiful day, no clouds to obscure a diamond sun set in sapphire sky. The moment she set foot outside the building she felt lifted. She chose to forget Newman and his reaction to the tape. A chilly breeze sent shivers through the Seine.

She crossed Pont Louis-Philippe and returned to Web 46 on rue du Roi du Sicilie, just five minutes away from the apartment. She didn't bother checking any of her own e-mail addresses. Instead, she used a neutral Hotmail address – Joan Appleby – to send a message to Cyril Bradfield.

> Cyril – having a lovely time in NZ. Off to Sydney next week. Then Melbourne, Alice Springs, Darwin. HK next month, then home. Hope you're well – Joan.

Then she created a new Hotmail address – no name, just a series of letters and numbers – and sent a second message to a third address. This one had been established by Bradfield but had never been used. He checked it twice a month to keep it active, but never did so from his own computer. A message from Joan Appleby would direct him to it.

> Cyril, Jacob and Miriam are dead. Whoever did it is after me. You're in danger. Everything's gone. If you can, contact me through our friend. Love, you know who.

When she'd finished, she went to a nearby café and ordered coffee, orange juice and an omelette. She hoped Bradfield would remember the process. When it came to technology beyond his own field of expertise, he remained stubbornly ignorant.

Apart from Stephanie herself, Bradfield was the only link between the Fursts and every version of Petra. Which meant that he was probably already dead. If he was alive and safe, he'd know what to do. And if he was alive and under duress, he'd *still* know what to do; she'd given him a secure way out.

> Contact me through our friend.

Any involved party reading that phrase would assume it referred to Petra. And Bradfield would confirm that. But he knew that in an emergency all Petra's addresses were to be considered redundant. If he was in trouble, he'd be able to warn her in his response.

*   *   *

124

Guy Grangé, an *immobilier* on boulevard Magenta in the *10ème arrondissement*. There were one-room and studio apartments for sale in the window. The digital images were fuzzy. The meagre rentals were hanging from a felt-covered board inside.

Central heating and cigarettes robbed the air of oxygen. The office was staffed by a middle-aged woman with tinted lenses in her glasses and tinted streaks in her hair. Defeated and grey, she was sitting beneath a cheerless property calendar with a photograph of a commercial rental. Nobody had bothered to turn the page since October.

Stephanie showed the woman the receipt she'd found in Golitsyn's attaché case. 'There's no address on this.'

'No.'

'And no phone number.'

'With short-term rentals, we keep the address and only issue the invoice number. It's a question of security.'

'Security?'

'This isn't the *16ème*, you know. The people we deal with, *well . . .*'

Somewhere near the bottom of the heap herself, she still found plenty of others to look down on.

Stephanie showed her the keys she'd taken from Golitsyn's case. 'I have these but I don't know where to go. My boss has gone away. I'm supposed to go over and check everything.' She glimpsed the signature on the bottom of the receipt. Medvedev's,

naturally, not Golitsyn's. 'You don't know how difficult these Russians are . . .'

The remark sparked a lightning strike of solidarity. 'Almost as bad as the Africans.'

Stephanie rolled her eyes in sympathy. 'Say one
thing, do another.'

'That's the least of it. You know something? We
lose money with them. Seriously. Even when we
take it in advance.'

'*No*. How?'

'The condition of the places when we take them
back – you wouldn't believe it. Disgusting. As for
the Chinese – I don't know where to start . . .'

She was in her stride now, reaching into the
memory bank for the worst offenders. And as she
did so, she gathered a scrap of paper and a felt-
tip pen.

New York City, 06:20

There was someone downstairs. John Cabrini sat
up in bed, ears straining for the sound inside over
the sounds outside; a distant dustcart, an alarm,
two Cubans arguing on the pavement beneath his
window.

The more he listened the louder the silence
became. Until it was broken by a second clunk.
Definitely inside.

He got out of bed and pulled on a grey towelling
robe he'd stolen from a hotel in Turin. He wasn't
going to confront anyone in a pair of navy boxer
shorts and a string vest. In the drawer of his

bedside table was a Ruger P-85. Evelyn, his wife, had never let him keep a gun in the house. He'd bought the weapon three months after she'd died. Unable to endure the prospect of a life without her, he'd intended to use it on himself. At the last moment – safety-catch off, forefinger squeezing – he'd hesitated.

That had been fourteen years ago. The gun had never been fired. But on four previous occasions he'd been ready to shoot, two of them in the last twelve months. Both times, the intruders had vanished by the time he'd reached the pizza parlour downstairs. Both times, there'd been broken glass on the floor and no cash in the till.

Angelo's on West 122nd Street in Harlem. Nothing fancy. Just good pizza and cheap prices. Part of a chain of seven Angelo's restaurants in Harlem and the higher reaches of the Upper West Side and Upper East Side. Michael Cabrini, John's younger brother, owned the business, employing his wife, two sons and a handful of nephews. As he was fond of saying, 'Franchises ain't worth shit unless you got someone you can trust running them. That means you, John. You and the boys. No outsiders.' Which was why the empire had halted at seven; his brother had run out of employable sons and nephews.

Cabrini tip-toed down the stairs and through the kitchen. He paused in the shadow of the doorway that led into the restaurant, his eyes gradually growing accustomed to the gloom.

The man was making no attempt to hide. He was sitting at a table in the centre of the room. In front of him, on the red check tablecloth, was a cup and saucer.

'Hope you don't mind. Made myself an espresso.'

Pale-skinned, the remains of black hair greying at the temples, bald on top, in his fifties, he was wearing a navy-blue overcoat over a suit. Even in the half-light Cabrini could see how polished the tips of his black shoes were. He approved. Beside the cup and saucer was a felt hat.

'I'm surprised you know how.'

A thin bloodless smile. 'My wife bought a smaller version of that machine at vast expense. Naturally, she never used it. Personally, I can't stand to see waste so I made the effort to learn myself. Now I use it every day.' He raised the cup, took a sip, then added: 'I'm sure we'd both be happier if you stopped pointing that gun at me.'

Cabrini laid it on the zinc counter. 'How'd you get in?'

'Far too easily. To your knowledge, have we met?'

'No.'

'But you know who I am.'

'I have an idea.'

Gordon Wiley. A man whose instincts were more at home in Washington DC than in New York.

Wiley said, 'Mr Ellroy is in Europe. I spoke to him earlier.'

'What are we looking at?'

128

'Salvage.'

'What kind of assistance are we going to get?'

'One hundred percent.'

'What's the damage?'

'*Who's* the damage? That's the question. She's a German named Reuter. Petra Reuter. I'd never heard of her until an hour ago. And now I wish I could turn back the clock. It's a hell of a mess over there.'

'What about Mr Ellroy?'

'He's staying. Which is why he wants his favourite anchor running the show.'

Wiley collected his hat. There was a black Lincoln waiting for him outside the door in front of a dilapidated white Datsun. Cabrini watched it leave through the first fall of the snow and felt relief rather than anxiety; no more pizzas. For a day or two, at least. And in a year or so, no more pizzas ever again.

It was quarter-to-seven when he phoned his brother. 'Michael?'

'Christ, John, you know what the time is?'

'I've got to go away.'

There was a long pause. 'When?'

'Now.'

'Is it serious?'

'Always. You know that.'

'How long?'

'I don't know.'

'You okay?'

'I'm good. You gonna take care of things?'

'Sure, sure. I'll get Stevie to look after your place.'

The youngest nephew. The next in line, if the Angelo's empire ever expanded to eight. After the call Cabrini went upstairs.

Salvage.

Well, he was the expert. Had been for twenty years. It was never pretty but then again it wasn't a beauty pageant. Besides, he hadn't had a failure yet. That was all that mattered.

He replaced the Ruger P-85 in the drawer of the bedside table. In the bathroom, he shaved. Most days, he didn't bother. Serving behind the counter he preferred to be unshaven, sallow, dreary. Invisible to his customers. A fifty-five-year-old man dispensing pizzas; hardly one of life's successes.

Beneath the weak light falling from the naked bulb was a lean man. The slight stoop and shuffle that his customers saw made him weak. But when he stood upright and walked with purpose, he appeared as he was: fiercely fit. He watched the welcome transformation in the mirror as he combed his hair and dabbed some Christian Dior aftershave on each cheek.

He returned to the bedroom, half-resurrected. Cabrini had always favoured fine clothes but almost everything he wore came from discount stores. In the back of the cupboard, however, was a tailored suit by Huntsman of London. Five years old, a masterpiece in fabric, Cabrini knew it would last the rest of his life. He laid it on the bed, then selected a pair of Lobb shoes and a black silk polo-neck that had been specially made for him by Clive Ishiguro.

His salvage uniform. He was the leader, he set the tone. It felt good to be able to shed the shoddy disguise from time to time.

When the farm overlooking Orvieto was ready, he would move to Italy and never return, content to comfort himself over the permanently painful loss of Evelyn by surrounding himself with beautiful things. A garden, porcelain, paintings, clothes, music.

The rusting white Datsun was twenty-one years old. Cabrini and Evelyn had bought it together. It was the only car he'd ever owned. He'd never wanted another. From Harlem to Brooklyn, he peeled off the Long Island Expressway and circled beneath it to the waterfront and a stretch of ware-houses that were still awaiting development.

Cabrini came to the loading bay of the third warehouse: R.L. Gallagher Inc. Noiselessly, a large gate lifted. Cabrini drove to the back of the docking area, parked and then stepped into the waiting cargo lift. On the fourth floor, he crossed a vast storage area that was deserted, except for two matt black cabins on steel struts. The large sets of wheels which were now six inches clear of the floor were only just visible in the draughty darkness. Up a flight of aluminium steps was a sealed door. Beside the door, mounted on the wall, was a matt grey panel. He placed his face in front of it and said, 'Cabrini, John, place of birth, Cleveland, Ohio.'

Cabrini had been born in New York but that didn't matter. The biometric plate analysed voice timbre, the pattern of blood vessels in the retina, and traces of breath composition, a process that currently took between two and five seconds.

When the door parted with a hiss, John Cabrini stepped into a sanitized airlock of ultraviolet light.

Stalingrad, at the point where boulevard de la Chapelle becomes boulevard de la Villette. Overlooking the steel delta of rail fanning out of Gare de l'Est, the crumbling building was itself overlooked by an elevated section of the Métro. As Stephanie descended to the street the iron struts overhead began to creak. A train on the Nation-Porte Dauphine line was approaching. Pigeons fluttered at her feet.

The address was five storeys of peeling plaster and broken windows. There were commercial premises at street level. Not that many looked very commercial. Rusting shutters hid half of them. The rest were not busy; discount stores peddling cheap clothing, Chinese luggage, basins and toilet bowls in avocado and salmon pink. There was a bar-nightclub at one end. Coral was the name stencilled on to the dirty red canopy beside a cream silhouette of two entwined women.

Stephanie walked through an archway into the

untended courtyard behind. Swing doors led to a staircase; unlit, cold, damp. The graffiti was as original as ever: *Marie Z, I love you, Antoine; PSG are shit; Jim Morrison 1943–1971; Marie Z is a fucking slut.* The apartment was on the third floor at the end of the corridor. From each door she passed came a different sound, a crying child, Arab rap, a barking dog. She smelt fried meat, sour tobacco, a pipe in need of a plumber.

The door had been recently replaced. The scratches on the frame hadn't been filled or painted. Both locks were still shiny. She knocked twice then tried the keys she'd found in Golitsyn's attaché case.

'Hello?'

No answer. She stepped inside. It was dark. Instinctively, she withdrew the Smith & Wesson from the pocket of her MaxMara coat.

There were two main rooms, the curtains partly drawn in both. A cramped living area overlooked the street, the bedroom overlooked the rail-tracks. There was a tiny shower cubicle next to a toilet and sink. The woman in the agency had already mentioned that; *a real luxury in that place – no communal toilet.* A greasy film of green mould was colonizing the shower curtain. In the living area, a portable gas stove sat on the floor beside a small fridge. In the sink was a cracked glass, cutlery and a dirty plate. Two cockroaches crawled over a sauce that had dried to a dark brown crust.

The air tasted stale. She examined the receipt again. Ten days old.

Into the bedroom; an olive-green canvas hold-all lay beside the bed. She rummaged through it. Women's clothes – two tatty jerseys, underwear, sneakers – a portable radio, a battered French copy of Donna Tartt's *The Secret History*. In the bathroom, a toothbrush sat in a plastic tangerine mug. There was a box of tampons on the floor by the toilet.

No sign of a man anywhere.

She peered through the bedroom curtains. A TGV emerged from beneath the bridge. In the living area, she checked the fridge: a plastic bottle of Orangina, a tube of tomato paste, three bottles of Amstel beer. On the table at the centre of the room was an old copy of *France-Soir* – 23 December – an empty box of cereal and a Samsung portable CD-player beside a few disks; *Colour of Spring* by Talk Talk, *Achtung Baby* by U2, Bob Dylan's *Blood on the Tracks*. Nothing recent, nothing French.

A woman, then. In an apartment paid for by Golitsyn, since the receipt was in his attaché case, despite Medvedev's signature. *Golitsyn floats above the world*. Wasn't that what Stern had said? Whatever that meant it presumably included not having to bother himself with signatures of this sort.

But what kind of woman? A lover? Not here. Money being no object, wouldn't he keep her in a discreet apartment in a classier area? Then again, perhaps Golitsyn liked to slum it. What do you give a man jaded by plenty? A taste of what it's like to have nothing, perhaps. Why not? A dip into the gutter to confirm and fortify the sweetness of his life.

She collected the Smith & Wesson, put it back in her pocket and let herself out. She double-locked, leaving the door as she'd found it.

'You're back.'

There were three of them blocking her path to the staircase. Clad and cropped in the homogenized uniform of the disaffected – Nike, Donnay, a scalp of fuzz – they were hard to source. Asian, perhaps. Two of them, anyway. The shortest of them, muscle-bound beneath the tight white T-shirt worn under his unzipped Adidas tracksuit top, might have been Arab. He had two zigzags shaved into the stubble above his left ear.

'You weren't here,' he said.

He was staring at her with matt eyes. She wondered how old he was. It was hard to tell. Somewhere between fifteen and twenty-five, she guessed. With an attitude somewhere between menace and slouching insolence.

'When?'

'When they came.'

'Who?'

'Want to fuck?'

The tallest one laughed, took a drag from a joint and passed it to the third of them, who was attempting to cultivate a moustache. He wore a baseball cap with 50 CENT picked out in gold thread.

Stephanie said, 'When who came?'

The short one looked her up and down, trying to make her nervous. 'You know who.'

Stephanie smiled coldly. *Of course I know.* 'What did they want?'

'To speak to you.'

'What about?'

'Get on your knees and I'll tell you.'

Another snigger from the tall one.

She returned the stare with interest. 'When was this?'

'Yesterday.'

Stephanie said, 'I haven't seen you around.'

'So?'

'How do you know I'm the one?'

'They had a photo.'

'Of me?'

'Who else?'

'You sure it was me?'

He nodded. 'What did you do?'

'Nothing. What else?'

'They said to call them if we saw you. Said there'd be money for us.'

'You going to?'

'We don't need their money,' he sneered. 'We have enough. And when we need more, we take it. Same with you. If we want you, we'll take you.'

'How many of them were there?'

'You don't think we would?'

She tried to pitch him a neutral look; no challenge, no fear. 'I don't know.'

He grabbed his crotch with his right hand. 'Come on, *putain*. There are only three of us. That's something for everyone, no?'

'How many were there?'

They stared at each other, neither blinking.

Eventually, he said, 'Two. One of the fuckers didn't speak French.'

'How do you know?'

He grinned, revealing capped teeth. 'The other one did all the talking so I called the silent one a stupid cunt. Know what he said?'

'What?'

'Nothing. He just nodded like a donkey. That's all the bastard could do.'

They let her leave but not without a grope. She struggled to suppress a violent reaction as she wriggled between them, eyes down, unhappy but determined. On boulevard de la Villette she waited for almost an hour until they emerged from the courtyard. When they entered Stalingrad Métro station she returned to the apartment.

In the living-room she went through every drawer and cupboard. Again, nothing. There was a tatty rug laid over floorboards. She dragged the table to one side and rolled it back. All the effort yielded was the dust from the gaps between the boards.

The sofa by the window was covered in chocolate velour. She tossed the cushions on to the floor and pushed her hand into the folds on both sides and along the back. Grime lodged beneath her fingernails. An old one-franc piece, a biro cap, a badly creased snapshot, a cheap silver necklace, a spent match. The necklace was broken, one link ripped open. She ran a palm across the photo; a collection of five grubby boys, aged seven or eight, all mugging for the camera. She didn't recognize them. The background was slightly out of focus; a dour grey building through a veil of falling snow.

Her second sweep of the bathroom was no more productive than the first. In the bedroom she emptied the hold-all on to the lumpy mattress and checked both side-pockets. In the lop-sided wardrobe was a dark grey overcoat on a hanger. She knelt on the floor and looked under the bed; a carpet of dust, a pair of jeans scrunched into a ball, a torn condom-wrapper.

The jeans were a pair of Levi's with nothing in the front pockets. In the back left she found a Métro ticket, a crumpled tissue and a scrap of paper with a message written in pencil: *Rudi, Gare du Nord, 19:30.* Beneath it was a phone number. From the back right pocket she retrieved a folded credit-card receipt stapled to a bill. She couldn't decipher the scrawled signature at the foot of the receipt. It was a Visa card transaction worth €75. The bill beneath was printed on laid white paper with blue embossed print. The name at the top was Augustine Villard. A physiotherapist on rue du Châtelain. Listed below was the service, an extended session to treat the neck, shoulders and upper back. The patient's name was printed at the bottom of the page.

Marianne Bernard.

Stephanie stared at it. Every time she blinked she expected it to change. *Willed* it to change. But it wouldn't.

She'd used several physiotherapists over the years but had never heard of Augustine Villard. And now she noticed that the address – rue du Châtelain – was not in Paris but in Brussels. She examined the receipt again and saw that Marianne Bernard *was* the name written as a signature. But it wasn't *her* signature.

She looked at the scrap of paper again. Rudi. Still meant nothing. But the phone number looked vaguely familiar. Or was she imagining it? It had seven digits. Numbers in Paris had eight. Brussels again?

Back to the living-room and the CDs on the table. Not hers, certainly, but all of them albums she knew. She picked up the creased photograph she'd found down the back of the sofa and studied the five young faces more carefully. They remained smiling strangers. But there was . . . *something*.

Realization crept up on her slowly. It wasn't the children in the foreground. It was the building in the blurred background. It was the snow.

Children's Home Number 23 at Izmailovo in Moscow. The orphanage that Konstantin Komarov had rebuilt. The orphanage to which Stephanie had contributed a million of Petra Reuter's contaminated dollars.

For a moment Stephanie truly believed she couldn't breathe.

This was *her* apartment.

Shaking, I leave the apartment and start to walk. I don't know where I'm going and I don't care. I just need to keep moving, to keep breathing.

It's my apartment. Or rather, Petra's. Although even that isn't entirely correct. It belongs to a version of Petra. A substantially accurate version that includes elements of Stephanie's history. A version created by someone who knows about Marianne Bernard in Brussels. In other words, the Petra I was the day before yesterday. Because today I don't know which Petra I am. Or whether I'm Petra at all.

They also know about the Petra I used to be when I was in love with Kostya. And, perhaps, when I was in love with Mark.

The CDs were familiar to me, although I've never owned any of them. But Mark did. My civilian lover, my one and only window on to the world of the normal. He had all three. Then again, he had dozens of albums. Under any other set of circumstances, I wouldn't even consider this but when I think about the photograph and the receipt, I can't ignore the possibility.

I cling to one thing: the errors. A personal photo-

graph left in an operational safe-house? Never. A credit-card receipt bearing an inactive name in the possession of an active name? Not a chance. This Petra is a cheap pastiche of the real thing. Not that it makes her any less of a threat.

I assume the clues in the apartment were planted so that they could be discovered. I think about the Sentier bomb. I imagine there must be a thread of evidence somewhere to point them towards the Stalingrad apartment.

From there, where do these clues lead? What do they suggest? What story is someone trying to tell? That the terrorist Petra Reuter planted the bomb in Passage du Caire? That it exploded prematurely, perhaps, killing her? Does the trail lead from here to Brussels? To Marianne Bernard and beyond? And where does Leonid Golitsyn fit into this? If it was his scheme, it's failed since he's dead. If it wasn't, then perhaps there is a bond between us, since I am also supposed to be dead.

All my adult life I've been two women, Stephanie Patrick and Petra Reuter. But now I'm three; the woman I am, the woman who was created for me, and the woman created to replace the first two. There's a dialogue going on inside my head. Petra and Stephanie are wondering how to proceed. From different angles, the pair are coming to the same conclusion: the key to their survival is the third of us.

The third woman.

The front door was still double-locked, just as she'd left it, the single hair in place, the oldest trick she knew. Stephanie entered as quietly as she could. There was a sound coming from the direction of the sitting-room. A struggle of some sort. She put down the bag of groceries and pulled the gun from her overcoat pocket.

Newman had his back to her. He was trembling violently, the shoulders of his shirt were dark with sweat. For several seconds, Stephanie watched in silence.

This is a trick.

He caught her reflection in a mirror. Still cautious, Stephanie approached. His face was beetroot-red, his skin slippery, the veins popping in his throat.

'I'm going to take the tape off. Don't shout.'

She ripped it away. There was blood in his mouth. Despite the warning, he cried out. A series of sounds, none of them a word.

Stephanie kept her distance. 'What is it?'

Through gritted teeth he hissed, 'My legs, my back . . .'

'What about them?'

'Cramp . . .'

'Cramp?'

'Get these goddamned things off me!'

It's still a trick.

She took a step back, deciding.

'For Christ's sake! Don't just stand there. *Do* something!'

Stephanie thrust the gun at him. 'Don't try anything. Okay?'

'*Okay!*'

She tore the tape from the ankles first, then untied the washing line securing his wrists, and stood back. He tried to get up but his legs wouldn't straighten. He pitched forward, hitting the carpet with a wheeze.

Human instinct compelled her to help but Petra was in the way. So instead she watched him wrestle with himself, as he tried to massage blood into anaemic blocks of rigid muscle. When the worst of it had passed, he relaxed and lay still on the carpet. Detached, Stephanie watched his breathing slow.

His eyes were still closed when he muttered, 'At least the other bastards let me move around.'

'What others?'

'Forget it.'

'*What others?*'

She offered him a banana. 'Here. Eat this.'

'I don't want a banana.'

Half an hour had passed. She'd decided not to bind him immediately. He needed movement. A circulation break. She didn't know – or couldn't remember – whether this was correct. And she didn't care.

They were in the kitchen. She was sorting through the bag of groceries she'd bought; fruit, orange juice, yoghurt, bread, cheese, salami. Newman was sitting on a stool on the other side of the island. Just where she'd ordered him to sit. She'd removed the knife-block and the half-empty bottle of Léoville Las Cases 1985 from his reach. The Smith & Wesson was on the counter behind her.

She set the banana in front of him. 'You should eat it anyway.'

He drank water from a plastic bottle. 'Oh yeah? Why's that?'

'For the potassium.'

'Potassium?'

'Potassium deficiency causes cramp.'

'Trust me, this kind of cramp has nothing to do with lack of potassium.'

'How do you know?'

'A doctor told me.'

She put the fruit in an empty china bowl and left the bread on the counter beside the gas rings. 'I've never seen anyone have a cramp attack like that.'

'Then maybe you should tie people to chairs more often.'

There was a phone on the worktop. The base unit was beside the Belfast sink. There were five messages waiting. Stephanie pressed play.

10:17 – Robert, your cell phone is switched off. Call me. You're late.

A female voice, seductively deep. A smoker, perhaps.

10:59 – nothing.

12:43 – Robert, it's Marie again. Where are you? Are you okay? I'll be here until one, then on my cell. Bye.

17:23 – Good afternoon. This is Jean-Claude Sardé. I would like to meet with you as soon as possible. Your secretary gave me your home number. I hope you don't mind. Could you call me when you have some time? Thank you.

17:34 – nothing.

Stephanie said, 'Who's Marie?'

'My secretary.'

'At Solaris?'

'Yeah.'

'Is it unusual for you to drop out of contact for twenty-four hours?'

'When I'm away, it's normal.'

'But here in Paris?'

'No.'

She took the orange juice, salami, cheese and yoghurt to the end of the island, next to the fridge. 'Then you need to call her. And you'd better think of something good. Who's Jean-Claude Sardé?'

'A business associate. A banker.'

She opened the fridge door. And for a second, as she stooped to put the orange juice carton on a shelf, her back was partially turned to him.

She'd cleared the obvious implements from his reach but had overlooked one. Sliding off the stool, Newman grasped with both hands the absurd chrome pepper grinder he'd been given one Christmas by a lover who hadn't made it to New Year.

He swung it like Babe Ruth. Aiming for the back of the head. Aiming for the cranial home-run.

*   *   *

145

Most petty crimes were crimes of opportunity. Newman had read that somewhere. Random acts of impulse. Yet even as the opportunity had presented itself, he'd felt caution kick in and had opted against it. But he was already moving, as though some other entity had control of his body. And once started, there was no retreat.

She seemed to fall in slow motion.

She'd turned at the last moment. He wasn't quite sure where he'd caught her. Across the top of the shoulders? Over part of the neck? No matter. He swung again, bringing the grinder down across her back. When he then kicked her it was hard enough to wrench his ankle.

He pushed away from her but didn't head for the front door. Instead, he went for the Smith & Wesson on the other side of the kitchen.

He heard her behind him. Clawing herself to standing, clawing through the pain. He picked up the gun and spun round. She was coming at him, eating up the space between them.

He started to squeeze the trigger. She skidded to a halt, eyes widening. For a second, she considered throwing herself at him. He saw it, she knew it. And then hesitated.

The gun was shaking in Newman's hand. 'Take one more step and I swear to God I'll kill you.'

New York City, 15:37
The construction was simple; two forty-ton haulage containers that merged to form a single

146

mobile operations suite. At the heart of the suite was the operations room itself with a curved command desk on a raised dais towards the rear. That was where John Cabrini sat. In front of him were two additional desks for the other members of the team, Steven Mathis and Helen Ito. Their desks had four retractable monitors each. Cabrini's had six. At the front of the room, the curving wall was lined with a membrane of slither screens, six by four, usable as one composite screen or twenty-four individual screens, or any combination between.

The two containers were coated in a special polymer that prevented thermal imaging from detecting human activity within. The colourless skin contained micro sensors that measured external air temperature so that the governing computer could cool or warm the container shells to match their environment perfectly. The containers also emitted a blizzard of impenetrable electronic signals to foil eavesdropping.

Gradually, all the facilities were coming on line, most of them courtesy of the National Security Agency (NSA), Cabrini's former employers. The top right screen at the front of the suite had coverage from the Defense Intelligence Network, the NSA's own version of CNN. It ran a contin-uously updated news service. Much of the time it rather resembled CNN, without the incessant adverts and self-promotion. But it also provided the viewer with real-time images from spy satellites and transcripts or recordings of intercepted conversations, as well as gossip from the global intelligence community. Of the two active screens on Cabrini's desk, the one on the left was hooked into Intelink, Crypto City's private intranet.

Not far from the small village of Annapolis Junction in Maryland lies a complex of about sixty buildings. They are hidden from public view by screens of woodland, protected by motion detectors, cement barriers, hydraulic anti-truck devices and barbed-wire fences. These buildings – offices, laboratories, factories, storage facilities and living quarters – constitute the home of the world's most technically sophisticated spying organization, the National Security Agency. The complex is known as Crypto City. Within Crypto City exists the most powerful army of computers ever assembled, augmented by some of the finest mathematicians and linguists on the planet.

Intelink is the NSA's own intranet service, although it is also used by other intelligence agencies, particularly those of Canada, Australia and the United Kingdom. Operating out of Intelink Central are four different services, each with its own security-clearance requirements. John Cabrini had access to all of them, including Intelink-P, a service intended for only the president, the vice-president, the national security adviser and a select handful of officials.

'How are we doing, Steven?'

Mathis looked back at Cabrini. 'Almost there, sir. Still waiting for INTELSAT and Echelon.'

A very poor image of Stephanie formed on the wall in front of them. The next shot also lacked clarity. They might have been different women. Nothing that followed was any clearer, including discarded passport photographs, all tailored to fit a specific look.

Cabrini read through the scrolling biography. 'Reuter, Petra. German national, born Hamburg, an only child. Father was . . . Reuter, Karl, a cop, moved to Stuttgart in 1959, married in 1963 to . . . Holl, Rosa, an archivist at the *Bibliothek für Zeitgeschichte*, deceased 1985, auto-wreck. Karl died in . . . 1987. Which seems to be where the trouble starts.'

A campus activist, then a left-wing anarchist. Later, a terrorist. Later still, a paid assassin. A shoot-out in Mechelen in Belgium had left her with her most distinguishing feature: a bullet entry and exit wound on the front and back of the left shoulder. After Belgium, she'd turned up in Brazil with Gustavo Marin, the arms-dealer. Later, there'd been an altercation with another arms-dealer, the flamboyant Russian Maxim Mostovoi. That had occurred in Marrakech. She'd worked in Russia, the United States, all over Europe, and across the Far East. A busy professional woman, then.

When Cabrini was first recruited to the commercial sector, he'd only agreed on the condition that he could bring his two NSA assistants with him. Steven Mathis and Helen Ito, both pre-eminent in their fields, had been encountering personal problems that were undermining their prospects at NSA. Mathis had debts and Helen Ito was under scrutiny after a deep search had revealed past membership of a disorganized socialist student body during her spell at Cambridge University. Although internal security at NSA had ultimately decided that neither Mathis nor Ito represented any immediate risk, they'd both hit the glass ceiling as a consequence. Their careers were going nowhere and they knew it.

Both had served under Cabrini. On one occasion, together. Cabrini had been running an operation in Beijing, eavesdropping on the PSB. The three of them had enjoyed the run of Room 3E099 of OPS 1, the centre of the NSA's global eavesdropping network. Professionally, Mathis and Ito had complemented each other perfectly.

Mathis was a linguist. Fluent in seven languages, he had an encyclopaedic knowledge of other linguists, allowing him to cover the tongues of the globe. Helen Ito's talents were mathematical. She'd been part of a team trying to develop a supercomputer capable of one septillion operations a second.

One septillion. A one with twenty-four noughts after it. In Helen Ito's world, time came not in hours, minutes or seconds but in femtoseconds, one femtosecond being one million billionth of a second.

Although Cabrini was no longer an employee of the NSA, he retained many of the contacts and privileges that he'd enjoyed during those years. There had been a time when that had been a source of contention. Indeed, it had been an issue of legality. These days, however, in an increasingly corporate world, it was no more than a matter of common sense. Now, more than ever, both communities shared common interests, common strategies, common resources.

And common methods.

'What are you going to do?' I ask him. 'Shoot me?'

He knows the response. 'You don't think I would?'

He might. He's more nervous now that he's got the gun than he was before. Emotionally, he's all over the place. I see it in his eyes, in the clumsy way he moves.

We're in the sitting-room because that's where I kept him. He can't think of a better alternative and has assumed that I knew what I was doing.

Blood is trickling from a cut behind my left ear. My neck and shoulder throb.

'You going to call the police?'

'When I'm ready. First, I want answers.'

'You can't do that.'

'Do what?'

'Call the police. They're looking for me.'

'So?'

'They'll kill me.'

'The police don't kill people.'

'You'd like to believe that, wouldn't you?'

I'm sitting on the sofa, which is where he told me to sit. He's pacing. If I made a move now there's a good chance he'd miss me but I stay still.

'Who are you?'

'Claudia Calderon.'

'Bullshit.'

'Then I don't know who I am.'

'Cute.'

He waves the gun at me. I've been scared of being shot before. But never by mistake. Then again, perhaps it won't be a mistake.

'I was set up and I don't know why. I got into your car because I didn't have a choice. Golitsyn and Medvedev were dead when I got to the room. The police were already on their way. Somebody called it in, knowing where I would be.'

'What about Sentier?'

'I was supposed to meet someone there. I went. The bomb went off. I was lucky to escape. That's all I know.'

He considers this for a second. 'You're lying. What about Golitsyn?'

'I never knew him. I went there because I had an introduction.'

'From?'

'Someone I thought I could trust. Turns out I was wrong.'

'And he was dead?'

'Yes.'

'That's convenient.'

'Not from where I'm sitting. Look, I wasn't even supposed to be here. I came to Paris to help a friend. We were due to meet in Passage du Caire and . . .'

'You're just a normal girl who ended up in the wrong place at the wrong time?'

I don't say anything.

'What friend?' he asks.

'An old family friend.'

'You spoken to him since?'

'No. He's dead. So's his wife.'

He snorts with derision. 'More bodies? You're kidding me.'

I'm not even going to try to counter his justifiable incredulity.

He stares at me scornfully, then says, 'Self-defence.'

'I'm sorry?'

'That's what I'll say. It was self-defence. I was abducted, then broke free, there was a struggle and I got the gun. If what you said is true, they're going to be delighted when they discover the body in my apartment is yours.'

'Trouble is, they'll kill you too.'

'Why? I'm the one person who can verify their version of events.'

'Trust me, that's not a good thing.'

'I'll be giving them what they want. Their bomber. Their killer.'

'You don't believe either of those things.'

'Why not? I know you're a liar.'

'That's not the same.'

He jabs the gun at me. 'You've got balls, I'll give

153

you that. What I've seen of you, you could kill in cold blood, no problem. You've got the look.'

'What look's that?'

'The disengaged look.'

I try something else. 'You're not going to kill me.'

'Why not?'

'The same reason I couldn't kill you.'

'Remind me.'

'We had something.'

He arches an eyebrow. 'At the Lancaster? Don't kid yourself. I had something with a woman named Claudia. Remember her?'

'You weren't talking to her. You were talking to me.'

'I'm talking to you now and I don't know who you are.'

'You felt a connection.'

'I don't remember what I felt last night. That was years ago.'

I can't disagree with that.

He steps back from his aggression for a moment. 'Go on, then. Convince me.'

A request, not an order, but from a man still on the edge. He's desperate not to pull the trigger but desperate enough to do it anyway. I need to give him something. I've got to keep this going. I can't let him come to a decision. Not unless it's the right one.

'I used to work for the government.'

'Which government?'

'The British government.'

'Doing what?'

'Undercover work.'

154

'That sounds like import-export. Could mean anything. What kind of undercover work?'

'Let me go,' I suggest.

He doesn't hide his disbelief. 'Let you go?'

'I'll be doing you a favour. You don't want me around.'

'You're not going anywhere. Not until I get some answers.'

'One: I don't have the answers. Two: even if I did, the chances are you'd be better off without them.'

'If you try to leave, I'll shoot you.'

I rise from the sofa. 'No you won't.'

He thrusts the gun at me menacingly. 'Hold it right there.'

'Go ahead. You'll probably be doing me a favour. You'll certainly be doing someone else a favour.'

'I'm serious.'

Our eyes meet. 'So am I.'

I turn my back on him and begin to walk. There's a little hot spot between my shoulder-blades like a reserved table for diners whose arrival is imminent.

'Last chance.'

He means it. I feel it in his voice and it's a genuine surprise.

I turn back to him. 'Fine. Shoot me. One thing, though: if you're going to fire that gun, you'd better remove the safety first.'

He glances at the Smith & Wesson but can't see one. And by the time he looks back at me, I'm no longer where I was.

* * *

155

She moved like a dust devil, an amorphous blur that danced over the ground without ever seeming to touch it. Until her left foot hit the carpet, just as her right caught him on the left knee.

He buckled and she managed to land two further blows before he hit the floor. Then she stood on his right wrist and his hand splayed. She kicked the Smith & Wesson clear of him. When he tried to push himself up she caught him on the side of the face with a ferocious backhand.

The blow hurt her. And felt good. A sure sign that Petra was back.

No matter how much she despised herself for it, there was pleasure in performance. There always had been. It didn't matter to her that Newman was no kind of adversary; you could only ever deal with what was put in front of you.

But with the pleasure came disgust. How had she been so inept? *Again*. She shrugged it off. The inquisition could wait.

She retrieved the gun and went back to him. She pressed a foot on to his chest. He groaned. There was blood coming from his nose.

'This is a Smith & Wesson Sigma .40. It has no manual safety-catch. The two automatic safety devices are incorporated in the mechanism. The first is in the trigger, the second is part of the firing pin system. Sorry.'

He looked up at her, full of resignation and rage, the two emotions blending to form a third: defiance. 'Fuck you.'

Day Five

She stood on the balcony overlooking Pont Louis-Philippe and the Seine. Three o'clock in the morning, the drizzle drifting. She lifted her face to it, closed her eyes and tried to ignore the persistent ache of her bruises.

A pepper grinder!

How depressingly amateur. She'd removed the knife-block and the bottle but not the large chrome pepper grinder standing next to them. There were reasons, naturally – exhaustion, the Stalingrad shock – but no excuses. Petra didn't believe in excuses. They were for other people. Weak people. Like Stephanie.

She'd moved just before the first blow which had probably saved her. With hindsight there was something vaguely comical about the idea of the great Petra Reuter being killed by a blow from a pepper grinder. Like Finnish sniper Juha Suomalainen dying in a bizarre gardening accident. Assassins were meant to be gunned down in a blaze of bloody glory. Not killed by condiments.

Why her? And why use Jacob Furst to lure her to Paris? She hadn't been brought here to take a contract. She'd been brought here to die. In Passage du Caire with Anders Brand, a famous man she'd never met. So what of Leonid Golitsyn? An afterthought, clearly, but whose? Stern's? Or someone else's? Someone who used Stern the way Stephanie used him, perhaps. At the moment, that made little difference since it failed to answer the only question that truly mattered: why?

In his office, there were shelves the length of one wall; books, mostly, a mix of fact and fiction in hardback and paperback. Most of the fiction was twentieth-century American; F. Scott Fitzgerald, Norman Mailer, Robert Penn Warren, Robert Stone.

Inside an oak cupboard she found crowded CD racks and boxes of old dog-eared vinyl albums, which she flicked through. Stephanie would have marked Newman as a jazz fan so his taste surprised her. Talking Heads, Patti Smith, lots of Rolling Stones, no Beatles. Pink Floyd was less surprising but *twelve* David Bowie albums? That made him more than a casual fan but was still less of a surprise than learning that an assassin like John Peltor made marmalade in his spare time. An admirer of Tchaikovsky, Mahler and Beethoven, she noticed, but not of Mozart.

On one wall were three framed drawings, pencil sketches on plain paper – a hand holding a tea cup, a solitary petrol pump, a nude woman sitting on the edge of a bed – all signed by the artist: Edward Hopper. Yet in the entrance hall the gilt-framed canvases were sixteenth-century Flemish.

A cultural scavenger, Stephanie decided. A man who enjoyed Mahler and the Thin White Duke, literature and pulp fiction, pop art and fine art. A man at home in tailored suits and threadbare T-shirts. A man who was comfortable with different versions of himself.

Just as she was.

Shortly before seven, she took him breakfast. When she untied his hands he thanked her. He didn't look at the raw scars. Stephanie gave him fruit and bread, and a cup of milky coffee.

She switched on the TV. The headlines were still dominated by the Sentier bomb and its repercussions. Overnight a mosque in the town of Annecy had been fire-bombed. Some saw it as the first sign of a backlash. Meanwhile the French President had declared that 'an attack on a Jew is an attack against France'. Which was not enough of an assurance for Benabdallah Bentaleb, president of the Muslim Association of Greater Annecy.

In the TV studio, Patrick Roth, a Paris correspondent for *The Washington Post*, was airing his own opinion: 'In the United States these days there's a feeling that it's not safe to be a Jew in

Europe any more. It's the old European disease and it's been around for a thousand years. The current situation in Israel is making it very easy for modern Europeans to resurrect old hatreds. What happened in Sentier is a tragedy. But seen from another perspective, it's nothing new. It's history repeating itself. It's Jewish businesses being destroyed. It's Jews being murdered.'

Beside Roth sat Alain Vega, the Swiss writer and intellectual. 'This is absurd, of course. To try and make a comparison with the persecution of European Jews in the nineteen-thirties is a gross distortion of the reality. If I may be blunt: there is a far closer comparison to be drawn and that is with the way the Israelis are treating the Palestinians in the Occupied Territories. That is the real comparison. An entire people geographically imprisoned and marked out for persecution. An entire people who – were it not for the inconvenience of satellite television – would be likely candidates for total eradication.'

Stephanie was aware of Newman looking at her and could *feel* his question: *where do you fit into all of this?*

He chose the indirect way to ask it. 'Are they even close?'

'I don't know.'

'This means nothing to you?'

'Nothing.'

'Well I wouldn't sweat it. These guys are paid for.'

Provocation dressed in the designer clothes of the casual aside.

'What do you mean?'

'I don't know who greases Vega but I can tell you that Patrick Roth is in the pocket of AIPAC.'

'AIPAC?'

'The American Israel Public Affairs Committee. A lobbying organization.'

'I haven't heard of them.'

'The American Association of Retired Persons is considered the most influential interest group in Washington. They've got thirty-three million members. AIPAC is considered the next most influential. They've got fifty thousand members.'

'How do they manage that?'

'They've got a lot of money and they're not afraid to use it. They spread it around. Directly, or indirectly, through astro-turf organizations . . .'

'Astro-turf?'

'Fake grass-roots groups. Like the Californian Retired People's Association for Better Government. Or the Texan Institute for Moral Conduct in Public Life. Anything, as long as it doesn't sound too Jewish. In Washington AIPAC lines up with many of the think-tanks that have helped shape the foreign policy of the current administration. Outfits like the Potomac Institute and the American Partnership Foundation.'

'The fabled neo-cons?'

Newman nodded. 'For lack of a better term. AIPAC can easily influence the appointment of

161

hardliners to key posts in the administration.'

'Like?'

'Richard Rhinehart, for one. A senior figure in the American Partnership Foundation but also a member of the Pentagon's Defense Policy Board.'

'That sounds convenient.'

'That's the way it works. Because that's the way they make it work. But it's an imperfect situation, having organizations like AIPAC running parallel to the Potomac Institute or the APF. They're staunchly right-wing. That's not the natural territory for Jewish interests in American politics.'

'What's *your* interest?'

'Easy. Oil.'

'Oil?'

'Well, the US's Middle-East policy is a blend of three things, above all: oil, Israel and Islam. And whichever way you cut it, you can't separate them. That's how I know about AIPAC. And that's how I know that Patrick Roth takes money from them. It's in my *interest* to know. I'll guarantee you this: if you gave me a telephone and an hour I'd be able to tell you who's paying for Alain Vega's retirement.'

At eight-thirty Stephanie made Newman call Marie, his secretary at Solaris. He told her he had influenza. Exhausted, he sounded convincing to Stephanie. But evidently not to his secretary: 'No, Marie. It's not a cold. Not even a heavy cold. It's influenza, okay? And that means I'm in bed. Which is where I'm going to stay . . . no, I don't need anything. Except sleep. I'll call you when I feel human again.'

They watched some more news. Later, Stephanie made him another cup of coffee and watched him drink half of it while he focused on the screen. She tried to remember how she'd first seen him; at the bar, a glass at his elbow, on the phone.

What were you really doing there?

They'd been together for thirty-six hours. Stephanie felt he'd adapted to their situation better than she had; the competent hostage and incompetent captor. Did the familiar surroundings of his own apartment make a difference? Did gender make a difference? Or had he detected in her something to ease his own anxiety? Whatever it was, she found his composure unnerving.

Eventually, she said, 'Your cramp yesterday – that was real?'

'You thought I was acting?'

'If you were, you should move to LA and get an agent. But I thought it might be a ploy to get you out of the chair.'

'I wish I'd thought of that.'

'The pepper grinder – you didn't plan that?'

He shook his head. 'It just happened.'

'You never worried it might go wrong?'

'There wasn't time. Besides, I figured you were going to kill me anyway so . . .'

'Wait a minute. Why would you think that?'

'Why *wouldn't* I? The fact that you're here. The fact that you were *there*. At the hotel. And the fact that I know who you are.'

Stephanie scoffed. '*I* don't even know who I am.'

'I've seen your face. You're on the run. You can't afford loose ends.'

'Listen to me. I'm not going to kill you.'

'Not unless you have to. Right?'

She didn't want to argue with him. She took his empty cup from him and said, 'For what it's worth, I'm sorry.'

'For what?'

'For getting into your car. I'm sorry it turned out to be you.'

Sutherland, north coast of Scotland, 09:25

The helicopter dropped out of the cloud, rain slithering over the glass bubble. They flew between stark mountains and over black lochs and rivers. Beneath them a single-track road meandered through the bleak rusted landscape and Rosie Chaudhuri realized the pilot was using it to navigate.

'Are we nearly there?'

He leaned over and prodded a finger at a winding line on the map, the B801 to Kinlochbervie. 'We're here. Oldshoremore's just a couple of miles on.'

He circled the beach twice at two hundred feet. Halfway along it, a rocky spit protruded into the sea, rising to its furthest point, from where it dropped vertically into the rioting swell. During the second pass, she saw people on the spit, black spots running over green grass towards the tip. There were three people on the stretch of beach from where the spit departed.

The pilot began to drop the helicopter, struggling to keep it steady in the wind. Before they'd even landed, Rosie saw one of the three coming towards them.

Iain Boyd. More than any other individual, he was the man who'd turned Stephanie Patrick into Petra Reuter. Rosie had heard plenty about Boyd but had never met him. Not as tall as she'd anticipated but broader, he looked five ten from top to toe, and from shoulder to shoulder. A product of the land that had nurtured him, his features and temperament had been weathered by climate.

They hit the beach with a bump. The pilot killed the engine. It died with a sad wail. Then he leaned across Rosie and opened the door, ushering in a blast of freezing ocean air. She stepped on to wet sand and her heels sank. She tottered forward a few steps before kicking off her shoes despite the cold and wet.

Ian Boyd watched her, unimpressed. She looked over his shoulder at the black specks nearing the rocky point. 'Friends of yours?' she asked.

He stared at her, not blinking in the horizontal rain.

'Sorry about this. We tried to get hold of you earlier. My name's Rosie Chaudhuri. We don't know each other but . . .'

'I know who you are.'

'You do?'

'Who else would land a piece of shit like that on a beach like this? I don't work for you people any longer.'

Rosie tried to keep the hair from blowing into her eyes. 'It's Stephanie.'

He shook his head. 'She's gone. *Vanished*.'

'She *should* be gone. But she's back.'

'Seen her yourself, have you?'

'No.'

'Then you've made a mistake.'

'Have you seen the news today?'

'I know we're a long way from Islington, or wherever it is you people come from, but we do get newspapers up here. Some of us can even read them.'

'The bomb in Paris . . .'

'Not her work.'

'How can you be so sure?'

'You know how. I made her.'

'There's been a lot of water under the bridge since you last saw her.'

'Then what the hell are you doing here?'

'I'm sorry?'

'Isn't that why you've come? For my opinion?'

'Partly.'

'Well, that *is* my opinion. It's not her.'

'But she was there. That's a fact. And it's not the only thing. Two nights ago there was a double strike in central Paris. Again, she was there. In both places.'

'She retired.'

'I know. But people come out of retirement. For all sorts of reasons. Anyway, she's the one the French authorities are looking for.'

'What do you want?'

Rosie looked out to sea where pewter waves rose and collapsed, their rumble drifting ashore between gusts of icy wind. 'Somebody has to talk to her.'

'Don't you have people to do that?'

She looked back at him. 'My people don't *talk*, Mr Boyd. You of all people should know that. Besides, you're the one she trusts.'

'I thought that was *you*.'

'It used to be. Maybe it still could be. I don't know. In any event, you're the only one who stands a chance of finding her before somebody else does.'

'If she's half the woman she used to be she'll evade the French authorities.'

'Maybe.'

'Definitely.'

Her fingers and toes were already numb. Boyd was wearing a worn sweatshirt – once dark blue, now pale grey – over a T-shirt. She could see the temperature was making no impact on him.

Rosie said, 'You're assuming they're the only ones looking for her.'

'There's someone else?'

'There could be.'

He looked annoyed. 'If I find her, and if I manage to talk to her, then what?'

'Bring her in.'

'To Magenta House?'

'It's not the same organization it used to be.'

His smile was one of the chilliest Rosie had ever seen. 'I heard that. Quite a coup the two of you staged. She put the bullet in Alexander, you took his position, and she got what the old man wouldn't give her: freedom. Very neat. For you, for her. But not for him.'

'It wasn't a coup.'

'Whatever you say.'

'It was neat for the organization, too. Alexander had become a serious liability.'

'I'm not disputing that.'

'Just find her and talk to her.'

'And if she won't cooperate, then what?'

'I don't have the luxury of a sentimental option, Mr Boyd. One way or another, she needs to be disengaged. If you won't do it, I'll send someone else. Someone who doesn't know her. Someone who'll do it the clinical way. Then you can go back and join your friends over there on the rock. It's up to you.'

I look at the scrap of paper from the pair of Levi's in the apartment at Stalingrad. Rudi, Gare du Nord, 19:30. *At the bottom there's a seven-digit phone*

168

*number. The Thalys service I took from Brussels to Paris
terminated at Gare du Nord. I dial the number using
the Brussels prefix but there's no answer.*

*Who is Rudi? What is he to me, since this message
was in my jeans, in my apartment? And what was
Leonid Golitsyn to me? He paid for the place and I lived
there. Was I the taste of the gutter for the man who has
everything?*

*There have always been versions of Petra and most
of them have been me. But now I've been stolen from
myself. I have no control over the Petra I discovered in
Stalingrad. I feel peculiarly violated by her existence. I
don't know what she's done but one thing is certain:
like every other version of Petra, she will have a purpose.*

*I'm in the office going through Golitsyn's attaché case
again; two packs of Philip Morris cigarettes, a Mont
Blanc pen, a leather pocket diary from Smythson's. I
flick through it. Since we're in January, there's not much
to look at. His entries are a mix of Russian and English,
with no apparent logic to either. There are several
appointments in New York before his departure five days
ago.*

Four days ago: 10.30 a.m., arrive CDG; lunch,
av. Foch, 1 p.m.; AB – the Meurice, 8.15 p.m.

*AB – Anders Brand. Stern told me that Golitsyn and
Brand dined together at the Hotel Meurice the night
before the bomb in Passage du Caire.*

Three days ago: blank.

Two days ago: blank.

*No mention of the Emile Wolf suite at the Lancaster.
Or of an appointment with Claudia Calderon at eight.*

Yesterday: 7.30 a.m., EL; Moscow, Air France; MosProm dinner, Café Pushkin, 8.30 p.m.

I know Café Pushkin in Moscow. A wonderful place to eat unless you're paying. Next to EL, which was written in black ink, the original time – 11 a.m. – has been crossed out in the same red ink that has provided the new time: 7.30 a.m. The unused Air France ticket is in a travel wallet with a black American Express card and a wad of roubles. There's a small plastic pouch containing three bottles of prescription medication; Golitsyn suffered from high blood pressure, inflamed joints and lack of sleep.

I look through some of his business correspondence; banks, security houses, lawyers. Much of it relates to the proposed Golitsyn Gallery on Cork Street in London. Then there's a plastic folder marked PETROTECH XIX. Inside, the top sheet is a letter from Agence Sirius on avenue de Wagram:

Sir,
We are pleased to confirm the following arrangements: a private aircraft, Moscow – Vienna – Moscow; a penthouse suite at the Hotel Bristol on Kärntner Ring for three nights; a private car and driver for the duration of your visit. Further details to follow.

There are five slim brochures beneath the letter. Four are American; two engineering firms, one aviation leasing company, one Florida-based deep-sea diving company. The fifth brochure is from a Russo-

French industrial design company called Mirasia. The product is Mir-3, a brand new service drone for oil pipelines.

Stern hinted at interests that ran beyond the world of fine art. First politics, now oil. Although perhaps it's naïve to consider them apart.

I glance at the final sheet of paper in the folder.

Entrance Hall, Yellow Level, 12:00.

Hall A, Red Level, 12:30.

Hall D, Blue Level, 15:30.

A schedule of some kind but with no names.

I return to the attaché case. There's a copy of The Economist, *a folder of clippings from newspapers and magazines – primarily gossip from the art-world – and the most recent Sotheby's catalogue. Stuck to the front cover is a yellow Post-it note with a scrawled name and address. Étienne Lorenz, Zénith Studio, rue André Antoine, Pigalle.*

I go back to Golitsyn's diary. EL – Étienne Lorenz?

The last thing I look at is the receipt I found yesterday from Ginzburg. And the message on the back:

Leonid, mon cher,

merci pour tout,

N x.

Followed, in Russian, by the curious addition:

Diamonds or bread? Only we know which.

Boulevard de Clichy in Pigalle on a wet mid-week morning, as close to a bad hangover as a street could

171

be. Metal shop-front shutters lifted with the creaking slowness of a drunk's crusty eyelid. At night, the sex shops looked their drab, seedy best. By the grey light of day, they had a look that seemed to smell.

Rue André Antoine was just off place Pigalle, a narrow cobbled street rising towards Saint-Jean de Montmartre. Just beyond the Hotel des Beaux Arts and Club Harmony, Stephanie came to Zénith Studio. Which didn't look like much of a studio. It appeared to be a cheap apartment block. On the intercom, there was a sticker over the top button: *Lorenz – Zénith*. It was hard to imagine Leonid Golitsyn standing where she was, although no harder than picturing him at the apartment in Stalingrad.

Stephanie tried three times. No answer. She tried the next button down.

A woman replied. *'Oui?'*

'I'm looking for Étienne Lorenz.'

'Who is this?'

'Celine. I have a delivery.'

'It's the top buzzer.'

'I know. I tried. He's not answering.'

'Maybe he's not there.'

'Will you let me in? I can't leave it out here.'

'What is it?'

A photo-flash from Newman's entrance hall: 'A bouquet. Casablanca lilies. It's too cold out here. They'll die. Perhaps I could leave them inside? I have a card.'

For a moment she thought she'd been cut off. Then there was a buzz.

A dark hall led to a gloomy courtyard. Rain fell from choked gutters, splattering on filthy concrete. There was no lift. A door was open on the third-floor landing, secured by two chains. A jaundiced eye watched her from the crack, smoke leaking from a cigarette.

'Where are the flowers?'

'Downstairs. Like I said.'

'So where are you going?'

Stephanie didn't stop. 'Up.'

The woman called after her. 'Lying bitch! I'm going to call the police.'

'I *am* the police.'

The door slammed shut.

There was a note taped to Lorenz's door. *Claudette – you fucking retard. Where are you? Where's my fucking money? Call me before midday. Or get out and don't come back. Étienne.* There was a mobile number at the bottom. Stephanie tore the paper from the door, left the building and found a France Télécom booth on boulevard de Clichy.

'Yes?'

There was noise in the background and the reception was poor.

'Étienne?'

'About fucking time. Where are you?'

'Is this Étienne Lorenz?'

He hesitated. 'Who's this?'

'I'm calling on behalf of Leonid Golitsyn.'

173

'Don't you read the papers? That old prick's dead.'

She decided to meet Lorenz in the sewer. 'That's why you're talking to me, you asshole.'

'Who the fuck are you?'

'A friend of his.'

'What do you want?'

'What do you think I want?' snapped Stephanie.

In the pause that followed, she could tell he was in a car, Eminem on the stereo.

'So . . . you still want to buy it?'

'Well, I'm not phoning for a date. You're not my type.'

'Same price?'

'Depends.'

'On what?'

'He never told me how much.'

'Ten.'

'That's way too high.'

'Too bad.'

'Okay. See you . . .'

'Wait.'

'What?'

'How much are you offering?'

Stephanie said, 'Five,' and wondered what she was offering for.

'Fuck you.'

'Fine. Forget it.'

'Seven-five?'

Her turn to hesitate. But not for too long. 'Maybe. When?'

'I can't make it today. What about tomorrow?'

'Here?'

'Where are you?'

'Rue André Antoine.'

Another pause. 'No. Place de Vénétie. You know it?'

He gave her instructions and they fixed a time. After the call she headed back along boulevard de Clichy towards place Blanche.

'Something I can do for you, honey?'

He was standing in the entrance to a sex shop. Fifty-something, small and wretched, in a dirty mustard sweatshirt and faded denim jeans with a bleached crease. The shop window was smeared. Behind the glass were gang-bang DVDs, crotchless knickers in scarlet PVC and a selection of monstrous matt black vibrators.

Stephanie smiled sweetly for him. 'Actually, yes.'

Inverness, 12:05

The private aircraft were parked to the left of the terminal building. By the time Rosie Chaudhuri and Iain Boyd had transferred from the heliport to the Falcon 2000, its engines were already running.

Boyd had trained more Magenta House operatives than anyone else but his association with the organization had effectively ended the moment Stephanie shot Alexander in a toilet at Zoo Station in Berlin. Alexander had approached

Boyd in the early days of Magenta House. Recently discharged from the Army, Boyd had been attempting to establish a corporately-orientated outward-bound centre in the Highlands. Short of cash, he'd been an easy target. The centre would be a perfect cover, Alexander had argued, providing him with a legitimate business in a part of the country far from prying eyes. For their part, Magenta House would subsidize the venture, contributing to initial costs, with occasional 'corporate bookings' to follow.

Alexander had always led Boyd to believe that he had selected him personally. Originally, Magenta House had been created by a small, secretive group known as the Edgware Trust. The anonymous members of the Edgware Trust belonged to the security services and oversaw Magenta House's creation and finance. One of the original trustees, as members became known within Magenta House, had been Sir Richard Clere, a man Boyd knew well from his time in the Special Forces. And it had been Clere, in an unguarded moment, who had let Boyd know that it was the trustees, not Alexander, who had decided that Boyd should be hired to train Magenta House's assassins. They'd wanted an outsider, a remote individual in a remote location. Clere himself had recommended Boyd to the Trust. Alexander had merely done their bidding by recruiting him.

Boyd didn't know how many trustees there

now were. As far as he was aware, none of the originals were still in place. He'd only ever come across three of them; Sir Richard Clere, who was now dead, Maurice Hammond and Elizabeth Manning. Clere had been a pivotal figure at Bletchley Park during the Second World War and had later headed MI6.

Boyd understood that the original trustees had been reluctant to establish Magenta House at all. It wasn't the illegality that concerned them. It was ethics. They saw the creation of Magenta House as a pact with the Devil. On the other hand, new threats in a new world required new counter-measures. In the end, it was decided that the unit should be quarantined from the established security services, which was a condition that had existed ever since. Now, looking at Rosie Chaudhuri, Boyd wondered who the current trustees were and whether their charter had altered since the dark days of Alexander's disintegration.

The Falcon 2000 accelerated down a fraction of the runway before soaring into the sky. It banked right over the Moray Firth. Boyd glimpsed oil rigs being towed towards the Cromarty Firth before the aircraft ploughed into turbulent cloud.

Rosie said, 'I thought you'd stopped doing the outward-bound courses.'

Boyd nodded. 'Packed it in after Berlin.'

'How come?'

'Didn't enjoy it much. Not my kind of people.'

'What about the money?'

'What money? I was in debt.'

'And now?'

'Now I'm okay.'

'So the people I saw on the beach – a new venture?'

'You could say that.'

'It looked to me as though you're still in the training business, though.'

'Maybe.'

'And making money out of it too.'

'How's that?'

'New 4x4 vehicles at your lodge. A new track leading to the place.'

They'd put down there for half an hour to allow Boyd to change clothes and gather a few things.

'You've not been there before.'

'I'm not without resources, Mr Boyd.'

'Been checking my bank accounts too?'

'Not yet. But now that you mention it . . .'

To his surprise, he found himself warming to her. 'More money, like you said, and my kind of people. A better deal all round.'

'Who are they?'

That raised an eyebrow. 'You don't know?'

'I've been a little preoccupied over the last twenty-four hours.'

'I'm doing private contracts these days.'

'Private *military* contracts? Trading on connections from the old days?'

'And the not-so-old days. That lot on the rock,

they'll be in Colorado next week for high-altitude training. In three weeks, they'll be in Colombia.'

A destination that covered a multitude of possibilities.

'Who's the client?'

'Paragon Resources.'

Rosie had heard the name but wasn't familiar with them. 'Where do they operate?'

'Former Soviet Union, Middle East, Far East, Latin America.'

'What are they into?'

'Oil, gas, gemstones, precious metals.'

'Sounds lucrative.'

'*Very.*'

Rosie gave him the updated dossier that had been handed to her as she'd left Magenta House. Boyd read it twice. When he gave it back to her they were approaching the Belgian coast.

He shook his head. 'I don't get it. From the moment I first met her she was looking for a way out. Tell me about the rumours.'

'They never stopped. Before Berlin, after Berlin.'

'And you didn't think it was possible that she could actually *become* Petra?'

'Frankly, no. Would you?'

'No. I wouldn't. And still don't.'

'But it *is* her.'

Boyd peered out of the window. 'What about money?'

Rosie shook her head. 'She'd made plenty

before Berlin. Somewhere between three and five million dollars, we estimate. Certainly enough for a new life.'

'Through you?'

'No. Independently.'

'Tell me something: why bother? So what if she's out there? She's not working for you any more. She's history.'

'Two reasons. One: her memory. She knows more about the sharp end of Magenta House than anyone alive. Frankly, if she *was* history, she wouldn't be a problem.'

'And two?'

'DeMille.'

Boyd hesitated. 'DeMille Corporation?'

Rosie nodded. 'Given your new line of business, I imagine you know more about them than I do.'

'I'm sure. What's the connection?'

'They're looking for her too.'

'Why?'

'Leonid Golitsyn. We're not sure of the exact reason but there seems to have been a link between Golitsyn and DeMille.'

Boyd sat back and wondered whether Stephanie knew how many hunters she had. The French authorities, DeMille Corporation and now Magenta House. Three trackers, three agendas. He understood Rosie Chaudhuri's concern. He and the French authorities were known commodities but DeMille was harder to quantify. Clandestine and vast, DeMille was an American weapon of commerce, not of state.

Forty minutes later, the brown fields to the north of Paris began to rise up towards them. Rosie looked at her watch. In two hours, she'd be back in her office overlooking the Thames.

'There's something I need to say before you go. If it comes to it, I want you to look at it this way: she may no longer be the woman she once was, which is a tragedy because more than anything else, she used to be a friend. To both of us.'

Stephanie entered place Vendôme from rue de Rivoli. Ginzburg was in one corner of the square, next to Dior, not much more than a hundred metres away from Banque Damiani. Not much more than forty-eight hours away, either.

The door, baroque curls of black wrought-iron over etched glass, was locked. She pressed the brass button, heard the click and was confronted by a large man in the overstated uniform of contemporary doormen; black Italian suit and unnecessary earpiece. Despite this, Ginzburg was a jeweller of the old school. No clean lines or halogen spots. Instead, burgundy silk wallpaper, heavy damask curtains, green marble shot through with veins of cream. Traditional settings were encouraged for sapphires, emeralds and rubies. More than anything, though, Ginzburg was diamonds. *They have both sizes*, Kostya had once joked, *large and enormous*.

A woman stepped forward to greet Stephanie; slim, in her forties, blonde hair stacked like whipped vanilla mousse.

'Is Madame Ginzburg here?' Stephanie asked.

The woman looked at her coldly. 'Not today. I'm sorry.'

'I have a message for her from Konstantin Komarov.'

Five minutes later, Stephanie was ushered into a sumptuous first-floor salon overlooking place Vendôme itself with marble busts between French windows, two Frans Hals canvases on the wall to her left and an alabaster fireplace to the right with a portrait of Aleksandr Ginzburg above it.

Natalya Ginzburg was in a high-backed chair to one side of the fireplace; tiny, bony, fiercely green-eyed with gathered white hair. Her extraordinary cheekbones had once been a feature of sharp beauty. Now they threatened to tear through her papery skin.

She was dressed in a black suit and was smoking the last of a filterless handmade cigarette. The smoke was tinged yellow, the scent of tobacco thick and sweet. Like inhaled toffee. She extinguished it in a soapstone ashtray. A single diamond hung from a platinum necklace; pear-shaped, twenty-eight carats, flawless, the Ginzburg Tear was a celebrated gift from her husband.

'You have a message for me from Kostya?'

Polished French spoken in a surprisingly deep voice.

'Only in the vaguest terms, I'm afraid.'

'Your name?'

A question that always snagged Stephanie. 'Petra.' No reaction. 'Or Stephanie.'

A pencilled eyebrow flickered. Ginzburg tilted her head from side to side, taking her time. 'So . . . you're the one. I never thought I would actually meet you.'

'You know who I am?'

'Who you are and what you are. You're not quite as I imagined you.'

A stern-looking woman with dyed red hair cut like a man's was summoned and dispatched. She returned with a lacquered tray bearing an antique brass samovar, two tall glasses in silver filigree holders, a silver sugar bowl and a silver armada dish of sliced lemon.

When they were alone again, Ginzburg said, 'I know that you are not here because of some message from Kostya so what is it that you want?'

'I'm here because of Leonid Golitsyn. I saw him the day before yesterday. Just after he died.'

'Just *after*? How soon after?'

'Let me put it this way: I think I'm supposed to be the one who killed him.'

She reached for a mother-of-pearl cigarette case. 'That sounds awkward.' The cigarettes were short and oval, the paper starched and sepia. She slipped one between crimson lips and lit it with a gold Cartier lighter. Stephanie watched blue veins rise off her spindly hand.

Natalya Ginzburg said, 'How do you know –
how *did* you know – Leonid?'

'I'd never heard of him until two days ago. But
we must have a connection.'

'And so you've come to me because you think
I might know what that is?'

'The two of you knew each other well.'

'You think so?'

Stephanie handed her the receipt with the
message on the back. 'Yes, I think so.'

Ginzburg examined the receipt. 'You took this
from him?'

'He was already dead.'

Her frosty stare seemed to last all winter.
'Leonid and I have lived in parallel. Born into
the same generation, we grew up in Moscow.
We fell out of contact during the war; I was a
nurse at the siege of Leningrad, Leonid fought
for the defence of Moscow in 1941, then served
under Zhukov, liberating the Ukraine and
Crimea. After the war, we met again, only to be
parted once more.'

'How?'

'The normal thing. The Gulag.' Said as a quip,
but there was no mistaking the gravity. 'I spent
seven years in Vyatlag, not far from Perm. Leonid
was sentenced to four at Minlag in the north, and
then five at Dalstroi in the east.'

'Why?'

'You imagine there needed to be a reason?'

'When did you meet again?'

'In 1957. Here, in Paris. Can you imagine that? Each of us believing that the other had died in the camps. Then to meet in *this* city, of all places.'

'What were you doing?'

'I arrived here from Switzerland in 1953, on the very day that Stalin died. By the time I met Leonid again, I was engaged to Aleksandr.'

'How did Golitsyn get here?'

'He never told me. I asked him once but he wouldn't say. There are some questions you don't ask more than once. These days, everybody is encouraged to talk about everything all the time. But some things are best left alone.'

'I agree.'

'Leonid had already buried his past by the time he arrived here. For us, our history was a dirty secret. We whispered in private and were silent in public. I never told Aleksandr anything. He grew up here. The Occupation couldn't compare. He knew that. And knew better than to ask. There would have been no merit in telling him about the things I had to do just to get enough bread to survive.'

'You're being remarkably candid with me.'

'Only because I know that you understand.'

'Diamonds or bread – only we know which?'

'Exactly. Among the circle of affluent acquaintances we acquired over the subsequent years, only Leonid and I knew which was the most precious. It was our little joke. And a reminder of the only valuable thing that we took from the camps.'

'Which was?'

'In every instance, to do whatever is necessary. In my case, I'm talking about the hardest substance known to man.' She fingered the diamond hanging from her neck. 'Not this, but a woman. Look at me. What do you see? An old woman? A rich woman?'

'I suppose so, yes.'

'Aristocratic, in a way?'

'Yes.'

She smiled. 'An illusion. The same with Leonid. In the camps, we did whatever was necessary to survive. It was as simple as that. After the camps, we became who we needed to be in order to live the lives we chose.'

'I understand.'

'Of course you do. Kostya told me about you.'

'Really?'

'You look surprised. Perhaps you considered him more discreet than that.'

'Perhaps.'

'Don't think poorly of him. It says more about our relationship than yours.'

'Did he mention that I didn't *choose* my life?'

'A point of pedantry, really. You've lived your life by being who you needed to be at any given moment. Why do you imagine I agreed to see you? Because you said you had a message from him? Of course not. In five seconds I can speak to him on the phone. I agreed to see you because I'm a curious woman. I wanted to see what a younger version of myself might look like these days.'

'What?'

Amused, she shook her head. 'No, no, I never did what you do. But I led a life no less unusual. I lied for survival. I lied for advancement. I used what I had to the full. When I met Aleksandr here in Paris, I made him fall in love with me, in the same way that I made other men fall in love with me. I made myself into something he couldn't defy. I let nothing get in the way. Leonid was the same.'

We're in her private office now, a small cube with a window but no view. This is the truth about Natalya Ginzburg; a woman in her mid-eighties, working every day, just as she always has. She fronts a business trading the world's finest gemstones. She dresses immaculately and throws off an air of impenetrable, aristocratic defiance. Yet her office is dark, dull and small. This is where the work occurs. And it's all about the work. For all her grandeur, she's the oldest whore in this city. She's been working Paris since the moment she stepped off the train.

She's brought me in here to look at photographs of her and Leonid. She shows me a scratched sepia print of them standing in front of the Cathedral of Christ the Saviour in Moscow. They are children, Golitsyn in knee-length shorts, Ginzburg slightly older in a pale dress.

'The original cathedral,' she stresses. 'This must have

been in 1929 or 1930. Before that mud-eating peasant Stalin destroyed it. He intended to construct a Palace of Soviets on the site but never got round to it. Typical. In the end, they built a swimming pool there once he was dead. Now the cathedral has been rebuilt. Not quite a replica, but close.'

'I've seen it.'

'Really? I've never been back.'

'It's very impressive.'

She nods. 'Important, too. The arrogance of it – only a Georgian could imagine that religion could be so easily crushed.'

As she shuffles through other dog-eared photographs, I ask, 'Did you know Anders Brand?'

She doesn't look up but nods.

'Were you aware that he and Golitsyn had dinner together four nights ago?'

'No.'

'But you're aware that he's dead?'

'Naturally. I must say, I was surprised.'

'I don't understand.'

'That he was in Sentier.'

'Why?'

'That was not really his . . . environment.'

'What does that mean?'

'Don't be cheap.'

I choose not to press it. Instead, I say, 'Were they friends, or was it a professional relationship?'

'Both. Anders was very well connected. He knew everyone. A cultured man, too. He and Leonid were similar in many ways.'

'A nice man?'

'Very. Polite but never dull.'

'Did Golitsyn have any business interests in Amsterdam?'

She hesitates. 'In Amsterdam?'

'Yes.'

'Not that I know of. Although I'm a little surprised at the way you ask the question. In what context does Amsterdam arise?'

'He was trying to tell me something.'

'Leonid?'

'Yes.'

'When?'

'When I found him.'

'I thought you said you saw him after he'd died.'

'He was dying. The damage was done.'

'By you?'

Asked with utter dispassion.

'No. He was alive when I found him. And dead within a minute or two.'

'This was at the Hotel Lancaster?'

'Yes.'

'What was Leonid trying to tell you?'

'I don't know. Amsterdam was the only word he managed. I was wondering if he had interests there. Personal, professional, anything . . .'

'You're assuming this has something to do with the city in the Netherlands.'

'I don't know of any other Amsterdam.'

Her look couldn't be more withering. 'Leonid had connections to the Amsterdam Group.'

'I'm not familiar with the name.'

'Based in New York. Or is it Washington? He did tell me once but I don't remember. A private investment house. They hire only the best people with the best connections. I don't recall how much they have under management but it's many billions.'

'What kind of connections?'

'Political, mainly.'

'And he was part of this group?'

She shakes her head. 'He had business dealings with them, certainly. But whether he was a member of Amsterdam or not, I couldn't say.'

'I thought his interests were in art.'

'On a personal level, yes. All his life he loved art. But Leonid loved to live a certain way. An expensive way. So he needed money. And he loved it. He loved what it did for him. He loved the acquisition of it – the deals – and the doors it opened.'

'I've heard he was close to Brezhnev, Chernenko, Andropov . . .'

Ginzburg looks bored by this minor revelation. 'Gorbachev, Yeltsin, even Putin – yes, yes, all of them. They were good for business.'

'Was that something Amsterdam valued?'

'Naturally. In Moscow and elsewhere. You have to understand that Leonid had no money at all in 1957, when he arrived in Paris. Ten years later, he was rich. And by 1970 he had what he really wanted. Influence. Silent power. All the things Amsterdam values. More than anything, though, Leonid had a talent for putting people together where others couldn't. He brokered

190

connections. And Amsterdam is a business built on a foundation of connections.'

Back in the salon, Natalya Ginzburg said, 'Recently Leonid had started to give away large amounts of his wealth. Mostly to Jewish charitable organizations.'

Streams of dying sunlight spilled through the French windows and across the carpet. Ginzburg had resumed her position in her favoured chair.

'He was Jewish himself?' Stephanie asked.

'Half-Jewish. His mother was Russian Orthodox.'

'What kind of organizations?'

'He was most interested in Russian Jews wishing to emigrate to Israel. He established a foundation in Moscow to assist those who couldn't afford the legal and practical costs. In Israel he funded two housing projects in Tel Aviv and one in Jerusalem, specifically for Russian immigrants. Not a universally popular move.'

'No?'

'No. There's a feeling in Israel that many of the Jews who emigrate from Russia are – how shall I put this? – from the bottom of the barrel.'

'I don't suppose he agreed.'

'I would say that he didn't feel there was anything wrong with coming from the bottom of the barrel. After all, that was where we came from. It's not where you come from that matters. It's where you go and how you get there.'

191

'And the will to do whatever is necessary.'

'Just so.' She smiled again, revealing fragments of failing teeth speckled red with lipstick. 'I don't believe Kostya ever bought anything for you from me, did he?'

'No.'

'He bought gifts for other women from me. Did you know that?'

'No.'

'Does it disappoint you to hear it?'

'Of course not.'

A lie so transparent that it prompted a look of pity from Ginzburg. 'For the ones who loved emeralds, he bought emeralds. For the ones who loved diamonds, he bought diamonds.'

Stephanie tried to shrug it off. 'I guess I should have told him what I liked.'

'You know the ones I mean. The willing ones. The beautiful, empty ones.'

'Is there a point to this?'

'You should feel flattered.'

'I should?'

'I asked him once whether it hurt that the two of you were no longer together. He said no. I was surprised. He said it was because you were always together. Even when he was with the truly beautiful ones and their diamonds. He loved you because you couldn't be bought.'

Stephanie smiled and hoped it didn't look as sad as it felt. 'It would have been nice if he'd tried.'

Natalya Ginzburg smiled too but also shook her head. '*You* have to be earned, Stephanie. That was what he told me.'

Earned by the good ones, bought by the bad. That was the painful truth.

Stephanie ripped the tape from his mouth. There was no cramp this time. Just as there'd been no protest when she'd applied the tape. But he looked ragged; bloodshot eyes, dishevelled hair, a dark shadow of stubble falling over his jaw.

'Are you okay?' she asked.

'Sure. I love being tied and gagged in my own home. Normally I have to pay for a service like that from a woman like you.'

'Talking of which, I've brought you a present.'

She took the blue plastic bag from her overcoat pocket and placed it in his lap. Then she unfastened his hands.

'What is it?'

'See for yourself.'

He picked at the bag cautiously, saw what was inside, then looked harder at it, as though his eyes had made a mistake. Finally, he reached inside and pulled it out; a pair of studded leather cuffs, a length of steel chain and a chunky padlock.

He looked up at her. 'You're kidding me.'

'It's up to you. But it's going to hurt a lot less than the washing line.'

'Where'd you get it?'

Under the circumstances, Stephanie found that

funny. 'A sex shop in Pigalle.' When Newman grimaced, she added: 'Look on the bright side. At least it's not Tommy Hilfiger.'

She escorted him to the bathroom, waited for him to finish, then returned him to the chair, where she fastened the cuffs around his wrists, before leaving the room. In his office, she sat down at his desk and switched on his computer.

The Amsterdam Group home page was matt grey with a central image of an impressive skyscraper wrapped in a mirror skin set against a deep blue sky. Regions of operation faded in and out like film credits; Asia, Europe, North America. And at the centre of the page:

THE AMSTERDAM GROUP
TOMORROW TODAY

She absorbed the facts; three continents, seventeen countries, almost four hundred employees, and over twenty-two billion dollars under management. Founded in 1983, Amsterdam currently operated eighteen funds, focusing on their preferred sectors: energy, property, telecommunications, aerospace, defence, technology. It claimed to have more than six hundred investors from almost fifty countries and to have invested more than eight hundred million dollars of its own capital to the funds.

She navigated her way through the site. The facts were predictably dry, the photographs predictably smug; wholesome executives who looked as though they had never consumed anything stronger than Evian. The pages were suffused with meaningless phrases:

IN A WORLD OF CHANGE, A CONSTANT PARTNER.
TOMORROW'S OPPORTUNITIES, YESTERDAY'S VALUES.
WELCOME TO THE WORLD'S PREMIER FINANCIAL FAMILY.

There was a directory of employees, from senior executives down to the new recruits. Leonid Golitsyn didn't appear on the list. Nor did Anders Brand. But she recognized several others: James G. Harris, a former US Secretary of State; Albert Raphael, the Canadian newspaper baron, now a US citizen; Allan Hunt, the retired head of NATO; Vladimir Kravnik, the long-serving chief of Gazprom, the giant Russian gas company. Former politicians included two European prime ministers, a president of South Korea and a vice-president of Venezuela.

She looked at the News section, which listed recent deals: the acquisition of Ballentyne InterMedia for $77 million; the opening of a new office in Singapore to coincide with the launch of a new fund for south-east Asia; a deal by Kincaid Pearson Merriweather, a wholly-owned subsidiary, to supply the Indonesian army with the Reaper IV missile-defence system.

Stephanie's attention drifted. On the desk, beside the screen were four DVDs; *Touch of Evil, Chinatown,*

Les Amants du Pont-Neuf, The Usual Suspects. On the shelf nearest them were some framed photographs: Newman ten years younger, shaking hands with an Asian man in a green military uniform and dark glasses, the two of them beside a Gulfstream V; Newman in a bar with friends, Tsingtao bottles on the table; Newman on a yacht with another man, both laughing, both tanned, a marlin suspended from a hook between them.

There was a black-and-white photograph of a man and woman with two boys standing in front of them. The backdrop was a garden, a farmhouse and a wood of mature pine. She looked at the boys. He was the taller of the two. Perhaps only nine or ten, yet there was no doubt about it; Newman as a young boy.

In a simple wooden frame was the same woman from the only photograph on the desk. Stephanie took the smaller picture from the shelf and compared it to the larger shot. Dark-skinned, thick black hair, eyes the colour of anthracite. The photo on the desk was a head-and-shoulders shot. Her mouth was sheer charity. She seemed to know it too. Something in her eyes promised trouble coupled to an assurance that it would be worth the effort.

The smaller print from the shelf was taken on a beach. Stephanie was transfixed by her figure. Waist, bust, hips, bottom. She looked fabulously sexy; strong but feminine. Not an easy balance to strike.

Stephanie thought she looked Mediterranean. Greek or Spanish, maybe. Or, perhaps, Italian. Stephanie wondered whether she was looking at Carlotta, the woman who'd given him the watch with the inscription: *Robert, with love, Carlotta*. In both shots her throat was encircled by a piece of orange coral suspended on a leather cord. The coral was in a tiny bowl of blue glass beside the lamp on the desk. Stephanie picked it up: It was smooth and cool to the touch.

Something sentimental, something precious.

New York City, 13:05

'No one disappears these days. You understand me? No one. It's just plain . . . *old-fashioned*.'

John Cabrini abruptly terminated the call to Steven Mathis because he could see Gordon Wiley, CEO of the Amsterdam Group, approaching the table. Cabrini began to rise from his chair but was waved back into it by Wiley.

'Sorry to drag you over here but I've only got an hour.'

Cabrini shrugged. 'No problem, sir.'

Wiley smiled thinly. 'I'm hoping that won't be the last time I hear that phrase during our conversation.'

They were at Quatorze Bis, a French bistro on East 79th Street. A waiter approached with two menus.

'It's okay,' Wiley said. 'We know what we're having. Fried chicken, fries, green salad.' He turned to Cabrini. 'Trust me. You won't be disappointed.'

Cabrini felt he'd just had a premonition of the kind of conversation they were going to have.

'So,' sighed Wiley, checking the screen of his phone so that he wouldn't have to make eye contact, 'how long's it been?'

'About thirty hours.'

'And how are we doing?'

'We're doing fine.'

'She dead yet?'

'Not yet.'

Another smile, equally bereft of humour. 'I'm kidding. But I won't be in another thirty hours.'

'I understand, sir.'

'I hope so. I spoke to Ellroy earlier. He was a little evasive. That's why you're here. He's your boss, but I'm his boss, so don't make me beg. I'm not in the mood.'

'We've only been fully operational for twenty hours.'

'What's the current situation?'

'We're moving in on her.'

'Do you know where she is?'

'Not exactly. But we have a good idea.'

'Where?'

'We're pretty sure she's still in Paris.'

Wiley raised an eyebrow. 'Nice work. That narrows it down to about seven or eight million.'

'We're still collating.'

'Collating? Then how do you know you're

moving in on her? She could be moving too. Anywhere on the planet.'

'We'll find her, sir.'

'You're not working for the government any more, Cabrini. You're in the private sector now. You get paid to deliver.'

'My record speaks for itself.'

Wiley sat back. 'True. But I need you to understand the position we're in. Our partners are asking questions. They've got itches that need to be scratched. The longer we wait, the worse they'll get. This has to be over in five days.' He looked at his watch. 'Less twelve hours.'

'That's plenty of time. She'll be cold by then. You have my word on it.'

'Do you want a shower? A change of clothes?'

He didn't jump at the offer. It felt like a trick. She looked surprised. Perhaps she expected him to dissolve with gratitude. He tried to ignore his aching exhaustion and reached for as much insouciance as he could muster.

'Sure. Why not?'

As though *he* was doing *her* a favour.

She escorted him to the bathroom, wedged the book into the frame and pulled the door behind her. Newman stripped slowly and then looked at himself in the mirror; five years older than the day before yesterday.

He ran the shower as hot as he could tolerate and leaned against the white tiles, letting the water sluice over his head, shoulders and back. His wrists stung. He watched pale pink water disappear down the plug-hole. When he'd finished, she allowed him a few seconds to wrap a towel around his waist before entering the bathroom.

'Okay if I shave?'

She couldn't answer. It was only once he'd started rubbing shaving foam across his jaw that she nodded. It wasn't just the wrists. There were scars across his back, over the ribs, on his shoulders, stomach and legs. Deep ones, shallow ones, clean and ragged, holes and slashes. She knew she was staring but couldn't seem to do anything about it.

Newman was as used to the reaction as he was to the scars. It took such moments to remind him quite how prominent they were.

'What happened to you?'

'You don't quit, do you? Haven't you got the message yet? It's not something I talk about.'

She watched him shave then brush his teeth. He took his time, squeezing as much pleasure from the process as he could. She followed him into his bedroom where he was equally slow in picking fresh clothes; a maroon T-shirt that had faded to raspberry, a worn grey sweatshirt with holes in each elbow and a pair of faded jeans that looked a little large for him.

He pulled off the towel and Stephanie felt surprisingly awkward. She half-turned from him and spilled the first sentence to form in her mouth.

Anything to break the silence, no matter how clumsy: 'So . . . you like Norman Mailer?'

He looked over at her. *'What?'*

'Norman Mailer. I saw *The Naked and the Dead* and *The Deer Park* on the shelf in your office.'

He looked faintly amused when he finally chose to reply. 'Yeah. I like Mailer. I like the way he writes, I like his views. I don't always agree with them but I admire a man who's not afraid to speak his mind. And who has the intellect and guts to back it up, no matter what.'

'My father had a signed copy of *Tough Guys Don't Dance.'*

'Did he read it?'

He saw her bite her tongue and was annoyed with himself.

She said, 'You've also got *All The King's Men*. That was the first great American novel I ever read. I'd never heard of Robert Penn Warren. I must have been about fifteen or sixteen. Later, I discovered Salinger, Steinbeck and Fitzgerald, but I never thought they produced anything as good.'

'Ever see the movie?'

She shook her head. 'I didn't know there was one.'

'It won two or three Oscars. Broderick Crawford got one for Best Actor.'

'Never heard of him. He played Willie Stark?'

Newman nodded. 'Crawford was a big star back then. This would be 1949, maybe 1950.'

'Oh. Right.'

And with that he saw that he'd lost her.

We're in the kitchen. One of his hands is cuffed to the cloth-rail on one side of the central island. The other is free. Clean again, he looks older than he did at the Lancaster. But age suits him. Some men wear experience like a subtle aftershave; it never overpowers, it just leaves a trace that invites investigation.

There are seven messages on the answer-phone, three of them blank. I delete those and replay the other four.

09:59 – Hello, Robert. It's Abel Kessler. I'm coming to Europe soon, for about ten days. It'd be great to catch up. Let me know if you're around. Hope you're still seeing whatever-her-name-was.

11:02 – (*first female voice*) Robert. Did you hear about the other night after we left? I can't believe it. Please call me. I want to talk to you about it.

17:29 – Robert. Jean-Claude Sardé again. I hope you got my message yesterday. I called your office today. Your secretary said you're not well. I hope it's nothing serious. When you feel better please call me. Thank you.

18:01 – (*second female voice*) Hey. It's me. I know it's been a while but . . . I just wanted to talk. You're probably away. Like always. I've been away too. I just wanted to . . . I don't know . . . catch up, I guess. Anyway, if you're around . . . well, you know my number.'

I run the second message for a third time. 'Who's that?'

'Scheherazade Zahani.'

'She didn't leave her name.'

'So?'

'I guess she felt she didn't need to. How do you know her anyway?'

'We've been close a long time. I knew her husband.'

'What did she say to you?'

'When?'

'At the Lancaster. When you went over to see her. The two of you looked back at me. She whispered something to you that made you both laugh. What was it?'

'She asked if you were a lover.'

'And you said?'

'Not of mine. And then she said she was sure she'd seen you before.'

'And that was it?'

'Yes.'

'And that was enough to make both of you laugh?'

He looks at me dispassionately. 'If you say so. I don't remember.'

'And the other female caller?'

'That was Anna. She's an ex-girlfriend.'

'Ex?'

'That's right.'

'She didn't sound too happy about it.'

'You should have heard her when we were together.'

I take an educated guess. 'Is she whatever-her-name-was?'

He manages half a smile. 'Very perceptive.'

'Mr Kessler didn't sound too happy about it, either.'

'Well, he has the luxury of living on the other side

203

of the world to her. Let me ask you something. Is your name really Claudia? And are you really from Argentina?'

'That's two things.'

'So pick one.'

I go for the softer option. 'I'm not from Argentina.'

'Then I'm guessing you're not Claudia, either.'

'Probably not.'

'So what should I call you?'

'Anything you like.'

'That makes you sound like a hooker.'

'I've been accused of worse.'

'For the sake of convenience, why don't you give me a name?'

'Marianne,' *I say, after some thought.*

'Is that your real name?'

'Sort of.'

'What kind of answer's that?'

'All the answer you're going to get. Okay, my turn. Ever hear of the Amsterdam Group?'

A question that represents a sudden shift in gear. But he takes it in his stride. 'Sure.'

Not the answer I anticipated, regardless of the truth. 'Ever done business with them?'

'Not directly.'

I pour us both a glass of water. He drains his and I refill it for him. I take some saucisson sec *from the fridge and begin to carve slices on a wooden board beside the sink.*

'What do you know about them?' *I ask.*

'They're based in Washington, which makes them*

slightly unusual. Most private equity firms – which is what they are – are based in New York. But they're very political so it makes a kind of sense.'

'How?'

'A lot of their investments are tied into government contracts. They spend a lot of time and money courting the right people on the right committees up on Capitol Hill. They're right in there, right in the middle of it.'

'In the middle of what?'

'The Iron Triangle.'

'Which is what?'

He seems surprised that I don't know. 'A three-way relationship between politics, big business and the military. It's cronyism on a massive scale because it's business on a massive scale. During the Reagan era, for instance, before the so-called Cold War peace dividend kicked in, the Pentagon was spending north of twenty-five million dollars an hour, every hour of the year.'

'Suddenly the attraction becomes clear.'

I scrape the slices of saucisson sec *on to a plate and place it between us. Then I refill my glass.*

He says, 'Over-spends on these contracts are normal and most budgets have vast profit-margins built into them because the companies submitting the tenders know that a final decision will rarely come down to cost. Almost always it's determined by influence and connections.'

'What the Chinese call guanxi.'

'Exactly. Even then, there are safety nets. Like Black Projects. These are deals that are kept secret because public scrutiny would jeopardize national security. At

least, that's the argument. Lawmakers and the media hate Black Projects. They suspect many of them are kept classified just to protect them from congressional review.'

'Any truth in that?'

'Plenty.'

With one hand fastened to the cloth-rail, he's struggling to peel the rind off the slices of saucisson sec but I'm not about to offer to do it for him.

'So, this Iron Triangle – how does it work?'

'Pretty smoothly because they have a system of checks and balances. Business, politics, military: the people who run this alliance are always coming at it from more than one angle. They're co-dependent. And that's their greatest security asset. Remember I was talking about Richard Rhinehart this morning?'

'The Pentagon?'

He nods. 'He sits on the Pentagon's Defense Policy Board. That makes him military. But he's also a big noise at the American Partnership Foundation, a right-wing political think-tank. This is how it goes: Rhinehart has a view of the world. It's a view shared by his colleagues at the APF. And because of the influence that Rhinehart and his kind have, it's currently a view reflected by the administration. And they're the ones who hand out the contracts that generate the money.'

'What about Amsterdam?'

'They're the business manifestation of his political philosophy.'

'How's that?'

'More than one member of the Amsterdam board is a member of the APF. Or the Potomac Institute, which

is another influential think-tank. So they're political.
But they're military too; they own Kincaid Pearson
Merriweather, one of the largest defence contractors in
the US.'

'And what about oil?'

'They have a powerful energy sector. And they're into
all the sectors that oil-rich states invest in. Then there
are Amsterdam's private investors: you can't just walk
off the street and ask them to invest fifty thousand here
or a hundred thousand there. As a private client, you
have to be invited to invest with the Amsterdam Group.
And that means you have to be very rich.'

'Oil-rich?'

'Precisely. So there's another relationship:
Amsterdam, the Iron Triangle, the oil industry. There's
an obvious synergy to it.'

'Because the current US administration is run by oil
interests?'

'When four percent of the world's population burns
a quarter of the world's oil I think it's fair to say that
every US administration is run by oil interests.'

I take a baguette from the paper bag on the counter,
tear it in two and offer him half. He asks for butter,
which I fetch from the fridge. Then I pass him a knife.
It never occurs to me that he will use it for anything
other than buttering the bread. Of course, he's cuffed,
but forty-eight hours ago – or even twenty-four – I
wouldn't have been so blasé. We're evolving.

'And your position in all this,' I say, 'how did that
come about?'

'Through Scheherazade Zahani's husband.'

'The Saudi oil billionaire?'

He nods. 'I used to work for him. I know about Amsterdam because he was one of their first investors. He knew Gordon Wiley from way back. He made a lot of money out of Amsterdam.'

'Who's Gordon Wiley?'

'One of Amsterdam's founders.'

'Is Scheherazade Zahani an investor today?'

'I don't know. But I wouldn't be surprised. She inherited everything from her husband. Including his investments. Of course she's a very shrewd investor in her own right so she may have had other ideas since then.'

I lean against the oven and fold my arms. 'This all sounds like one gigantic conspiracy theory.'

He smiles at the suggestion; he's heard it before. 'It does, doesn't it? But that doesn't mean it isn't true.'

'What's your view?'

He shrugs. 'I know these people. I meet them in Washington. I meet them in Riyadh. In Jakarta and Shanghai. They don't care about anything except money.'

'And you?'

'I'm the same. That's how I know.'

Even as he says it, I find two reasons not to believe him: the fact that he says it at all, and the fact I can tell there's something more important that he's not saying.

'Doesn't the climate change?'

He looks puzzled. 'How do you mean?'

'Depending on the presidency.'

'You mean Republican or Democrat?'

'Yes.'

'It makes no difference.'

'Why not?'

'Because America's not a democracy. It's a plutocracy. Whichever party gets its candidate into the White House, they're still going to be surrounded by many of the same people. The same power *people with the same agenda.'*

'Which is what?'

'Well, they have a vision about the way the world should be run in the twenty-first century. They believe it should be run their *way. The* American *way. They regard the twenty-first century as an American century.'*

'It doesn't sound as though you agree with that.'

'The twentieth century was America's century. I don't know who the twenty-first century will belong to – China or India, maybe – but it won't be America. Empires are like innovations in technology; the next version is quicker than the last version. The Roman Empire – several hundred years. The British Empire – at its height, say, one hundred years. The Soviet Empire – about seventy. America's already in decline. It just doesn't know it yet.'

Day Six

Steven Mathis was asleep in one of the two cots in the sleeping area. Helen Ito was at her desk but John Cabrini wasn't sure she was awake, even though he could see that her eyes were open.

Cabrini was familiar with this. During his years with the NSA he'd run many operations where hours had slurred into days. Within the sterile operating suites of Crypto City, nights had ceased to exist in a world of artificial light. In those days he'd lived off green tea and taurine tablets.

He enjoyed the sense of dislocation that came with this kind of work. To him, it was no more perverse than pulling a day-shift at a pizza parlour in Harlem; both environments felt equally surreal.

On the screens in front of him were the names. All in Europe, all unaware but available, some retained, others independent, all through the books of DeMille. It was twelve hours since his lunch with Gordon Wiley. In that time, there had

210

been no sign of Petra Reuter. Not a single trace.

Inevitably, this had led to doubts. Perhaps she'd left Paris. But Cabrini was reluctant to believe this. He'd had access to an SIS file from London. Their profile suggested she would lie low, wait for the worst of the aftermath to pass, then try to gather as much information as possible, before performing one of two executions: the source, or an exit. In that order of preference.

Patience under pressure, the mark of a professional – looking through the SIS document one thing was clear: Reuter wasn't prone to panic. Which was why Cabrini was convinced that she was still in Paris, even though it was almost four days since the Sentier bomb. He'd hoped to locate and terminate Petra Reuter using an in-house DeMille team before the French authorities got to her. Or anyone else, for that matter. But that hadn't happened and it was now more than forty-eight hours since Leonid Golitsyn's death.

Cabrini had spent much of his life fighting distant wars from sealed control suites, for the government, then for corporate America. There were similarities – methods of operation, the physical dislocation that made brutal choices and costly mistakes so much easier to make – and there were differences. The largest of these was in regulation. In the corporate world, there was no serious threat of judicial enquiry, no threat of congressional review. When necessary, an operation could be shifted to a neutral territory. Or out-sourced.

Cumbersome notions of legality were bypassed in the interest of more practical concerns. This extended to the free-market recruitment of independents, allowing contracts on individuals to be put out to tender.

Time to widen the net.

Newman looked incredulous. 'You want me to do *what*?'

'I want you to arrange for me to meet Scheherazade Zahani.'

'No way.'

'It's not a request.'

'Why would she agree to see you?'

'Because you'll ask her.'

'I don't know her well enough to do that.'

'That's not how it looked the other night at the Lancaster. The two of you seemed close.'

Newman was lying on a mattress in the spare bedroom. Stephanie had dragged it off one of the two beds in the room. He had a pillow and a blanket. The leather cuff was attached by its chain to the radiator. The new arrangement had allowed him to sleep overnight. Stephanie had slept on the bed closest to the door but had only managed two hours' sleep.

She'd spent most of the night in thought. Zahani's husband had been one of the Amsterdam Group's original private investors. Golitsyn had also had some kind of connection to Amsterdam. And both had been at the Lancaster. As had

Newman. She'd thought about him at the bar. Then with Zahani. Then in the Audi, coming up the car-park ramp. She still couldn't convince herself that it was a coincidence. Or that it wasn't.

Newman said, 'I'd need a reason.'

'So think of one. But I'm going to see her one way or the other. Do it my way and I give you my word that no harm will come to her.'

He stared at her for several seconds. 'Bitch.'

'I know.'

When the time came they went into his office. His mobile phone was on his desk. He put it on speaker-phone.

'Go ahead. Dial the number.' As Newman reached forward, Stephanie added: 'Her *private* number.'

Scheherazade Zahani answered at the fourth ring. 'Robert. How are you? You got my message.'

'Yes.'

'So you know about Leonid?'

'I only just heard. I'm not in Paris.'

'Where are you?'

'New York. I've been out of reach.'

One lie, one truth; Stephanie could hardly tell the difference.

'God, what time is it with you?'

'Two-thirty. I just got in.'

'Living the Manhattan high-life?'

'If only . . .'

'Where are you staying?'

'With some old friends.'

Another quicksilver lie.

'You never mentioned New York the other night.'

'It was last-minute. Something came up. You know how it is.'

'So secretive, Robert.'

'Aren't we all?'

Zahani laughed softly. 'Very true, very true. When are you coming back?'

'I'm not sure. A few days.'

'Have the police been in contact?'

Instinctively, Newman and Stephanie glanced at each other. Stephanie made a circular motion with her finger to encourage him to continue.

Newman nodded and said, 'No. Why? Have they been in contact with you?'

'Yes. Well through Balthazar, actually . . .'

Newman mouthed the word 'lawyer' to Stephanie. 'What did they want?'

'Just a few questions. To see whether I could assist them with anything. I'm afraid I wasn't much help.'

Stephanie prompted him again.

'Did you say you'd seen me?'

Zahani paused. 'No.'

'They haven't left a message for me yet. I better call them when I get back.'

'You better call me too.'

'I will. We'll have dinner.'

'I look forward to it. I can't tell you how much this has unsettled me.'

'It's a great shock,' Newman confirmed.

'Thank you for calling, Robert. You better get some sleep.'

'Before I do, the real reason I phoned: I have a favour to ask.'

Résidence Sienne was a dreary tower-block on place de Vénétie, east of avenue d'Italie. The square itself was small and mostly concrete. Patches of grass and asthmatic trees were cast into shade by the surrounding high-rises. The entrance was cramped between a laundromat and a Vietnamese restaurant. Stephanie spoke into an entry-phone that crackled with static.

'I'm here to see Étienne Lorenz.'

'The elevator doors don't open on the fourteenth. Go to the fifteenth and walk down.'

The skinny man who opened the door was wearing a lime-green poncho, black leather trousers with large silver studs down each leg and a pair of Aviator Ray-Bans. He smelt of dope and dirt.

'Étienne Lorenz?'

'He's asleep.'

'Who are you?'

'Pico. You?'

'He agreed to see me.'

'Today?'

Stephanie nodded. 'Now.'

Pico led her to a living-room at the rear. Stephanie looked out of the window at place de Vénétie. She watched people scuttle in and out of the large supermarket, its garish scarlet and blue neon providing the only brightness on a dismal morning.

She heard movement behind her and turned round. He wore a dark grey towelling dressing-gown over pale grey skin. He yawned, scratched his genitals through the dressing-gown, then looked at her properly.

And was astonished.

His eyes widened, over-exposing two bloodshot whites. But he didn't say a word. Instead, the surprise mutated into curiosity before subsiding into something inscrutable. Stephanie watched the transformation without comment. She'd always favoured tactical silences.

Étienne Lorenz patted both pockets fruitlessly before finding a pack of Merit cigarettes on the smoked-glass table. He lit one, coughed furiously, wiped the tears from his eyes, then took two drags as deep into his lungs as he could.

Stephanie wondered how Lorenz had ever drifted into Leonid Golitsyn's refined orbit.

'Have we met?'

She shrugged. 'You tell me.'

'I'm asking, cutie.'

'I don't think so.'

He glanced at Pico, who'd entered the room and was leaning against the wall by the door. 'She doesn't think so.'

Pico smiled. He had two gold teeth. The rest were brown.

Étienne Lorenz's initial shock now dissolved

into sly pleasure. 'Well, well, cutie – how come you knew the old man?'

'It's a long story.'

'Ever meet any of his friends?'

A strange question, Stephanie felt, but she played it straight. 'No.'

'You sure about that?'

'I think I'd remember.'

'How about modelling?'

'What?'

'Ever done any modelling?'

'Very funny.'

'I'm serious. You look fit.'

'I am fit.'

'You should think about it. With a little work on your face . . .'

Pico sniggered in the corner.

Stephanie said, 'I'm sure we're all busy so why don't we get on with it?'

Lorenz shrugged, mimicking disappointment. 'Okay. Just asking. Want some coffee?'

'Only if you're making some.'

The kitchen opened on to a small balcony that was fully occupied by a ferocious *fila brasileira* with a stainless-steel choke-collar. The moment the dog saw Stephanie it started barking, pressing its face against the glass door, which shuddered under the assault.

'Easy, Giselle,' Lorenz murmured, before turning to Stephanie with a grin. 'Just as well you're a friend, no?'

Stephanie smiled lamely. 'So, what line of work are you in?'

'You don't know?'

'That's why I'm asking.'

'I'm a photographer. I thought you were at the studio yesterday.'

'Could've been an artist's studio.'

'In a way, it is. I'm a photographic artist. Mostly.'

'Mostly?'

'I have other business interests. Commercial property, cheap rentals. I got a couple of cafés along avenue d'Italie and a share in two night-clubs. One over in Montreuil, one in Saint-Denis.'

'A busy man.'

'That's why I have people working for me, cutie.'

'People like Pico over there?'

'Pico knows things about Paris that nobody else knows.'

'I can imagine.'

'In answer to your question, I'm an entrepreneur. An *impresario*.'

'Run out of this very impressive office?'

Lorenz spun round, the good humour gone. 'This is my home, cutie.'

'Sorry. I hadn't realized you were the sensitive type.'

He waved the insult aside, his mood swinging back, just as wildly. 'My office is on the other side of the *périphérique*, in Kremlin-Bicêtre.'

Pico loitered in the doorway, rolling a cigarette with crooked fingers. Although she was now sitting still, Giselle continued to growl on the other side of the glass, pools of glossy saliva forming on the concrete directly beneath her mouth.

When the water had boiled Lorenz poured it into the cafetière. 'You don't look like the sort of bitch who'd be a friend of the old man's.'

'Nor do you.'

'That's because I only met him once and it was business. *This* business . . .'

'Since you've raised the subject . . . shall we?'

Lorenz reached into his dressing-gown pocket and produced a DVD in a see-through plastic wallet. He smirked at her. 'Here. Enjoy it.'

She took it and followed him back into the living-room. There were no markings of any kind. 'This is it?'

'What were you expecting? Ninety minutes of 70mm in a can?'

Stephanie put the disk in her pocket.

Lorenz began to depress the cafetière's plunger. 'You have something for me?'

She handed him a five-euro note, two euro coins and a fifty-cent piece. 'Seven fifty, right?'

'Hilarious,' he sneered. 'Now where is it?'

'That was the price we agreed.'

'Seven thousand five hundred, cutie.'

'Are you out of your mind? It's a DVD.'

He stuck out his hand. 'Okay. Give it back.'

'Take the money, Étienne. And be grateful.'

She feinted to her left. Pico's wild lunge from behind missed her and his momentum threw him off balance. Stephanie caught him with a reverse sweep of her right arm, the elbow clattering into his teeth. There was a loud crack. And then he went down.

Lorenz jumped back. *'Merde!'*

Pico cupped his face. Blood dribbled between his fingers.

'Not on the floor, Pico! The carpet's new. Get off the floor!'

Lorenz charged at her. Stephanie leapt out of his way, grabbed the cafetière and swung it at him. It shattered, throwing hot coffee over him.

Trapped on the kitchen balcony, Giselle started howling. Stephanie could hear her thumping the glass door. Lorenz was trying to wave coffee off his scalded hands. Pico was crawling off the carpet on to linoleum tiles, leaving blood and tooth chips in his wake.

Stephanie stepped over him and said to Lorenz, 'Keep the change.'

Down to the last set, the muscles in his arms and shoulders aflame. Which was good. Which was *beautiful*. The pain was the point. His face was puce, sinews and blood testing the skin, sweat dribbling into his eyes.

Manu, a doorman at Le Cab on place du Palais-Royal, stood over him. When Lance Grotius completed his final set of presses, Manu guided the bar and weights back into the cups of the stand.

Grotius sat up on the bench, panting heavily, enjoying the sensation of the tangerine vest sticking to his skin. Manu flicked him on the thigh with a hand-towel.

'Not bad for an old man.'

'Get lost.'

Manu grinned and leaned forward, lowering his voice. 'Got anything new?'

Grotius looked up at him. 'Like what?'

Manu shadow-boxed a little. 'Anything that gets the blood cooking.'

In the past, uncontrolled aggression had been regarded as an unwelcome steroid side-effect. But tastes changed. Especially in body-building. A new generation of steroids had been engineered specifically to enhance aggression.

Grotius shrugged. 'Depends.'

'On what?'

'You don't like needles, do you? They're syringe administration only.'

Manu grimaced. 'I'll think about it.'

'Do you really need to? You're in great shape.'

'All the other pricks are into it. You know how it is. Too much is never enough.'

An incontestable truth in the murky underworld of body-building. The gymnasium sound-system echoed off hard surfaces. Between tracks came the rumble of traffic on avenue du Président Wilson two storeys beneath the wall of blacked-out windows. Grotius drank from a plastic bottle

221

of mango juice. He'd read somewhere that mangoes delivered energy to the body swifter than any other fruit.

He'd been coming to Adonis for a year. He'd tried other places, closer to home, but they were filled with amateurs who never broke sweat. Adonis was hardcore weight-lifting. Neither he nor Manu wanted to be surrounded by old men on treadmills, or ladies in leotards doing Pilates. They wanted weights, muscles, grunts and the pungent aroma of stale sweat. All of which were abundant at Adonis.

In the locker room, his phone was ringing; *Sweet Child O' Mine* by Guns N' Roses. He reached into his sports bag. It was a text message sent as junk mail.

SPECIAL DEAL! ALL SUBSCRIBERS!
Lucrative offer, immediate availability.
Secure downloads.
Confirm application by return.

He sent a blank reply.

Secure downloads. Two words that propelled a frisson of excitement through Grotius, the trigger for that feeling being the word 'secure'. In other words, the information was not to be downloaded at all. Instead, it would have to be collected in person. Which meant it was too sensitive to be disseminated over the security-sieve of the internet.

By the time he was out of the shower, there was another text.

Collection ready.
Usual outlet.
Offer ends 12:00.

Grotius looked at his watch. Five-past-ten. No problem. He took the Métro to Les Sablons and walked back along avenue Charles de Gaulle towards the Arc de Triomphe. He entered a nondescript apartment block with a car dealership at street level. In the stark entrance hall, pigeon-holes were suspended from the wall on the right. Grotius opened 3C. There was a sealed, padded envelope inside.

Three floors above, apartment C was empty. He knew that; he'd checked once, out of curiosity. Forty-five minutes later, as he'd strolled down a sun-drenched rue du Faubourg Saint Honoré his phone had rung. When he'd answered it a man had muttered softly into his ear.

'This is the only warning you'll receive. Your collection point is in the entrance hall. Don't stray to the upper floors. Do it again and you'll be dead within sixty minutes.'

Before he'd had the chance to apologize the connection had been severed. Grotius wasn't scared of anything in life but he'd never been tempted to repeat the transgression.

It took less than ten minutes to return to his

sixth-floor apartment on avenue des Ternes between boulevard Pereire and place du Général Koenig. He dropped his sports bag in the hall, collected a bottle of beetroot and carrot juice from the fridge and went into the living-room, where he tore open the envelope.

As ever, there were two things inside; a single sheet of paper and a smaller, second envelope, which would contain details of the target. Grotius put it to one side and turned his attention to the sheet of paper and the most crucial item on it.

It was in the regular place, close to the bottom. He'd had a five before. With noughts after it. But never six of them.

Five million US dollars.

He looked at the conditions, near the top, just below the instruction to burn the paper as soon as possible.

Status: open.

He wasn't alone. The contract was out to tender. It was a free-for-all. What did that mean? How many were there? Who deserved *this*?

He read the rest of the sheet – contact procedures, request procedures, a terse set of instructions – then set light to it with a match. Inside the information envelope were five stapled pages, a collection of photographs and a CD.

The first photograph was a terrible shot, blurred black-and-white, taken across a busy street, traffic in the way. A woman. That was as much as Grotius could tell. The second wasn't much better. She

224

was sitting in a car. It was a long-lens shot through diagonal rain at dusk.

He looked at the top sheet of five and saw the name.

Reuter, Petra.

Lance Grotius whistled. In admiration, at first. Then in anticipation.

I go into Robert's office and slip the DVD I got from Étienne Lorenz into the computer. A luxurious sitting-room fills the screen; two sofas, armchairs, heavy curtains framing French windows. Some rich person's apartment, or a room in a grand hotel, perhaps. There are three people, a man and two women, one black, one white. They're drinking champagne from tall flutes. The bottle is in an ice-bucket, a starched linen napkin draped over the top.

The man is middle-aged, tall and slender, with a pleasant face. He wears khaki slacks, slip-ons and a pale blue button-down shirt, rolled up at the sleeves. The white woman has short, dark hair. She wears black jeans and a turquoise top. The black woman, who's several inches shorter, is extremely attractive and wears a slinky black dress. She's already kicked off her shoes.

It doesn't take a genius to predict what's going to happen.

The first thing I notice is that nobody appears to be aware of the camera. The body-language is wrong. Which means at least one person's about to get set up. Almost certainly the man. I look at him with a measure of pity, which is when I notice the second thing.

It's Anders Brand.

It has to be a mistake. I look again as the party of three move through to the bedroom. A new set of cameras are in place to greet them.

There's no mistake. It's him.

They carry their glasses, Brand carries the bottle. He puts it on a bedside table. The white girl is unbuttoning her jeans. When he turns round Brand wears a sheepish grin. Pretty soon, that's all he's wearing; with varying degrees of imagination, the three of them fumble their way towards nakedness.

It's like watching a car-crash unfold in slow-motion. Three vehicles skidding out of control, the outcome inevitable, the tangled contact a mere formality.

Most clandestine films are poorly shot. Not this one. Now that we're in the bedroom there are several cameras operating, some capable of motion, all capable of zoom. The sound is as clear as the image. I can see and hear everything. Including the syrupy moans of the black girl as she sinks to her knees at the foot of the bed to give him a blow-job. He's kissing the other girl, running a hand over her breasts.

Everyone moves on to the bed. For a while Brand is content to let the girls have sex while he drinks a glass of champagne. Then he joins them.

Anders Brand, The Whisperer. The former Swedish diplomat. The former UN negotiator. A man universally trusted and respected. Lying on his back with his head lost between a pair of muscular black thighs, his penis lost between a pair of muscular white thighs. Not quite the image of Brand that Kofi Annan holds in his memory, I suspect.

Golitsyn agreed to buy this disk from Étienne Lorenz. The night before Brand died in Passage du Caire, he and Golitsyn had dinner at the Hotel Meurice. Did they talk about this?

Now Brand is taking the black girl from behind with impressive vigour. His eyes are transfixed by the sight of himself sliding in and out of her. Drops of sweat fall from his brow on to the small of her back. She, in turn, has her mouth buried between the white girl's legs. Their moans and gasps sound comical, like a wretched performance from a tone-deaf choir of three.

Time for a change; the white girl slides into position and waits for Brand to enter her. Which is when I notice something on her left shoulder. A blemish of some sort. At first I think it's a tattoo. But when he pulls her towards him I see that it's a scar. Ragged and round, a couple of centimetres across. By the time he's fully inside her, I can see the back of her left shoulder, where there's another scar, same shape, same size.

It's startling how similar we are.

It's startling that I never noticed before.

Perhaps it was because I knew it wasn't me. Perhaps it's because her hair is shorter. Perhaps it's because I was so surprised to see Anders Brand on screen.

It doesn't matter. Now that I know who she is, the likeness is astonishing. I watch her – or do I mean me? – for a couple of minutes, trying to establish some differences. At first, there don't seem to be any. Later, gradually, one or two suggest themselves. Her figure is a little fuller, perhaps. Maybe her breasts are a little larger. Maybe she's sexier, I don't know.

227

And I don't really care. I'm well beyond that.

Étienne Lorenz's reaction to me begins to make sense. The look of amazement the moment he saw me. The snide questions that he and Pico found so amusing.

Ever done any modelling?

First Stalingrad, now this.

Am I looking at the woman who's supposed to live in that apartment? An apartment paid for by Leonid Golitsyn, the man who agreed to buy this disk.

My mouth is dry. I feel nauseous.

Golitsyn. Brand. Me. Or rather, her. *Neither Stephanie, nor Petra, but the third of us.*

Why?

The sexual crescendo reaches its noisy, sweaty climax-in-triplicate and I find I'm reminded of something Robert and I saw on television. It was a news programme. The great and the good were mourning Anders Brand's death. They were paying solemn tributes. One of his former UN colleagues said, 'His greatest skill was being able to make different people come together.'

How true.

At five-to-two Pierre Damiani's dark green BMW 750 was waiting for him outside 16, place Vendôme. By the time the chauffeur opened the door for him outside the entrance to his apartment overlooking Parc Monceau it was almost quarter-past.

Damiani favoured the stairs over the lift, a small daily concession to the concept of exercise. The five-bedroom apartment was on the second floor; large rooms, tall ceilings and fabulous views of the park. Damiani loved it. Yet when Alia and the children were away it felt as soulless as a disused movie set. He let himself in and tossed his keys into the porcelain bowl on the marble sideboard. He had fifteen minutes.

Out of the corner of his right eye there was a smudge of movement. The blow caught him just above the right temple, knocking him to the floor. A powerful hand grabbed the collar of his jacket and dragged him across polished stone. Along the hall, then right, into the salon, where he was dumped at the foot of a French Rococo chair.

'Get up and sit.'

Still reeling, Damiani clawed himself on to the chair and melted into its green silk damask uphol- stery. The man wore a black fleece zipped to the chin, denim jeans and a pair of walking boots. In his right hand was a gun, in his eyes the will to use it.

Adrenaline nullified the pain but not the fear. Damiani said, 'I'm expecting my wife back at any moment. My wife and two children.'

'Your wife's in Gstaad. At your chalet. With your little boy and girl, and your wife's parents.'

'What do you want?'

'You're due to join them in five days. After your trip to Beijing. Which is why you're here. To collect a bag and some papers.' The man looked at his watch. 'You've got ninety minutes; Air

229

France flight AF128, departing Charles de Gaulle at five-to-four. Your pre-reserved seat is 2A.'

'Who are you?'

'You're going to miss that flight. Unless you're very lucky.'

Damiani's questions were multiplying but he stayed silent. He knew his role; to provide answers.

Iain Boyd said, 'Three days ago Stephanie Schneider walked into your bank.'

'Who?'

Boyd fired the gun.

Pierre Damiani leapt.

The bullet hit the wooden frame of the chair, beside Damiani's left shoulder. The impact reverberated through him. Splinters scattered as far as the window behind.

'I haven't got time to screw around. That means you don't either. So . . . she's got a safe-deposit box there, right?'

Damiani didn't answer immediately. Boyd prepared to shoot again.

'What's in the box?'

'I don't know.'

'But she *does* have a box?'

A small slip of acknowledgement. Damiani tried to make amends and shook his head. 'I have no idea.'

Boyd stepped forward and struck him across the face with the gun. The blow parted the skin by the right ear.

'Sooner or later, I'm going to run out of patience. Probably sooner. When I do, I'll use the gun again. And not on your fucking chair. Got that?'

Damiani swallowed. 'I can't help you.'

Boyd shook his head in disgust. 'Bankers . . .'

'You don't understand.'

'I understand more than you think. She entered the bank from place Vendôme. But that's not how she left.'

'So?'

'Is that normal? Do all your clients go in the front and leave by the back?'

'Look, I don't know anything . . .'

'Who are they?'

Damiani ran his fingertips over the graze by his ear. 'Who are you talking about?'

'You know who. The ones who set her up. The ones who set *you* up.'

'Who are *you*?'

'Someone she used to know.'

Not an answer Boyd expected Damiani to take on trust. The banker took his time deciding how to play it. Boyd didn't mind, as long as he came to the right decision.

'You can threaten me all you like but I can't tell you anything about the bank's clients.'

'I'm not asking you to.'

Damiani nodded a little. They understood each other. 'The man who came to my office was American.'

231

'Name?'

'Ellroy. Paul Ellroy.'

'Go on.'

'I only met him once.'

'What happened?'

'He made an appointment to see me. He came to my office under false pretences, masquerading as a potential client. He checked our security procedures thoroughly. I dealt with him personally. Then he told me he was interested in one of our other clients. Naturally, I told him nothing. And when he became persistent, I asked him to leave. As he got up, he said we could expect a visit from the authorities.'

'What did you do?'

'Nothing.'

'What happened?'

'Two officials from the *Gendarmerie Nationale* came to see me. They asked about her.'

'What did you tell them?'

'Nothing.'

'Nothing?'

'Since when do the *Gendarmerie Nationale* take instruction from Americans? I told them to return with an order from a higher authority. The *highest* authority. They didn't.'

'You weren't worried by that?'

Damiani couldn't have looked more disdainful. 'My family have been in the private banking business for three hundred years. First in Beirut, then here. Ours is a business made out of trust, not legal documents. When we give our word, it's unbreakable. It would take a lot more than some governmental department to change that.'

'You'd sooner put your own life at risk?'

'Don't be fooled by the cut of my suit. I'm a peasant. I don't value my own skin so highly. The only thing I have of worth is my word. Without it, I have nothing.'

'Then what?'

'A problem with the phones.'

Boyd nodded. A ploy as old as Alexander Graham Bell. 'And a knock on the door from some France Télécom engineers?'

'Naturally. With perfect documents.'

'And you told them to get stuffed.'

'Get stuffed?'

Despite himself, Boyd smiled. 'To go away.'

Damiani shook his head. 'On the contrary. We let them in. We let them do their work.'

'Why?'

'You know what they say: keep your friends close, keep your enemies closer. We have our own clandestine devices at the bank. We were able to watch them installing their equipment to monitor us. On balance, we felt it was better to let them believe they'd succeeded. And to know the limit of their imagination.'

Boyd shook his head in admiration, then lowered the gun. 'You're running out of time.'

Damiani frowned, not understanding.

'If you want to catch that flight to China.'

Damiani pulled a silk handkerchief from his pocket and began dabbing the graze. When he stood up, he moved a little unsteadily.

Boyd said, 'Take a good look at me. If you see her again, or even hear from her, just tell her this: Iain is looking for her. And then describe me. And if she's still in doubt, say this: Laxford Bridge. She'll know.'

Avenue Foch. Scheherazade Zahani's building wasn't far from the Arc de Triomphe. One of the two uniformed porters escorted Stephanie into the lift. She could smell different polishes for the brass and mahogany.

Zahani's penthouse apartment was spread over two floors. The grand entrance hall had a check floor of black-and-white stone. Two bodyguards led her through a long Neoclassical reception room. Stephanie counted five different chess boards, the pieces in play on all of them. She wondered whether the entrance hall floor was an extension of the theme.

The next room they came to was a total contrast; no windows, walls of a deep lacquered red, muted light falling from recessed spots on to specific targets; paintings, sculptures, artefacts. Scheherazade Zahani was at the far end with a Chinese woman. They were in earnest discussion over a piece of marble frieze hanging from the wall.

Stephanie had no strategy. All she had was an

idea. That Scheherazade Zahani and Golitsyn had something concrete in common.

Zahani came towards her in a simple cream blouse and black linen skirt. She wore no jewellery. The effect was understated but there was no mistaking her pedigree. She wasn't tall – Stephanie had six inches over her – and she wasn't as pencil-thin as women of her wealth often were. She emitted a kind of sexual confidence that Stephanie recognized immediately: it was the property of women who'd prospered in a predominately male environment.

She had pale grey-green eyes – *les yeux pers* – and a mouth as generous as Stephanie's, although a little broader. Cut to the shoulder, her rich, thick, dark hair had a slight tint.

Scheherazade Zahani didn't offer a hand. 'Marianne, is it?'

Stephanie nodded. 'Madame Zahani. Thank you for agreeing to see me.'

'I've known Robert a long time.'

A silence developed. Stephanie considered herself an expert but in Zahani she found an equal. A woman who could smile pleasantly, say nothing, and feel no discomfort.

It was Stephanie who finally fumbled for small talk. 'This is quite something . . . this apartment . . . this *room*.' And who immediately despised herself for it.

'My Chinese room,' Zahani said. 'Everything you can see is from one of two dynasties; the

T'ang or the Sui. I keep these pieces here for senti-mental reasons. Most of the collection is on loan. The British Museum, the Shōdō in Tokyo, the Museum of Fine Arts in Boston. We're just hanging a new piece. A seventh-century frieze of the cosmic Buddha Vairocana.'

'Really?'

A reply that sounded resolutely ignorant.

'One of the Five Celestial Buddhas,' Zahani explained.

They walked to a small library overlooking avenue Foch. A servant appeared without being summoned. She wore a uniform of purple silk; a Mao jacket, buttoned to the throat, narrow-legged trousers and matching slippers. She brought coffee on a silver tray. She poured a cup for both of them.

When they were alone, Zahani said, 'I've seen you before, I think.'

Half a statement, half a question. Stephanie provided an answer. 'At the Hotel Lancaster.'

'Ah yes. I remember now.'

Except that wasn't what she remembered. Stephanie saw that quite clearly. But only because Zahani had made sure she saw it.

'So, tell me. You're a good friend of Robert's?'

Stephanie suddenly recognized how sly his amorphous introduction had been over the phone. *She's a friend, Scheherazade. A good friend. And yes, she's . . . well, you'll see for yourself.*

'An *old* friend, would you say?'

'Not really,' Stephanie said.

'A new friend?'

'Sort of.'

The smile was in Zahani's eyes, not on her lips, when she said, 'A friend made at the Lancaster *that* night, perhaps?'

'Perhaps.'

'You didn't go there to meet him, then?'

Stephanie shook her head. 'I went to see someone else.'

'*Another* friend?'

Teasing her, taunting her; time to play a higher card. 'Of yours, I think. Not mine.'

'How intriguing.'

'It gets more intriguing. I went there to see the man who was killed.'

'Two men were killed,' she remarked pointedly.

'I went to see Leonid Golitsyn.'

She didn't look surprised. That fell to Stephanie who hadn't expected her answer to be predictable.

'And did you see him?' Zahani asked.

'Yes. But he was dead.'

'Well, that doesn't really count, does it? Had you met him before?'

'No.'

'But you knew Anders, of course.'

The connection. Or rather, the confirmation of *a* connection.

Stephanie was about to deny it. But instinct interceded; Zahani wasn't probing. She thought she knew. And, slowly, Stephanie saw that she did.

When she'd asked Newman what Zahani had said to him at the Lancaster, he'd replied that Zahani had thought she'd recognized her. That fitted the beginning of the current conversation: *I've seen you before, I think.* Now, however, Stephanie realized that Zahani hadn't been referring to the Lancaster. She'd been thinking of something else.

The DVD. *But you knew Anders, of course.*

Gradually, almost painfully, it dawned on Stephanie that Scheherazade Zahani thought she was talking to the woman from the film. And why wouldn't she, if she'd seen it? It had been hard enough for Stephanie to pinpoint the differences between the two versions of herself.

No wonder Zahani was so amused by the idea of Stephanie being a friend of Newman's. An old acquaintance of hers fooling around with . . . what, precisely? An *actress*? Only in the loosest sense of the word.

Once the fog of surprise had cleared, Stephanie saw that Zahani's assumption had provided her with a new and unexpected option: to *be* the third woman. She chose to take it. To play the part. To blush.

Zahani said, 'There's no need to look so coy, Marianne. What happened at the Lancaster?'

'I went upstairs to see him but he was dead. They were both dead. Then I came downstairs. Robert was leaving. It was a coincidence. He asked me if he could give me a lift and I said yes.'

'Just like that?'

238

'Just like that.'

'Did you tell him what you'd seen?'

Stephanie shook her head. 'I told him nothing. I let him drive me away.'

'To his apartment?'

She nodded. 'The next morning he was already awake. He was packing a bag. He said he had to leave for America.'

'What did you do?'

'I went home. And there were people waiting for me.'

'Who?'

'I don't know. But they attacked me. I can show you the bruises, if you like.'

'That won't be necessary. Where do you live, Marianne?'

'Stalingrad.'

'Your own place?'

Stephanie side-stepped the question. 'A rental. It's a dump.'

'Have you been back since?'

'No. I've been living rough. I'm used to it. It's no big deal. I lived for three years on the streets.'

'And so after you got away from them, you did what? You called Robert?'

'I tried. I even went to his place.'

'Even though you knew he'd gone to America?'

'I didn't know what else to do. I left messages for him. Then I finally got through to him – this was last night – and he said he'd try to do something.'

'Who do you think was waiting for you at your apartment?'

'I don't know. The people who killed Golitsyn, I suppose. And Anders.'

'The two of them and you? That's quite a conspiracy.'

Zahani's tone seemed to be shifting. Stephanie thought she detected less amusement than before. And less judgement.

'What are you going to do?'

Stephanie shrugged. 'Disappear, I guess.'

'Where will you go?'

'It doesn't matter. Anywhere.'

'So what do you need me for? Money?'

The obvious first assumption. 'No. But it wouldn't hurt.'

'What, then?'

'It's easier to run away from something if you know what it is.'

'What makes you think I know?'

'Nothing. I'm just doing what Robert suggested. But it seems to me that you knew both men. And that you've seen me before. So maybe you can think of something. Anything . . .'

Zahani stood up and smoothed a crease in her skirt with the palm of her hand. 'Wait here.'

Stephanie was alone for twenty minutes. She stood by the window watching cars throw up tails of spray along avenue Foch. The road itself was suitably distant, the building separated from it by a ribbon of dirt, a ribbon of grass and a screen of trees.

When Scheherazade Zahani returned she was holding a small leather bag by Tumi, which she handed to Stephanie. 'It's not much. Not to me. More valuable, perhaps, is what I can tell you. Then again, perhaps it will be of no value at all.'

'Can I ask a question first?'

'By all means.'

'How well did you know Golitsyn?'

'Not that well. At least, not personally.'

'Yet he was here two days before he died.'

She stiffened, then tried to conceal it, but the damage was done; Stephanie's guess was confirmed. She'd remembered the entry in Golitsyn's diary for the day of his arrival in Paris from New York. *Lunch, av. Foch, 1 p.m.* That evening, he'd had dinner with Anders Brand at the Meurice. There'd been no name or number by the entry but as soon as Newman had told her where Zahani lived, Stephanie had been confident of Golitsyn's lunchtime appointment.

'How do you know that?' Zahani asked tersely.

'I took his diary from his hotel room.'

There was a stony silence. Then: 'Did you take his wallet too?'

'Yes.'

'Maybe you don't need my money after all.'

'I panicked.'

Zahani inclined her head to one side. 'I doubt that.'

241

'I took what I could. It goes with the life.'

'I'm sure.'

'Do you know why Golitsyn was killed?'

'No. Nor do I know why Anders was killed. Or even why anybody would want to kill you.'

'But you've seen the film, haven't you?'

'Yes.'

'How?'

'Leonid showed me a copy.'

'So you knew that he was negotiating to buy it?'

'Yes.'

'But I thought you didn't really know him.'

Stephanie's impertinence was greeted by more silence, followed by the curtest of nods. 'I bought art from Leonid. I knew him professionally. But over the years we became friends of a sort. However, I was never as close to him as I was to Anders, whom I first met through my late husband.'

'Can I ask why Golitsyn showed you the film?'

'Out of concern for Anders. They were good friends. And since Anders and I were also close Leonid wanted to discuss with me what he should do.'

'Did Anders know about the film?'

'No. Did you?'

'Did I what?'

'Know about it. While you were . . . *starring* in it.'

Stephanie had to shake off her mental lethargy to resume the role. 'Not at first. I found out afterwards and I was angry. But then there was the money, so . . .'

'Nevertheless, you were there. How did that happen?'

Time for the lies. 'The other girl asked me. It was her show. I didn't know anything about it. She described the deal – but never mentioned any filming – and then offered me two thousand euros. Naturally I jumped at the chance.'

'Naturally.'

'We've worked together before. We get on well. I trust her, more or less.'

Zahani couldn't quite conceal her distaste. 'How did she get the job?'

'She never said and I never asked. For two thousand euros – best not to.'

'Have you spoken to her since then?'

Stephanie shook her head. 'She's gone.'

'Where?'

'I don't know. And I don't want to guess.'

Zahani nodded grimly. 'No. I can imagine.'

'Was Anders being blackmailed?' Stephanie asked.

'I have no doubt that was the intention. Why else would anyone go to all that effort? But as far as I know, he wasn't aware of the film when he died.'

'Who would have used it against him?'

'Do you play chess, Marianne?'

'No,' lied Stephanie, 'although I see that you do. You have a lot of boards.'

'I have nine in this apartment. Each one is a separate game.'

'All on-going?'

Zahani nodded. 'More than anything, chess is a game of pressure, in my opinion. You have a strategy. Within that strategy specific pieces, or specific squares, are subjected to varying degrees of pressure. Sometimes a single square – occupied or unoccupied – can come under pressure from a great number of pieces. You might describe it as compound pressure. That was the kind of pressure Anders was under. The film would have been just one element of the pressure he bore.'

Stephanie heard herself say, 'It didn't show.'

Despite herself, Zahani found that funny, then said, 'Whatever your opinion of Anders, Marianne, he was a remarkable man. A lovely man. Talented, too. He could make God and the Devil sit at the same table. Recently, he'd spent a lot of time in Iraq trying to mediate between the Iraqis and the Americans.'

'That sounds like a tougher challenge.'

'I think he would have agreed with you.'

'He never told me what he did.'

Zahani smiled sympathetically. 'Under the circumstances in which you met him, that's probably not a great surprise.'

'What has this got to do with me?'

'Nothing. It's to do with Anders and Iraq.'

'But they're after me too.'

'I'm sorry, Marianne, but you're just a detail. A "t" that needs crossing.'

'I've never been to Iraq.'

'Then I shouldn't start now.'

'What kind of pressure was he under?'

'He wouldn't tell me, even though we were friends. The only person who knew was Leonid and he's dead.'

'So who can I turn to?'

Zahani shrugged. 'Someone who knew Leonid a lot better than I ever did. And at the risk of offending your feelings, Marianne, I think it unlikely that you'll know anyone who falls into that category. And that even if you did, they might not want to discuss something like this with someone like you. I'm sorry if this sounds blunt.'

Blunt but honest. Stephanie nodded a little forlornly.

Zahani said, 'I've told you all I can usefully tell you. Perhaps more than I should have. However, my advice to you is this: take the money and vanish. Start again somewhere a long way from here.'

I walk down avenue Foch in a cold drizzle that I hardly feel. The hiss of passing cars drowns out the rest of the city. Every time I think about the film my stomach tightens. On the screen behind my eyelids Anders is having sex but he's no longer with my clone; he's with me. I'm a woman with two bodies. Or even three. Or am I three women occupying a single body? It's getting harder to tell.

245

When I think about her – the other me – I feel bitter at the violation but I also feel worried. I'm meant to be dead. That means she should be dead too. Does that terminal sentence extend as far as the woman who played the role, or is it limited to the on-screen character?

Zahani says the answers will come from Iraq. Whether she's telling the truth or not makes little difference; if I'm to find them they'll need to be closer than that. The woman on the disk is a starting point. I need to find her in order to find myself. I need to know whether she's alive or dead.

I head home. Home. That's a strange way to think of Robert's apartment. A haven, perhaps, but hardly a home; I've been there for less than seventy-two hours. Yet the place feels familiar. And safe.

Zahani, Golitsyn, Brand. Where does Robert fit in? Does he fit in? I don't know, although it occurs to me that there is one thing I've overlooked.

He's asleep when I get back and I don't wake him up. His mobile phone is still on his desk. The only call he's made from it since I got into his car was to Scheherazade Zahani this morning. I look at the call before that and remember what he told me: that the man he was due to meet called to cancel him. I check the time at which it was made. 20:28. That corresponds. I hit the button to call the number.

'Hi. This is Robert Coogan. Please leave your name and number and I'll get back to you. Thanks.'

An American. The name means nothing.

I unzip the Tumi bag that Zahani gave me. Ten thou-

sand euros in twenties and fifties. It's not much. Not to me. *Next, I look for the note that was pinned to Lorenz's studio door in Pigalle. I find it scrunched into a ball in the back pocket of the trousers I was wearing.* Claudette – you fucking retard. Where are you? Where's my fucking money? Call me before midday. Or get out and don't come back. Étienne. *The number's at the bottom. The man who answers doesn't sound like Lorenz. It could be Pico.*

'*I want to speak to Étienne.*'

'*He's . . . uh . . . he's kind of . . . busy. Who's this?*'

'*Claudette.*'

He doesn't question this. Which means he doesn't know her. At least, not well enough to identify her voice.

'*Where are you?*'

'*With his money.*'

'*About time.*'

'*Can I bring it over?*'

'*We're not around.*'

'*When, then?*'

'*We're back tomorrow.*'

'*I can't do it before?*'

'*Sure,*' he sniggers. '*If you want to fly down to Marseille.*'

'*What time are you back?*'

'*In the morning.*'

'*Can I come over then?*'

'*I guess so.*'

'*To Pigalle?*'

'*He won't be there. He'll be over at Kremlin-Bicêtre.*'

'*Give me the address again.*'

'What's the matter with you? How many times you been there?'

'Listen, monkey boy, if you think he wants his money just give me the address.'

She seemed anxious when she came into the room and knelt beside him to unfasten the leather cuffs. Newman stretched on the mattress and then rubbed his raw wrists. He ached, particularly through the shoulders and down the spine. The mattress was better than the chair but without his daily regime of stretches the damaged muscles and sinews swiftly resorted to discomfort. He got up slowly and stiffly, taking care to let nothing show on his face.

'How was it with Scheherazade? She any help?'

'She gave me some advice. And some money.'

'How much?'

'Ten thousand euros.'

'Just like that?'

Stephanie nodded.

'Maybe I should ask her myself.'

'Who's Robert Coogan?'

'Coogs? He's an old friend. Why?'

A publisher from New York, it turned out, just passing through for a couple of days on his way to Switzerland. They'd decided to go to the Lancaster because 'Coogs' wanted to try the restaurant, which was now under the direction of a star-spangled Michelin chef Stephanie had never heard of.

No connections at all, it seemed. *Except that Newman had still recognized Zahani.* Stephanie couldn't let go of that fact even though chance encounters happened all the time. She thought of herself and John Peltor; on two separate occasions, thousands of miles apart, so why not Newman and Zahani? They both lived in Paris, after all, not so far apart. Statistically, it wasn't that unlikely; it just felt that way.

They went through to the sitting-room. There was a cup of tea waiting for him on the table. He thanked her, picked it up and sat on the sofa.

It was dark outside. Another day gone. More than anything else he wanted fresh air. A cold wind against his skin, with rain or sun. Anything that invigorated.

To Newman, Stephanie seemed less vigilant than the day before. On their way to the sitting-room she'd walked ahead of him, not behind him. He couldn't decide whether she was softening, or whether she was simply distracted. The second time she'd gone out she hadn't gagged him. She'd been beside him on the bed and had picked up the roll of tape and bitten off a six-inch strip. But as she'd leaned over him to apply it, she'd hesitated.

'If I don't do it, will you shout?'

He'd shaken his head – what other response was there? – and she'd screwed the tape into a sticky ball and tossed it aside.

'I believe you,' she'd said.

He'd heard the front door close and had decided to wait. It had to be a trap. A test. She hadn't gone out at all; she'd be waiting out of sight. The moment he opened his mouth she'd reappear. He was sure of it.

Five minutes drifted by. Still nothing. He'd listened to the city; sirens in the distance, cars crawling along quai d'Orléans, a couple arguing in the street. Then another five minutes. Followed by a further five. Gradually, he'd realized two things. One: she wasn't in the apartment with him. Two: her trust wasn't misplaced.

He wasn't going to shout. He wasn't sure why not. Every time logic argued the prosecutor's case, instinct leapt to the defence. It didn't make sense; he owed her nothing. But there it was.

He wondered how she'd known. Or had she simply gambled?

At some point he'd drifted back to sleep. When he next awoke, she'd returned. And she didn't seem remotely surprised to find nothing had changed. At least, not with him. But there seemed to be a change within her.

For the first time, Newman thought he detected a serious sense of doubt.

Five-to-eight. The buzzer sounded. They both looked at each other and saw genuine alarm. Stephanie picked up the Smith & Wesson. They went into the hall. The entry-phone was to the right of the door. The black and white image was a little fuzzy but Stephanie saw a slender woman with long fair hair in a dark overcoat.

'Shit,' muttered Newman. 'Anna.'

'Anna the ex-girlfriend?'

Newman nodded.

'What's she doing here?'

'I don't know.'

They watched her reach for the button on the panel. The buzzer sounded again, longer this time.

'Don't answer. She'll go away.'

But she didn't. She waited, then opened the small bag she was carrying and began to rummage through it. Stephanie and Newman watched in silence as Anna pulled something out and turned to the door.

'A key,' Stephanie whispered. 'She's got a key. Why's she got a key?'

'Do we have time for this?'

'*Why?*'

'I guess I forgot about it. Maybe she's bringing it back. Christ, I don't know. I'll make her go away.'

'How, exactly?'

'I'll take the key and . . .'

'Walk out with her? I don't think so.'

'Trust me.'

She wanted to. And she did, up to a point. Hadn't she proved that by not gagging him? But Petra was in the ascendancy now.

'Don't hurt her, Marianne. We can work something out.'

'Like *what*?'

Stephanie looked around the hall, then opened the front door a few inches. Nothing yet.

'Go into the sitting-room. I'll leave the door open. When she gets here, call her in. Talk to her, take the key from her, then show her out. She won't see me but the moment she steps inside I'm going to see both of you. Got that?'

'Yes.'

'Whisper anything, I'll shoot her. Pass her anything, I'll shoot her. Do anything – *absolutely anything* – and I swear to God I will.'

Newman went into the sitting-room. Stephanie retreated to the kitchen. The lift doors parted. The bell rang and the front door squeaked on brass hinges.

'Robert?'

From the sitting-room: 'That you, Anna?'

'You didn't answer.'

English with a European accent.

'I'm on the phone. Be with you in a second. Come on in.'

Stephanie heard the heavy clunk of the front door closing. She tip-toed in the wake of Anna's footsteps as far as the sitting-room doorway. She watched Anna shed a leather overcoat. Bootcut jeans and a mauve long-sleeved T-shirt heightened a fabulous figure.

Newman pretended to finish a call. 'Hey. How are you?'

'I'm fine, Robert. God, you look terrible.'

'Thanks.'

'What's wrong?'

'Nothing. It's just . . . *work*. You know how it is.'

She smiled sadly. 'Sure. The way it always is. And always *was*.'

'How did you . . .'

'I saw the lights. And I still have a key.'

'You didn't say you were coming over.'

She shrugged. 'I wanted to surprise you.'

'Congratulations. You've succeeded.'

'You haven't called me.'

'I've been away.'

'Me too. Where?'

'All over. Jakarta, Kuala Lumpur, Tehran. You?'

Newman's lies flowed as smoothly as Petra's.

'Milan and New York,' Anna said. 'I'm here for ten more days, then back to New York. How come you never called?'

'You know, this isn't a good time right now.'

Anna looked around. 'You have someone else here?'

'No. Nothing like that.'

Anna was tall – five ten or eleven, Stephanie estimated – with the type of buttery pale skin that tanned easily. Her beauty was so pure it bordered blandness.

'I just wanted to see you again,' she said. 'I miss you.'

'Anna . . .'

'Aren't you going to offer me a drink?'

He couldn't quite bring himself to say no. 'Are you okay?'

She bit her lip. 'Not really.'

'What is it?'

'I'm sorry. I should have called you first.'

He said, 'Tell me what it is.'

She said, 'It's Karl.'

Newman looked stung. Stephanie saw his concentration slip, his concern extending beyond Anna's immediate safety.

Time to intervene.

Stephanie swept silently down the hall to the bathroom, kicked off her shoes and socks, ran a basin of water, pushed her head into it, then grabbed a towel, before padding back to the sitting-room.

Barefoot, towelling her wet hair, she called out to him. 'Robert, darling, there's a problem with the shower. I think you . . .'

She halted in the doorway, faking surprise. Anna was now sitting on the sofa, visibly subdued. Newman was still standing, consumed by uncertainty. Startled, they both looked at Stephanie.

'I'm sorry. I didn't hear . . . I was in the shower and . . .'

Anna looked at Newman for an explanation. But he was looking to Stephanie for guidance.

Anna introduced herself. She was close to tears but determined to retain as much dignity as possible, no matter how uncomfortable the moment. She rose from the sofa. 'I'm sorry. He

254

never said. I wouldn't have come if I'd known.'
She turned to Newman. 'You didn't have to lie,
Robert. You could have just said.'

He shook his head. 'Anna . . .'

'Don't make it worse. Don't say anything.'

'About Karl. If you want . . .'

'Forget it. It's not your problem any more.'

Stephanie said, 'I thought you were letting the
situation slip. I had to do something.'

Newman was sitting, elbows on knees,
hunched forward, despondent. Five minutes had
passed since Anna had let herself out of the apartment. Stephanie was standing by the window
looking across at the floodlit cathedral of Notre
Dame.

'Is she okay?'

He shook his head.

'What's the problem?'

'It doesn't concern you.'

'Docs it concern *you*?'

'Indirectly.'

'You still care about her.'

His accusatory glance was confirmation.

'Then I'm sorry.'

He shrugged off her apology.

She said, 'If it's any consolation, you did okay.
It could've been a lot messier.'

His smile was laced with bitterness. 'Easy for
you to say.'

* * *

Newman said, 'I'm hungry.'

Stephanie was relieved; the sound from the television hadn't succeeded in crushing a silence that had persisted for half an hour. When she'd looked at him she'd seen worry, not petulance. The longer the freeze, the worse she'd felt, even though she knew there'd been no alternative.

'Okay. I'll make us something. What do you want?'

He looked directly at her. 'I want to go out.'

'What?'

'I want to eat out.'

'You mean leave the apartment?'

'Yes. I want to walk in the rain. I want to breathe fresh air. I want a proper meal. I want something alcoholic to drink.'

Impossible. That was her initial reaction. But she tempered it instantly. 'I don't think that's going to work.'

'You don't trust me?'

'It's not that.'

'Sure it is. What else could it be?'

'It's not safe.'

'Bullshit. Nobody knows where you are, do they? There are places round the corner – small, discreet, dark – no one's going to know.'

'I just don't . . .'

'This isn't a trick, Marianne. I give you my word. Come on. You owe me.'

Irrelevant yet incontestable. She felt the protest from every part of her that was Petra. Which, perhaps, was the reason for her answer: 'My name isn't Marianne, Robert. It's Stephanie.'

It was still raining and the air froze their breath. They headed down rue Saint Louis en L'Île, a narrow, cobbled lane bisecting the island, and stopped at the Auberge de la Reine Blanche.

The *patron* greeted Newman enthusiastically, glanced at Stephanie and then suggested a cosy table towards the rear. Newman seemed to find that funny – *merci, Fabrice, merci* – and they traded conspiratorial winks.

Water and bread arrived, Newman ordered some vodka, a candle was lit. The air was warm and tasted of tobacco. Stephanie suggested he choose for both of them; carrot soup followed by quail, with a bottle of red burgundy. Stephanie had decided not to drink but when the waiter poured some into her glass anyway her resolve weakened. Heavy and spicy, it burnt a little magic from tongue to stomach.

'How come you told me your name was Marianne?'

Stephanie shrugged. 'Spur of the moment.'

'Okay. How come you told me your name was Stephanie?'

Another shrug. 'I guess it was a gesture of some sort. An olive branch.'

'Is it your real name?'

'I think so. Sometimes it's hard to remember.'

'That an occupational hazard?'

She nodded. 'One of many. Tell me about Anna.'

'What do you want to know? She's Danish, she's a model . . .'

'What a surprise.'

'. . . and what you see is what you get.'

'Which isn't bad.'

Newman saw through the remark. 'I know. Shallow middle-aged man falls for youth and beauty. What can I say? It's better than buying a Porsche.'

'I won't argue with that.'

'And I won't apologize for it, either.'

'Why should you? Actually, it was an education. I've never seen anyone so perfect. So flawless.'

'She's not flawless. She has a birthmark.'

'I didn't notice. Where?'

Newman reached for his glass. 'Don't ask.'

'Not for public consumption?'

'More public than you might imagine.'

'Really?'

'Anna's got a good heart. And she's smart. But she's also a highly strung mess. The coke doesn't help. I didn't mind it in the beginning. We had fun. For me it was a kind of wake-up call. Something different, you know?'

'The coke?'

'No. Anna. I don't do coke. I don't do anything. Doing coke in your forties is like buying that Porsche. It's as sad as it looks.'

'I've known girls like Anna. They discover their beauty will get them through so they let it. Before long, they come to rely on it.'

Newman nodded. 'The way she looks gets her into trouble. It draws the wrong kind of people to her. Without it, she'd be safer.'

'From people like Karl?'

'You don't miss much, do you?'

'In my world, it pays not to.'

'Karl's a party animal. A rich playboy who lives in a narcotic blizzard. Very good-looking, very charming.'

'Eurotrash.'

'That's a polite way of putting it. He's mean to her, then he spoils her. Anna knows he's no good but she can't get him out of her system. Except, it turns out, when she's with me.'

'How come it didn't last?'

'Come on, Stephanie. We're never in the same place. We're thousands of miles apart. And twenty years apart.'

'Still, nice if you can get it.'

For a moment, he looked offended, and then chose not to be. 'Of course. But the truth is this: the first thing she stimulated was my mind.'

Instinctively, Stephanie wanted to contest that but found she couldn't quite bring herself to. 'Maybe. But intellect or no intellect, the body helps. Right?'

'Only for a while. In the end there has to be more.'

'And there wasn't?'

'There could have been. But I didn't let it get that far.'

'Why not?'

'It wouldn't have been fair on her. Not today or tomorrow, but somewhere down the line. So I gave her the choice.'

'Keep it casual or take a walk?'

'I didn't put it quite like that.'

'Is that what happened to Carlotta?'

Irritation flickered. 'What is it with you and her?'

'I saw the inscription on the back of the watch. Things like that – it's the history behind them.'

'What about it?'

'It's nice. It matters. The *past* matters. It defines who we are.'

'I hate to disappoint you but my relationship with Carlotta was no more significant than my relationship with Anna.'

'That's a shame. She looks lovely.'

'*Looks lovely?* Have you met her?'

'I've seen her.'

'Where?'

'In your study. The photograph on your desk.'

'That's not Carlotta.'

'*No?*'

'No.'

When the food had gone, Newman ordered coffee for both of them. The *patron* placed a bottle of armagnac and two small glasses on the table. Later, when Newman asked for the bill, the waiter placed it in front of him and he put down a credit-card. Stephanie reached across the table and replaced it with cash.

'No credit-cards,' she said, smiling sweetly. 'I insist.'

Five-to-midnight. Newman was on the mattress, waiting for the cuffs. Stephanie felt acutely awkward; after Anna, then dinner, now this? A retrograde step, surely, yet one she knew she should take.

He sensed her discomfort. 'If it makes you sleep easier, you can do it. But if you don't, I won't try anything.'

'Why not?'

He propped himself up on one elbow. 'I'm not sure. I mean, I don't know who you really are, or what you've done, but I don't believe you killed Leonid Golitsyn or the other guy.'

'And Anders Brand?'

'If you say you were there, I guess you were there. Why would you make up something like that?'

'Exactly.'

'I'm just going by instinct.'

'Then that makes two of us,' Stephanie said, switching off the light.

Day Seven

It's five-to-six and the hot-water pipes are creaking.
I watch the DVD again on his computer with the sound
muted. It's me, it's her, it's me again. She's so like me,
the differences no more than marginal, it would take
close inspection to tell us apart. I look at Anders Brand.
Is it him? Or is he a fake too?

'Hey. What're you looking at?'

He's standing in the doorway, still drowsy.

'Nothing,' I blurt, as I thrust my mouse towards the
stop icon. I miss it, hit the mute icon – which reintro-
duces sound – and then frantically try again. All I
succeed in doing is drawing attention to myself. The
sound of the DVD drive ejecting the disk fills the silence
between us. As I pick it out of the tray I say, 'By the
end of today I'll be gone.'

A remark designed to deflect that also happens to be
true.

'Where are you going?'

'Does it matter? I'll be out of your hair. You can have
your life back.'

'I thought that happened already.'

'You can have all of it back.'

'Maybe I don't want all of it back.'

'That's up to you.'

'What's changed?'

'Almost nothing. That's why I have to go.'

'I'm not with you.'

'I can't stay here for ever.'

'When will you leave?'

'Tonight. I have two people I need to see first.'

He rubs his face, trying to shed the remains of sleep. *'Well, this is . . .* abrupt. *What do I do?'*

'Whatever you want.'

'And today? I mean, are you going to cuff me again when you go out? Or are we past that? And if we are, what can I do? TV but no phone? Computer but no internet? Free movement but don't open the door or go on to the balcony?'

Good point. And not something I've considered. Perhaps I should *cuff* him. If I don't, does it matter what I say?

'After all, you're still the boss,' he reminds me. *'Aren't you?'*

She crossed the *périphérique* to Kremlin-Bicêtre at Porte d'Italie, the grumble of traffic rising up from the congested lanes beneath her. Stephanie doubted Kremlin-Bicêtre looked any better in dazzling sunshine. Not a fresh face to be seen anywhere, cheap shops lining avenue de Fontainebleau: Balkan phonecard booths; north-African clothing stores; Resto Istanbul, a Turkish sandwich shop. On rue du Général Leclerc Stephanie glanced over her shoulder and saw the tower-blocks of place de Vénétie, east of avenue d'Italie. A fifteen-minute walk away but she doubted Étienne Lorenz ever made the journey on foot.

The building was at the junction with rue de 14 juillet, four storeys rising from the L'ambassade brasserie, a newsagent, and a toy shop with windows opaque with dust. Stephanie walked past the entrance twice, loitered outside La Maison du Couscous to check for muscle, then went inside. She climbed a staircase missing half its banisters. The door on the top floor had no buzzer so she hammered the zinc sheet bolted to it. There was a sign beside it: Zénith Production SA.

Pico was still wearing his lime poncho, wrap-around sunglasses and studded leather trousers. His split lip was badly swollen. A blast of hot, sour air washed over Stephanie, driven by the amplified pulse of Busta Rhymes.

'I'm here to see Étienne.'

If he was angry, it didn't show. In fact, she wasn't sure he recognized her. Which, after a moment's thought, was only a partial surprise. 'He's not here.'

'Of course he's here. *You're* here.'

'He didn't say you were coming.'

The sudden absence of two teeth lent his voice a peculiar whistle.

'Sure he did,' Stephanie retorted, pulling the

Smith & Wesson Sigma out of her coat. 'Here's my invitation.'

Pico took two steps back. Stephanie made a circle with a finger. He turned round and led the way down a narrow passage; purple drapes on the walls, red light bulbs overhead, dope fumes corrupting the air.

Lorenz's office was pure pimp; two black leather sofas, a kidney-shaped desk made of smoked glass on a chrome frame, three zebra skin rugs on the floor. A massive entertainment system filled one corner. Behind the desk, the window had been boarded over and painted silver. On either side were two large panes of glass over a selection of VHS and DVD covers, naked starlets prominent in all of them. Half the titles were in French, the others in English or German.

Lorenz looked relaxed in a tilting chair of squashy tan leather, his feet on the desk. He was wearing crocodile-skin cowboy boots. A can of Diet Coke sat beside two copulating gnomes carved out of ebony.

He played it as cool as he could. 'Hey, cutie . . .'

He was trying to roll a joint with burnt fingers. The boiling coffee had left livid raspberry patches over the backs of his hands. He picked up the remote and lowered the volume a little but the sound was still loud enough to rumble through her.

Stephanie looked around for the *fila brasileira* with the foaming jaws. 'Where's Giselle, Étienne?'

'At home. That's where I keep all my bitches.'

Stephanie sighed. 'Oh, Étienne, please. Normally I don't shoot dumb animals. But in your case I might be open to persuasion.'

Lorenz bristled with bravado. 'You here to bring me the rest of my money?'

She gazed at the framed covers and shook her head sadly. 'Étienne Lorenz, porn producer. I missed that before, when you were running through your long list of business interests.'

'I like to keep different areas of business separate. Anyway, I'm not a porn producer, cutie. I make motion pictures.' He patted a pile of manuscripts on the desk to emphasize the point. 'Some of them have a high erotic content, it's true. But I do other stuff too.'

'Really?'

'Sure. Horror, thrillers . . .'

Stephanie looked at the VHS covers again. '*Virgin Bodyguards III* – that would be a thriller, would it?'

'An *erotic* thriller, yes.'

'And *Star Whores: the Phallic Menace* – what would that be, exactly?'

'The same. An erotic adventure. In outer space.'

'Jesus, Étienne. If it's got a tail and it barks, it's a dog.'

'*What?*'

'Forget it. Tell me about the disk.'

'What can I say? You've seen it, right? It's all on the screen. Wall-to-wall fucking, cutie.'

She prodded Pico in the ribs and told him to sit on the sofa closest to Lorenz, who now leaned forward into the upright position.

'Where was it filmed?'

'The George V.'

'The hotel?'

'No. The monastery. Of course the hotel. In one of the suites.'

'Who arranged it?'

Lorenz shrugged. 'I don't know. But the guy who paid me got me in there the day before to set up the cameras. Said he wanted a real smooth job.'

'Who was he?'

'Look, cutie, what's the problem? You wanted the disk. You got the disk.'

'I said, who was he?'

'Never saw him before. A big bastard. Spoke like a flushing toilet.'

'Not French?'

'Not unless he was putting it on.'

'Nationality?'

'How would I know, cutie?'

'You couldn't tell from the accent?'

'Do I look like an expert?'

'Why did Golitsyn have your number?'

Lorenz cocked his head to one side. 'How come *you* have it? That's the real question.' He pointed at her accusingly, ash falling into his lap from the tip of the joint. 'Maybe you had something to do with his death, huh?'

Stephanie thrust the gun at him sharply. 'How badly do you want to find out?'

Lorenz squirmed but Pico didn't react. Behind the lenses, Stephanie envisaged pin-hole pupils.

'Okay, okay,' muttered Lorenz, 'take it easy, cutie.'

'Don't call me cutie.'

'How about bitch?'

'Much better.'

'What do you want, anyway? You got everything for nothing.'

'Did Golitsyn organize it?'

Lorenz sniggered. 'No way. He just wanted the disk.'

'Why would *he* want a copy?'

'A *copy*? He wanted the original.'

'And this is the original?'

Lorenz shook his head.

Stephanie saw the predictable truth. 'But he thought it was.'

'Right. Dumb Russian bastard.'

The CD changed. On came David Holmes, *All Bow Down To The Exit Sign*.

'Who has the original?'

'I don't know. The big man, I guess. I had to send the original to an address in Vienna.'

'What was the name?'

'No name, just a box number.'

'And you did that? No questions asked?'

'No questions asked.'

She shook her head. 'A maggot like you always

has an angle. That's why you lied to Golitsyn.'

'Golitsyn I could lie to. But not this one. He said he'd be able to tell if it was the original or not.'

'Yet you made a copy.'

'I always make copies. Two, generally. One for insurance, one for the right opportunity.'

'Which was what Golitsyn was?'

'Right.'

Lorenz took a deep drag from the joint, held it in his lungs as long as possible, then exhaled slowly. He offered it to Stephanie. When she declined, he passed it to Pico.

'Who was the black girl?'

'Angeline.'

He let the name hang between them, hoping it would be enough.

'Don't stop now, Étienne. You're on a roll.'

'Just a girl I know.'

'Personally or professionally?'

Lorenz grabbed his crotch. 'Both.'

Pico giggled, then lapsed into a creaking cough.

'An easily pleased woman, then,' Stephanie said. 'What about the other one?'

Lorenz scowled. 'You mean the bitch who looks exactly like you?'

They traded stares for a moment.

'Étienne,' she hissed, 'do yourself a favour: *don't.*'

Her tone was sharp enough to puncture him, his sigh an act of deflation. 'I didn't know her. It was the first time I'd worked with her.'

'Local?'

'No. Not French. But she was staying here.'

Stephanie arched an eyebrow. 'Here with you?'

'No. In Paris.'

'Where?'

'Stalingrad. That's what she said. Somewhere around avenue de Flandre, I think. She never gave me the address.'

Stephanie pursued the inference. 'But you asked for it.'

Lorenz shrugged. 'Sure. Why not? We went out for a couple of drinks. We had a good time.' The sick smile returned. 'Anyway, you saw for yourself. She's a natural. She could fuck a man to death and he'd die grinning. I thought we might do business together.'

'Business?'

Another shrug. 'And pleasure. In my line of work business *is* pleasure.'

Stephanie winced. 'You're a class act, Étienne.'

'I wish I could say the same about you.'

'You said she was staying in Paris. Where'd she come from?'

'Vienna.'

A mistake, she saw, the confession too swift for caution.

'The same place you sent the original disk.'

'A coincidence.'

'Really? Did she give you a number?'

'No.'

'An address?'

'No.'

'How were you supposed to get in touch?'

'I wasn't. She didn't want to see me.'

'I thought you went out. I thought you had a good time.'

'*I* had a good time, cutie,' he confirmed, before attempting a look of sorrow. 'But she didn't. So . . .'

Stephanie fired the gun three times, once after each word: *where – is – she*?

The front of the amplifier dissolved into a shower of sparks and black plastic splinters. Lorenz kicked back, the chair skipping across the floor until it clattered against the board over the window. Pico still didn't move.

'Crazy bitch!' screeched Lorenz.

'I told you not to call me cutie.' Stephanie stepped forward and pointed the gun at his head. 'I'm not going to ask politely next time. Where can I find her?'

'Club Nitro.'

'In Vienna?'

'Yes.'

'What's her name?'

'I don't know her real name.'

Through clenched teeth, Stephanie muttered, 'I'm losing my fucking patience, Étienne.'

'She said to call her Petra.'

Stephanie said, 'Thank you for agreeing to see me at such short notice.'

'I can't pretend that I was surprised by your call. I had the feeling we would see each other again. Although I'd rather hoped we wouldn't.'

She wore a black suit and black shoes. On the left lapel of her jacket was a large brooch, a swirl of square-cut emeralds framed by diamonds. Stephanie couldn't help but stare at it.

'The Spirit of Mercury,' Natalya Ginzburg said. 'A piece originally designed by my husband for Audrey Hepburn.' She was sitting in the chair closest to the window overlooking place Vendôme. 'I'd foolishly imagined that you might do the right thing and disappear. You'll need to be brief. I don't have much time.'

'I'm wondering if Anders Brand would have regarded Golitsyn as a confidant. I know they were very close; you said so yourself.'

'This was your idea?'

'Yes.'

'So not Scheherazade Zahani's, then?'

Stephanie couldn't disguise her surprise.

Natalya Ginzburg said, 'I hear more than I should. My husband, Aleksandr, was a peddler of precious stones but he also traded in a commodity far more valuable: information.'

'As did Golitsyn.'

'Precisely. And as I have, in my own small way.'

Stephanie said the first thing to come to mind. 'Do you know Stern?'

'I know *of* him, naturally. But I've never met him. At least, not to my knowledge.'

'Well he told me this: *Golitsyn floats above the world.*'

Ginzburg raised an eyebrow traced in pencil. 'Did he? Not bad for a man with so little panache. Perhaps even accurate. When was this?'

'Four days ago.'

Ginzburg looked as though she was recalling a time far more distant. 'Leonid lived among people for whom the normal rules don't apply. They're too rich to pay tax. They live in too many houses to have a home. They leave the constraints of the law to those who can't afford the best lawyers.'

'Do you float above the world too?'

The smile was cold. 'I prefer to think of myself as someone who occupies a unique and solitary environment.'

'You said you hear more than you should. What have you heard about the Sentier bomb? Or Brand. Or even Golitsyn.'

She sighed theatrically. 'Assuming for a moment that you find the answers to your questions – a rather rash assumption, I feel – what will you do with them? How will they benefit you?'

'I want to know the reason why.'

'But you already know the answer to that: it is because you are Petra Reuter.'

'I need to know who's responsible.'

'So that you can exact bloody revenge for your inconvenience?'

'I regard what happened at Sentier as more than an inconvenience.'

Ginzburg took one of her handmade Turkish cigarettes from a silver box on the table to her left. 'And your *alter ego* – Petra – how would she regard it?'

As nothing more than an inconvenience; Ginzburg, it seemed, understood both sides of her.

Stephanie said, 'I've changed. Or I'm changing. One or the other, I'm not sure which.'

Ginzburg lit her cigarette and peered at Stephanie through thick twists of golden smoke. 'I saw Leonid the morning he died.'

Stephanie felt a rapid patter beneath the breastbone. 'You never mentioned that before. Where did you meet?'

'Here. When he phoned in the morning he sounded awful. I said I'd go to him but he wouldn't let me. He insisted on coming to see me. *It'll appear normal* – that was what he said. A visit to an old friend; what could be less suspicious?'

'Did he mention that he was going to the Lancaster that evening?'

'No.'

'Did he mention Scheherazade Zahani?'

'No.'

'How about Robert Newman?'

'Who?'

'An American businessman.'

'No, I don't believe so. I don't recognize the name.'

'How much do you know about Zahani?'

'Over and above what one reads in the papers, only this: that she has a ferocious intellect. And that she's surgically shrewd.'

'Surgically shrewd?'

'Zahani has always thrived in hostile environments whether they've been physical, political, commercial or cultural. She has an astonishing capacity for analysis. A country or an individual – it makes no difference to her. She's a consummate chess player – it's her passion – and in many ways, she conducts her life on a board of sixty-four squares. She's a woman of infinite analysis, a woman of infinite options.'

There was a knock at the door. When it opened, a squat man in a black suit and white shirt appeared. He gave the slightest nod and then vanished without a word.

'I have to leave for the airport. If you wish, you may accompany me part of the way so that we can talk some more.'

The car was a black Zil limousine. Dark grey curtains were half-drawn across the windows. On the back shelf was a single red rose in a silver cup. A thick sheet of glass partitioned them from the chauffeur.

'A gift to my husband from Leonid Brezhnev,' Ginzburg explained. 'Or rather, from the grateful people of the Soviet Union. Aleksandr sent it straight to Stuttgart and had the people at Mercedes recondition it. In other words, it's not what you see. It's a glossy lie.'

They crept out of place Vendôme towards boulevard des Capucines.

'What did the other Leonid tell you?'

'We discussed the dinner that he and Anders had shared at the Meurice the day he arrived from New York. Anders was in a shocking state. Very despondent, very distracted. Leonid said he was deathly pale.'

'Did he offer a reason?'

'Iraq. Commuting between Baghdad and the United States was taking its toll. Anders was under pressure from the State Department, the Pentagon, even from the White House. That was what he told Leonid.'

'What kind of pressure?'

She peered through the window at the passing of rue Marx Dormoy. 'Are you aware of Butterfly?'

'No. What is it?'

'It's a regeneration programme for Iraq, centred on the city of Mosul, in the north. It's an aid project, essentially, with guiding principles not dissimilar to the oil-for-food programme instituted under Saddam. The difference is that the revenues are to be administered by a neutral third party to ensure that all the money reaches its intended targets.'

'At the risk of appearing naïve, that sounds like a good idea.'

'I thought so too.'

'So what was the problem?'

'Anders didn't see it that way, according to Leonid.'

'Why not?'

'He felt – no, he *believed* – that the Iraqi people were being misled.'

'I have to confess, I never really understood why his opinion was quite so important anyway.'

'Anders was a man the current US administration trusted completely, despite being European, and despite his long association with the UN. At the same time, in Iraq, he was also the one man – the one *westerner* – who was trusted by the Kurds, the Sunni Muslims and, in particular, the Shia Muslims. Can you think of another individual for whom that would be true? Can you even imagine such a person?'

'Perhaps not.'

'So you begin to see the position he was in: on this matter, his patronage was essential. The Americans felt they could rely on his endorsement of Butterfly and that once the project was running, everyone would be able to see the benefits, as vast amounts of investment were generated for Iraq's social infrastructure.'

'A massive PR exercise, then.'

'On an unprecedented scale. But with the bonus of integrity.'

'What went wrong?'

'He wouldn't even take it to the Iraqis.'

'Why not?'

'Anders said he could deliver the factions but what he also said was this: if he was to act in good faith – to be the honest broker the Americans wanted him to be – he would recommend that all parties reject Butterfly.'

'Why?'

'He said it was a smokescreen.'

'For what?'

'He wouldn't tell Leonid. He said it wouldn't be safe.'

'Why didn't he put it to the Iraqi factions and let them decide for themselves? I'm sure they would've viewed the proposal from a starting point of sufficient scepticism.'

'I'm inclined to agree with you. But he didn't.'

'And so when Anders died, Leonid came to see you because he needed someone to talk to.'

'Yes.'

'If you don't mind my asking, why you?'

Ginzburg offered haughty amusement. 'This surprises you?'

'Frankly, yes.'

'Leonid was always candid with those he trusted. But he was never cheap with his trust.'

Stephanie wondered whether Ginzburg knew about Brand and the call-girls. Probably, she decided. She was, after all, a woman who heard more than she should.

'Is there anything else I need to know?'

'Butterfly was due to be ratified four days from now.'

'Due?'

'Anders was supposed to be present. As a guarantor of good faith, you might say. I assume his

278

death has cast a shadow over Butterfly. Although whether that will change anything, I couldn't say.'

'Where was the signing to take place?'

'In Vienna. At the conference.'

'What conference?'

'Petrotech. It's some kind of oil forum, I think. Leonid did explain it to me but I have to confess that I didn't pay full attention. It sounded very dull.'

Vienna. For the second time that morning.

There was a small tortoise-shell control panel built into the arm-rest next to Ginzburg. She pressed a red button and the Zil glided to the kerb beside the slip road to the *périphérique* at porte de la Chapelle.

'I've told you all I can regarding Leonid and Anders. What you do with the information is up to you. But when you make your choice, there's one more thing you should know: you're under contract.'

Stephanie stared at her for several seconds. 'How do you know?'

'Why do you suppose Brezhnev gave Aleksandr this car?' Her parched face cracked into a humourless smile. 'It wasn't because they were friends. They weren't. It was because each had something the other wanted. And when the price was right, they traded. I've been asking questions about you. Calling in old favours.'

'Why?'

'You know why, Stephanie. We're the same, you and I.'

She couldn't deny it but spoke her mind anyway. 'Is that enough?'

'At my age? Certainly. I feel I can be as indulgent as I wish.'

'How liberating.'

'It is. *Very.* I hope you'll live long enough to experience it yourself.'

'You never know.'

Ginzburg was holding something back. Stephanie was sure of it. As Petra, she would have too.

'Five million dollars.'

'I'm sorry?'

'The price on your head,' said Natalya Ginzburg. She let it sink in and then offered a suitably sympathetic nod. 'I understand how you must feel. I imagine it's more of an insult than a threat.'

'Who's putting up the money?'

'I haven't been able to establish that. But it's open. First come, first served. A race, a free-for-all.'

Stephanie reached for the door. 'Well . . . thank you anyway.'

'Don't thank me. Listen to me, instead. You can't see them. You don't know how many of them there are. Or how well connected they are.' Ginzburg leaned over and took her by the hand. 'Run, Stephanie. Realistically, it's all you can do.'

It's still raining when I surface from the Métro at Châtelet Les Halles but I don't mind. I've always liked rain; it lifts my spirit. I stroll down boulevard de Sébastopol, then quai des Gesvres.

Natalya Ginzburg is right, of course. I've seen her and I've seen Étienne Lorenz and all I have are more questions than answers. So tonight I'll head for Italy. I know of a document forger in Turin, another of Jacob Furst's apprentices. From Italy, I'll fly to the States where I'll dissolve into a big city. Los Angeles, most likely. Nowhere has so many lost people as Los Angeles. I'll drift with the nomadic flotsam on the margins of the city. And as the hazy weeks bleed into one another a long-term plan will form. Australia, maybe. Or New Zealand. Anywhere that's a long way from here. And from her.

I don't need to find the other Petra now because I'm no longer interested in this Petra. I've seen enough. I don't want this life any more. More importantly, I don't need it. Whatever the illness was, I'm cured.

The police could be waiting for me when I enter the apartment on quai d'Orléans since I didn't cuff Robert before going out. Yet I have no hesitation in opening the front door and stepping inside. Half of me trusts him, the other half doesn't care. I wouldn't call it a death wish, exactly. Just an acute sense of fatalism. Which is proof, if I ever I needed it, of Petra's waning influence.

She's making the transition from reality to memory. She's a snapshot where age has begun to bleach the colour. In time, she'll be nothing more than an amorphous blur over a blank background.

Robert is in the sitting-room. The curtains are open, the lights are on. He's reading a copy of The

Economist. *He wears a pair of old denim jeans and a crisp cream cotton shirt with the sleeves rolled up. His hair is still damp from the shower. He's clean-shaven and barefoot. Technically, he's still a hostage but to the casual observer I could be a wife coming home to her husband.*

'You look relaxed,' I say.

'As prisoners go, I feel pretty relaxed. Did you get what you needed?'

'Yes. What about you?'

'I've just been hanging out here. I spoke to Marie.'

'Your secretary?'

He nods. 'I thought I should. I'm supposed to be ill, not away. And then I called Yvette. She's coming the day after tomorrow.'

'You didn't go out?'

'You asked me not to.'

'I know.'

He recognizes the surface absurdity of our situation. 'Look, Stephanie, the way this has worked out . . . I don't know what I was expecting when you jumped into my car but it wasn't this.'

'Join the club.'

'I just didn't see any point in doing anything. Not now. Not with you leaving.'

'Thanks.'

'There is one thing, though.'

'What?'

His expression is pitched somewhere between embarrassment and pain. 'I went into my office to check my e-mail.'

'That's okay.'

He avoids looking at me directly. 'The disk was beside the computer. The one you were watching this morning.'

More than anything I feel disappointed. Not by him. By me. Even though it's not me. I just don't want him to think of me that way, no matter who it really is. I tell him it's not me but can see that he doesn't believe it.

'She looks like me because she's supposed to.'

'I shouldn't have watched it, okay? I'm sorry.'

'If you look close enough you'll see the differences.'

'It's all right, Stephanie. I believe you.'

The lie only makes it worse. He wants to believe me but he knows what he's seen. Which is exactly why the disk was made. I could prove it to him if I wanted. But that would mean sitting beside him as we watched it together and I'm not sure I have the stomach for that. Not right now. And in an hour or two, when I've gone, what difference will it make?

Stephanie made tea for them and brought it to the sitting-room on a tray. As she set it on the coffee table in front of Newman she said, 'Have you ever heard of something called Butterfly in relation to Iraq?'

'No. What is it?'

'A regeneration programme based in Mosul. An oil-for-cash scheme.'

Newman's soft laugh was sarcastic. 'Born within the Beltway?'

'I think so. Why?'

'I don't know. I just wish some of the people who dreamt these things up took the time to find out what life's like on the ground.'

'Are you talking about Iraq, or generally?'

'Both.'

She poured tea into a blue mug and handed it to him. 'You don't approve of what happened in Iraq?'

'The way you say that makes it sound like you think I should.'

'You're an oil-man.'

'First: I'm not an oil-man. I'm just someone who happens to do business with oil-men. Second: no, I don't approve of what happened in Iraq.'

'So you don't believe the reasons for war were right?'

'I don't know what I believe any more. Except this one thing: the world is a better place without Saddam, Uday or Qusay. There was only ever one legitimate argument for going into Iraq and that was humanitarian. And no one bothered with that until all the other reasons had been discredited.'

'Do you know Iraq well?'

'Not really. I used to go in the Eighties. Between the wars, I only went twice. Since then, not at all. I know other countries in the region much better.'

'That still gives you a view.'

'Sure it does and it's this: it's a mess. And there's no way out.'

'Except to leave, of course.'

'That's not a way out. It wouldn't be the end of it.'

Stephanie poured a mug of tea for herself and took it to the other sofa. She kicked off her shoes and sat at one end, her legs folded beneath her. 'How can you be so sure?'

'Because America wants democracy for Iraq. If it succeeds in establishing it Iraq will become even more of a regional lightning-rod for anti-American, anti-democratic militancy than it is already. And if democracy fails in Iraq, America will have failed too. And all it will have achieved is a legacy of intensified hatred.'

'Do you believe democracy is actually possible in Iraq?'

'In the long-term – maybe, but probably not.'

'Why not?'

'Basically, Islam and democracy are incompatible. If you accept that democracy gives power to the people. And that in Islam, power belongs to God alone.'

'So any attempt to establish democracy in Iraq – or anywhere else in the Arab world, for that matter – is doomed to failure?'

'It depends on how Islamic or democratic Iraq is going to be. But it's naïve and insulting to assume that Iraq can't be a successful society without democracy. Or that Muslims generally can't establish successful non-democratic societies. Historically, they have. On the other hand, with the exception of Turkey, almost every Muslim state in the world today is a despotic failure. But that's not Islam's fault. It's the fault of the leaders of those countries.'

'So you presumably consider Butterfly nothing more than an exercise in cynicism?'

Newman drank some tea. 'Take it from someone who knows this industry. Iraq is about oil. Nothing more, nothing less. Even though the oil industry denies it.'

'Well they would, wouldn't they?'

'Yes. But they're also right.'

'Now you're contradicting yourself.'

'Not really. Look, oil companies argued against the Iraq war. They warned that it would lead to regional unrest, instability in Saudi Arabia, and rising prices of crude. Which is what happened. But the politicians went ahead anyway. It was the same when the British initiated the Suez conflict in 1956. That led directly to the rise of Arab nationalism which brought about the formation of OPEC and the 1973 oil crisis.'

'So it really is about oil, after all.'

'Yes. But at governmental level, not corporate level, as the conspiracy theorists would have you believe. The US wants – *needs* – a permanent foothold in the region. If a better alternative presented itself, the US would switch to it in a shot because they really don't give a fuck about anybody else.'

'You know, sometimes I find it hard to believe

you're an American.'

'Why? Because I don't wave a little flag? Because I'm not a NASCAR dad? Don't patronize me, Stephanie.'

'Come on. You're hardly your average American.'

'I accept that. I've lived abroad almost half my life. I've travelled all over the world. I'm lucky I've never had to rely on Fox News for real news. But that doesn't invalidate me as an American.'

'Perhaps not.'

'Maybe I'm just not that mainstream. Maybe I'm just a little too . . . *tangential*.'

Just as she was. Was that it, then? Were they the same? Strip away the professional veneer – the business suit, the gun – and what was left? An evasive core.

'Tangential. That's a good word. Your relationship to Solaris – is that tangential too?'

'Now you mention it – yes, it is.'

'What is Solaris, exactly? You never really told me.'

'You never really asked.' He placed his mug on the side-table. 'Technically, it's an international law firm. Its head office is in Zurich and it has offices on five continents.'

'Technically?'

'Solaris is more than a law firm. Or less, if you're a purist. I'd say it was somewhere between a law firm and an investment house.'

'That trades in oil.'

'Not exclusively. Although in the United States, most Solaris work is concerned with oil. Around the world, it wears a lot of hats. It instigates and handles mergers and acquisitions. It's a lobbying organization. It's a firm of industry strategists. It's a firm of financiers. It's a law firm. Take your pick.'

'So what are you, then? A lawyer?'

'First patronizing, now aggressive. What next? No, I'm not a lawyer.'

She recalled that he hadn't answered the question at the Lancaster, either. At least he was consistent. 'A strategist?'

'No. And I'm not a financier, either. Not really. I'm just someone who puts people together.'

'That sounds amorphous.'

'I guess that's why I'm a consultant to Solaris and not an employee.'

'Yet you have a secretary.'

'Considering the amount of money I've generated for Solaris I'm probably entitled to a Gulfstream. But I'm happy to settle for Marie. She imposes order on a chaotic life.'

'I'd like to see her try now.'

'Good point,' Newman conceded.

'But your background's in oil, isn't it? That's what you said.'

'I worked for oil companies when I was younger. In the United States and the Middle East. And that's why Solaris approached me. Essentially, they wanted to exploit my contacts which were – and still are – pretty good.'

'And you didn't mind that? Being exploited?'

'Why would I? Contacts are currency, nothing more, nothing less. Trading them is like trading dollars for euros. It's a simple transaction where the exchange rate is determined by degrees of urgency.'

How true. Wasn't that how Stern had conducted himself? And if that principle remained true, where did that leave Natalya Ginzburg? She'd supplied information to Stephanie. Why? So that she could disappear, as Ginzburg had belatedly suggested?

Unlikely.

She took a pair of scissors and a newspaper to the bathroom. She closed the door and stripped, then ran a basin full of warm water. She ducked her head into it, making sure all her hair was immersed, then ran a comb through it. She looked at her dripping reflection and tried to decide where to make the cut. Shoulder or shorter?

Over the years, Petra had worn her hair shorter than Stephanie. Petra tried colours and styles – including a total shave on one occasion – while Stephanie preferred the natural look; dark and thick with a few curls when she grew it long enough. In recent months, however, it had been Petra who'd had the long hair.

She cut it short and thought it hardened her features. That was good. She needed to be Petra now. Just for a day or two, until she was someone else. Then she could lay her to rest and contemplate the rest of her life.

She supposed it would feel peculiar to have only one life to lead. The last time she'd been in that position she'd been eighteen. Since then, she'd been partitioned. As an adult, she'd never lived any other way. She wondered how she'd adapt to reunification.

When she'd finished cutting, she wrapped the damp hair in newspaper and dropped it in the bin, then took a long shower, washing away the remainder of the cut.

In the bedroom she put on the clothes she'd laid out; a pair of Anna's olive combats, a black T-shirt, a turquoise cotton shirt, a pair of trainers, tennis socks and black underwear. Next to the clothes was the small Tumi bag containing Scheherazade Zahani's cash. In the hall was a thick jersey and a coat. And that was it. She didn't intend taking anything of Golitsyn's, apart from his cash. There was no point. Not any more. Best to travel as light as possible.

Newman was still on the sofa in the sitting-room when she returned. He'd finished *The Economist* and was flicking through a copy of *The New Yorker*.

When he saw her he said, 'That's radical.'

She ran a hand through the damp cut. 'I'm supposed to be radical.'

'Then it suits you.'

'And if you met me in a bar? At the Lancaster, say?'

'It would still suit you. But not Claudia Calderon. She was a different kind of woman.'

'True. She was classy, sophisticated and elegant.'

'She was see-through.'

'In my line of work, see-through can be good.'

He smiled at her. 'Since you're leaving, I can say this: despite everything, I'm going to miss you, Stephanie.'

'No you're not. You're going to miss a version of me that exists only in your imagination. You don't know me.'

'I know what you're not. You're not the woman who got into my car.'

'Don't get misty, Robert. I'm not worth it.'

Quarter-past-nine. Stephanie entered the kitchen. Newman was standing by the island. Bloomberg was playing on the TV suspended over the slate top, stock prices scrolling across the bottom of the screen. He poured Glenlivet into a tumbler then offered her the bottle.

She shook her head. 'I don't drink and drive.'

'Drive?'

She smiled sweetly for him. 'I need your car, Robert.'

'Sure. Why not? Have I ever denied you anything?'

'I'm sure your insurance company will take pity on you.'

She put a pan of water on a dancing blue gas

ring and opened a pack of spaghetti. Food for fuel. No point in leaving the sanctuary of Newman's apartment on anything less than a full tank. She took a bottle of virgin olive oil from the shelf to the right of the sink, laid it next to the thick board and began to chop an onion with a Sabatier carving knife.

He sat on one of the stools. 'Where will you go?'

'Tonight? Holland. I have contacts there. After that – who knows?'

She didn't want to lie to him. Not now. But it was a necessary piece of chicanery for both of them.

'I need a few hours, Robert.'

He was still watching the wafer-thin Loewe screen. 'How many?'

'As many as you can give me.'

'You want me to wait until morning?'

'Would you?'

He nodded, then peered into his glass. 'If you're about to leave, I might make some calls.'

Stephanie stiffened, then felt ashamed, anxious and confused in quick succession.

'Business calls,' Newman assured her. 'I mean, I could wait half an hour if you want. But I'd like to catch New York before four.'

'You've had all day to make the calls but you waited until now?'

'I said I wouldn't when you asked me not to.'

'You know what I mean.'

'When I give my word, I keep it.'

'An honest man.'

'When I have to be.'

'And you felt you had to be even under duress?'

He looked at her. 'What duress?'

'Go ahead. It's your place again.'

She watched him leave the kitchen. For some reason, she expected him to turn round. To say something else. But he didn't.

She scraped the chopped onion into a pan with a little oil, then pushed a garlic clove through a pristine crusher, turning the pulp to paste. She added that to the onion, which began to sizzle. The water started to splutter. She salted it and put the spaghetti in.

Having ended so many other lives, now she was ending one of her own. She was already in limbo, stranded between Petra's world and a post-Petra world. When she left the apartment, Petra would begin to disintegrate. With every mile she put between her and Paris the greater that disintegration.

The future, huge and empty, was simultaneously seductive and alarming. She saw herself softer. She pictured herself alone. Or with friends she hadn't yet made. But she knew there would be parts of Petra that she'd never purge.

Which was why instinct cut in a moment before the sound.

It wasn't loud – she barely heard it over the kitchen TV – and it wasn't startling. A thud of some sort. Something knocked over. A common household noise.

But she *knew*.

It wasn't taught. Boyd had told her that much. It developed after all the teaching had finished. It developed with experience. There was no short cut.

The temptation was to call out, to locate Newman, but she resisted it. Nor did she quieten the TV. Where was the gun? In the sitting-room, which was the approximate source of the sound. She listened for further noise. Nothing.

She picked up the carving knife, then examined the other Sabatier blades in the block, selecting a paring knife as a second weapon.

The kitchen had two doors. The main door led into the hall. The other led to the utility room, which was an effective dead end. She couldn't cross the hall or go down it. Not if there was a gun out there.

She heard movement. A squeak. Rubber soles on stone, perhaps?

She grabbed the bottle of olive oil and poured it over the tiled floor. When the bottle was empty she retreated to the far corner of the kitchen. She took a look beneath the sink for disinfectant. None.

She tried the utility room and found a plastic bottle of bleach. And the fuse-box, mounted in a beige case over the ironing-board hook. She abandoned the bleach and turned off the power.

Eyes open, shapes forming, the Bloomberg

commentators cut off in their prime. She edged out of the utility room. The only light in the kitchen came from the two blue gas rings. They whispered to her. She crouched by the island, her head just below the lip, the carving knife in one hand, the paring blade in the other.

In the new silence, the city outside was suddenly inside; cars cruising along quai d'Orléans, sirens in the distance, muffled music from a passing boat. And a trace of movement entering the kitchen.

The slip sounded like a squelch. A male voice grunted. The body hit the ground, the gun discharged. A flash, a muted percussive thump – *there's a silencer attached* – and the slap of a bullet biting into the wall.

She was moving. And so was the intruder. Unbelievably quick, already up on one knee, the gun coming round towards her. The second shot flew so close to her she could feel it part the air beside her left shoulder. She lashed out with a foot, knocking the weapon from his grip. Then she hurled herself towards him, both blades forward. And missed.

He moved like a spirit, vanishing in a moment, reforming in another place an instant later. In the blue darkness, she caught a glint of light on steel. A dagger, longer than her carving knife, twice as broad, both edges serrated.

He was a big man. Six-three, six-four, trim, all in black, including the balaclava. He jabbed the dagger at her, trying to suck her into a strike. She held back, holding the carving knife to the fore, keeping the paring knife to the rear for close work.

When his right heel hit olive oil again, he skidded, losing his balance. Stephanie surged forward and he moved inside, lashing at her. She twisted to avoid the knife, losing her footing in the process. Her momentum carried her into him.

They both lost a blade in the fall, leaving Stephanie with the paring knife. She thrust it at him but he parried with his forearm, then grabbed her left wrist, crushing it in his hand. His free fist landed a series of staccato punches to her body, each blow powerful enough to send a shudder right through her.

She leaned over and bit the hand gripping her wrist as violently as she could, her teeth sawing through glove, skin and sinew. His grip loosened for a moment. Which was all it took to throw herself – her whole body behind the movement – and head-butt him in the face.

Beneath the black balaclava, his nose buckled. It sounded like footfall on gravel. Momentarily stunned, he allowed Stephanie a little space. She lashed backwards with her elbow, catching him full in the mouth. She crawled clear and gathered the carving knife. He rolled over, retrieved his dagger and sprang to his feet. He plunged, she swivelled. The tip of his blade smacked against slate and squealed across the worktop.

In the flickering blue gas-light, she noticed a

circular wet patch forming just beneath the bala-clava's eye-slits. He came at her again, one knife being no disadvantage to her two. There was a dazzle of steel in front of her. She deflected, metal biting metal, then tried a jab of her own with the paring knife. He swatted it away with his left arm. It skittered across the floor.

The force of the backhand unbalanced her again. He pitched forwards once more. She tried to spin away but was too clumsy and slow. She felt the contact ripple through her left side, the knife so sharp it cut through material and flesh without significant protest.

A sticky wet heat gripped her left side.

The next thrust missed but he was close enough to kick her in the knee. Down she went, her wrist smacking the corner of the worktop, the carving knife spiralling into the dark.

He lunged at her. She scrambled backwards, ignoring the pain in the joint, the soles of her shoes repelling two knife strikes. He was stepping through the blood she was leaving on the floor, closing in on his target, the arc of his blade swinging ever closer, his confidence on the rise.

Just too much.

She stopped retreating. He stepped forward. She kicked up with all her force, catching him in the testicles with enough power to lift him off the ground.

She didn't wait for the reaction but heard the wheeze. She dragged herself to standing. The knives were out of reach. He over-rode his pain and advanced. Which was when she heaved the pan of boiling water at him.

He howled. Stephanie reached for the knife-block on the other side of the island and grabbed the first handle she could. A meat cleaver.

Slower now, less nimble, he was coming at her again. She stepped to one side, wrapped both hands around the handle and swung it into him, catching him on his right flank, just below the ribs, the force of her blow barging him into the sink. She let go, leaving the blade embedded. He staggered, slipped on her blood, and fell.

She saw his gun under the island beside the swing-bin. When she bent down to retrieve it she felt the full protest of the tear in her own side.

A Heckler & Koch USP with a sound suppressor. The anti-corrosion finish over the synthetic polymer frame gave the gun a silvery gloss in the half-light. She pointed it at the back of his head and squeezed the trigger.

But only a little. She needed him alive. For a while, anyway.

Stephanie kicked his dagger away, stepped over his prostrate body, grabbed a fistful of balaclava and yanked it off.

A large square head emerged. Ruddy skin, short blonde hair, not entirely unattractive at first glance, if one discounted the rhubarb crumble nose. And not unfamiliar, either.

'Grotius,' she whispered. 'Lance Grotius.'

*   *   *

I flip the switch on the fuse-box. The lights come on, the Bloomberg broadcast resumes. Grotius is a mess but his attitude remains intact. Somehow, he manages a smile through a parade of broken teeth and steaming spaghetti.

'Hey, Petra,' he gurgles. 'Long time, no see. We could still have that drink, if you want.'

'Drink? That wasn't what you promised me, Lance.'

A former soldier with the South African Army, Grotius was born to fight. He served in Namibia and Angola before leaving South Africa for a life of freelance violence; Sierra Leone, the DRC, Somalia, the Balkans.

We met at a bar in Cyprus – the Mistral – more than a year ago now, not long after my reincarnation. Cheap drinks, cheap lighting, the rotor-blades doing nothing to stir the humid heat. I was there to meet three Russian human-traffickers.

The second thing Grotius said to me was: 'My name's Lance.' The first thing he said to me was: 'My God, man, you're beautiful.'

It's hard to imagine how those words could sound so ugly. But even now, the memory of them repulses me. Which makes the task ahead a little easier. His guttural, machine-gun accent, the waft of body odour beneath cheap aftershave, the hand he pressed on to one thigh, then the other, then between – I've forgotten none of it.

The third thing he said to me was: 'Can you guess why they call me Lance?'

I tried to head him off at the pass. 'Because you work for free?'

Confused, he frowned, his brow casting his eyes into

shadow.

Over-excited, lacking any hint of social restraint, he pawed me continually. At first, he was merely persistent. Later, his bloodstream infected with alcohol, he became insistent. At one point, he pulled me close to him, kissed my neck, then tongued my ear before whispering to me, 'One more drink then I'm going to take you back to my place. I want you now. Let me show you.' Beneath the table, he took my hand and guided it to his stiffening crotch.

'You'll cry,' he promised me.

I couldn't react violently, not with the Russians at the table. But when Grotius staggered away from us in search of the urinals, I left. Back in my hotel I scrubbed my skin raw in the shower; a narrow escape and I still felt contaminated. Later, I realized why. It wasn't me. It was the thought of those anonymous others. The ones who must have been in the same position. The ones who hadn't got away. The ones who'd had no choice.

That's what I'm thinking about as I ask him, 'Who's with you, Lance?'

'I'm alone.' Despite the pain, he manages a smirk. 'Like you, Petra.'

I fire the Heckler & Koch. The bullet tears through his left ankle. His whole body convulses. When the air flees his lungs it sounds like a kettle's whistle. Splinters of bone stick to the kitchen unit by his soggy foot.

'Now I know why they call you Lance. Because that's where you get the next one. Who's with you?'

I aim at his bruised balls.

'No one,' he gasps. 'I swear it, man. No one.'

I leave him writhing on the kitchen floor. Robert is on the sitting-room floor. He's trying to haul himself on to his hands and knees. I kneel beside him.

'It's me. Are you okay?'

He chokes, streaming saliva from his mouth and tears from his eyes. 'Never better.'

'What happened?'

He tries to speak again but his voice is an incomprehensible rasp that disintegrates into another retch.

I see the delivery device lying by the sofa. Not dissimilar to the one in my safe-deposit box at Banque Damiani. I remove the opaque plastic cartridge and turn it over; Avrolax, engineered ketamine, instantly effective. The drug begins to break down the moment it enters the body leading to a recovery that is as swift and unpleasant as its administration.

'Lie down,' I tell Robert, 'and stay still. Focus on your breathing. You might puke but it's going to pass, I promise.'

I help him on to his side which is when I notice the discoloured skin above the right ear and around the temple.

'You'll be okay. I'll be back in a minute. Don't move.'

When I return to the kitchen, Grotius has dragged himself halfway down one side of the island, the meat cleaver handle still protruding from his side. I stand on his fingers.

'Questions, Lance.' I pick up the Sabatier paring blade from the floor and crouch beside him. I rest the tip on his bloody ankle. 'Who sent you?'

He clenches his teeth. 'No one.'

I thrust the blade into the bony lattice. He tries not to cry out. But does.

'Do yourself a favour. We know the way it works. If our positions were reversed, you'd do the same to me.'

Through his grimace, he mutters, 'No way, man. I'd have you first.'

'Better than after, I suppose.'

'That depends.'

'Drop the act, Lance, and I promise I'll make it quick.'

His breathing is already turning shallow.

'They'll never stop looking for you, Petra.'

'Who?'

'That's the beauty of it. I don't know.'

'Well, they can try. But they won't find me.'

'One day they will.'

'How did you get the contract?'

'The usual way.'

'Electronic dead-letter drop?'

He manages the slightest shake of the head. 'Text and e-mail.'

It takes me a moment to understand. 'You're not free-lance any more?'

'For you, I'm . . . retained.'

'By?'

'You're not listening. I told you. I don't know.'

'You're on someone's books but you don't know who they are?'

'Better for everyone.'

It sounds plausible but he's lying. 'How long have

you been in Paris?'

'Eighteen months.'

'Where do they send you?'

'Africa. The Middle East. Central and South Asia.'

'What about me?'

'You're out to tender.'

'I heard. Five million. I wasn't pleased. How did you find me?'

It takes several painful prompts to get the answer: a CCTV tape the police missed. Housed over the entrance to a jeweller, micro-lenses pointing both ways, one of them covering the junction between rue de Berri and rue du Faubourg Saint-Honoré. A shame we didn't head right down rue d'Artois, I tell him. He explains how he retrieved the tape with particular glee, how he narrowed it down to five vehicles within the time-frame, and how he sent their licence plates for identification. Robert's name and address came back next to one of them, with independent verification, which was why Grotius was given the green light.

'Congratulations, Lance,' I say, as he watches me adjust my grip on the Sabatier paring knife. 'What does it feel like to be five million dollars richer than you were an hour ago?'

Stephanie tucked the Smith & Wesson Sigma into the waistband of her trousers and moved through the apartment with the Heckler & Koch USP at the ready. She assumed Grotius had come in through the front door; her sweep provided no sign of an alternative entry or of

303

any accomplice.

In the sitting-room Newman was on the sofa, hunched over a wastepaper bin.

'How are you feeling?' she asked him.

'Marvellous. Next stupid question?'

She gave him a glass of water. 'Drink this. Don't gulp it.'

When he looked up at her his eyes widened, revealing bloodshot whites. 'Shit – are you okay?'

'I'm fine.'

'You're covered in blood.'

Stephanie gave him a look that belonged to Petra. 'It's not all mine.'

'Jesus . . . is he . . .'

'Don't worry about him. He's in the kitchen wearing my spaghetti.'

She went to the bathroom. The left side of her shirt was soaked. She unfastened the buttons and peeled the material away. The cut was almost six inches long. Grotius could easily have sliced through to the spine; a moving target, a matter of inches. The blood flowed freely. She rinsed her hands in the sink and investigated the laceration with a forefinger. The central third was deeper than she'd expected.

She looked in the cupboard; Nurofen, a half-used pack of plasters, an out-of-date strip of anti-inflammatory pills, a box of unused antiseptic wipes.

She returned to Newman. 'Do you have a first-aid kit?'

His eyes were drawn to the gash between her bra and the olive combats. The blood was turning the waistband black.

'Answer the question, Robert.'

'Uh . . . no. I don't think so. I mean I got some Band-aids . . .'

'I found those. Apart from them?'

'No. Sorry.'

'It's not as bad as it looks. Have you thrown up yet?'

'No.'

'Then you probably won't. Not now. Drink some more water. It'll help.'

She found a small white hand-towel in an airing cupboard and two silk ties in the wardrobe in his bedroom. In the bathroom, she stripped off her combats, washed the blood from her skin, used three antiseptic wipes over the cut, then pressed the folded hand-towel to the wound and secured it with the ties.

As makeshift medicine went, it wasn't the worst she'd known. Once, in Romania, she'd had to use superglue to secure a deep cut on the back of her right calf. It had been three days before she'd managed to get to a hospital at the port of Constanta. The remedial work carried out by the doctor had been more painful than the original injury.

She pulled on a pair of clean jeans and one of Newman's shirts, then a thick navy jersey and a leather jacket.

'Better?' she asked Newman, when she went

back to him.

'Yeah. I only feel like shit now.'

'Can you drive?' His sweaty skin was grey, his breathing short and sharp. Stephanie recognized the symptoms. On the verge of shock, he hadn't heard her. She repeated the question with added urgency. 'Can you drive?'

'I guess so.'

'Good. We're leaving.'

'*We?*'

'I need you to drive me.'

'I thought . . .'

'Well don't. There isn't time. I know what I said and I meant it. But right now, we need to get out of here.'

'Where are we going?'

'Get your stuff together.'

'What stuff?'

'All the money you have. Clothes, if you want.'

'Wait a minute . . .'

'We don't have a minute. Do it. *Now.*'

On the way to Grotius's apartment they stopped at a twenty-four-hour pharmacy, where Stephanie bought all she needed to dress the cut properly.

'You've been here before?' Newman asked, as they parked on avenue des Ternes outside a branch of Crédit Agricole.

'Of course not.'

'I thought you said you knew him.'

'I met him once. Not here.'

'You sure this is the place?'

'This is the address he gave me.'

'Maybe he lied.'

'If he did, it was only at the beginning.'

Plane trees shivered in the wind. They sat in the car for a while watching the entrance to the building.

Newman's demeanour had changed the moment he saw Grotius on the kitchen floor. Not a word had passed his lips, his eyes never straying from the twisted corpse, the blood or the blades. Afterwards, he'd gathered his things and had followed her out of the apartment in total silence.

She pressed the buzzer marked Sturgess, which was the name Grotius had given her. No answer; good. She tried the code, 1736, and the door opened into a dark, dank hall. They rode the lift to the sixth floor. The number Grotius had given her was along a short passage to the right. When they reached his door, she pressed her ear to it but heard nothing. The TV was playing loudly in the apartment to the left, a sitcom, cheesy banter preceding canned laughter.

Stephanie looked both ways, then took out the key and the gun. Inside, she fumbled for a light switch, then closed the door behind them. It was stuffy, as though it had been empty for months, yet the bottom of the glass coffee pot beside the stove was lukewarm.

The bedroom and bathroom were to the right.

Stephanie saw twenty years of neglect; patches of wallpaper peeling from rotten plaster, discoloured light-shades, black cigarette burns peppering a dark green, nylon carpet.

There were dumb-bells on a triangular rack along one wall. In the bathroom were tubs of supplements to aid muscle growth. Taped to the wall was a picture ripped from a magazine; Jennifer Lopez in a bikini. Stephanie laid the things she'd bought at the pharmacy on the cabinet beside the sink and was about to remove her shirt when she heard Newman.

'In here.'

He was in the bedroom. Stephanie picked up the gun and went through to find him standing in front of an open cupboard.

'I was going through his things and the clothes rail came away. It's on a hinge.'

He showed her: when he pulled, the back of the cupboard swung forward. Stephanie peered inside the hidden compartment. There were three shelves for Grotius's professional equipment: boxes of .45 ACP ammunition for the gun, which she took; two passports – one Australian, one American, both in the name of Wayne Sturgess; a dozen miniature steel darts; two mobile phones; a selection of knives; another gun – a Spanish Star Megastar; brass knuckle-dusters; three canisters of pepper spray and one of CS gas; a box containing six Avrolax cartridges.

The bottom two shelves revealed the true

Grotius: thirty or forty well used hardcore pornographic magazines; seven DVDs and a dozen VHS
tapes – all with pornographic covers; some rolled
plastic-coated cord; a box containing a variety of
lubricants and vibrators; a see-through plastic
wash-bag with a capped needle and four small
phials containing a colourless liquid with two
cotton-wool balls, both pricked with rusty blood
stains.

Newman shook his head. 'What a sweetheart.'

Stephanie nodded. 'Maybe I let him off too
lightly.'

'Guns and porn. In Louisiana, he'd be
governor.'

In the bathroom she dressed her cut again. Then
she searched the living area. Cupboards and
drawers yielded nothing but there was a Toshiba
laptop attached to a Nokia mobile phone on the
table beside the fridge. She touched the finger-
pad and the machine awoke from slumber.

Newman came back with the two passports and
some documents. 'I got statements from France
Télécom and Crédit Lyonnais in the name of
Wayne Sturgess. But the electricity and gas are
addressed to Emeline Duprée.'

'A sub-let, maybe.'

'Or a girlfriend?'

'I doubt it. I don't see any female influence
here, do you?'

Stephanie began to sort through the files on
the computer. Predictably, his e-mails had been

deleted. She could find no personal data anywhere. She examined the mobile phone; no numbers held on the handset or on the SIM card. She tried to retrieve the last ten numbers dialled and the last ten received. All erased. She tried direct last-number redial. No response.

'We should get out of here,' Newman said.

'I can't leave empty-handed.'

'I thought you were going to vanish.'

'I am. But I need to know.'

'Know what?'

She wasn't sure. Perhaps it was just because it was Grotius.

They started in the kitchenette. In the fridge Newman found more than two kilos of beef, four bags of spinach leaves and half a dozen cartons of high-protein soya milk.

'I'm surprised he didn't kill himself with his diet.'

She checked beneath the sofa and armchair, beneath the green carpet, beneath the floorboards. Newman unscrewed the bath panel, examined the cistern, the bathroom cupboards, the vent. He turned the bed over, cut open the mattress.

'Found anything?' Stephanie called out from the kitchenette.

'A lot of black silk . . . I don't know what you call them exactly . . . kind of like . . . *G-strings.*'

'A woman's?'

'I'd like to say yes. But I don't think so.'

The neighbour turned off the television.

Stephanie looked at her watch. Ten-past-eleven. She peered out of the window. It was starting to rain again.

'You might want to take a look at these.'

She turned round. Newman was holding two disks.

'They were in one of the DVD cases. They've got no marks on them.'

Stephanie slipped the first disk into the Toshiba, fearing the worst: something 'homemade' by Grotius. The laptop whirred and a window formed on the screen, revealing a large data directory. The folders were colour-coded: red, green, blue. There were nine of them. She dipped into four at random and scrolled over the files. Most of the filenames were letter-digit combinations. Unintelligible to her, they clearly had order. She investigated a selection. Saved e-mail, information downloads, photographs, some of them timed and placed, some not.

'Any idea what it is?' Newman asked.

'If I had to guess, I'd say it was an insurance policy.'

In one folder, Stephanie found files documenting banking transactions. Cash deposits, wire transfers, even cheques, all paid into a series of holding accounts, then transferred and rolled. She knew the process well. Dirty dollars reclaimed their virginity, commissions were paid, proceeds invested.

Another folder contained scanned documents;

311

medical bills, property contracts, three insurance claims and several invoices for transport. She opened one, a claim from Calloway Transport Inc. of Trenton, New Jersey, billed to a company in Paris named Duprée. The billing address matched Grotius's apartment. It was marked for the attention of Wayne Sturgess and listed container numbers bound by sea for Rotterdam, then overland to Paris. It priced for shipping, handling charges, import duty tariffs and local taxes. It didn't specify what was in the containers.

'Look at that,' Newman murmured. 'Calloway *and* DeMille.'

'Calloway and DeMille?'

He leaned over her and retreated through several open documents until he came to a piece of faxed correspondence between two companies. One of them, Red Line Aviation, was demanding compensation for a delay in payment from a firm called Gilchrist Marine Services of Miami, Florida. Red Line was requesting seventy-five thousand dollars for private aircraft and helicopter transport in Indonesia. It asked for the bill to be settled immediately and in full at the offices of its parent company, the DeMille Corporation of Houston, Texas.

Newman pointed to the reference number on the scanned fax and then at the corresponding reference on the invoice from Calloway Transport. 'See that. RW/434/DeM/CTI. The *DeM* part, that's DeMille. It's on both.'

'DeMille. That sounds familiar.'

'The DeMille Corporation. Private military contractors for those who can afford it. Like the Saudi royal family. DeMille helped establish and run SANG, the Saudi Arabia National Guard. They've also trained the Indonesian army.'

'What about Calloway?'

'Calloway Transport is a wholly owned subsidiary of DeMille. DeMille is wholly owned by Kincaid Pearson Merriweather. KPM is one of the largest defence contractors in the States and is owned by the Amsterdam Group. KPM's CEO, Kenneth Kincaid, is a political heavyweight. A member of the American Partnership Foundation in Washington, he's a friend of this president, the last president, *every* president.'

'So there's a food-chain?'

'Right. Running from the top: Amsterdam – KPM – DeMille – Calloway.'

'And at the bottom we go from Calloway to Grotius.'

'Looks like it,' Newman admitted.

'But Calloway's a transport group.'

'Sure. And Voice of America is a public service radio station.'

'How do you know about DeMille?'

'Look at where they operate. Saudi Arabia, Indonesia, Nigeria, Venezuela.'

'Oil?'

He nodded. 'They're not involved in oil directly. But those who *are* tend to be the ones who can afford – and who *require* – the services that DeMille offers. They're not a secret. But they *are* secretive. They were the original pioneers of military privatization. No one's as good, no one's as big.'

'They must have a lot of people.'

'They have *access* to a lot of people. It's kind of like running a modelling agency. You don't own the models. They're on your books and you get them work. For a fee.'

'How many?'

'Thousands. Twenty, thirty. Maybe more.'

'An army, then.'

'Several armies.'

'How can a company so large be so . . . *quiet*?'

'Because it operates on a micro-level, through small outfits like Calloway. Companies that don't have premises. Companies that can be folded in the press of a button.'

'Companies that can't be connected to DeMille directly?'

'Right. Except when someone like your friend decides to keep a piece of information to himself.'

'Lending credibility to my theory that this disk is insurance.'

Stephanie began to search through other files. Newman said, 'Why don't you just take the laptop and disk? I don't think he'll be needing it.'

'In a minute.'

She tried the second disk. The directory revealed the most recent transfers; three folders copied to the disk within four minutes of each other, less than seventy-two hours ago. She opened one of the folders. There were four files inside. She picked one at random. Names, numbers and addresses formed on the screen.

Newman was still talking to her but she could no longer hear him.

She stared at the first name and felt queasy. She looked at the next name, then the rest. She knew them all.

Mark Hamilton, Konstantin Komarov. Not just people she knew. People who mattered to her. The cast of her life. Except for Cyril Bradfield and Albert Eichner. They were enigmatically absent.

She looked at Komarov's address; Kutuzovsky Prospekt, Moscow, the same as it had been when they'd been lovers. She remembered her first night there, how reckless she'd been and how right it had felt. There were three other contact addresses for Komarov in Moscow; his office, the orphanage in Izmailovo and a third she didn't recognize. Ulitsa Pyatnitskaya. There was a name and phone number to go with it: Ludmilla Ivanova.

A geologist fluent in four languages and perhaps the most beautiful woman Stephanie had ever seen. In her darker moments, she'd imagined that Komarov would have moved on by now. No – that wasn't quite correct; she'd *hoped* he would have moved on. That was the truth. But why would he?

She looked at Mark Hamilton. Still living in Queen's Gate Mews in London. The phone number was the same.

Her head was spinning.

Her fingers moved over the mouse-pad. A new page of information filled the screen. A sea of black on electronic white. She couldn't take it in. Except for one thing. Two thirds of the way down the page was a sequence of letters and numbers: M-E-1-1-6-4-R-P.

Her Magenta House clearance code.

Day Eight

They were on the A6 *péage* south of Auxerre. Newman was driving the silver Audi, Stephanie was in the back, the laptop on the leather seat beside her. She knew the numbness would pass but that wasn't enough to make it happen. For now, confusion reigned and she made little attempt to counter it.

Of all the recent surprises – the apartment at Stalingrad, the clandestine film – the exposure of her Magenta House clearance code was the most shocking because it was more than a mere security designation. It was Petra Reuter's DNA. And who else could have provided it but Magenta House itself?

Someone on the inside.

Would Petra Reuter now be revealed as nothing more than a ghost? A legend of convenience designed to smoke out potential targets. Possibly. Except, of course, Stephanie had allowed Petra to transcend the limited scope of Magenta House's imagination.

Ironically, the code's very existence might now lead to the conclusion that Petra Reuter had never existed. But what about Otto Heilmann? Who'd killed him? After Magenta House, Stephanie had allowed life to imitate art. Then to better it.

But why? Staring into the darkness, she found she couldn't remember.

They were heading for Switzerland, then Italy, from where she'd make her way to the United States. She wondered where Newman would go, how they'd part. She wondered how it was they were still together.

She tried to impose order on Paris: the bomb in Passage du Caire, the Lancaster, the apartment at Stalingrad, the film. And then Grotius. She was supposed to have died in Sentier. Having survived, she'd been set up to take the fall for Golitsyn. Having survived that, they'd tried to kill her again.

Her thoughts strayed to Newman. He'd recognized all the names on Grotius's laptop; DeMille, Calloway, KPM. He knew that Amsterdam owned them. He'd been at the Lancaster. And in the car coming up the ramp. He said he didn't know about Butterfly but was very familiar with the geopolitical background. She couldn't pin a single suspicion to him. It was just a general feeling. Or maybe it was because she was tired. It was getting harder to tell.

She pressed her face to the glass.

Newman was watching her in the rear-view

mirror. 'You okay? Maybe we should stop for coffee. I'll need gas in less than eighty kilometres.'

She didn't answer and he didn't press it. There were questions he wanted to ask – *needed* to ask – but now wasn't the time. When he got his answers, he wanted them to be coherent.

He couldn't purge the image of the body in his kitchen. The blood, the knives, the *injuries*. During the days they'd shared there had been times when he'd doubted her capacity for serious violence. Perhaps it was an illusion he'd encouraged. Now he knew better.

New York City, 20:50

Paris-2, the South African Lance Grotius, had been granted a termination order shortly after 21:05 CET. John Cabrini had allowed for the fact that Grotius might wait until late at night but in Paris it was now ten-to-three in the morning and there was still no confirmation from him.

When Grotius had posted the licence plate applications the last thing Cabrini had expected was a connection. But there it was: Robert Newman, a Solaris consultant. That description had sent a shiver through Cabrini; in his world 'consultancy' covered a vast range of options, none of them savoury.

Solaris had acted as informal advisers to companies controlled by the Amsterdam Group, though not to Amsterdam itself. Newman had been involved personally on two occasions. Once in Kuala Lumpur, once in Caracas. But that was it. There were no other leads to follow. Until the vehicle licence plate. Followed, shortly afterwards, by Helen Ito's Internet trace.

Cabrini had always been amazed by the ignorance of the public. The Internet had allowed people to assume the illusion of privacy. He was reminded of small children who put their hands over their eyes and imagine that because they can't see anyone else they can't themselves be seen. But every connection and movement on the Internet left its own personal fingerprint. With the right technology and sufficient power, any single piece of Internet activity could be traced back to the monitor of origin.

Hooking into the NSA and their vast network of INTELSAT eavesdropping stations, Helen Ito had initiated the search with key words and phrases. At the NSA, analysts gave each word or phrase a four-digit number – a one-time search code – before passing them through the Echelon computer system to listening posts around the world, where a programme called Dictionary hunted among millions of transmissions caught by the interceptors. The hits came from Menwith Hill in England, the largest surveillance station in the world, a 560-acre site of satellite dishes belonging to the NSA.

By the time Lance Grotius's request had reached New York, Ito had established a list of seventeen origins of heightened activity. When the names and addresses of the vehicle licence plates came back, the only name on both lists had been Robert Newman's.

I walk from the washroom to the canteen and head for the table where Robert is. He's leaning over the back of his chair, talking to a man from the next-door table. A man dressed in dark blue. A man who has three friends at the table, also dressed in blue. A man with a holstered gun on his hip. A man who starts laughing at something that Robert has just said.

Now they're all laughing.

We're at Le Chien Blanc service area. At ten-to-four in the morning, it's simultaneously cheerless and welcoming. A haven from the windswept dark of the road, yet soulless, the skeleton staff drifting beneath lights that drain life from even the heartiest face.

The Petra reflex offers two solutions. One: turn around and leave. But Robert has the key to the Audi and at this time of the morning there aren't many viable alternatives in the car-park. Two: take the gun out of my leather jacket, shoot everyone in sight, collect the key and leave.

Fortunately, I'm not half the woman I used to be so I do neither. Robert sees me and smiles. A relaxed man without a care in the world, as long as you don't ask about the nasty graze above his right ear. Which, by turning to me, he presents to his new friend, the police officer, for closer inspection.

He introduces me as Anna. When I shoot a glance at

him, there's definitely a glint in his eye. The police officers shake my hand, pleasantries are exchanged. I sit down
and the conversation resumes. Everyone's in a good mood.
I imagine they have X-Ray eyes, that they can see the
Heckler & Koch USP through the bulge in my coat pocket,
and the cuts and bruises that have discoloured my skin.

When they stand to leave, I have no idea how many
minutes have passed. Handshakes all round, they wish
us a safe journey, then go. I watch them from the canteen
to the two patrol cars outside, waiting for it to turn sour.

It never does.

I give Robert a look that's supposed to convey annoy-
ance. 'Anna?'

He shrugs. 'All I could think of on the spur of the
moment.'

'That makes it even worse.'

'Would it have been better if I'd used your name?'

'It would have been better if you'd chosen not to
engage the local gendarmerie in some friendly banter.'

'What was I supposed to do? Get up and move to
another table?'

'You could have ignored them.'

'Even when they spoke to me?'

'What did they want?'

'The paper.'

I frown. 'What paper?'

'There was a copy of France-Soir on our table. One
of them asked for it. Then we got talking and he picked
up on my accent. I told him I was American and he
said he loved New York. One of the others has a sister
who married a dentist in San Francisco.'

'What were they laughing about?'

Robert shifts awkwardly. 'Well . . . I told them you were my secretary. And that we were going away for a few days.'

A partial explanation if ever I heard one. 'Go on.'

'One of them asked where I was taking you.'

'And you said?'

'From behind.'

For a moment, I'm too stunned to say anything at all. When the words eventually form, they line up in regimental fashion. 'You. Are. Joking.'

But he's not. What's more, he seems to find it funny.

I shake my head in a feeble attempt at disapproval. 'From behind?'

Another shrug. 'Again, all I could think of on the spur of the moment.'

'That really does *make it worse.'*

Quarter-past-four and my coffee's cold but I drink some of it anyway. 'I still need your car, Robert. And if you could give me an hour or two to get down the péage that would help. Maybe you could have another cup of this lovely coffee.'

'What a prospect.'

We look at each other for a while, neither finding it necessary to break the moment. We're beyond such petty embarrassments now.

'Before I steal your car, I want to thank you.'

'For what?'

'Making it interesting. Making it a lot easier than it could have been.'

'You had a gun.'

'You know what I mean. With Anna. With the police just now.'

He doesn't look elated. Or even relieved. Just tired.

I fidget with my coffee cup, avoiding eye contact. 'Talking of the police, you should go to them.'

'If only you'd mentioned it ten minutes ago . . .'

I give him a leaden smile. 'I'm serious. Tell them what happened.'

'Everything?'

'Yes. Or as much as you want. Whatever works for you.'

He peers out of the window. 'And that's it?'

'Yes.'

Now that the fog of Paris has lifted that's the conclusion I've reached. Grotius was right: they probably will find me. Generally that's a gamble I'd take. But his disk has changed everything. It's no longer just my life in the balance.

Robert shakes his head. 'No deal.'

I assume I've misheard. 'Sorry?'

'You got me into this mess. Now you're going to get me out of it.'

'You don't understand. My plans have changed.'

'Because of the disk?'

'Partly.'

'Is this what you've been thinking about since Paris?'

'Yes. I can't run. Not now. I need to go to Vienna.'

'Then we'll go together.'

'Are you out of your mind? Have you forgotten what happened in your apartment?'

He looks cross. 'What do you suppose I've been doing since Paris?'

'Driving?'

'I know I'm only a man, Stephanie, but I can do two things at once.'

'Congratulations. Evolution at work.'

'I can't go home.'

'Of course you can,' I reply, before I've even considered it. And then, in an attempt to qualify the blunder, I compound it. 'Go to the police.'

'The same police who tried to kill you in Passage du Caire?'

'Come on. There are thousands of cops in Paris.'

'How am I supposed to tell which ones are which? And does it matter anyway? The moment I walk into a station and mention my name, it'll leak out, won't it? Somehow, sooner or later.'

I can't deny it.

'How long do you suppose it'll take?' he asks. 'An hour? A day? Tell you what. If you think it's safe for me to go back to Paris I'll let you have a three-hour head start. Then I'll make the call. All you have to do is tell me it's okay.'

I neither speak . . .

'Or you can just nod,' he suggests.

. . . nor move.

They climbed into the Audi. The car-park was almost deserted. Newman slid the key into the ignition, then stopped.

'Before we go on, there's something you need

325

to know. You're not going to like it but since we're in this together now . . .'

'What is it?'

'The Lancaster. I went there to see Scheherazade.'

Stephanie nodded slowly. 'And your friend – Robert Coogan? The one who called you on the phone?'

'Coogs did call me. But it had nothing to do with any meeting.'

'So you lied.'

'Of course.'

Stephanie rubbed her face with both hands.

Newman said, 'Look, I'm sorry. Maybe I should've said something. But I didn't know who you were. You were just a woman with a gun.'

'And you wanted to protect Scheherazade.'

'I wanted to protect myself.'

'Forget it. Tell me about the Lancaster.'

'I went there to meet her.'

Stephanie replayed the scene in her mind. Zahani entering the bar, Newman excusing himself to join her, the two of them sharing a joke.

'You were gone when I came downstairs.'

'We were going to see Golitsyn.'

Startled, Stephanie looked across at him. 'You were going to see Golitsyn?'

'That's the real reason I never said anything. As far as I was concerned, you'd just killed him.'

'So you *did* know him?'

Newman shook his head. 'Scheherazade was going to introduce us.'

'Why?'

'Leonid was well connected. So am I. She thought we'd get on.'

'And that was it?'

'Yes. She was a good friend to both of us.'

'But a better friend to you.'

She regretted the comment the moment she'd made it. Newman looked annoyed but said nothing.

'What happened?' Stephanie asked.

'She got a call saying Golitsyn wasn't going to make it.'

'From Golitsyn himself?'

Newman thought about it. 'I don't think so. She didn't say.'

'Then what?'

'There was no point in hanging around. I suggested a drink but she passed. She said she had plans for later. That was okay by me. She hadn't been intending to stay after the introduction anyway. So that was it. We left.'

Stephanie digested the disclosure slowly, running through the sequence of events as she remembered them. She couldn't find anything to contradict Newman's confession. On the contrary. His explanation made better sense than any elongated notion of coincidence.

'Did she set up the meeting or was it Golitsyn?'

'I don't know. But I guess we could find out.'

Another thought occurred to Stephanie: some-body else had also known about the meeting unless Zahani had been responsible for the murders of Leonid Golitsyn and Fyodor Medvedev. Stephanie wondered who that might be. Someone she'd already encountered? Or someone new? In other words, someone invis-ible. She replayed the scene. From the bartender handing her the house phone to the Audi on the ramp – how long? Five minutes? Probably less.

'How did she get home?'

'She has a chauffeur.'

'Of course she does.' Stephanie smiled in the darkness. 'Just like me. Let's go.'

Boyd got the call at four-fifteen. Ninety minutes later, he was in. Magenta House had provided the code to the building, Boyd had picked the front-door lock. Inside, the lights were on. He closed the door and took the Browning BDA9 from the interior pocket of his coat.

He stayed in the hall for more than a minute, adjusting to the stillness, waiting for sounds, then crept forward. The kitchen was the fourth room he came to. There was blood everywhere, much of it now a dark scum with a black crust.

He checked the rest of the apartment, then returned. He didn't recognize the corpse at first. It was only when he crouched beside it that he saw it was probably Lance Grotius. The face was badly disfigured.

He'd met Grotius once. In Kinshasa, back in 1992. Boyd hadn't liked him at all; immensely arrogant with no reason to be so. It hadn't been a surprise to learn of his conviction two years ago in Antwerp for statutory rape. Or of his escape from prison. Grotius had been a hard and resourceful man.

His skin had been scalded. He wore a wig of spaghetti, now brittle. There was a meat cleaver embedded in his right side but Boyd could see that hadn't been the fatal wound. Grotius's throat had been cut. The cleaver might have proved fatal had it been removed. Leaving it in had slowed the loss of blood. Boyd wondered whether that was deliberate, bearing in mind the other injuries, particularly to the left ankle and face. Broken nose and broken teeth were to be expected, perhaps, but there were more sinister wounds, none of them post-mortem as far as he could tell.

He recognized them because he'd taught her how to inflict them. Interrogation fast-track. He had no doubts concerning the identity of Grotius's killer. He checked Grotius's clothes. Nothing, not even a set of keys. She'd taken everything, which was correct.

Boyd left the apartment shortly before six and walked back along quai d'Orléans to rue des deux Ponts, where he climbed into the rented Renault and took the portable INMARSAT phone from the glove compartment. Recently, Rosie Chaudhuri had told him, Magenta House had been using customized phones that transmitted via the spacecraft belonging to the International Maritime Satellite Organization. Very useful, Boyd had replied, as he'd stepped out of the Falcon 2000 four days earlier, if you're under the stars in Afghanistan. Rather unnecessary in Paris, though. She'd agreed and they'd both smiled.

Rosie was already at her desk in London. 'Is it her?'

'It *was*. She's gone.'

'And the American – Robert Newman?'

'No sign of him. What about Paul Ellroy? Anything on him yet?'

After his confrontation with Pierre Damiani, Boyd had sent Ellroy's name to Magenta House for a deep search. He'd expected a swift reply but had heard nothing in the subsequent sixty hours.

'We've had some hits,' she said, 'but nothing useful to you. Not yet, anyway. We'll let you know as soon as we do. Is there anything else at your end?'

'There's a body.'

'Anyone we know?'

'Someone *I* know. Grotius, Lance, ex-South African Army.'

'Ex?'

'Last I heard, he was a mercenary. I'm surprised to find him in Paris but he was in Belgium a couple of years ago.'

'Any sign of any damage to Stephanie?'

'None that I can see. Anyway, Grotius is damaged enough for two.'

Boyd finished the call and sat in the car for a while contemplating Grotius and the DeMille Corporation. A perfect match, in many ways. A borderline psychopath on the books of an entirely amoral entity. In this line of business it rarely paid to take the moral high ground but every now and then a justifiable opportunity presented itself.

'You've been a hostage before, haven't you?'

Newman's face was marked by the warm red glow emitted by the dashboard. Stephanie saw no reaction at all. Which was at least consistent with his silence.

She said, 'I'll take that as a confirmation.'

Heading south towards Lyon, they passed a couple of articulated lorries, their mighty wheels throwing up walls of spray. The worse the weather, the more snugly insulated Stephanie felt inside the car. The feeling reminded her of her childhood in the rugged countryside of north Northumberland, not far from the border with Scotland. Wild weather had been normal, especially during the long winters. She recalled with absolute clarity the sensation of being inside the family home as storms raged outside; the permanent heat of the kitchen, the smell of it, the crackle and dance of the fire.

Until recently, she'd avoided such rose-tinted memories. They'd felt stolen; dreams ripped from another woman's life. Now, when she thought of those times, she remembered only the good things, and it occurred to her that perhaps they were the seeds of a change within; perhaps her moment was coming.

'Your scars.'

Newman sighed irritably. 'What about them?'

'In particular, the scars on your wrists. They're from bindings. When I tied your hands behind you, they rubbed the scar tissue along the same lines.'

'Is that right?'

'Not approximately. *Exactly*.'

'You're guessing.'

Stephanie shook her head. 'Over the last four days there was only one of us who knew what they were doing. Who knew the procedure. The *tricks*. It wasn't me.'

'Beirut,' Newman said. '1985.'

More than ten minutes had elapsed. If silence could sound painful it just had.

'You must have been very young.'

'I was in my late twenties.'

'You were one of *them*? McCarthy, Anderson, Waite . . .'

'No way. Not at all.'

'But you *were* a hostage?'

He nodded. 'But not like them.'

'Why not?'

'I was just . . . well . . . it wasn't the same.'

'Why not?'

'They were . . . *involved*. All of them, somehow.'

'And you weren't?'

'Not in the same way.'

'What was different?'

'I wasn't supposed to be there.'

'How come? Were you political?'

His laughter was suffused with regret. 'I thought I was. I thought I was right on the pulse. Turns out I was a tourist. Just a naïve boy.'

'I've only read about that period in Lebanon.'

That prolonged the laughter. 'No shit. You'd have been a baby at the time.'

'I was at school, thank you very much.'

'Doing what?'

'Pretending to enjoy Stendhal, smoking, listening to the Clash. And secretly fantasizing about John Taylor.'

'Who?'

'Duran Duran.'

'Duran Duran from the movie?'

'What movie?'

'*Barbarella.*'

'No. The rock band. The New Romantics?'

'Oh yeah. I'd forgotten about them.'

She wasn't sure whether it was a slip of the memory or no memory at all.

'They're back in fashion,' she said.

'First I was square. Now I'm cubed.'

Stephanie smiled. Sometimes the gap in ages melted away, sometimes it was reinforced. 'Was I right about the scars?'

Newman nodded.

'Sorry.'

'Forget it. I don't know why I didn't tell you. The truth is I don't mind them so much. The physical scars. The pain that caused them, the way they look, I can rationalize that. It's the other stuff I find tougher.'

'What stuff?'

'I get claustrophobic. Even now, twenty years later. And that thing with the tape across my mouth – that's a kind of hangover from what happened.'

'How?'

'You don't want to know.'

'Tell me.'

He was glad to have to keep his eyes on the road. 'Probably the closest I've ever been to death was the first time they taped my mouth.'

'Why?'

'Because of an involuntary reflex. I threw up, then choked. And nearly drowned. No reason for it. It just happened. Again and again. Every time they did it. Eventually I learned to do the only thing I could do. I took it back down.'

Stephanie wanted to apologize but knew it would sound trite.

'For a long time, I couldn't take darkness; for months I was in a basement with almost no light. After I was set free I had to sleep with the light on. I remember going to stay with some friends in Maine, just outside Bar Harbor, about a year after I got home. There was a power-cut in the night and I was just . . . *back there.*' He clicked his fingers. 'Like that. In the dark. My wrists bound by wire. The sound of rats I couldn't see. The smell of my own shit.'

'How did you get over it?'

'I had a lot of counselling. That's what everyone recommended. And it helped, in its own way. I guess time had as much to do with it as anything. But I still get caught out, even now. Not very often, although that makes it more of a shock when it *does* happen.'

'Like when some psychotic woman jumps into your car and sticks a gun in your ear?'

He nodded. 'That usually does it.'

Stephanie shook her head. 'Of all the people I could have chosen to kidnap, I had to pick someone who'd been a hostage before. Why were you in Lebanon anyway? Not exactly a tourist hot-spot in the mid-Eighties.'

'*That's* the reason I was there. Because I had ideals. Because I was an idiot.'

They drove into the centre of Lyon and parked on place des Célestins beside the theatre, which was under refurbishment. Stepping on to the damp pavement, Stephanie stretched, arching her back until the tear in her side began to protest. The air was damp and chilly.

Brasserie des Célestins had stone walls, exposed beams and a waiter with a bony grey face. His narrow shoulders were set at the same acute angle as his sloping silver hair. The skin around his eyes appeared to belong to someone else; crude grafts of dark papery tissue.

'What's Petrotech?'

Newman yawned. 'It's the annual conference for the oil services industry.'

'Oil services as opposed to oil?'

'Yeah. Engineering, design, marine, aviation, pipe construction, platforms, terminals, human resources, legal, accounting, security. Anything but the product. Each year Petrotech happens in a different location.'

'Do you know where it is this year?'

Stephanie watched him make the connection. 'Is that why we're going to Vienna?'

She nodded. 'One of the reasons. Have you ever been to Petrotech?'

'Three times. Dubai, Caracas, Las Vegas. Always as a guest, though. Solaris isn't represented.'

'Will DeMille be represented?'

'I don't know. But others in that industry will be.'

'It's not a world I know.'

'Until recently, it wasn't a world many people knew. But it's become a massive growth industry. You have the established players like Kroll, DeMille, DynCorp and ArmorGroup. Then you have the smaller outfits, sometimes just five or six people.'

'What kind of money are we talking about?'

'Depends. You want to hire a four-man ex-SAS team? That'll cost you $5000 a day. A company like DynCorp probably runs about $1 billion of contracts at any given moment. DeMille's portfolio is larger but they're more diverse. Baghdad's been a boom town for the industry. The British, in particular, have profited, mainly because ex-SAS soldiers have a great reputation. The British sector was earning around $300 million a year before Iraq. Now it's closer to $2 billion.'

'How does it work on the ground?'

'In Iraq most outfits are running a three-tier structure. At the bottom you have local Iraqis. They get paid around $500 a month. They're the foot-soldiers. Next you have "third-country nationals" – Fijians, Ukrainians, Russians – and they're paid between $2500 and $4000 a month. At the top, you have the "internationals"; the Brits, the Americans. They get paid around $15,000 a month. For example, US contractors like Bechtel and KBR are protected by Ghurkhas supplied by ArmorGroup.'

'Sounds lucrative.'

'That has to be the understatement of the year. The US Program Management Office is handling the aid budget for Iraq. That's almost twenty billion dollars. At least ten percent of that will go on security. On top of that you can factor in cost over-runs of twenty-five percent. And that's just for Iraq.'

Their cadaverous waiter appeared with croissants. Stephanie asked for butter which brought a glance of disapproval. Newman poured them both coffee.

'Ever hear of a company called Erinys?'

Stephanie shook her head.

'Set up by a Brit. Ex-SAS. It won a contract to protect oil installations in Iraq and Jordan. You're talking north of $100 million running 14,000 people. Our analysts estimate there are more ex-SAS soldiers in Iraq today than there are in the regiment itself.'

'And London's the centre for this industry, is it?'

'London and Washington. But the manpower comes from all over.'

'And the conventional military – how do they feel about it?'

'Conflicted, mostly. Especially when their areas of operation converge. People like Donald Rumsfeld don't see it that way, though. He feels armies should specialize and then contract out everything else. The problem is a legal one. Regular soldiers are subject to law. Could be a court-martial, could be international law. But no one seems sure what kind of law applies to these firms. Generally, it's not local law. And probably not American law, either. As for international law – despite the best efforts of the International Red Cross, it's too hazy on this matter.'

'Isn't that part of the appeal?'

'Sure. You contract out to save money for the taxpayer and at the same time it allows you to wash your hands of responsibility. Take it one stage further and you're handing these private contractors the jobs you don't want to take on yourself.'

Stephanie understood that principle perfectly. That was why Magenta House existed. To perform the tasks the conventional security services wished to avoid.

Her thoughts turned to Grotius. Initially, he'd insisted that he didn't know whose books he was on, that anonymity was in the interests of all parties. But the blade had teased some of the truth from him before he died.

Grotius had been a DeMille employee. His payments had come through Calloway Transport to an account in the name of Wayne Sturgess; phantom imports under invoice. He'd admitted to being recruited by a friend from the South African Army during his time as a mercenary in Bosnia.

The butter finally arrived. The waiter looked surprised, then annoyed, that she'd waited. She smiled for him, which seemed to make it worse.

'How does DeMille stack up against these other outfits?' she asked.

'Bigger, better. And richer. It was a construction company originally, back in the Sixties. Based in San Diego, they were into large civic projects – airports, hospitals – but they always had a military angle too. They built at least three air force bases. Sometime in the late Sixties they stepped out of the limelight and stopped tendering for civic projects. But the company continued to prosper. On the few occasions the name surfaced in public it was usually in connection with foreign projects. Airstrips in Vietnam or the Congo, that kind of thing. But in 1976 it got involved in a scandal that generated a lot of publicity and revealed what it'd really been doing.'

'Which was what?'

'Pioneering the sale of military services overseas.'

'Pioneering?'

Newman nodded. 'We're not talking about American companies selling equipment overseas. We're talking about training men for combat using American hardware and tactics. Men who might, somewhere down the line, use that training against the US or its allies. DeMille signed two contracts, initially: with Iran for about $60 million and with Saudi Arabia for about $80 million.'

'And the publicity?'

'There was a lot of it, none of it good. Articles in the media, TV documentaries, questions in Congress. Especially when it was alleged that DeMille had agreed that no Jews should be employed on either contract.'

'Was the allegation true?'

'Yes, it was. Although it was never proved. The agreement had been verbal. And in the long run, it turned out to be a blessing in disguise.'

'How?'

'The hysteria surrounding the Jewish issue deflected attention from the real issue: the business that DeMille was actually creating.'

'What happened?'

'What always happens. DeMille was rescued by the shrinking attention span of the public. When they got bored, the media dropped it and the storm passed. And the people at DeMille made sure they learned from their mistakes. They were already masters of the low profile. The scandal was a huge embarrassment. After it, the company took discretion and silence to new levels. In a way it's a paradox; the bigger they've become, the more invisible they've become. And they spend millions of dollars a year to make sure it stays that way.'

'That is curious; enhancing one's reputation by concealing it,' murmured Stephanie, as she sipped some coffee and considered Petra's professional parallel.

Newman yawned again, apologized, and then said, 'These days, they recruit from around the world but the services they offer are based on the US military model. The latest tactics, the latest weapons, the latest instructors. Whatever the client can afford. Which is just about anything, since most of DeMille's clients are oil-producing states.'

'And it's owned by the Amsterdam Group.'

'Technically, yes. DeMille is very secretive. Sure, they have a chairman and a CEO like everyone else. But nobody really believes they're running the company. Or that Amsterdam has too much of a voice. The point is this: DeMille can't afford to be transparent. But as long as they deliver, no one's going to rock the boat. That's not to say it doesn't have its problems.'

'Like?'

'They tend to operate in volatile environments. The work they do draws attention. Remember the coordinated Saudi attacks last April?'

Stephanie's memory was vague. 'Remind me.'

'Three bombs within five minutes. The first went off at a compound in the Ghawar oil field, the second detonated close to Thirty Street in Riyadh, the third demolished an office block in Jeddah. Twenty-five dead, another hundred injured. Seventeen of the dead were American, employees of Elkington McMahon, an oil-services conglomerate based in Houston.'

'So?'

'Elkington McMahon, DeMille, Calloway Transport: same difference. They all exist under the umbrella of the Amsterdam Group. DeMille uses companies like Elkington McMahon to get men into countries where there's a tolerance issue. Saudi Arabia's the obvious example. They come in as mechanics, engineers, support personnel.'

A common ploy, Stephanie supposed. Like being posted to a foreign embassy as the cultural attaché; everyone knew you were a spy.

Newman leaned across the table to refill her cup. 'What now? Vienna?'

'Not yet. Not until we have a new car.'

'What's wrong with mine?'

'Somebody knew where you lived. That means they know what you drive.'

'Then why did we take it in the first place?'

'Because the night was our friend. Whoever sent Grotius is probably going to wait a while before trying to find out what's happened to him. But they won't wait for ever. We had a period of grace but I think we should assume it's over. When they trace the car – and somebody will – we need to think about where it is. What message it sends.'

'I'm not with you.'

Stephanie smiled. 'You don't need to be. Leave it to me. I'll dump it and get a new one. We'll meet later.'

'You don't want me to come with you?'

'It would be better if I did it alone. We'll meet outside St Nizier church. Starting at ten, be there every hour at five minutes past the hour. Or at the junction of rue Dubois and rue de Brest at thirty-five minutes past the hour.'

Stephanie found an internet café nearby, Connectik on quai St Antoine, where she checked Petra's AOL and Hotmail addresses for messages. There were several from Stern, the content the same in all of them – *we need to talk* – and one from Cyril Bradfield.

> I've been away. Bad news but I'm okay. I had no contact from J or M beforehand. No contact for months.

343

Nothing unusual anywhere else. What can I do?

Stephanie had introduced Bradfield to e-mail and the art of electronic brevity. He'd resisted both. She felt relief flood through her and wondered whether his lack of contact with the Fursts had saved him.

> Nothing. Don't trust any messages from me. No phone, no notes, no e-mail. The next time we have contact, it'll be in person. I'll come to you. Until then, stay safe. And forget me.

She drove Newman's Audi to Croix Rousse, took the leather bag from the boot and abandoned it. She walked back towards the centre of the city and later caught a tram to the Centre d'Échange at Gare de Perrache, where she boarded a bus for Lyon-St Exupéry airport, arriving fifty minutes later. She spoke to the driver twice; once to ask how long the journey took, once to ask if they were going to be late. Both times, her smile bordered flirtation.

She went to P5, the long-term car-park, where she waited, ignoring all the vehicles that were already there since there was no way of knowing how soon their owners might return. Cars came and went, none quite suitable, until, shortly before eleven, a dark blue Peugeot saloon arrived at the barrier. A single middle-aged man was driving. From a distance, Stephanie watched him park. He took an attaché case from the front passenger seat and a suitcase from the boot. He locked the car and dropped the key into the right pocket of his brown jacket before heading towards the terminal.

Stephanie closed the distance between them so that by the time he entered Terminal 2, she was only a couple of metres behind him. As he joined the queue for the check-in, the eleven o'clock Air France flight to Paris, she bumped into him, turning to apologize – *'pardon, monsieur'* – as she walked on. Another sweet smile, this one reciprocated, the key secure in her hand as she pushed it into her own pocket.

She left the terminal building and waited another fifty minutes in sight of the car-park. The man didn't return. Inside the terminal again, she checked the departure board. By five-past-eleven, the Air France flight had gone.

Less than twenty minutes later, so had she.

They took the A42 and the A39, heading north, before veering east on the A36 towards Besançon and Mulhouse. Stephanie was driving, keeping just short of the speed limit. The radio was on. They listened to the news, neither of them saying what they were both thinking: *will we recognize ourselves in the bulletins*? The weather reports warned of storms blowing in from the east.

Stephanie rummaged through the CD cases. 'The Doors. I don't believe it.'

'Why not?'

'You should've seen the man who got out of this car. He looked like an accountant. Or an undertaker.'

He'd certainly been a smoker. Stephanie had emptied the ashtray of its cigarette butts on the way into Lyon but the Peugeot still smelt of stale smoke.

Newman said, 'Are you familiar with the phrase "never judge a book by its cover"?'

'I'm familiar with the phrase "mid-life crisis". Then again, I would never have had you down as a David Bowie fan.'

'I'm sorry?'

'When I was looking through your office, I came across your albums. All that vinyl . . .'

'I don't play them any more. But I like to keep them. Anyway, what's wrong with Bowie?'

'Nothing. God, nothing at all. I love Bowie.'

'Okay. What's wrong with me?'

'Look at where you live. The *way* you live, what you do. Everything.'

'When I was growing up, he was the deal. I was the right age at the right time. I loved the music, the way he looked, his attitude. And that most people hated him.'

'In New York? I'm surprised.'

'Mostly I grew up in Maine. The Thin White Duke went down well in Manhattan but not in Bangor or Bar Harbor. You know, it's stranger that *you* should like Bowie's music than me. When I bought his albums they were new. *You* buy him the way I buy Tchaikovsky.'

'Or read about Lebanon? As a matter of history?'

'Ouch.'

'You never did say why you went there.'

'For all the wrong reasons. But mostly because of my old man.'

'What does that mean?'

'It doesn't matter.'

'You can't say something like that and then drop it.'

'Why not?'

'It's . . . *unethical*.'

'Unethical? That puts it in the same ballpark as what you did to the guy in my kitchen.'

'That wasn't unethical. That was unavoidable.'

'Well, it's a long story.'

'This is a long road.'

'Okay. My father was a professor of politics at Harvard. An academic liberal. A socialist, I guess, though he never liked the word. He was also a fierce critic of Israel. Not of its right to exist, but of its conduct as a state. And he was equally critical of America's unqualified support for Israel, and of the pro-Israeli bias in the media. He thought it was absurd that you couldn't criticize Israel without being branded anti-Semitic. All these things he put in a paper in 1980; *The Illness Inside*. Professionally speaking, it was a thirty-seven-page suicide note.'

'Proving his point about the press?'

'Ironically, yes; they rounded on him and accused him of being anti-Semitic. Just as he'd predicted. They character-assassinated him and it cost him his job.'

'I would've thought a place like Harvard . . .'

'The pressure. Financial, political, all from the invisible above. Even a place like Harvard isn't immune. You know it happens. Everyone does. And he swallowed it. Said he had no interest in being part of an institution that didn't have the guts to stand up to tyranny.'

'A strong stance.'

'No. A weak stance dressed to look strong.'

'What did he do?'

'He went back to Maine. Back to the house where I grew up. To the house where my mother died from cancer the previous summer. And on the last day of October, he committed suicide.'

'Just because some half-wit journalists bad-mouthed him?'

Newman shook his head. 'That's what I thought back then. Now, I don't think it had anything to do with that. I think he killed himself because he was broken-hearted.'

'Yet you still ended up in Lebanon because of him?'

'That's right. I wanted to be a journalist. I wanted to redress the balance somehow. To be the Woodward and Bernstein of the Middle East.'

Stephanie rolled her eyes. 'A crusader in Lebanon? Smart thinking. Is this a genetic thing, chasing lost causes?'

'Could be – I'm still with you.'

'Very amusing.'

'Trouble was, I couldn't write for shit.'

'A slight drawback. What did you do?'

'I became a photo-journalist instead.'

'Just like that?'

'My mother was a portrait photographer. Quite well known in her own field. So I knew what an aperture was. The rest was bullshit. But it was enough to get me into an agency and to get assigned.'

'To Lebanon.'

'I would've gone anywhere. Europe, the Far East, Africa. But Lebanon came up. It was 1982. The Israelis had just invaded. Dad had been dead for less than a year. It just seemed to come together.'

'In a war zone?'

Newman smiled. 'I was an idiot with spots. It seemed like an adventure.'

'I'll bet it didn't disappoint on that score.'

'Damn right. So off I went.'

'To take pictures.'

'To document the truth. To be neutral.'

'How was it?'

'Extraordinary. Not another country, really. More like another world.'

'And did you succeed in remaining neutral?'

His laugh was simultaneously weary and nostalgic. Like the lines at the corners of his eyes, it was a scar of experience for which there was no short cut.

'Of course not,' he said. 'Nobody who was there

was neutral. That didn't mean you had to be on anybody's side. You just couldn't be neutral. There was no neutral. I felt for the eighteen-year-old Israeli boys bullied into the IDF to fight a war they didn't understand. I felt for the Palestinians. Most of all, though, I felt for the Lebanese. Caught in the crossfire – literally and politically – their country ruined by a conflict between outside parties. You can't believe the mess it was.'

'Sounds like a non-stop adrenaline rush.'

'Right. I never had a dull day. Could never relax, never wanted to. From one day to the next, you never knew what you were doing. No matter how much you resisted it, you got sucked in. Sooner or later you were bound to make a mistake. It was inevitable.'

'What was yours?'

'Falling in love with the wrong woman.'

New York City, 09:15
'We've got the footage from Lyon-St Exupéry airport coming through any moment now, sir,' Steven Mathis said. 'Five, four, three, two and . . . here we go. We're in Terminal 2.'

The active screen configuration at the front of the suite was two by two, the dividing lines between the four screens almost invisible. Each screen showed a different angle. The time was recorded in the bottom right-hand corners and was synchronized between the four. The pictures were almost five hours old. Since their recording,

350

Cabrini had learned that Grotius was dead; Paris-1 had confirmed it. There had been no sign of Newman in the apartment on quai d'Orléans.

'I don't see her.'

'Top right. Crossing now, in front of the taxi. Behind the guy in the brown suit. She's carrying a leather bag, two loop straps.'

'Okay.'

'Now she's inside. Go to the bottom left. You can see her coming into the terminal, towards us. Looks like she's in a hurry.'

Cabrini watched her until she disappeared through the bottom of the screen.

'Top left,' Mathis said. 'From right to left, beneath the departure board . . . now.'

Certainly in a rush, Cabrini thought. Where was she heading? Weaving in and out of passengers, she brushed against the man in the brown suit, just as he joined the short queue for check-in desk 25. She turned to apologize but didn't stop. Then she was scurrying forward again, towards the far end of the building, and was gone.

The four screens were refreshed with a fresh quartet of camera angles. Cabrini picked her up easily this time; the jeans, the leather coat, the scamper. Mathis gave the commentary that was no longer needed. When she vanished from the top right, she didn't reappear. Cabrini asked what was next.

'Nothing,' Mathis said. 'That's all we got. The

passenger manifests are being scrutinized as we speak.'

As she would no doubt have expected, Cabrini thought. 'Let's assume she drove to the airport. Can we find Newman's car?'

'We're on to it.'

'And what about the hook-up in Paris? Any more on that?'

'No, sir. No one saw it.'

'No cameras?'

'Only what Grotius stole. Nothing from the car-park.'

Cabrini sat back. How had it happened? Why Newman? It couldn't be a coincidence. Not with his connections.

'We've overlooked something,' he concluded.

'Maybe he was the first person she came across?'

'And she just climbed into his car? *His* car, of all people? Look at who he is. We know why she was at the Lancaster. Why was *he* there?'

They hadn't moved for more than two hours. Somewhere ahead of them in the gathering gloom, two lorries had collided. One had turned over, the other had jack-knifed. A dozen other vehicles had crashed into them. The road was shut. Air ambulances were ferrying the injured to hospital. Three were in a critical condition. Stephanie turned off the radio.

At first, there had been an inclination to panic:

they weren't moving yet they had to keep moving. Perhaps they should abandon the car? Of course not. The moment they got out, they'd draw attention to themselves. What could be more anonymous than sitting in kilometres of stationary traffic? Then again, what if the licence plate was recognized? By whom? Almost certainly, the owner didn't know that his car had been stolen. Besides, the cars in front and behind were so close that neither driver would have been able to make the plate.

They were circular arguments. After a while, by force of will, she abandoned them. 'I'm going to sleep,' she'd told Newman, when the radio had confirmed the carnage ahead. 'I suggest you do too.'

To his surprise, she'd managed more than an hour. Her first waking thoughts had centred on the other Petra. Étienne Lorenz had said that she could be found at Club Nitro in Vienna. Stephanie hoped that was true. A persistent knot of dread suggested it might not be. Women like her were always expendable.

Now it was after six. The last of the daylight was long gone. Belching exhausts threw a fog around them, engines running to keep their drivers warm.

Stephanie said, 'If you had to pick another life for yourself, what would it be?'

'The one I was having.'

'As a photo-journalist?'

'Yes.'

'With the wrong kind of woman?'

'Yes.'

'She can't have been that wrong.'

'What about you?'

What a question. It was impossible to imagine how her life might have unfolded. A university career taken to its conclusion? A good job, then a husband and children? She supposed that was the fate that had befallen the majority of her contemporaries. Would it have been hers? Impossible to say now. She was too far away from the girl she'd once been to make that leap. But in theory . . .

'Like you, the life I was having.'

'Which was what?'

She looked out of the window. The first snowflakes were falling. They were blurred.

Around seven-thirty the traffic began to crawl forward. Close to Mulhouse, they stopped at a service area for fuel and something to eat. They rejoined the *autoroute* just after ten and headed north on the A35 towards Strasbourg. Down to thirty kilometres an hour in places, the snow dancing over the windscreen, a strong wind driving it across the open plain. All the bulletins were advising against travel. Just after Colmar they saw a car on the other side of the barrier slide into a three-sixty spin before veering off the carriageway.

'We're too exposed. We need to let the worst of this pass,' Stephanie said. 'We can't afford a collision.'

They came off the *autoroute* and made it to Ribeauvillé at the foot of the Vosges mountains. Stephanie drove through the picturesque town centre. Restaurant windows glowed in the darkness. Light seeped from the cracks in curtains. The pavements were deserted. When they reached the far side of town, Stephanie took the road for Sainte Marie.

'We're not stopping?'

'We can't take a room.'

'Where are we going?'

'No idea.'

They began to climb, the road twisting through steep slopes of mature forest. Despite this, Stephanie found the conditions marginally easier; the terrain shielded them from the worst of the wind. Fat snowflakes fell vertically through the cones of light cast by the headlights. Occasional houses came and went, emerging briefly from the darkness like passing ships in fog. There were intermittent turnings, some signposted, most not. After eight kilometres, she took one.

It was a rough track, marked out only by the alternatives: a steep rise on one side, a steep drop on the other, both through towering trees, their branches already sagging under the weight of snow.

'Know where we are?' Newman asked, after ten minutes of total darkness.

'No. But look on the bright side: if we don't, it's extremely unlikely anybody else does.'

'I like a woman who's glass-half-full.'

'What are you? The glass-half-empty type?'

'Not normally. What are we looking for?'

'Nothing.'

'I thought we found that already.'

Even as he said it, it was clear they hadn't. As they lurched around a rocky corner, a shack came into view, light spilling from fractured shutters, smoke curling from a chimney. Beside the shack was a rusting 2CV on bricks, a discarded refrigerator and an upturned bathtub.

It was barely a hamlet. A few creaking dwellings on either side of the track, wooden telephone poles running along one side, the lines looping from house to house. They crept on, the track turning sharply to manoeuvre around one house, then the next.

A cross appeared, gradually, then sharply, as it drifted into their light. A roadside shrine; a wooden crucifix with the gleaming white body of Jesus. Within twenty yards, there was another; a wooden box with a glass front, Mary holding the infant Jesus in her arms, illuminated by guttering candles. Despite the weather, somebody had persevered. In all, Stephanie counted seven shrines and a dozen houses.

They negotiated another tight bend and were

in darkness again. As though the hamlet had been nothing more than a momentary flight of imagination.

Five minutes later, they spotted a dilapidated barn in a small clearing just off the track. Stephanie killed the lights and engine, took the hold-all from the boot and climbed back in. She handed the Smith & Wesson Sigma to Newman and kept the Heckler & Koch for herself.

'Ever used one of these?'

'All the time. They're useful in the boardroom.'

'Not even in your colourful past?'

'Never,' he insisted, before adding: 'but I know how to. Providing there's a safety-catch, of course.'

'Smart-arse. I'm going to check the barn.'

She circled it twice, peering through the gaps between the rotten planks. No livestock, no machinery. The front of the barn had two doors secured by a wooden beam dropped into iron cups. She removed the beam and tried to pull the doors open but the snow was banked too high. She managed to squeeze through the gap she'd created. The lack of wind made it comparatively warm. A few snowflakes fell through holes in the roof. There was no sign of recent use.

Using planks ripped from the rear wall, they scraped clear enough snow to allow the doors to open. By the time they'd finished, their hands were red, their fingers numb. Steam rose off them. Newman reversed the car into the barn and

Stephanie pulled the doors closed as the headlights threw creamy pools on to gnarled wood.

'What was her name?'

'Who?'

'The wrong woman.'

We've been here half an hour. I don't expect him to answer. He's avoided talking about her every time I've given him the opportunity. But he surprises me.

'Gabriella.'

'Italian?'

'Spanish.'

I can see her immediately. 'The woman in the photo on your desk?'

'That's right.'

'Wow.'

He arches an eyebrow. 'Wow?'

'That she still has pride of place twenty years later. Very impressive.'

He doesn't have an answer for that.

'How'd you meet her?'

'In the bar at the Commodore Hotel in Beirut. That's where all the journalists drank.'

'She was a journalist?'

'For Associated Press. I was working for the SIPA Photo agency at that time. A French firm. The moment I saw her at the bar – I knew.'

My sigh is more wistful than I'd like it to be.

'You've had it too?'

I nod. 'Once. In New York. He was Russian.'

'Then you'll know. It's a feeling you can't forget.'

'Or fake. He was supposed to be an adversary but if he'd asked me to make love to him there and then, I would have.'

Robert nods and looks down at his hands. 'The thing is, Gabriella wasn't Spanish. Or a journalist. Her name was Rachel and she was Israeli.'

'Ah.'

An utterly inadequate response but I can't think of an alternative.

Robert looks across at me. 'In the end, though, it didn't make any difference.'

'Why did she tell you she was Spanish?'

'She was half-Spanish. And half-Israeli.'

'That's only half a lie, then. In fact, it's not even a lie. It's an omission. What about the journalist part?'

'She was a Mossad plant. Being Spanish allowed her to appear impartial. Meanwhile, her work – sometimes hers, sometimes not – was picked up by papers in the States. On the surface, she looked good for it. But she was doing a lot more reporting than any of the other journalists realized. Mossad wanted information on all the foreign press stationed in Beirut.'

'Including you?'

'The writers were the main target.'

'And you bought that?'

'I fell in love. She fell in love. Neither of us bought it. We just put it to one side.'

'Is that really possible?'

'When nothing else matters, sure. Why not?'

How true. We sit in the darkness for a while, listening

to the wind battering the barn. The whole structure groans.

'Is that why you never married?' I ask, eventually. 'Nothing could compare?'

'I guess that's part of it.'

'No children, no ex-wives, but plenty of girls like Anna.'

'The life I lead now is not exactly conducive to family stability. I've been living out of a suitcase for twenty years. I've spent more nights at thirty-five-thousand feet than in my own bed. That's not good for a marriage. Or parenthood.'

'So you change your job.'

'If I'd met the right person, I would've.'

'Sounds like a vicious circle.'

'Maybe. But I'm not complaining. For all the things I've missed out on, I've been lucky.'

I nod. 'And nobody has it all.'

'Right. So what about you? Ever been married?'

I laugh. 'God no.'

'What's so funny?'

'Nothing. Nothing at all.'

'What about children?'

'Please.'

'You never considered it?'

'Of course I've considered it. It's just . . .'

'Just what?' he prompts, when I falter.

'It doesn't matter. You wouldn't believe me.'

'Try me.'

I avoid looking at him. 'No matter what you think about me, I'm actually rather conventional.' I wait for

a snort of incredulous laughter that never materializes.
'So without a husband . . .'

I let my shrug finish it off. He's a little embarrassed.
He nods thoughtfully and then cushions the blow so
clumsily that he makes it worse. 'Well . . . you have
plenty of time on your side.'

'So what happened with you and Rachel?'

'In the end, it didn't work out.'

'How come?'

He considers it for a moment. 'The star that burns
twice as bright burns half as long. The way we were
living was unsustainable. We were like drug-addicts.
We had to have the fix. We were out of our minds. That's
what it was.'

'Life in a danger zone? Every adrenaline-fuelled expe-
rience sharpened?'

'That's it. We thought we were the only people in
the world who understood.'

'I know what that's like.'

He looks at me in the darkness. 'It's something like
this, isn't it?'

New York City, 20:35
When John Cabrini returned to his desk, Steven
Mathis was waiting for him. 'We have the results.'

'And?'

'There were only three cars to enter the long-
term car-park at Lyon-St Exupéry airport this
morning and to leave by 15:00 CET. One of them
was a mistake; an Italian tourist who parked in
the wrong car-park. The second was a local

361

woman – Marie Sylvain – who was due to fly to London. She was actually checking her bags with British Airways when her office in Lyon called her back. Some kind of crisis, nothing important to us. The third car belongs to Alain Fabius, a cosmetic surgeon at the Morgenthau clinic in Lyon. He boarded an Air France flight to Paris with an onward connection to Chicago, where he's attending a conference.'

Mathis handed Cabrini the photograph. A gaunt, humourless man. The man in the brown suit. The one she'd brushed against. Not just an assassin; a pickpocket too.

'Did he make his connection?'

'Yes.'

'And his car?'

'Left the long-term car-park while his flight was en route to Paris. We have a positive identification.'

'How?'

'She didn't have a ticket for the vehicle. She made some excuse to the official about losing it. She had to pay the maximum charge. She was okay with it, though, which isn't the normal reaction. The guy remembered.'

'Was she alone?'

'Yes. Also, we have another positive identification from the driver of the bus she took from Gare de Perrache out to the airport.'

'So she dumped Newman's car first,' Cabrini mused. 'Probably somewhere in the city.'

'That's what it looks like.'

'Was she alone on the bus?'

'The driver said so.'

So far, so conventional. Cabrini felt uncomfortable; Reuter wasn't the kind to go by the book. Or to leave a trail.

'So we have neither Newman nor his car. Raising a number of possibilities.'

'They could've separated.'

'Possibly.'

'Or Newman could actually be *in* his car.'

'He could be,' Cabrini conceded. 'Dead or alive.'

Mathis frowned. 'You think she would have done that? After the way the police officers said they were?'

There had been an earlier identification. Four *gendarmes* had encountered Reuter and Newman at Le Chien Blanc service station on the A6 in the early hours of the morning. When questioned later by DST agents, they'd reported that the American had done the talking. The mood had been jovial, there'd been laughter. Although the woman had seemed slightly tense, neither had given cause for suspicion.

Cabrini had been intrigued by their account. Newman had been alone with the officers and had said nothing. Either they were lying in order to cover themselves for some greater transgression or Newman and Reuter had some form of relationship. Which was a possibility that returned him to his original theory: Newman was involved

363

somehow. What other plausible explanation could there be?

On the other hand, involved or not, he'd always be expendable to a woman like Reuter. 'She killed Grotius,' Cabrini pointed out. 'Viciously.'

'Yeah, maybe. I guess once Newman had outlived his usefulness . . .'

'What car is she in now?'

'A dark blue Peugeot,' said Mathis, handing Cabrini the details. 'This is the registration.'

'Has Fabius arrived in Chicago yet?'

'About ninety minutes ago. He was met by security at O'Hare. The CPD spoke to him first, then the FBI.'

'Anything useful come out of it?'

Mathis perked up; this was his moment. 'Actually, yes. One thing . . .'

Day Nine

Ultimately, there were three of them. Initially, however, there had been only one. And one would have been enough had Stephanie been asleep.

But she couldn't sleep; her body was too cold, her mind too hot. Newman had been dozing in the front seat, she'd been across the back. In the frozen darkness, she'd glimpsed movement. The barn door shifting, a tiny squall of snow breathing through a narrow gap. Very slowly she'd leaned forward, touched Newman on the shoulder and had whispered to him.

'Don't move. Don't say anything. We've got company.'

The headlights were Newman's idea once Stephanie had thrown open the back door and scampered across the ground, the Heckler & Koch ready. Suddenly there was light. And the cough of a cold engine. The stunning brightness bought her precious moments of advantage.

Movement and gun-shot. She couldn't recall the exact sequence of events. She supposed the second one had been coming through the door as the first one went down. She felt him before she saw him, a heavy boot kicking the gun from her hand. But she'd stayed close and even though he'd managed to fire his weapon, she'd deflected his arm with her body. Bullets sprayed the barn roof.

There had been hand-to-hand combat. She'd fallen and he'd kicked her, catching her exactly where Grotius had cut her, the sutures exploding as the injury ruptured. The pain had paralysed her for a second. Then they'd struggled on the ground. She'd heard shouts in a language she didn't recognize. Then gunfire from outside the barn, splinters flying, more shouts.

She'd prodded her attacker in the eyes. He couldn't defy instinct, his hands automatically shielding his face. His supremacy interrupted, Stephanie had grabbed the gun. He'd understood instantly and had tried to claw back some parity but it was too late. She shot him from less than a metre.

A moment later, a final shot. It wasn't hers.

When she looked up there was a body by the barn door. Beside it, Newman stood completely still, the Smith & Wesson Sigma in his hand.

The third attacker was dead. One shot to the head, blood everywhere. Newman couldn't take his eyes off it. Until Stephanie rolled on to one side and cried out. Then he looked over at her.

'Are you hit?'

Through clenched teeth, she muttered, 'No. It's the cut.'

The second attacker was dead too. His throat looked like a crimson rhododendron in full bloom. The first attacker, and the only one of them to take more than a single bullet, was still alive. Just.

The interrogation was brief. At first, Stephanie couldn't understand him. She tried French, English and German. Nothing. He spoke basic Russian, however, but not for long. Within a minute he'd slipped into unconsciousness.

'Who is he?' Newman asked.

'An Albanian.'

'Jesus.'

'One of them's his brother. The other's a Turk.'

'What else?'

'Nothing.'

'Come on, Stephanie. He said more than that.'

She leaned against the car and tried to regulate her breathing. 'He said they'd be waiting.'

'Who?'

Stephanie shrugged and winced at the discomfort it provoked. '*That* was the last thing he said. I'm going to check outside.'

'I'll come with you.'

'No. Stay here. In the corner there. When I get back, I'll call your name before I come in. Anybody else comes, shoot them. Don't wait to see who they are.'

It took ten minutes to trace the tracks back to

their point of origin. It had stopped snowing. The ground looked ultraviolet beneath the moon. A gentle breeze whispered among the trees. It was bitterly cold, clouds of frozen breath encircling her head like a shroud.

Over rough ground, then through dense wood, she came to a narrow clearing. The three sets of footprints stopped where the tyre-tracks started. Broad wheels with a chunky bite. A four-wheel drive. She read the prints; the vehicle had arrived, dropped its cargo, turned around and gone back.

Which meant there was at least one other person. And if the Albanian was to be believed, perhaps more.

But where?

'Are you okay?' Stephanie asked

Newman nodded. Despite the darkness she could see he wasn't. He was looking through her, not at her, to the body beyond. She wondered if he'd moved in the ten minutes since she'd left him. She looked at her watch. Twenty-past-five.

She said, 'We need to go.'

He nodded again.

'Robert, look at me.'

He did.

'I understand what's going on in your mind. But we need to leave right now. I need you to come with me. *All* of you.'

'I'll be fine.'

'Good. Then help me get the body out of the way.'

They dragged the third corpse into the barn to clear the exit. Newman seemed to recover but Stephanie guessed the shock would return later. It usually did. They climbed into the car. Stephanie clutched the wheel for support as she got in but failed to suppress a gasp.

'How bad is it?' he asked.

'It's okay. It just hurts, that's all.'

'You want me to drive?'

She arched an eyebrow. 'I hope this isn't a gender thing.'

'I know how to drive on snow.'

'And you think I don't?'

'From what I saw last night . . .'

'I was taught by an expert.'

'So was I.'

Stephanie felt her temper rising. 'Oh yeah? Where?'

'Finland. Outside Rovaniemi. You?'

'Scotland. Sutherland.'

'Who taught you?'

'A former member of the Special Services. You?'

'A former World Rally champion.'

She glared at him. 'Rubbish.'

'I'm serious.'

'Well . . . you're not in any shape to drive. Look at you. You're shaking.'

'And you're bleeding. Now move over and fasten your seatbelt.'

* * *

Newman saw the lights first. They'd only been going for a couple of minutes and hadn't yet reached the hamlet.

'Shit.'

'What?'

'Up ahead on the left. Through the trees, coming down to the track.'

Stephanie saw immediately. Glittering pin-pricks of light winking at them through a web of black branches. 'Could be anyone.'

Newman accelerated as much as he dared. 'Could be.'

The closer they got, the less likely it seemed. The other vehicle was gathering speed. On a snowy surface that meant dangerous momentum.

'If he gets to the junction before us, we're screwed.'

'So don't let him,' Stephanie suggested.

'You got any more useful advice?'

'Yes. Don't do their work for them.'

Newman kept accelerating, even as the wheels beneath him began to slide.

'Robert . . .'

'I know, I know.'

They made it to the junction first. The other vehicle missed the rear end by a metre. It skidded wildly, ploughing into a bank of snow before righting itself. A black Range Rover. The driver switched his lights to full-beam. Newman pushed the rear-view mirror away.

They reached the hamlet. One or two lights

were on, smoke puffing from an occasional chimney. The Range Rover was catching them. Newman wrestled the wheel. The car slipped left and right, the brakes shuddering. He used drifted snow to slow down then swung to the left, past the first house. The back stepped out. He couldn't retrieve it so he didn't try. Instead, he accelerated again, just as they hit a fence. The nudging impact corrected their alignment. The Range Rover dropped back a little, then surged closer.

Newman used whatever he could; ruts, banks, the upturned bathtub, a tree stump. Anything. Stephanie looked over her shoulder and saw the Range Rover crash into one of the roadside shrines. There was a shower of glass and wood in the cast of the headlights.

'They're dropping back.'

'That's because the guy can't drive. But he's got snow-tyres. When the track straightens he'll be all over us.'

They clipped the corner of a house as they tried to negotiate a right-angle bend. The Peugeot slid sideways into a plump hedge with a resounding thump. A wing-mirror snapped off. Snow sprayed across the windscreen. The engine stalled.

Newman turned the ignition. Nothing. The Range Rover approached, aiming directly at the Peugeot.

'Robert . . .'

Another failure. Stephanie clutched the door-handle, a futile brace.

'*Robert . . .*'

The engine sparked, the Peugeot shifted forwards. The Range Rover driver tried to turn too violently. The wheels lost grip and the vehicle powered straight through the hedge. The driver kept going, spinning the machine around.

Newman cleared the hamlet and they were in total darkness again, a steep bank rising to the left, a steeper bank dropping to the right. The inside of the Peugeot grew brighter as the Range Rover closed in.

'What are we going to do?'

Newman said nothing and focused on keeping the drive as smooth as possible.

Stephanie looked over her shoulder again. 'Oh God . . .'

The Range Rover was upon them. The first contact propelled them towards the ravine to the right. Newman over-compensated. The car lurched. He turned into the skid and accelerated through it. Then had to brake immediately for a sharp left turn. Which was when the Range Rover hit them again. Missing the apex of the corner, Newman pulled at the wheel to send the Peugeot into a lateral skid so that they hit the oncoming tree side-on, not head-first.

The collision hurt. Stephanie felt pain ripple through her left side. Newman was already thinking ahead, nosing the Peugeot back onto the road as the Range Rover came at them again.

'For God's sake!' Stephanie cried. 'We can't out-run him!'

'Wait, goddamn it.'

'*Wait?* For what? Roadside assistance?'

'Exactly.'

They slithered down a gentle banana-shaped curve to the right which then opened on to a straight. Newman pressed his foot down. The Range Rover matched him, then bettered him, swallowing the distance between them. With the full-beam on, Stephanie saw clearly the turn ahead. A sharp left that suddenly grew far too quickly.

'Robert . . .'

'Hold on.'

They were past the braking-point, travelling at their fastest yet, everything a blur. All she saw were mighty tree trunks and blackness.

'Robert . . . please . . . oh my God . . . *no*!'

Suddenly they were off the road. But not ahead, or to the right. To the left, instead. Newman had driven at full speed into the ditch. The car ricocheted over snowy stones and stumps. The deceleration was massive, hurling Stephanie forward, the seatbelt biting into her collarbone.

And then they veered right into the side of the Range Rover, which was overtaking them despite every effort to slow. There was an almighty crunch that killed the Peugeot's momentum. The Range Rover spun out of control. The driver stamped on his brakes but the snow-tyres made no difference. The vehicle reached the turning and sailed straight ahead into the darkness.

The cartwheel descent was marked by headlight spirals against the trees, and a procession of crunches that grew fainter the further the Range Rover fell.

We drive back through Ribeauvillé in silence. There are vines in the snowy fields beyond. They look like barbed wire on a battlefield; branches bent around miles of wire between thousands of stout wooden posts.

The tracks we leave don't exist solely in the snow. They're also in my mind and I can't brush fresh snow over them. The suspicion persists.

'We should get something to eat.'

'We'll be in Strasbourg soon.'

'Before then,' I suggest.

'You in trouble?'

'I'm okay. But food and drink would help.'

'You need a doctor.'

'First things first. Are you okay?'

'Me? I'm fine.'

The lie's so naked it makes us both smile. Even in the dark of the car I can see how pale he is. He looked better when he was standing over the remains of Lance Grotius. He's clutching the steering wheel as tightly as he can but he can't pacify the shakes.

'It's normal,' I tell him.

'Did it happen to you?'

'Yes. The first time.'

'Not any more?'

You only lose your virginity once. That's what I'd

tell him if I answered the question. And that too much of anything can become routine.

It's still dark when we creep into Obernai, about thirty-five kilometres south of Strasbourg. We head for the centre and park the Peugeot on place du Marché outside Arc en Ciel. We cross the square to the Hôtel La Diligence. The wound hurts when I walk, forcing me to limp.

The snow has barely been disturbed. It's so quiet the air feels brittle; it seems to fracture when a distant dog barks.

Behind the hotel's reception desk sits a weary-looking woman counting down the final minutes of the night-shift.

'Is it possible to have breakfast?' I ask her.

'Are you guests?'

'No.'

'I'm sorry. We are not open for breakfast.'

Not to us anyway. I don't suppose we appear the most appealing prospect. I try to stand straight to conceal the injury.

'Is there anywhere in Obernai where we could get a cup of coffee?' Robert asks. 'We've been driving all night.'

Her eyes widen. 'Through the storm?'

He nods. 'All the way from Rotterdam.'

Without so much as a blink. I'm impressed. He's learning. Although why should I assume that he can learn anything from me? Perhaps we're equals. Perhaps he's better.

Out of the corner of my eye, I catch movement. Robert

*is still talking to the woman behind the desk and she's
beginning to thaw. Through the window, across the
square, a figure circles the Peugeot once, then twice.
Dressed in dark clothing, a black satchel slung over the
right shoulder.*

Not again. It's not possible. Not already.

*He moves away from the car and I begin to think
I've made a mistake. Then he returns to the Mercedes
in front of our car, looks as though he's about to get
into it, his head flicking from side to side, before nipping
back to the Peugeot. He pretends to drop something
before dipping into a crouch to search for it. He puts
one hand against the Peugeot for support. The other
hand pulls something from the satchel. I can't see what
it is. I don't need to. He reaches under the Peugeot,
attaches it, and then disappears. Five seconds from start
to finish; a magnetic clamp, most likely.*

*I put my hand on Robert's arm. 'Just going to the
car for a minute, darling. Back in a moment.'*

*Before he can ask why, I'm outside. Fresh footprints
in the snow cut diagonally across place du Marché
towards the corner to my left. I head right and turn into
rue de la Paille, which allows me to curl around the
outside of the square. On rue Dietrich, I approach the
corner with caution and peer round it. There are several
vehicles parked along the kerb of rue Sainte Odile. All
have snow on them. Except one. A black BMW X5 with
tinted windows.*

*It's parked outside a small bookshop, from where it
has a partial view of the square. The Peugeot is visible
but the entrance to Hôtel La Diligence is not. I memo-*

rize the registration then return to the shadows.

Three threats before dawn. Part of me feels flattered.

Robert's charm has failed. He's still talking to the receptionist but there's no chance of breakfast. I smile sweetly. 'Well, we'll find somewhere else.'

Outside I take him by the arm and steer him sharply to the right.

'Where are we going?'

'To the station.'

'Why?'

'We're leaving the car,' I tell him as we exit place du Marché. 'It's wired.'

Exasperated, he shakes his head. 'I know the feeling.'

'We should have got the bag from the trunk.'

Stephanie shook her head. 'Couldn't risk it. We don't know what kind of device it was. Could've been a timer, could've been a motion sensor. Or a remote; there was a clear line of vision between the two vehicles.'

Newman watched the emerging landscape lumber past, early daylight staining it deep blue. They were on the local train, the 06:47 to Strasbourg, a few early commuters with them, none sitting too close to their end of the carriage.

Stephanie was aware of the weight of the Heckler & Koch in her coat pocket. In a low voice, she said, 'Have you got the Smith & Wesson?'

He shook his head. 'I put it in the trunk. With the bag.'

'What did you have in the bag?'

'Some clothes, some money. You got Scheherazade's cash?'

Stephanie patted her jacket. 'In here.'

'How the hell did they find us?'

'I don't know. You're not carrying a mobile, are you?'

'No.'

'Anything electronic?'

'No. Although we have the laptop.'

'I haven't turned it on since we switched cars in Lyon.'

'Can it be traced anyway?'

She'd been told that the technology to track mobile phones when they were switched off already existed, although not yet in operation. 'I don't know. Maybe.'

'Then we better dump it. Just to be sure. Is that what Obernai was about?'

'It was just a feeling,' Stephanie replied. 'An instinct.'

'You could've said so, you know. What's your instinct telling you now?'

'That we must be doing something right.'

The train pulled into Strasbourg at 07:27. They left the laptop under the seat. Stephanie checked that she had the disks in her pocket, then found a France Télécom phonebooth and called the police.

'Place du Marché, Obernai. There's a dark blue Peugeot outside the shop Arc en Ciel. It has a bomb attached to the underside, controlled from a black BMW X5 that was parked on rue Sainte

Odile. Maybe it's still there. If not, the registration is . . .'

As soon as she'd given it, she put the phone down.

Half an hour later, they left Strasbourg in an old grey Saab, stolen from the car-park beneath place du Gare. Stephanie's wound was padded with hand-towels taken from the station washroom. Newman drove. They crossed the Rhine into Germany at Kehl, then headed north for Mannheim.

From Mannheim, they caught a high-speed ICE train for Munich. Their carriage was less than half full. Outside, intermittent snow squalls sped past the window. Inside, it was quiet and warm. Stephanie felt nauseous and exhausted. She knew her body needed a boost which was why she'd bought a sandwich but she couldn't yet bring herself to eat it.

'So how come you're friends with a World Rally champion?'

'A *former* World Rally champion.'

'That doesn't make it any more likely.'

'Then the truth won't either: I borrowed his girlfriend for a few months.'

'Actually, that's something I *can* believe. Nice of him to lend her to you, though. I hope you returned her in the same condition you received her.'

'He didn't know about me.'

'Did you know about him?'

'No.'

'This wouldn't be Anna, would it?'

'No. Carlotta.'

'I was wondering when she'd come around. What happened?'

'She got careless with her diary. I was at her place when he turned up.'

'Sounds messy.'

'It could've been. But it wasn't. We left together and as we were walking down the stairs, he suggested a drink. You know – no hard feelings, that kind of thing.'

'And that was it?'

'Not exactly. He's Finnish so one drink turned into a weekend. We've been friends ever since. He lives down in Monaco now but we still see each other a couple of times a year.'

'And he taught you how to drive like that?'

'That's right. He has this place in Finland near Rovaniemi. He used to have these great long weekends; lots of friends from all over the place, great food, plenty to drink, no time to sleep. We used to drive on frozen lakes. Or through the woods. Any time of the day or night.'

'Sounds as though you had more fun with him than you did with Carlotta.'

'Actually, I did. And in return, I used to help him manage some of the money he'd made. These days he makes more through his investments than he ever did as a driver.'

Stephanie raised her cup. 'Well, here's to

Carlotta. Without her we'd probably be wrapped round a tree.'

Newman raised his own cup. 'To Carlotta.'

'I'll bet that's not something you ever expected to hear yourself say.'

As their train pulled out of Stuttgart station, Stephanie said, 'A euro for your thoughts.'

'It's not a thought. It's a question.'

'Let's hear it.'

'You sure you want to?'

She placed a euro coin on the table. 'Tell me.'

'Okay. Who are you? *What* are you?'

'That's two questions.'

'You've already used that on me. Don't be cheap.'

'And I've already told you.'

'You told me you used to work for the government.'

'That's true.'

'That's *an* answer. Not *the* answer. Tax officials work for the government. Teachers work for the government.'

'You've seen what I can do.'

'I've seen all kinds of stuff. And I'm just about as confused as I'm ever going to be. So what I want more than anything right now is a straight answer.'

She'd always hated the sound of it. It sounded like a lie. Or, even worse, a boast. Either way, something that had nothing to do with her.

She gave it to him as plainly as she could. 'I was an assassin.'

There was no outrage, not even surprise. It was the answer he expected, it appeared. Perhaps even the answer he'd hoped for, confirmation of anything being better than doubt.

'For the British government?'

'Yes. But not officially.'

'Is it ever official?'

'The organization I used to work for doesn't exist. It never did.'

'But you retired from it?'

'I tried to.'

'What does that mean?'

'I'd rather not talk about it.'

Her stock phrase whenever a difficult situation presented itself.

'I'm not surprised.'

That annoyed her. 'Are you going to take the moral high ground with me now?'

'Do I need to?'

Stephanie thought about it, then looked directly at him. 'Until a couple of years ago, I'd spent my entire adult life as a highly trained slave. I followed orders. Those orders usually culminated in killing. That takes a toll. At first, it erodes you. Later, it consumes you because it's all you have left. It's what you become. But I never stopped dreaming about an after-life. And in the end, I got my chance. There was a situation in Berlin. When it was over, I was offered my freedom with no comebacks. I didn't have to be asked twice.'

'You left it all behind?'

'I did. And that should have been it. I had what I'd wanted right from the start. The chance to begin again.'

'What did you do?'

'Initially, I travelled. I took a long holiday. South-east Asia, backpacking like a student, no fixed itinerary. The sea on my skin, the sun in my hair. It was lovely. I read books, took trains, slept, ate, put on weight. I felt relaxed, sexy, happy. All that good stuff. All the things I used to dream about when I was freezing in a storm-drain in Grozny.'

'I wish I'd met you then.'

'In Grozny?'

'In south-east Asia.'

'You wouldn't have liked it.'

'Why not?'

'No first-class travel, no five-star hotels.'

'We're not travelling first-class now, are we? And last night definitely wasn't the Ritz. Tell me what happened.'

She found she didn't have an answer straight away. 'I suppose I slipped. Regressed. How it happened is a mystery but I can tell you *why* it happened. Shortly before I killed him, Alexander said to me that I would never be able to lead a regular life.'

'Who was Alexander?'

'My boss.'

'And you killed him?'

'In a loo at Zoo Station in Berlin.'

Newman raised an eyebrow. 'I guess it's true what they say; worker loyalty ain't what it used to be.'

'I owed him nothing. He used to say that he'd saved me. On one level, that was true. He turned me from a wreck into a high-precision instrument. Superficially, that was an improvement. But at least I was no harm to anybody other than myself when I was a wreck.'

'That sounds like self-pity to me.'

'I don't really care what you think it sounds like. Alexander said it wouldn't be the killing that I couldn't live without. It would be the life. That adrenaline that you tasted in Beirut? The same thing, only magnified. It was everything. The assignments; preparation, execution, extraction. Then the down-time; neatly cut fillets of civilian life. Usually just long enough to relax but never long enough to get bored. The truth is that when you're the best at something, it kills you to give it up.'

'So he was right.'

Stephanie nodded. 'I was the sports star who can't live without the crowd.' She let the analogy linger then changed her mind. 'Actually, I was more like an alcoholic. When I walked away from Magenta House, that was rehab. But I couldn't make it stick. I began to falter. Then I fell off the wagon.'

'How?'

She shrugged. 'The way an alcoholic does, I guess. One sip. It was the stupidest thing possible. I was in Barcelona. It was late at night and I got attacked by four men. I was scared – I mean really terrified, the way any normal person would be – and I didn't think I'd be able to fight them off. I thought I was cured. But it came flooding back. It was so easy. So effortless. And it felt good. Physically and emotionally.'

'And that was it?'

'That was the start of it. Except this time, it was even better than before because I was nobody's slave. I was a perfect killing machine unburdened by the restraining influence of a controlling entity. It's one thing to fall off the wagon. It's another to discover you no longer suffer hangovers.'

'What about now?'

She sighed slowly. 'Now I'm waking up to the *real* truth.'

'Which is what?'

'That it was an illusion. It was a device to conceal the truth. I don't need the killing *or* the life. I just need time to make the adjustment away from them. The woman I was in south-east Asia – that was the real me. I just didn't recognize her.'

New York City, 06:05
John Cabrini had been in a deep sleep when the call came through and was still trying to gather

his senses. Steven Mathis passed him the handset as he swung his legs off the cot. His mouth was dry due to the artificial air pumped into the operations suite.

A voice boomed in his ear. 'What's the latest?'

'Paris-1 has a fix on her.'

'Where?'

'South of Strasbourg. I've green-lighted an interception. An assessment is being made as we speak.'

'When can we expect some kind of resolution?'

'Within the hour. No more than two.'

'Are you sure?'

'Positive, sir.'

'Do you know where I'm calling from?'

Cabrini glanced at Mathis who mouthed the answer that he repeated. 'Paris?'

'That's right. I'm at Charles de Gaulle, waiting for a flight. It's been delayed. All this snow we've had . . .'

'Sorry to hear that, sir.'

'Well, it's allowed me a little time to catch up on the news. That's what I'm watching, by the way. The news. On a TV in the departure lounge.'

Cabrini felt an unpleasant shift in the pit of his stomach. Behind the voice, he heard a flight announcement in French. He clutched at something neutral to say. 'I hope you won't be delayed too long, sir.'

'Yeah? I hope that's true for Paris-1.'

'I'm sorry?'

'I hope he won't be delayed too long.'

'I don't think I understand, sir.'

'He's in custody, you asshole. I'm looking at his black BMW. It's on goddamned TV, surrounded by *gendarmes* who look about as happy as I feel. What the hell's going on, Cabrini? Paris-1 is in a Strasbourg police station and I have to hear the news from the France-3 network?'

Cabrini was moving through to the control suite, trying to impose order on runaway thoughts.

'We're . . . we're looking into it . . . right now, sir.'

'No, Cabrini. I'm the one looking into it right now. You're the one who couldn't find his dick with a six-man search party. They picked Paris-1 up in some shitty little town. The whole place is cordoned off. A car bomb, for Christ's sake! This isn't fucking Israel, Cabrini. Who the hell is Paris-1, anyway?'

'Gavras, sir. Rafael Gavras.'

'The *Cuban*?'

'Yes, sir.'

'Jesus H. Christ, Cabrini! You picked a Cuban to go up against Reuter. First a South African, then a Cuban. Who's next? Gwyneth-fucking-Paltrow?'

'Gavras has never let us down in the past.'

There was another pause, long enough for an entire flight announcement. When the voice returned, the rage was undiminished but under control, which only served to add some menace. 'You just make sure he doesn't get the chance to let us down again.'

Stephanie was asleep but it didn't look peaceful. She was twitching. Newman watched her over a cup of coffee. Outside the carriage the landscape remained defiantly white. He thought of the shot, the jolt, the body creasing. He'd never seriously contemplated shooting anyone. Not even in Beirut. Now, two decades later, he had and what disturbed him most was the numbness. The lack of any sense of reality.

Perhaps if his victim had cried out. But he hadn't; he'd fallen silently. Perhaps if his victim hadn't been so anonymous. But he had been; dressed in black from head to toe, no features to focus on. A cartoon character from a computer game.

This was the real shock; the shakes had gone and there was nothing left.

Stephanie woke with a start. Then gasped, as the sudden movement pulled at her cut. For a moment, she looked utterly disorientated. Then she saw him and relaxed.

'Where are we?' she asked.

'About an hour from Munich.'

'What've you been doing?'

'Nothing. Thinking.'

She sat up, slowly and stiffly. 'Tell me about Lebanon. About Rachel.'

'You sure you want to know?'

She said she did. Until recently, she'd been ambivalent at best. But now she felt she *needed* to know.

She clung to the details. The taste of coffee in a café on a corner. The heat of the arrivals hall in the damaged terminal building at Beirut airport. The French contraband smuggler who worked out of an apartment on rue Australie. Long lunches with friends in the Chouf. The characters in Rachel's AP office – Greek Catholics, a Palestinian Sunni, an Irishman, an Armenian, an Iranian, a Maronite – all of them stuffed into a warren of rooms in a crumbling apartment block. Arabic *mezze* dinners with fellow journalists at the Grenier restaurant.

'One time, she took me to the cedars of Lebanon. It was winter; there was snow on the heights of the Sannine. We drove up into the Lebanon range. Around 3000 feet, the trees stopped. The track got worse. We reached 6000 feet. It was freezing. There was nothing but rock. Then we went round a sharp corner and there they were, three thousand feet after the last of the other trees. Fifteen hundred years old. We stood among them, looking out over the land below. Rachel was happy. She said that no matter what happened, we'd survive.'

Stephanie saw Newman slip back through time.

It was 18 September 1982 and he was walking through Chatila camp, stepping over the body parts of the women and children murdered by the Phalange with the permission and encouragement of the onlooking Israeli forces. That had been his baptism of fire. Then it was 23 October 1983 and he was shooting roll after roll of 35mm film amid the smoking ruins of the US Marines base. No longer the novice, seasoned in a year.

He described his down-time. It wasn't like Stephanie's had ever been. Petra's pleasure had been orchestrated as part of a mechanical process. His had been grabbed wherever it could be found.

'By late 1984, early 1985, the threat was changing. Westerners were being targeted by Islamic Jihad. There were killings, kidnappings. In the beginning, we didn't worry too much. Two of the first four were released unharmed. But then it got serious. When the CIA's Beirut chief William Buckley was taken and tortured to death, that was a real wake-up call. By the time Terry Anderson was taken, people were already leaving. Charles Wallace of the *Los Angeles Times*, the NBC crew, CNN's Levin. When SIPA instructed me to get out, Rachel and I talked about it and we decided I should go. We didn't want to be separated but she had back-up. I had none. And we knew that I'd never be able to rely on hers because she'd had to keep our relationship a secret from her superiors.

'So I left. Paris first, then New York, where I

waited for a new assignment. At first I was relieved. But by the time I reached New York I was desperate to get back. Like you, I fell off the wagon. In the end, I was away for less than ten weeks. The moment that shitty MEA 707 hit the ground I was home.'

'Did you tell your agency you were going back?'

'No. I left them. I was independent. Like you. And also like you, I found it liberating. But it turns out I was already marked.'

'How?'

'Two weeks before I left Beirut we went to see an Islamic Jihad leader in Bourj al-Barajneh, one of Beirut's slums. There was the usual bullshit security; boys hanging around with AK-47s, acting all aggressive. Anyway, they were the ones who kidnapped me when I returned.'

'They must have thought they'd missed their chance when you left for Paris.'

'Yes.'

'And that they'd won the lottery when you came back.'

'Except I was an invalid ticket.'

'Why?'

'I was an American but I had no value. I wasn't supposed to be there. So nobody cared. I was just some idiot who got caught up in something. But that's not the way it played out.'

'How come?'

'They interpreted the fact that nobody knew I was there differently.'

She understood immediately. 'They thought you were undercover.'

'That's right.'

She thought of his scars when she asked, 'How long did it take for them to find out that you weren't?'

'I don't remember.'

'How did it happen?'

'I was driving on the airport road, going to collect a friend of ours. A Lebanese guy coming in from Jordan. The airport road was a favoured hijack point but I was driving a borrowed car so I didn't expect a problem. Anyway, suddenly these guys appeared in the road, pointing guns at me. I knew if I stopped I was in serious trouble so I tried to drive out of it. They shot out the wheels and I crashed. They dragged me out of the wreckage and threw me into the trunk of a Datsun. When they closed the trunk that was the last daylight I saw in a year.'

The train began to slow. They were approaching Munich.

'Do you know where you were held?'

'All over. Tyre and Sidon. Beirut itself. The Bekaa Valley. Usually in a basement or cellar. Always tied to something solid. When they moved me, they'd tape my arms to my body, like I was in a strait-jacket. Then the ankles, the knees and finally the mouth and eyes. They'd leave a slit in the tape so I could breathe through my nose. Then they'd toss me in the back of a vehicle and drive like crazy. Every time I was transferred I got bruised and cut. But I was used to that. After a while, it doesn't really register. Like the beatings. You find you slip into some kind of catatonic state. You feel the pain and yet you don't feel it, not the same way you're used to feeling pain.'

'Were you with any other hostages?'

'Twice. Once in the Bekaa. He was a German. And once in Baalbek. He was Dutch. Both times, it was a few days. The first time could've been longer. I'm not sure. I wasn't in great shape.'

Their imminent arrival was announced as the train slowed to running pace.

'Why did they release you?'

'I've thought about that so often and I honestly don't know. By then, they knew I wasn't worth anything. The only conclusion I can come to is that they couldn't be bothered to kill me. I don't think I was worth the bullet and no one wanted to do it any other way.'

'How long were you held?'

'Twenty-two months and nine days.'

'And afterwards?'

Robert rose out of his seat as the train shuddered to a halt. 'What afterwards? The damage was done.'

It was already dark when the train pulled out of Munich: 17.23. They crossed into Austria and stopped soon after at Salzburg, then later at Linz. The American tourists who shared their six-seat compartment as far as Salzburg tried to engage them in conversation but Stephanie and Newman repaid them with French and haughty incomprehension. After Salzburg, they were alone.

'The people you went after,' Newman said, 'were they political?'

'In the sense that terrorists are political – yes.'

'Were they all terrorists?'

'Nearly all. Or criminals with terrorist associations. Financiers, lawyers – there were a few of those.'

'Any from al-Qaeda?'

'Not directly. But there have been one or two Islamist terrorists.'

'How do you feel about that? The whole Muslim thing.'

'Much the same way I feel about the whole Jewish thing. Despondent. But when I was working, I never let that get in the way.'

'Really? There weren't times when you thought you were doing the world a favour?'

'I understand what you're saying. But I never let myself see it in those terms. I like to think I was like a lawyer with an unpleasant client.'

'Okay. But if you had to kill a suicide-bomber just before they detonated . . .'

'Bad example.'

'Why?'

'If I felt anything for a suicide-bomber it would be pity.'

'You don't buy it?'

'Not at all. Martyrdom isn't sacrifice. Not if you believe that your life has no worth. Not if you profess to love death. Then martyrdom becomes a fast-track to an easier, more pleasurable existence. Where's the heroism or bravery in that? In fact, if you accept that your reward will be an eternity in Paradise in the company of seventy-two virgins, then that seems like no sacrifice at all. That reduces suicide-bombing to an act of naked self-interest. The criminals are the manipulators. The clerics, the teachers, the ones who call for martyrs but who lack the conviction to lead by example.'

'But they're mostly volunteers, the bombers.'

'Makes no difference. They're still manipulated, no matter what they think. You should see the few who don't go through with it and aren't then killed by their minders. They're disorientated. There's no religious fervour, no sense of certainty. They feel guilt and shame but are too confused to know why. It's mind-control, just like they use in cults. The same techniques, the same victims.'

'That sounds pretty cynical to me.'

'It's a cynical business. Not even the Koranic glimpse of Paradise is immune.'

'What do you mean?'

'It's a matter of dialect and translation. Depending on the tradition of interpretation, seventy-two virgins in Paradise could in fact be seventy-two pieces of exotic fruit. It's all in the interpretation and more recent fanatical spin has tended towards the lurid.'

Newman considered this. 'I guess that would put a different spin on it.'

'Certainly. Can you imagine how disappointing that would be? You blow yourself up thinking you're going to spend eternity with a bevy of beauties but what you get instead is *Groundhog Day* with a fruit salad.'

Stephanie was sorting through the pockets of her leather coat. She emptied them of everything except the Heckler & Koch: the bus ticket from Gare de Perrache to the airport; the Peugeot keys; the Saab keys; till receipts from *Le Chien Blanc* service station and the brasserie on place des Célestins; train tickets and loose change; the Tumi bag of cash; extra-strength Nurofen bought in Munich.

Newman said, 'I wonder how many were in the Range Rover.'

'It doesn't matter.'

'That the way it works in your world?'

'Yes. Absolutely. We're savages, Robert. Savages in suits, but still savages. Don't be fooled.'

He dropped the subject and looked at the items she'd spread across the table. He picked up the Peugeot car keys and examined the key-ring. 'At least we know how they found us.'

There were three tags on the key-ring: Peugeot, Nexus, Olympique Lyonnais.

Stephanie said, 'What am I looking at?'

'Nexus. A French car security firm. A microchip

concealed within the vehicle. As soon as it's reported stolen, the car can be traced by satellite.'

'I'm familiar with the technology, thank you. I just didn't expect it to be in that car. I deliberately picked an old vehicle.'

'Never underestimate a man's affection for machinery.'

'And now we've lost the computer.'

'Do we need it?'

'Perhaps not. Anyway, it's not all bad. If we'd got out of Obernai in one piece we wouldn't be safe. They'd still be following us. Taking the train has made us invisible again. For a while, anyway.'

It's been on my mind since our train pulled into Munich. 'When you said the damage was done, what did you mean?'

It takes him a moment to work out what I'm talking about. And another moment to decide whether he's prepared to tell me. 'Rachel was dead. I didn't find out at first. I got transferred to a base in Germany. Darmstadt. Nobody there knew anything. No one around me, no one I called. I only found out when I got back to New York.'

It's not a shock to hear it. He told me the star that burns twice as bright burns half as long. That's not an explanation for the end of a relationship. Even as he said it, I felt something in my stomach.

'How?'

He inhales slowly. And exhales slowly. 'Killed.'

'In Beirut?'

'Probably.'

'When?'

He looks at the carriage floor. 'Less than six months after my abduction.'

'She was abducted too?'

He nods. 'Three months after me.'

I can't possibly ask about the three months between.

'How'd you find out?'

'I was debriefed by the CIA when I got back to the States.'

That would be standard, under the circumstances.

He's still looking at the floor when he says, 'Turns out I was the one who betrayed her.'

'What do you mean?'

'I gave her up to them. At least, I guess I did.'

'You don't know?'

'It's what they said.'

'You won't get far in life believing anything that comes out of the CIA.'

'Maybe. But when I was being tortured, that's what they wanted to know. I was an American but not part of the regular press corps. That was the bone they clung to. It meant I was a spy. And that meant she was something too because they already suspected she wasn't part of the Spanish press.'

'This doesn't sound like your fault, Robert.'

Now he looks up at me. 'They sent her back to Israel in pieces. Literally.'

'Are you listening to me?'

He nods. 'You're right. I know you're right. But that

didn't change the way I felt about it back then. Or even now.'

'I understand.'

He looks dubious. 'Really?'

'I shot an innocent man once. The truth is I saved him from a worse death. That he would have died anyway is beyond question. You might call it a mercy killing. But it didn't feel like it. It felt like the most cold-blooded thing I've ever done. And believe me, as a single act of violence, that's up against some pretty stiff competition.'

Robert stares into the passing blackness. 'It's funny. I've never talked about this with anyone. Not my friends, not my family. No one.'

'I'm sorry. I shouldn't have pressed it.'

'It's okay. I wouldn't have answered if I hadn't wanted to. Or felt able to. I don't know. Maybe it's because . . . well, you know, you've been there. I don't know anybody else like that. Like you.'

'Believe me, that's a good thing.'

'Talking about it now – here with you – it feels like I'm talking about two people I heard about a long time ago.'

'I know that feeling too. My whole life feels like it belongs to someone else.'

'When I got back to the States I made the decision to change. I had to. I couldn't carry on thinking about what had happened. To her, to me. I needed a new life. Something completely different to the one I was having. And different to the one I'd always imagined.'

'A life in oil.'

He smiles. 'As it turns out, yes. Could have been in an investment house, or hotels, or steel. But it was in oil.'

'Not exactly the last bastion of the liberal altruist.'

'That's what made it so perfect.'

'Didn't any of the old instincts survive?'

'I guess they did. But I threw myself into it. And pretty soon I was so busy I didn't have time to think. And when I did, there was always something to distract me.'

'Something like Anna?'

'Yeah. And the ones before her. Then there was the money. The travel. The whole deal. It was very seductive.'

'Was?'

'Probably still is. I don't know. I've been a nomad for twenty years now. Physically and emotionally. I got used to it and then I liked it. So much, in fact, that I could never stand to be tied down.'

'After being tied up for two years, I'm not surprised.'

Talk about a joke in poor taste. To his credit, he doesn't take offence. After a moment's uncertainty, he actually laughs.

But not much.

Then he says, 'I don't know what's going to happen when this is over but my life won't be the same.'

'It probably could be.'

'Probably. But I don't think I want it to be. I've been everywhere, seen everything. I've made more money than I'll ever need. I've lost count of the beautiful lovers – I don't even remember half their names. Since I left

400

Lebanon I've had a great life but I still can't get the cedars out of my head.'

I know exactly what he's talking about. 'Why would you want to?'

We've taken a different route but we've arrived at the same destination.

I lean over and kiss him.

Vienna, 22:10.
The train pulled into Westbahnhof five minutes late. They decided to look for a cheap hotel close to the station. A stiff wind raked litter down Felberstrasse overlooking the rail-tracks. They settled for the Hotel Lübeck on Pelzgasse, its two-storey classical façade in ochre making a first impression that subsequent impressions couldn't match.

Their second-floor room looked on to the street. Stephanie drew heavy crimson curtains to preserve what little heat there was. The room was dominated by a large mahogany double-bed. They both pretended not to notice it, in a way that made Stephanie feel as gauche as a teenager. Although not the teenager she had ever been.

It had been comfortable in the train, cocooned in their own carriage, insulated from the freezing darkness outside. After the kiss, Newman had put his arm around her. For a while, neither had spoken. It hadn't felt awkward or contrived.

Stephanie turned on the light in the bathroom. Off-white mosaic tiles covered the floor and walls. Where pieces had come away the gaps had been

401

filled with poorly painted cement. The basin's enamel was stained green around the plug-hole. She took off her shirt then peeled away the soggy paper towels. Filaments of torn sutures protruded from the cut like monstrous eyelashes. In the mirror she saw Newman standing in the doorway.

'You were right,' she said. 'I need to see a doctor.'

'You could go to a hospital.'

'No.'

'Where are you going to find a doctor at this time of night?'

'I didn't say I needed to go now. Tomorrow will be fine.'

'Maybe we should get some food and rest.'

'We should. But I need to go out.'

'We only just got here.'

'There's someone I need to see.'

'Who?'

'A woman I know.'

'You want me to come?'

'I think it'd be better if I saw her alone.'

Later, as she headed for the door, Newman said, 'Who is she?'

'She's me,' Stephanie replied.

He didn't look surprised. 'Aren't they all?'

As soon as Gordon Wiley had been shown to his suite at the Imperial Hotel on Kärntner Ring, he ordered some room service, took a shower then made one phone call. Room service arrived;

smoked salmon, bread, a mixed salad, mineral water. He unpacked between mouthfuls, arranging the contents of his attaché case on the desk beside the window. Packing, unpacking, packing again; as a founder of the Amsterdam Group, travel had become as routine as brushing his teeth.

It hadn't always been so. Wiley had started out as a foreign policy adviser to Gerald Ford in 1975, stuffed behind a desk in an office with no window, earning $45,000 a year. Not a fortune, to be sure, but more than he'd needed since his dedication to the job consumed eighteen hours a day seven days a week. Time away from the office had been divided between sleep and marathon training. Not that he'd ever had the time to participate in a marathon.

The Amsterdam Group had been founded in 1983, just in time to catch the tidal wave of lever-aged buy-outs that had dominated that decade. From the start, though, Wiley had entertained grander ambitions. Quick profits and a dazzling lifestyle held no interest for him. He wanted longevity and solidity, to be outlived by his creation. He craved a reputation.

He was nauseated by the excess of the Eighties and took genuine pleasure from the fall and disgrace of men like Boesky and Milken. He loathed corporate extravagance. These days, when Wiley took one of Amsterdam's corporate jets, the justification for doing so was always economic; an equation that factored in time and money but not

403

prestige. Not unless prestige itself could be demonstrably converted into dollars and cents.

Amsterdam had been one of the first institutions to recruit former government officials to help deliver commercial patronage in areas under the direct control of federal government. The logic was simple: federal government is where the money is. More than anything, during the Reagan era, that had meant defence. Later, Amsterdam had moved into transport, technology, health care, energy and power, financial services and telecommunications. As the age of the leveraged buy-out imploded, Amsterdam had expanded into Europe, then Asia, recruiting only the most powerful and best-connected people in those regions. Acts of economic alchemy had then followed, transforming those connections into equity.

At ten-forty-five, he took the lift to the ground floor, crossed the marble lobby and entered the Maria Theresia bar. Paul Ellroy was waiting for him, his vast frame squeezed into a fragile nineteenth-century Viennese armchair. In front of him was a small circular table with a candle and the remains of a dry martini. A waiter came to take Wiley's order.

'Any single malt, no ice, still mineral water.'

His only alcoholic vice.

Ellroy ordered another dry martini and then said, 'You just got in?'

Wiley nodded. 'An hour ago. We put down in Paris this afternoon. I lit a few fires on avenue

404

Kléber then we flew here. What's the situation?'

'I spoke to Cabrini earlier. I told him how unhappy we are.'

Wiley looked around the bar for familiar faces and was surprised there weren't any. There were no spare rooms at the Imperial. Petrotech XIX had made sure of that. He'd expected at least one or two to be testing the tolerance of their expense accounts.

'Sayed and Fahad are asking questions. About Paris, about Golitsyn, about what went on in Alsace today. Five dead and one in custody?'

Ellroy was dismissive. 'Don't worry about it. Alsace is dealt with. It's a drugs story now. Turks and Albanians. No one wants to know.'

'What about the one in custody?'

'We've got a lawyer working on it right now. A real hot-shot.'

'And?'

'He's gonna make bail. Once he does, we'll deal with it.'

'The bigger picture is a concern.'

'I appreciate that. And I know it's tight. But we'll deal with that too.'

'You better. After Brand, they're nervous. And I can't say I blame them.'

'Like I said, when it's time to sign, everything will be fine.'

'Where's Reuter now?'

'Best guess: Germany.'

'Best guess?'

'After Sentier she was always going to be kind of . . . *elusive*.'

Wiley made no attempt to hide his alarm. 'So she could even be here? In Vienna?'

Ellroy laughed. 'That bitch is a lot of things but she ain't an idiot. Why would she be here? If she knew what was here, she'd make sure she was anywhere else.'

Day Ten

The taxi dropped her on a soulless stretch of Wagramer Strasse; car dealerships, UNO City in the distance, dreary hotels. A piercing wind ruffled the broad Danube. From the outside, Club Nitro lacked promise; a large concrete shack painted deep yellow, with a corrugated-iron roof. On top of it was a flashing neon sign: N-TRO. The letter 'I' was broken. The car-park, a patch of rough ground at the rear, was full.

The interior wasn't an improvement but the clientele didn't seem to mind, a curious mix of clubbers, drunks, pimps and pushers. It was very hot, the sour aroma of stale sweat seeping from the structure, cigarette smoke as thick as margarine. There were two bars, both crowded, all the tables taken. Again, Stephanie was surprised; it was such a desolate location. But when she looked more closely, an explanation emerged and brought with it a stab of weariness. Young girls, some beautiful, most bored, and older men, some selling, some buying; the Balkan infection, spreading everywhere unchecked. In the corners, where the management had thoughtfully provided only the dimmest of lighting, deals were swiftly negotiated and concluded.

Stephanie took a stool at the less busy of the two bars. The bartender – almost seven foot tall, a skeleton in a T-shirt with an emerald fuzz mohican – gravitated towards her, ignoring a parade of hands waving euros at him.

'What do you want?' he shouted over a booming Paul Oakenfold track.

'Vodka.'

'And?'

'Vodka.'

'Oh-la-la,' he said, with a surgical lack of enthusiasm. 'You alone?'

'Do I look alone?'

He gave an exaggerated glance over each of her shoulders. 'You shouldn't be. But I don't see anyone with you.'

'Then I guess I'm alone.'

'If you're looking for company I can help.'

'I'm looking for Petra.'

'Who?'

'Petra. About my height, about my build.'

'Don't know her.'

'She's my sister.'

'Still don't know her.'

Stephanie produced a print from the DVD for

him. He gave it a cursory glance, then took it for closer inspection into the cone of red light spilling from a spot above the bar.

'She never mentioned a sister.' It was impossible to tell whether he was too stupid to stop himself or simply too bored to carry on with the pretence. 'But I can see the resemblance. What did you call her?'

'What do *you* call her?'

'Julia. And she's not here.'

'You sure?'

'When she comes in she always says hello to me.'

'Aren't you the lucky one. You work here every night?'

'Six a week.'

'Know where I can find her?'

'That depends.'

'On?'

He offered her a lop-sided smile. The best thing about it were the gaps between the teeth. 'On whether you earn your favours the same way your sister does.'

'Hilarious.'

'I'm serious.'

The music changed to some euro hip-hop confection. Stephanie tried to look alluring. 'Well, I'm not her sister for no reason. I'm Maria.'

'Kurt.'

'When was she last here?'

'Three or four days ago.'

'How often does she come?'

'Considering you're her sister you don't seem to know her very well.'

'I don't live here. I live in Hamburg. I haven't seen her for a while.'

'No shit.'

'We fell out.'

'That's her speciality.'

'So, how often?'

'Depends. Sometimes three or four nights a week. Sometimes not for a month. You know how it is.'

They were interrupted by the sound of an empty bottle being smacked repeatedly against the bar. 'Hey, three beers here.'

'Fucking Albanians,' muttered Kurt. 'Monkeys in suits.'

'I need to find her, Kurt. Our mother's sick.'

'She told me her mother died when she was a child.'

Stephanie drilled him a sarcastic smile. 'She also told you her name was Julia.'

He looked left and right. 'I get off at two.'

'I can't wait.'

'Then I can't help you.'

Stephanie leaned across the bar. 'Don't they allow you five minutes for a cigarette break?'

Two minutes later, she was following him down a passage behind the bar. Crates of empty bottles were stacked along one wall, the waft of stale beer competing with the urinals for odour supremacy.

They entered a cold, cramped storage room by a fire-exit that had been welded shut. Kurt switched on the overhead light, a penetrating fluorescent tube, then closed the door.

Stephanie tried a pout. 'So, Kurt, where can I find her?'

He began to unbutton his khaki cargo pants. 'Afterwards.'

'Why not before? I promise I'll make it better for you.'

'Not a chance. Not if you're really Julia's sister.'

'We may be sisters but we're not the same.'

'In advance or you can fuck off.'

'Oh Kurt . . .'

Ninety seconds later, Stephanie was back on Wagramer Strasse, letting the freezing air purge Club Nitro from her lungs. Kurt was looking for the remains of two brown teeth on the storage room floor.

It was shortly before two when Stephanie entered their room at the Hotel Lübeck. Newman was asleep beneath the bedspread but above the sheets. His coat was draped over the chair by the window, his shoes and socks on the floor by the radiator. He lay on his side, his face to the far wall. For several moments she watched the slow rise and fall of his breathing.

In the bathroom was evidence of an excursion; a paper bag in the bin and a few items on the glass shelf over the basin. Shaving foam, a razor, toothpaste, a comb, *two* toothbrushes. The fact that hers was smaller and pink made her giggle. He'd also bought Band-aids, antiseptic cream and sterile tissues. She was touched by the gesture and amused by its inadequacy. The wound ached more than before. The time for makeshift medicine was coming to a close. She did her best to clean and dress the cut.

Newman hadn't drawn the bedroom curtains. Maybe he'd been waiting for her. She went to the window and watched a police car patrol Pelzgasse. She drew the curtains, shrugged off her coat, kicked off her shoes. She wanted to wake him but resisted. They were both short on sleep and she had nothing to say that couldn't wait.

She pulled off her jersey, unfastened the buttons of her jeans, let them drop then stepped out of them, leaving them on the floor. Wearing knickers and a T-shirt, she slipped beneath the sheets. They felt cold and brittle against her skin.

'Robert?' she whispered.

No response.

'Goodnight.'

Newman felt Stephanie shift beside him. He'd been asleep when she'd entered the room. He thought he might have heard her when she was in the bathroom but he wasn't sure. The sounds seemed to be mixed up with the dream he'd been having; he'd imagined he'd heard a faint trace of muffled laughter. Later, he'd been aware of her in the bedroom. Which was when he'd opened his eyes a little. She'd been stepping out of her jeans, her back to him.

He'd felt he should say something. But what, exactly? And perhaps now wasn't the moment, as she undressed for bed. She thought he was asleep so why not fuel the illusion? Besides, morning would bring clarity.

'Robert?'

He almost replied.

'Goodnight,' she whispered.

He mouthed it back to her. Half an hour later he was still awake.

The first thing she became aware of was the weight of his hand. The second was its location: her right thigh. She opened her eyes. He hadn't moved much but she had; she'd crept closer to him in the night, kicking off most of the bedding.

For a while, she lay there, happy for the physical contact. It was seven-fifteen. She could hear traffic outside. Someone walked past their room, whistling tunelessly.

She thought about the kiss on the train. It had felt natural. Now, the following morning, she thought it might feel awkward. It depended on him. For her, there were no regrets, which was a surprise. In their place was a question: what happens now?

When he rolled on to his side, dragging his hand with him, Stephanie got up. She wondered what it was like to lose someone like Rachel. Someone who could cast a twenty-year shadow. Who, in all probability, would cast a shadow as long as Newman lived.

Dorotheergasse, a narrow curve of street favoured by antiques dealers at the heart of the *Innere Stadt*. The sign above the shop looked decades old but Stephanie knew it was an art effect, a single word in gold German Gothic script on black wood: Kleist.

The shop shimmered. Standard lamps, hanging bowls, table lamps, chandeliers, sconces, candle lights, all of them on. A jungle of light, the dense refracted undergrowth generating a suffocating heat; horizontal surfaces were overgrown with lamp bases, the ceiling masked by vines of cable.

An elderly couple stood by the small table at the back of the shop talking to Bruno Kleist. He'd lost weight in the years since Stephanie had last seen him. Now he was almost as slender as he'd been in the days of the dreaded Stasi. Stephanie had seen photographs of him from that era; athletic-looking, straight dark hair cut short and neatly combed, deep-set hazel eyes.

In his Stasi prime, Kleist had controlled an espionage network that had covered western Europe. Stephanie had been in school at the time. While Kleist had run agents out of Paris and Bonn, Stephanie had smoked stolen cigarettes in the school cloakroom between classes.

At the time of Josef Kanek's assassination in London, Stephanie's main concern had been which boyfriend to choose. Popular Stephen Calder or unpopular Bernd Hass? An easy choice, in the end. Recently arrived at school and German, Hass had been an easy target for the other boys. Going out with him had irritated more of them than Stephanie had expected, which thrilled her. But when it turned out that Hass was a superb footballer, his popularity soared and her interest in him waned. By that time, Bruno Kleist had moved to Moscow for six months to let the Kanek affair blow over.

He'd been one of the Stasi's most effective agents, forging his reputation during the Seventies in Poland, Czechoslovakia and Hungary, before moving west in 1981. By 1989, few were as well positioned to take advantage of the coming chaos.

Stephanie watched him talking to the couple. His thinning snow-white hair was plastered to a scalp peppered with liver spots. A pair of tortoiseshell half-moon glasses hung from a blue ribbon around his neck.

Nobody from the Stasi had bleached their past from the collective record as thoroughly as Kleist following the collapse of the Communist regime in East Germany. And no former Stasi operative had profited quite so rapaciously in the confused years that followed. Kleist had seen the disintegration coming and had decided not to let three decades of state servitude go to waste. In the final days of the regime, he'd plundered Stasi archives. Not in the manner of a casual looter, though. He'd been more like a surgeon, expertly excising specifically targeted material.

The shop on Dorotheergasse was a retirement gift to himself. A passion indulged. After a lucrative decade in the private sector, Kleist had retired, opting for a quiet life in Vienna, immersed in the consuming love of his life: antique lights.

Since his retirement, Stephanie had visited him on one other occasion. He'd been wary of her at first, knowing her to be a client of Stern's. Stern and Kleist had been competitors, although in vastly different ways. Kleist had always dealt with his clients face to face. None of Stern's clients had ever met him. Kleist's openness had made him vulnerable to the ghosts of the past which, perversely, had worked to his advantage. In the twisted world of the information broker, it had bestowed upon him a reputation for reliability.

I'm an easy man to find.

That had been his catchphrase. In a business where most people hid, Kleist had been happy to stay in the open. It was a gamble that had paid off. Except once, when the past had collided with the present in order to extinguish the future. The doctors treating his bullet wounds hadn't expected him to survive. Six months later, having confounded them, he decided to quit.

The couple thanked Kleist and left. Stephanie

stepped forward. Kleist saw her and said, 'I'm sorry but we're closing.'

Not so much as a flicker. As though they'd never met.

She smiled coldly. 'That's not what the sign on the door says.'

'I have to go out.'

'We won't take much of your time.'

'I don't think I have anything you could possibly want.'

'With so many tasteful things in one room? Why don't you let me be the judge of that?' Then, in English, Stephanie said to Newman, 'Lock the door, will you?'

'Please leave,' Kleist snapped.

'Don't worry. We will. Very soon.'

Despite himself, anger succumbed to anxiety. 'What are you doing here?'

'I'm a customer, Bruno. Like anyone else who comes through that door.'

He pulled a pained face. 'I think about you, Petra. From time to time. I think how nice it would be to see you again.'

'How touching.'

'Then I remember. And I think no, it wouldn't be. Not at all.'

'If I was a different kind of girl, I might take offence.'

'Who's your friend?'

'He's . . . a lawyer.'

'Can he understand us?'

'He doesn't speak German.'

'Since when did the great Petra Reuter feel the need to resort to a lawyer?'

'I need *your* help, Bruno.'

'I thought you were one of Stern's.'

'Not any more. I got set up.'

'By Stern?'

'Yes.'

Kleist looked dubious. 'Are you sure?'

'I wouldn't be here if I wasn't.'

'Why?'

'Money.'

'You know that for certain?'

'I know that everything Stern does is motivated by money.'

Kleist considered this. 'It seems the environment has altered since I left. It was a more respectable business when I . . .'

'Save the sermon, Bruno. Poisoning Kanek in London? He took four days to die. It's always been a revolting business. New allegiances evolve, old ones dissolve. That *is* the environment. Always has been.'

'What do you want?'

'The face behind Stern.'

'You don't think it was his idea?'

'No. That would make it personal. Stern doesn't do personal. Somebody paid him to set me up. I need to know who and I need to know why.'

He was more relaxed now. He began to play

with his half-moon glasses. 'I'm not sure how much help I can be to you.'

'They're coming at me from every angle, Bruno. I'm blind.'

'And I'm retired.'

'That makes you an amateur instead of a professional. But you're still an easy man to find.'

The phrase made him smile. Nostalgia, perhaps. Then he remembered where he was. 'Only if you want a nineteenth-century French chandelier.'

'Come on, Bruno.'

'I don't have the contacts these days.'

'The Oracle doesn't talk to anybody any more? I find that hard to believe.'

'Why? Because you assume I found it hard to leave the life behind?' The remark slipped between her ribs and Kleist noticed. 'Do you never think of the after-life, Petra?'

'All the time.'

'Take it from someone who's tasted it. All the stuff that seemed so important before falls away.'

'To be replaced by old lights?'

Kleist chuckled. 'Yes. Exactly. Old lights.'

'I ran into a friend of yours not long ago. Otto Heilmann.'

She saw that he was about to deny all knowledge of Heilmann, before realizing how stupid that would sound. They had risen through the ranks of the Stasi together. Two shooting stars on parallel trajectories.

'Where?'

'Near St Petersburg.'

'I'd heard he was in Russia these days. How was he?'

'Strangely lifeless.' She let the answer gnaw a little before qualifying it: 'Although not at first. No, then he was in rude health. But by the time we parted . . .'

Kleist licked parched lips. 'Well, the path he took after we went our separate ways was quite different to mine.'

'Not that different, Bruno.'

'Look . . .'

'The contract came through Stern.'

'So?'

'It doesn't worry you that a former competitor is trading contracts for Stasi veterans?'

'A coincidence.'

'Someone I used to know told me that in our business a coincidence is an oversight.'

'Who?'

'Doesn't matter. He's dead. Like Otto.' She stepped closer to Kleist. 'Now, are you going to help me or not?'

I'm sitting on a treatment bench in a cramped room with no windows and grey-green walls, on the third floor of an anonymous block on Wallensteinstrasse, close to Nordwestbahnhof. This is the Fischer Clinic, although calling it a clinic lends it a veneer of sophistication it doesn't deserve.

Dr Rudolph Fischer was Kleist's response to a request

for a discreet doctor. No questions asked, he assured me. Wounds treated, abortions administered, pharmaceuticals dispensed. Anything you like for cash.

It takes him half an hour to treat the cut properly. He watches me dress, making no attempt to conceal his pleasure. I can't be bothered to react. In the adjoining office, where Robert has been waiting, I hand over the cash and pocket the drugs.

We return the way we came, stopping to buy clean clothes from a row of shops close to Franz-Joseph-Bahnhof. Then we catch a cab back to the Hotel Lübeck.

Robert says, 'You think Kleist'll come up with something on Butterfly?'

That was one of the things I asked.

'Possibly. He used to be very good. Stern rated him.'

'Who is Stern?'

'Someone I thought I could trust.'

'Past tense?'

'As far as I'm concerned.'

'But not dead?'

'Why should he be dead?'

'Sounds like the two of you fell out.'

'I don't kill everyone I disagree with, Robert. If I did, this continent would be littered with bodies. Tax officials, politicians, Parisian waiters. Who knows where it would end? Even you.'

'I doubt that.'

'You seem very sure of yourself.'

'I've never been less sure of myself. But I'm starting to feel sure about you.'

* * *

They changed into fresh clothes and left the hotel. The Austria Center Vienna sat between the skyscrapers of Donau City and the United Nations headquarters. It was a large hexagonal conference centre spread over four colour-coded levels. As Stephanie and Newman approached the main entrance, workmen were erecting a large sign overhead. The background was black, the letters blood red.

PETROTECH XIX
THEIR FUTURE IN OUR HANDS

On fluttering banners that fell either side of the entrance were the conference dates – three days starting tomorrow – and a long list of sponsors.

They walked into the cavernous main entrance. Gleaming stone floor, bright light everywhere, escalators directly ahead, no security. They were ignored by those at the main reception desk. Builders and technicians scurried past them. Half the stands in the entrance hall were incomplete.

To their left was a long counter of desks; tickets, transport, information, hotel and restaurant reservations, messages, groups, companies. Newman went to the last desk. A bored woman in a blue suit was shuffling paper.

He gave her a practised smile. 'Have you got a list of exhibitors?'

'Are you accredited?'

'I'm press. I just want the information-pack.'

'One moment, please.'

She disappeared.

Stephanie said, 'Very impressive.'

'Not if you've been before.'

The woman returned and handed him a slim black plastic folder with the same scarlet lettering that had been on the sign outside. They decided to look around. No one asked them what they were doing. The place was busy, a dozen languages to the ear.

The red level was the uppermost floor of the complex and housed a huge auditorium. The seating had been converted to a parliamentary format. Newman checked the programme. There were three debates scheduled, one for each day of the conference. The three topics were predictable: the relationship between the oil services industry and the environment; the relationship between the oil services industry and the political background in those areas where the industry was most prominent; the future of the oil services industry.

Spread over the three levels below – green, yellow and blue – was a mixture of conference rooms, offices and large foyers. Scheduled events included public discussion forums and private meetings, lectures and sponsored sales pitches. The open spaces were cluttered with corporate stands.

The colour-coded levels meant something to Stephanie but she couldn't remember why. The harder she concentrated, the further the answer receded. As they headed for the exit, she noticed a coffee shop to the right. They went in, ordered two cappuccinos and sat down at a table.

Newman said, 'I think I know how we could get some accreditation.'

'How?'

'Abel Kessler.'

Stephanie shook her head. 'Remind me.'

'He was one of the guys who left a message on my answer-phone in Paris.'

'So?'

'He said he was coming to Europe for ten days. Said he wanted to meet me in Paris. Hoped I was still seeing what's-her-name.'

Stephanie remembered now. 'Go on.'

Newman opened the press pack and sorted through a sheaf of papers, two brochures and a stack of inserts. He found what he was looking for inside the back of one of the brochures.

'Abel works for a firm of maritime lawyers in Singapore. He specializes in oil transport. They always take a stand at Petrotech. If he's in Europe this'll be one of the reasons.'

He showed her the full-page advert. McGinley Crawford, founded in Houston in 1937, now based in Washington DC, with twenty-four offices spread across the United States, Europe and Asia.

'I could call him,' Newman suggested.

'That might not be a good idea.'

'I know what you're thinking. But I'm about

the only person he knows in Paris. No one's going to make the link. Anyhow, I could go through his office in Singapore. Get his cell. Then call him from a payphone here.'

Stephanie ran through it in her mind. 'Okay. But not *right* here. Somewhere else in the city.'

The address Kurt had provided at Club Nitro was off Mexikoplatz by the Reichsbrücke; an area of dismal shops peddling counterfeit watches, cheap kitchenware and cut-price clothing. Despite the persistent cold drizzle, the pavement was busy with Russians, Albanians, Serbs. Stephanie and Newman circled the square once, then paused outside Krystyna, a shop offering tacky china figurines, before circling a second time. Stephanie understood the glances they attracted as clearly as the snippets of Russian; this part of town was not Vienna. It was somewhere further east, south and north. Anywhere but west.

Julia's address was a four-storey pistachio building on the corner of Engerthstrasse, above the Aktionsmarkt discount store. The apartment was on the third floor, halfway along a corridor with dark brown walls and a flecked black linoleum floor. Stephanie rang the buzzer three times and knocked twice. There was no reply. She pressed her ear to the door; silence inside. She looked at the lock and ran a finger over it, then placed both palms on the door and pressed. It moved but didn't open. Along the corridor

425

another door opened, just wide enough for a face to fill the gap.

'She's not there.'

Beginner's German uttered by a small woman with the complexion of a walnut. She wore a headscarf with a mauve and magenta floral print. From behind her came a chorus of squabbling children.

'Do you know where she is?'

The woman shook her head. 'She comes. She goes. Different times. Different days.'

'Do you know when she'll be back?'

'Later.'

'Today?'

'Yes. Maybe.'

'What time?'

'Don't know.'

'When did you last see her?'

She shrugged. 'The day before yesterday. The day before that. I don't remember.'

Stephanie felt a shiver; she was alive, it seemed.

'Do you know her?'

The woman closed the door.

'Tell me about Petra.'

'What?'

'Kleist called you Petra. Several times.'

They were eating in the Café Bräunerhof on Stallburggasse. It was a sedate place, especially now, at two-thirty, with most of the lunch-hour crowd back at work. Curtains over the lower windows shielded diners from the street. The lunchtime mist of cigarette smoke had yet to dissipate. Conversations were sprinkled with the clink of cutlery. A waiter brought clean glasses and a carafe of water.

'Well, well,' Stephanie murmured, 'what else did you pick up?'

Newman looked a little surprised. 'Mostly everything.'

'I didn't think you spoke German.'

He turned to the waiter and said, in German, 'What's the special today?'

'Cauliflower soup then chicken and rice.'

'That would be fine. And a beer. Ottakringer, if you have it.'

Stephanie ordered the soup followed by spaghetti with ham zucchini, and a bottle of sparkling mineral water. When the waiter had left them she said, 'You never said anything.'

'You never asked.'

'Did I really need to? We've been in German-speaking territory since yesterday morning.'

'And the only conversation I've had has been with you. Anyway, as you can tell, my German's not that good.'

'But good enough. Any more surprises?'

'I think I should be asking that. First Claudia, then Marianne, then Stephanie, now Petra.'

'That's different.'

'Sure is. Not disclosing bad German is a lapse. Operating under three different names seems more serious.'

'Don't be cute, Robert. You know what I do.'

Newman nodded. 'But what's the deal with Petra?'

'What do you mean?'

'Who's being cute now? *The great Petra Reuter*. That was the phrase Kleist used.'

The waiter brought bread. When he'd gone Stephanie said, 'My entire career – if that's what you want to call it – has been based on a lie called Petra Reuter.'

'How?'

'She never existed. She was a role created for me.'

'You never did any of the things you said you did?'

'Don't get me wrong. As Petra, I've done plenty of stuff. But her history – her *reputation* – all of it was manufactured. Like some second-rate boyband.'

Their drinks arrived. Stephanie swallowed some antibiotics and painkillers. Newman took a piece of bread from the basket and watched Stephanie, who looked over both shoulders and then at the remaining diners. Next to them, an elderly man leant across the table to offer a light to a younger woman. His hand shook. The woman had to hold it to steady the flame. For a moment she saw a younger version of herself with Albert Eichner.

'You okay?' Newman asked.

'I'm fine. Why?'

428

'You look kind of . . . *sad*.'

She peered into her glass, watching the bubbles rise. 'Actually, I'm scared.'

'That's not what it looks like.'

'That's Petra for you. But she's disintegrating. I'm not the woman she once was. I don't feel in control. I'm not even sure I want to be in control. I just want to . . . *stop*.'

The waiter placed two steaming bowls of soup before them.

'Isn't that why you're here? Why *we're* here. To make it stop?'

She nodded and began to eat.

'What are you not telling me, Stephanie?'

'Nothing. Forget it.'

After their main courses, Newman went to the washroom and then found a payphone. By the time he returned to the table, two cups of espresso had arrived.

'Any luck?' Stephanie asked.

'Yes. Abel Kessler is here in Vienna. He's arranged accreditation for us through McGinley Crawford.'

'Good.'

'It gets better. He's asked us to the pre-conference reception. Before Petrotech opens there's always a reception. Invitation only, very select. It's at the Hotel Bristol, tonight at seven.'

'Who did you say I was?'

'An associate.'

'Not Anna again, I hope.'

'Not this time.'

The Hotel Bristol. Why did that sound familiar? Stephanie sensed it had something to do with the colour-coded levels of the Austria Center. But how were the two connected?

It was after five when they arrived back at the Hotel Lübeck. After Café Bräunerhof they'd gone shopping on Graben for clothes better suited to a reception at the Hotel Bristol. They'd paid for them with Scheherazade Zahani's diminishing cash reserve.

Newman kicked off his shoes and lay on the bed. 'I'm going to sleep. Wake me in half an hour.'

Stephanie decided to take a shower. She water-proofed the new sutures and spent ten minutes cleansing herself. Afterwards, she stood in the wet heat. Gradually, the steam began to clear from the mirror. Now the cut had been treated it was the bruises that caught the eye. Across her stomach, encircling her cosmetic scar, down her right thigh.

She looked at herself and thought of Julia. It helped to have a name. She wondered whether the apartment overlooking Mexikoplatz was a true home, or just another dressed set like the apartment at Stalingrad.

Who was Julia? Or would she turn out not to be Julia? Would Julia be no more real than Marianne? Nothing more than an airlock between two identities, one genuine, one artificial. Now

430

that Stephanie knew she was alive, she wasn't sure how much she wanted to find her. Was this how the adopted child felt before the reunion with the blood parent? Simultaneously keen and reluctant?

She dried herself and brushed her teeth. There was a tightness in her stomach that left her slightly nauseous. The thought that continued to form felt alien. Her life had been governed by regime. Even her instincts were a product of conditioning, which was why it took her time to recognize it for what it was: the threat of spontaneity. A similar sensation to the one she'd experienced on the train the moment before she'd kissed him, but greatly amplified.

Her knickers and T-shirt were on the bathroom floor. She stepped over them and entered the bedroom.

She sat on the edge of the bed. He opened his eyes, saw she was naked, and didn't react at all. She started to unbutton his shirt. He looked a little uncertain. She ran a hand across his chest and stomach, against muscle and sinew that weren't immune to age, and across scar tissue that was; it hadn't softened with time. Then she saw that Newman was looking at *her* scars.

He said, 'I thought I was the only one.'

She shook her head. 'We're everywhere. We move among the flawless, undetected. Until we're naked. And then we're *really* naked.'

She kissed him. On the train, there had been

431

poignancy. Here, on the bed, it was surprisingly tentative.

'Touch me,' she whispered.

'Wait,' he murmured. 'Is this a good idea?'

She put a finger to his lips. 'Robert, I just want to make love with you. No strings, nothing complicated.'

It's dark outside. And inside. We haven't bothered with the lights. We lie together, our bodies gently cooling, relying on the grubby excess of the streetlamps. I look at my watch. It's six, an hour until the Petrotech reception starts.

'Do they bother you?' I ask, softly.

'What?'

'Your scars. Don't they take you back?'

'Not any more. Twenty years of the high life have eased the pain.'

I'm not sure I believe him. 'Did you ever consider doing something about them?'

'Like what?'

'I don't know. Cosmetic surgery, maybe . . .'

'That's just another kind of scar. Anyway,' he says, touching the ruined tissue on my left shoulder, 'you should talk.'

'This scar is cosmetic.'

'What do you mean?'

I explain it to him.

'Well, there you go,' he concludes. 'My point proved.'

'How?'

'Cosmetic surgery is a lie. I don't want to live like that.'

'You're right,' I concede. 'It eats away at you.'

'I don't like the scars but they're part of me. And I'm okay with that.'

'Then I envy you. For being comfortable with the way you are.'

'It wasn't always like this. It took time.'

'Don't they ever make you feel self-conscious? Mine are insignificant next to yours but there are times when I really detest them.'

'I'm only really aware of them when other people react to them.' He smiles a little awkwardly. 'Of course, if you're naked, that can make it worse. There've been one or two who found them hard to get used to. There was also one who said she found them sexy.'

I pull a face. 'How long did she last?'

'She didn't make it to breakfast.'

I giggle, then land the sucker punch. 'What about Scheherazade Zahani?'

'What about her?'

'Was she one of them?'

'Why?'

'I was thinking about her. Actually, I was thinking about the way we met. And trying to think of what might have happened if it had been different.'

'And she fits into that how?'

'She doesn't. Not in my new version. She's just an interloper from reality.'

'So how do you see us now?'

'We meet on a plane. Which means we're confined but not like in your apartment. It's something more natural,

433

more . . . organic. *It goes from there. A chance meeting.'*

'The Lancaster *was a chance meeting,'* Robert points out.

'But we're dropping that. This is the new version. Where we talk like normal people. By the time we get to our destination we agree to meet for a drink and trade phone numbers.'

'That's it?'

'No. Then we decide to share a taxi into town from the airport.'

'Which town?'

'It doesn't matter. Any town.'

'You have to make it real. Pick one.'

'Okay. Madrid. Or Nice. Wait – no – make it New York.'

'Why New York?'

'The traffic. It takes for ever to get to Manhattan from JFK.'

'So?'

'More time together in the taxi.'

'Ah.'

'And then, when we get there, we decide not to wait for that drink.'

'Sounds nice.'

'It could have happened like that for us.'

Robert considers it. 'I guess so.'

'We'd have stood a chance, too.'

'We're not dead yet, Stephanie.'

'Not yet.'

The pause that follows is filled only by the applause of the rain.

'Anyway,' he says, *'the longer the odds, the better the pay-out.'*

A string quartet was playing in one corner. Beneath glittering chandeliers the Hotel Bristol's staff dispensed Krug 1985 and canapés. Stephanie reckoned there were one hundred and fifty guests in the Festsaal. Less than one in ten were female. Newman took two glasses from a passing waitress, handed one to Stephanie and guided her into the gathering.

'Robert – there you are!'

He was a short man with tight black curls oiled to a scalp that grew visible towards the very top. Thick, tinted lenses couldn't conceal a slight squint.

Newman shook his hand. 'Abel. Good to see you. It's been a while.'

'Most certainly. Jakarta, two years ago, I think.'

'Actually, it was Kuala Lumpur. The Grand Prix. Petronas?'

'Of course. How could I forget?'

'This is Marina Schrader. Marina, meet Abel Kessler.'

Newman and Kessler started trading news. Stephanie drifted away from them. She recognized a few faces among the strangers. Albert Raphael, for one, the Canadian newspaper baron who'd recently become an American citizen. His wife, the socialite and self-appointed intellectual Paula Kray, stood beside him. They were talking to

Richard Rhinehart. Newman had told her that Rhinehart was a member of the Pentagon's Defense Policy Board and a leading light at the American Partnership Foundation. Stephanie now remembered that Albert Raphael had appeared on the list of Amsterdam directors she'd seen.

'Hi. I'm Elizabeth Weil. I don't believe we've met.'

She had heavy features and a mouth even more luscious than Stephanie's. Her beautiful cream-coffee skin was made for gold. Stephanie felt dour beside her.

Weil said, 'I think I know every other woman in the room.'

'I'm Marina Schrader. How do you do?'

'Could be better. Could be somewhere else,' she said, her voice a gentle purr, the accent East Coast American. 'I hate these things, don't you?'

'So how come you're here?'

Weil swept thick black hair out of large anthracite eyes. 'I'm taking part in a debate tomorrow. Then I'm scheduled to deliver a paper the day after.'

'At Petrotech?'

'Where else?'

'What's your subject?'

'The curse of oil.'

'That sounds like a humorous topic. What do you actually do?'

'A question my accountant always asks. I guess I'm an academic. That's what people say.

Or a freeloader, depending on your point of view. I work for the Potomac Institute in Washington.'

'I'm afraid I haven't heard of it,' Stephanie lied.

Weil's definition varied from Newman's. 'Basically, we promote the export of responsible democracy.'

'*Responsible* democracy? You mean, like having one glass instead of the whole bottle?'

She considered the comparison for a moment. 'Actually, that's a pretty accurate representation of what we believe in. Especially in those areas of the world that hold our attention.'

'Which areas would they be?'

'Primarily the Middle East and Asia. What do you do, Marina?'

Stephanie had an answer ready. 'I'm a lady of leisure.'

Weil laughed. 'I wouldn't say that in this room. You'll see a lot of men reaching for their wallets.'

'I'm an investor. A *private* investor.'

'In this environment that's a quick way to make friends.'

They talked for an hour and laughed more than those around them. Stephanie allowed Weil to feed on a sense of solidarity that didn't exist. But she liked her and could see why Weil felt isolated. The other women in the room looked humourless; career addicts too busy to know they were miserable.

People gravitated towards Weil to pay their

respects or to flirt: Brian Grabel, a senior executive with Halliburton; Azzam Fahad, number two at the Iraqi Oil Ministry; Lauren Dougherty, an executive with Bechtel; Jean-Claude Fernandez, owner of a French construction firm.

At nine Weil said, 'I'm afraid I have to go. I have a dinner at the American Embassy and I'm very late. It's been a pleasure meeting you, Marina. If you hadn't been here, I'd have been on time for the ambassador.'

'Glad to be a hindrance.'

'Will you be at Petrotech tomorrow?'

'I expect so.'

'If you're around in the afternoon come to the debate. It should be lively.'

'If I'm around, I will.'

Weil handed Stephanie her business card. 'I'll write it on the back for you. Hall D, Blue Level, 15:30.'

Stephanie didn't really notice Weil's farewell or departure. Instead, she stared at what was written on the card and knew that she'd seen it before.

Leonid Golitsyn.

His name was a prompt. The colour-coded levels of the Austria Center. The Hotel Bristol. She'd seen these details together. Slowly, it came back to her, from the apartment on quai d'Orléans in Paris, four or five days ago. A note from a travel agent, an itinerary. A private aircraft – Moscow-Vienna-Moscow – and a reservation for a penthouse suite at the Bristol. She couldn't remember how long Golitsyn had been booked in for.

There had been brochures with the itinerary. She could only recall the content of one: Mir-3, a new drone for oil pipelines designed by a Russo-French company whose name escaped her.

There had also been a brief schedule attached; three items, each with a colour-code, each with a time. And although she couldn't swear that 'Hall D, Blue Level, 15:30' had been one of them, in her bones, she knew it had been.

She found Newman, who was still talking to Abel Kessler, made an excuse and left. She returned to the Lübeck, collected the gun and walked to the U-Bahn, taking the U3 from Westbahnhof to Stephansplatz, then the U1 to Vorgartenstrasse.

Mexikoplatz was almost deserted. The rain had stopped but a bitter wind was blowing. By the time Stephanie reached the building on Engerthstrasse her fingers were already numb. She looked up at the pistachio façade. The lights were off.

The suffocating heat of the entrance hall was a pleasure. She took the stairs to the third floor. Using two short pieces of wire cut from a coat-hanger at the Lübeck she addressed the lock. She wasn't an expert but she didn't need to be; it took forty seconds to let herself in.

She pulled the Heckler & Koch from her coat. The music coming from the floor below was

Serbian pop. The kitchenette had a gas-boiler attached to the wall. A blue flame threw feeble light over an empty sink. There was no food in the fridge, just juice and Diet Coke. In the bedroom a blue check duvet was scrunched into a ball at one end of a single mattress. Dirty clothes covered the floor. An upturned cardboard box doubled as a bedside table. There was a German copy of *Vogue* on it, beside an empty pack of Marlboro Lights and five foil condom wrappers, four of them torn open. By one wall was a cheap black suitcase. Stephanie bent down to look inside – more dirty clothes – and noticed a book on the other side of the upturned box, its pages swollen by moisture. It was a Russian edition of a cheap horror novel called *Glittering Savages* by an English author she'd never heard of. There was a photograph between the damp pages.

An improvised bookmark or an attempt to conceal?

She examined the picture. Damp and age had distorted the colour. The edges were yellow and there was a strange purple glow over the centre of the photo, like a chemical bruise. But none of this distracted from the content.

Curiously, she wasn't shocked; it was almost a relief.

Konstantin Komarov, standing by a Mercedes outside the Hotel Baltschug. The hotel she had stayed in when she first went to Moscow. How long ago had that been? Four years? Five? She turned the photograph over.

Petra –

I love you. Today, tomorrow, for ever.

Don't forget.

Kostya.

It wasn't his writing. But it felt like it. Just to see the words written. A declaration of love from one phantom to another. Artificial in every way yet still capable of making a deep cut.

First Stalingrad, then the film, now here. Petra, the third woman, the link. But why the second apartment? Was it merely another stepping stone for the posthumous enquiry that should have been well under way by now?

She went into the living-room. Overall, the place seemed more like a home than Paris. There were coins on a coffee table and cartons of Chinese food, half-eaten. On the sofa was an out-of-date TV schedule and a bottle-green jersey with holes at the elbows. There were a dozen paperbacks on a DIY shelf, nine of them Russian, the others German.

She looked at the CDs. Bjork, Air, The Cardigans. Less of a plant than the music she'd found in Stalingrad. Unlike the letter she found among the mail stacked on top of the TV.

It was from Grumann Bank on Singerstrasse.

We are pleased to confirm the arrangements that you and I agreed upon yesterday. Should you

441

require further facilities here in Vienna, or in
Brussels, or further afield, we will be only too
happy to offer our services.
* Yours faithfully,*
* Gerhard Lander.*

The letter was addressed to Marianne Bernard.
But as Marianne Bernard, Stephanie had never
been to Austria. She checked the date – 4
December – then heard the scrape of metal against
metal.

A key sliding into a lock.

'Who are you? What are you doing here?'
Her hair was dyed black and cut in a bob.
Despite the night, a large pair of black sunglasses
masked a third of her face; she looked like a fly.
She wore a tartan mini-skirt, black tights, black
boots, black leather jacket. She clutched a brown
paper bag in her right hand, which was grazed
raw across the back. Crimson lipstick was plastered across a broad mouth.

Stephanie was standing in the kitchenette,
which had allowed the woman to close the front
door and move into the living-room before seeing
her. The gun was out of sight but in reach, just
behind the kettle.

'I said, what are you doing here?'
Stephanie stared into the curves of matt black
glass covering her eyes. 'Perhaps that's a question
I should be asking you.'

'Get out.'

'We need to talk.'

'How did you get in here?'

'What's your name?'

She reached into the brown paper bag.

Stephanie grabbed the gun from behind the kettle. 'I wouldn't if I were you.'

'Fuck!'

'Put the bag down. Slowly.'

'It's just some shit from the store.'

'Put it down.'

'I was reaching for cigarettes.'

'I don't want to shoot you in the hand. But I will. *Put . . . it . . . down.'*

She did so.

'Now take off your glasses.'

'Why?'

'It's the middle of the night.'

'So?'

'I'm not going to ask you again.'

She pulled them from her face and Stephanie felt a pang of guilt. The right eye was swollen, a broad palate of colours rising through the skin.

'What happened?'

'None of your business.'

'What's your name?'

'That's none of your business either.'

'The quicker you answer the questions the quicker I'll leave. But I'm not going until I have my answers. And I'll get them one way or the other. So do both of us a favour. Now what's your name?'

'Petra.'

'Small world. So's mine.'

She looked at Stephanie more carefully and it began to sink in. She focused on the face first, then the rest. Similar-looking, similar build. In fact, more than similar. Her indignation melted away but there was no comfort in the comparison.

'Got any other names?' Stephanie asked.

'Julia. You?'

'One or two. But you can stick with Petra.'

'What are you doing here?'

'Take off your leather jacket.'

She did. Underneath she wore a grey polo-neck.

'Take that off too,' Stephanie said.

Julia hesitated, then said, 'I don't do women.'

'Is that right?'

'Not usually.'

'Take it off.'

'You gonna pay me?'

'No. But if you play your cards right I won't shoot you.'

Julia pulled the polo-neck over her head. She was wearing a cerise and black leopard-skin print bra. The scar was neat. A small rough circle on the left shoulder.

'Turn round.'

The exit wound was an exact copy of the entry wound. Amateur, but good enough for a clandestine film. Stephanie noticed other marks. A couple of large red welts, two bruises over the ribs, lateral scratch marks over the lower back.

444

Stephanie took off her coat, put the gun on the sideboard by the kettle, and pulled off her sweat-shirt, revealing her own bullet-wound through the left shoulder.

Julia whistled softly. 'Holy Mother . . .'

Stephanie pulled the sweatshirt back on. 'One of us is a fake. The other's a killer who got shot through the shoulder during a shoot-out with Belgian police about eight years ago. Do you know which one you are?'

Julia tried to muster a smile. 'Well . . . you're the one with the gun. Where'd you get the cuts and bruises?'

'France. Where'd you get yours?'

'Don't ask.'

'What about the scars?'

'An operation.'

'I'll let you into a secret. Me too.'

'I don't understand.'

'Sure you do. It's a question of false identity. Like appearing in a movie, pretending to be someone else.'

Julia shifted uncomfortably. 'Can I smoke?'

'Yes.'

'My cigarettes are in the bag.'

'Better show me first.'

She did. Three packs of Marlboro Lights, a bottle of vodka, some bread and a tube of Pringles. She tore the cellophane from the first pack and lit a cigarette, the ritual restoring some self-confidence.

Stephanie said, 'You can put your top back on, if you want.'

Julia pouted cheaply. 'Is that what *you* want?'

'Yes.'

'Another time, perhaps?'

She pulled on the grey polo-neck. She had a fuller figure than Stephanie's. The kind of figure Stephanie had once enjoyed over a long, idle summer. She'd been happy while it lasted but a strenuous training regime that autumn had reduced her to a muscular hardness that had stayed with her ever since.

Stephanie said, 'Why'd you agree to your operation?'

'Money. Why else?'

'You agreed to be scarred for money?'

Julia was contemptuous. 'I've been scarred for no money. So this was better.'

'That's nice.'

'Why did *you* agree?'

'I didn't. I wasn't given a choice.'

'How come?'

Stephanie ignored the question. 'How much money?'

'A lot. Enough to reverse most of the damage when the time comes. And plenty more.'

'Tell me how it happened.'

'I went to a clinic here in Vienna. The Verbinski. Do you know it?'

'No.'

'Doctor Müller had photographs of a woman –

you, I guess – and she matched the scars from the prints.'

'Did you get a look at the photos?'

'Sure.'

'And it was definitely me?'

'Yes. I mean, I guess so. This was back in October. I remember the face because it looked a lot like me. And like you, if you know what I mean. I didn't recognize the man, though.'

'What man?'

'The man you were fucking.'

Stephanie took a moment to try to sort through her thoughts. 'I was having sex with someone?'

Julia nodded. 'There were about six or seven prints, I think. And in most of them you were doing it. In the others it was just before or after. The point is, you were naked.'

'So you could see the scars?'

'Yes. Front and back. The quality wasn't great. I think they were stills taken from a film. They had that kind of grainy look.'

'But you could see enough?'

'Enough? Too much.'

What were the odds on another Petra clone with replicated scars? Almost beyond calculation. Yet how could it be her?

'If I'm honest,' Julia was saying, 'I was a little jealous.'

'Why?'

'The guy you were with – he was good-looking.

447

I wouldn't have said no. Not even with all those tattoos.'

Stephanie felt a chill thicken her blood. 'I'm sorry?'

'Normally I don't like tattoos. And I've never seen anyone covered the way your friend was. Not in the flesh, only in pictures. But I'd have gone with him.'

Komarov, again. First the note inserted in the book, now this. When she'd first met him he'd worn corporate armour; suits by Brioni, shirts from Brooks Brothers, ties by Hermès. But beneath the silk and cotton he'd worn his history across his skin. The tattoos that covered him were badges of honour from the years he'd lost to the Soviet penal system.

Stephanie wanted to tell Julia it was a mistake. That there were no pictures featuring her. But it wasn't true. A memory was seeping back; film footage taken by concealed cameras in an apartment in London. Her and Kostya secretly recorded for leverage.

That had been a Magenta House apartment. And the woman who had showed her the film, when the time for leverage came, had been Rosie Chaudhuri. She'd been a mere employee then, working directly for Stephanie's nemesis, Alexander.

But he was dead. Rosie was the head of Magenta House now. And Magenta House owned more of her past than she did.

*   *   *

Julia giggles, then says, 'This is weird, isn't it? Up close, there are some differences between us – I mean, you're older, right? – but we do look like each other, don't we?'

'Yes. We do. But we sound different. Did you know that you're supposed to be German?'

'I was told that. Are you German? You sound German.'

'I'm more German than you.'

Julia nods. 'Well that's because I'm Austrian.'

I switch to Russian. 'And I'm the Virgin Mother. Where are you from, Julia? Moscow?'

She stares at me for a long time, deciding how to play it. 'Nizhny Novgorod,' she confesses, eventually. 'But I was living in Moscow for five years before I came here. How can you tell?'

'Your accent. It's not bad but it's not native.'

She acknowledges the criticism with a casual shrug. 'Actually, I usually say I'm Polish. They can't tell the difference.'

'Do you want to speak in Russian or German?'

'Russian. I miss it.'

'Me too.'

'Want a drink? Vodka and orange juice? Vodka and Diet Coke?'

'No.'

'Is it okay if I do?'

'Sure.'

She picks up the brown paper bag and squeezes past me. There's barely room for both of us in the kitchenette. She seems unfazed by the gun. Unfazed by anything, really; when I ask her what she's doing in Vienna, she says, 'I'm a prostitute.' No lies, no clumsy euphemisms. She gauges my reaction and sighs. 'Come on, what did you expect?'

She unscrews the cap on a bottle of supermarket vodka, pours three fingers into a dirty tumbler then adds orange juice from the fridge.

Her story is depressingly familiar. A cold childhood in Nizhny Novgorod improved only by dreams of a better world beyond the city limits. At fifteen, she left for Moscow.

'It was easier there. No one knew me so it didn't matter what I did. I still have family back in Nizhny Novgorod. I didn't want them to know.' She blows smoke towards the damp ceiling. 'Even though I don't give a fuck about them. Bastards.'

Five years in Moscow, on her back and out of her head, then Vienna.

'I wanted to go to Germany. My father taught me German when I was younger – about the only decent thing he ever did for me. And since that's where the money is I thought Germany would be good. Alexei said he'd arrange it and we ended up here in Vienna.'

'What went wrong?'

'Nothing. At least, not from Alexei's point of view. He thought Austria was a region of Germany, and that Vienna was the regional capital.'

We both laugh at this.

'Who's Alexei?' I ask.

'An ex-boyfriend.'

Who, it transpires, was also her pimp. She doesn't see the contradiction in this. Yes, he used to beat her *when she wouldn't sleep with his clients but he took care of her too. He showed her a good time, gave her drugs; she never had to pay for coke or speed when it came from him. I ask if he's still around and she nods, looking into the living-room. 'Over there.'*

'Where?'

'On the shelf. See that ceramic pot? In there.'

'Not a large man, then.'

She giggles. 'Those are his ashes.'

'What happened?' I ask, expecting an answer riddled with bullets.

'Car accident. To be honest, I'm surprised he survived as long as he did. Back in Moscow he and his friends used to race stolen cars through the city at night. I mean really race. A lot of guys used to do it back in the Nineties. One hundred and fifty kilometres an hour, the police after them, completely fucked out of their heads. He never drove fast when he was sober. Never. But with a neck full of vodka and a head full of glue . . .'

When she's finished unpacking the brown paper bag we go through to the living room. She starts to sort through her CDs and tells me about her life in Vienna. She's so candid I can't help warming to her. And the more I warm to her, the sadder I feel. She doesn't seem to notice. Even if she did, I doubt she'd care. I wouldn't have, not when I was like her.

'Tell me about Paris.'

Julia pulls a face. 'I don't really know what it was all about.'

'What about Étienne Lorenz?'

'That prick.'

'He told me the two of you got on well.'

'That's because he's more of a whore than I am.'

'How did it start?'

'It was here in Vienna. I got introduced to this big American guy. Paul Ellroy.'

'Who introduced you?'

'Rudi.'

'Who's Rudi?'

She pauses, wondering how much to tell me. Or whether she should tell me anything at all.

'Rudi the cockroach. Rudi Littbarski. Lives in a train carriage.'

'A train carriage?'

'In a railway siding out at Unter Purkersdorf.'

I ask for precise directions. She hesitates, then changes her mind and seems happy to give them to me. I write the details on an empty cigarette pack. As I put it in my pocket, I ask, 'So, who is Rudi?'

Her expression grows solemn. 'In this city, he's anything you need him to be. Whatever you want, Rudi can get it. He knows everybody but nobody admits to knowing Rudi. When the tourists come to town, they see beautiful architecture and eat Sacher Torte. But that's not Vienna. This city is the darkest place in Europe and nobody is more at home in it than Rudi.'

'What happened?'

'There's a place out on Wagramer Strasse . . .'

'Club Nitro.'

'You know it?'

'I've been there.'

'Rudi goes there for the traffic.'

'Traffic?'

'Girls. Anyway, that's where he found me.'

'What happened?'

'He said he'd been looking for me. Made a real scene out of it. That was bullshit. I'm not that hard to find. Then he said he had something special for me.'

'The American?'

'Yes.'

'What was special about him?'

'He wanted me, not anyone else.'

'Did Rudi say why?'

Julia shakes her head. 'But the money was good so I agreed to meet him. And he seemed okay.'

'Then what?'

'What do you think? He became a client. I saw him when he came to town.'

'He didn't live here, then?'

'No. But he was a regular visitor.'

'Where was he from?'

'All over. He travelled the whole time. I never paid much attention. You hear all sorts of shit. You ask the questions – to be polite and make conversation – but you don't bother listening to the answers.'

'I can imagine,' I remark, shamelessly crossing the divide between understatement and dishonesty.

'Anyway, Paul asked me if I'd be prepared to change my appearance. I thought he was talking about cutting my hair or dyeing it. You know – the usual things. Then he mentioned surgery. That's when I said no. But when he mentioned a hundred thousand euros I said I'd think about it.'

'Which you did.'

'For a little scar? A hundred thousand in cash? Why not?'

'Did he give a reason?'

'He'd already mentioned that it was for someone else. I didn't mind that as long as the money was right. When I asked why I needed the scar, Paul just said that it would make an old man happy because I looked exactly like somebody he'd once known.'

'And that was enough for you?'

'I've been involved with stranger stuff than that. And the more I thought about the hundred thousand, the less I thought about the reason.'

'So you went to the clinic and they performed the procedure?'

She nods. 'It was nothing.'

'Then what?'

'I got a ticket to Paris and a phone number to call when I got there.'

'Lorenz?'

'Right.'

'And he was in charge?'

'Yes. At the George V hotel. With this other girl. Angeline. She was nice. We got on. We both thought Étienne was a jerk.'

'You knew the cameras were rolling?'

'Sure.'

'You didn't mind?'

Julia shakes her head. 'It was kind of fun.'

'And the man?'

'He wasn't that old, after all. Anders.'

454

That surprises me. 'He told you his name?'

'Somebody did. Maybe him, I don't remember. Anyway, that's what we called him and he was happy enough with it. He was nice. Fit for a guy of his age too.'

She finds the memory amusing.

'It was just the one time?'

'That's right. Afterwards, I hung around Paris for a day or two then I came back.'

'You've been paid?'

'Half. That was the deal. Half before, half after.'

'Why the delay?'

'That was part of the original arrangement. That I might have to wait for the second half. Paul said that right from the start. That it might be a few weeks. Perhaps even a month or two.'

'Doesn't that worry you?'

She shakes her head. 'He paid the first half on time. Everything has happened just the way it was supposed to.'

How strange to be sitting here with Petra. Or, at least, a passable physical version of her. In terms of character, though, she's more like the girl I used to be before Petra. Hard on the outside, the soft inner core rendered numb.

Julia is the third woman in my life. She's the woman I left behind for Petra. She's a version of Stephanie I barely recognize any more.

'What are you going to do with your hundred thousand?' I ask.

'Disappear to a new country. Make a new life. That's what I've been looking for. The chance to begin again.'

That makes me smile. 'Then we've got more in common than just a name.'

'What are you thinking?' Julia asked. She was kneeling on the carpet, changing the CD, the discs scattered around the machine like loose change. 'That I'm an idiot? That they're not gonna pay me the second half?'

'I'm thinking the only reason you're still alive is because I am.'

'What are you talking about?'

'The cuts and bruises you saw earlier: I've had more than one lucky escape over the last few days. Someone wants me dead and, if I had to guess, it's your friend Paul. Or people he knows.'

'Why?'

'I'm not sure. But the question you need to ask yourself is this: if they succeed in killing me, what do you think's going to happen to you?'

Julia shook her head. 'No way. It was just a role. When it's over I'll cut my hair, change its colour, get the scar fixed – suddenly we're totally different.'

'Except that you were there. You're a witness to the lie.'

'I don't know anything. Besides, they've already paid me fifty thousand euros. Why would they do that if they were planning to stiff me?'

'Maybe they know where it is.'

'No chance.'

'You never let it slip to Paul?'

'Never.'

'Maybe they don't care. Maybe it's worth writing off.'

'Fuck you.'

'We're on the same side, Julia. We're the same woman, remember?'

'The only person on my side is me. And the only person I distrust more than a man is another woman.'

'What you do is up to you,' Stephanie said. 'I just need answers so I can make my own way.'

'I've told you what I know.'

'What about Gerhard Lander at Grumann Bank?'

'What do you know about that?'

'I read the letter on the TV over there. Addressed to Marianne Bernard. Any idea who she is?'

'No. But I had to use her name when I saw Lander.'

'*I'm* Marianne Bernard, Julia.'

'I thought you were Petra.'

'I am. I'm both.'

'Look, I didn't know anything about that.'

'Because you weren't supposed to know. The letter mentions "arrangements" and "further facilities". Any idea what those were?'

'I guess they were in the letter I was carrying.'

'Who arranged this? Paul?'

Julia nodded. 'He came with me to the bank. It was complicated. I was Petra but I was also Marianne. Like you.'

'Exactly. What about Paul?'

'For the purposes of that meeting, he was a lawyer. I didn't say anything. Paul spoke on my behalf. We both dressed up – smart clothes, formal-looking.'

Stephanie sat back and pictured the scene. Julia as Petra, a lawyer at her side. It made a certain kind of sense; Petra would keep physical and verbal contact to a minimum and yet some kind of meeting would be necessary. Stephanie thought of the way she conducted business with Albert Eichner; Lander would need to recognize her himself.

'Have you ever heard of Butterfly?'

Julia looked genuinely puzzled. 'There was a nightclub called Butterfly in Moscow. But that was a long time ago. It got burned down.'

'Did Paul or Gerhard Lander mention Anders?'

'No.'

'Did you know who Anders was?'

She shook her head. 'Just some rich guy who liked good sex in good hotels.'

'I'm sure that's what he would have wanted on his tombstone.'

Julia's eyes widened. 'He's dead?'

Stephanie nodded. 'Just over a week ago. In Paris.'

'How?'

'Don't you read the paper?'

'Was he famous?'

'You don't watch TV, either?'

458

'MTV sometimes. But not much. TV's boring. I prefer movies.'

'Never mind.'

'No. I want to know. What happened?'

Stephanie told her but Julia didn't seem particularly shocked. Perhaps it was too remote.

She said, 'You think Paul had something to do with that?'

'I don't know. What I do know is this: I was supposed to die in the explosion. Ever since then, someone's been trying to put that right. Your little sex party at the George V wasn't a memento for an old man. It was part of a set-up. My guess is the film was supposed to come out after he was dead.'

'Why?'

'To discredit him, most likely.'

'Why hasn't it?'

'Because I'm still alive. The film is part of something larger. With me dead, there'd be no one left to raise awkward questions.'

'Apart from me.'

Even as she said it, she got it.

Stephanie nodded. 'That's right. Apart from you.'

'And Angeline, of course.'

'Maybe, maybe not. But you're the one that matters. You're the one who's me.'

She let silence do her work for her. Julia started to chew a nail. When she'd smoked her cigarette to the stub, she used it to light a fresh one.

'What can I do?'

'First things first. Where can I find Ellroy?'

Julia picked at the stitching on her mini-skirt. 'When he comes to Vienna he stays at the Imperial.'

'Do you know where he is now?'

No answer.

'Is he at the Imperial?'

She shook her head. 'Not at the moment.'

'When did you last see him?'

Julia half-turned away from Stephanie, who couldn't decide whether it was deliberate or involuntary. It didn't matter. The effect was the same, drawing attention to the bruise she tried to hide.

'When did you last see him, Julia?'

Her answer was little more than a whisper. 'This afternoon.'

'At the Imperial?'

'Yes.'

'So he *is* there.'

She shook her head. 'Not tonight.'

'What about tomorrow night?'

She looked at Stephanie but wouldn't say it.

'Did he give you the bruise?'

Julia nodded.

'What did you do?'

'Nothing.'

'He did it for no good reason?'

A question that rekindled her defiance. 'He did it because he wanted to. Okay? Because he likes that kind of thing. That's the reason.'

460

'That's still not a *good* reason. If I go to the Imperial tomorrow night, will I find him there?'

'Yes.'

'You're sure?'

'I'm sure. He told me to be ready for him.'

'What time?'

'He didn't say. He just said I had to be on call. All night.'

'And you agreed?'

'Of course I agreed,' Julia snapped.

Stephanie felt gauche. What was a black eye to Julia of Nizhny Novgorod with fifty thousand euros on the line?

'You should think twice,' Julia said. 'He's a big bastard. Muscles everywhere.'

'I can look after myself.'

Julia shrugged. 'It's your funeral.'

'We'll see about that.'

'There's one more thing.'

'What?'

'When you ask for him at reception, you need the name. Paul doesn't register under his own name.'

'What is it?'

'Stonehouse. Alan Stonehouse.'

Julia was still talking but her voice was little more than the soft drone of a bee on a warm summer afternoon. It took Stephanie a while to connect the name but the moment Julia had mentioned it, she knew she'd heard it before.

Munich, late September. Just after her meeting

with Otto Heilmann at the Café Roma on Maximilianstrasse. A chance encounter with John Peltor, who'd suggested breakfast the following morning at his hotel, the Mandarin Oriental. The name Peltor had registered under had been Alan Stonehouse.

So, Alexander was right again. In their world, coincidence was still oversight. If the encounter in Café Roma had been planned did that mean that Peltor knew about Otto Heilmann? Not definitely. But probably.

Another memory was resurrected: an e-mail message in Brussels after her return from Turkmenistan. Peltor again:

I see you chose not to take the advice I gave you in Munich.

Having cast her mind forwards, she now cast it back again. The advice given in Munich – what had that been? She couldn't remember.

'You okay?' Julia asked her.

'Just thinking.'

'That's when the trouble starts.'

'Has he ever mentioned Munich?'

'He mentions a lot of places. Maybe. I don't know.'

'You said he was nice.'

Julia got up from the floor and headed for the kitchenette. 'That's right.'

'Even though he hits you.'

'He was nice in the beginning. That's what I meant. When he was paying me.'

462

'And now?'

'Now he's a bastard.'

'But he's still paying you?'

She shook her head. 'He doesn't have to.'

'Because he's got your money.'

'Right. Actually, no. That's only part of it.' She came back into the living-room with the vodka bottle and the orange juice carton. 'Things have changed.'

'How?'

'Since I became you, he's changed towards me.' Julia poured more vodka into her glass and offered it to Stephanie. 'You might want this.'

'Not at the moment.'

'You'll change your mind, I promise you. When I first started seeing him it was business as usual. He was Paul, I was Julia. He paid me the going rate. We had sex. It was fine. You know – nice hotel, clean sheets, a hot shower and fluffy towels. Maybe even a drink or two. Then the Petra thing happened. Before Paris it was okay. When I got back it was different.'

'In what way?'

'I wasn't allowed to change my appearance. I had to look like . . . well, like you. I was Petra, not Julia. And he was John, not Paul. The sex changed too.'

'How?'

'For one thing, he stopped paying me.'

'Because he was holding on to your second fifty thousand.'

463

Julia looked into her glass. 'That's true. But it's not the reason.'

'What is the reason?'

'He won't pay me because that makes it a transaction.'

'And?'

'And the scenario won't allow that.'

'What scenario?'

Julia forgot to add orange juice and drank some vodka. 'Please . . .'

'I need to know.'

The carapace was starting to crack. When she looked up Stephanie saw tears forming. Julia spoke very softly. 'He likes to take me by force. When he hits me, I have to fight back. If I don't, he makes it worse for me. I have to convince him that I'm you.' She sniffed loudly, then wiped her nose with the back of her hand. 'He mutters your name. It's like a mantra. Petra, Petra, Petra. He's obsessed with you. With fucking you. With hurting you.'

Stephanie thought of the bruises on Julia's body, and of those on her own body. They matched in more ways than Peltor could have imagined. Directly or indirectly, he was responsible for both sets. Stephanie felt sure of that. Beyond the shock, a more sinister sensation festered in the darkest corner of her mind.

Then she remembered the subject of Peltor's message: retirement.

That was what he'd suggested in Munich. He'd

surprised her by telling her that he was no longer in the front line. How had he put it? *I'm kinda drifting into something new right now. Something . . . corporate.*

Something corporate. Like DeMille, perhaps?

'Did you ever try to say no?'

'Only once. He said if I tried again, there'd be no second payment. And that I wouldn't get to spend the first.'

Stephanie considered the contrast between the aggressive Julia who had breezed into the apartment an hour earlier and the subdued version sitting cross-legged on the floor in front of her. They were as different as Stephanie was to Petra, or any other brand of her.

'Sometimes there are other men,' Julia said. 'He likes that. They all get into me together. There's one guy, a real bastard – a South African, I think – and he . . .'

'Tall with short blond hair? Good-looking in a nasty way?'

'You know him?'

'I'm afraid so. His name's Lance Grotius.'

Julia shuddered. 'He's the worst. Even Paul finds him creepy.'

'If it's any consolation, you won't be running into him again.'

'Really?'

'Not unless you own a funeral parlour in Paris.'

*　*　*

Five-to-midnight. Julia poured vodka into both their glasses. Stephanie had succumbed and was glad she had.

How many times had she and Peltor met in total? Three or four? No more than that. Fellow professionals in a lonely business. She'd never thought of them as anything more than that. They chanced across one another in airport departure lounges, in hotels. They swapped gossip then went their separate ways. Business executives with appointments to keep.

What was she to make of Munich? When she'd gone to the Mandarin Oriental she'd been directed to the roof where Peltor had been swimming outdoors on a freezing morning. At the time, she'd put that down to an ex-Marine's machismo. Now she suspected a more deviant motive; something to send Peltor's lift to the penthouse.

'What should I do?' Julia asked.

'You have fifty thousand euros already?'

'Yes.'

'In cash?'

'Yes.'

'How quickly can you get hold of it?'

'One hour.'

'My guess is you're safe until tomorrow evening. If I were you, I'd run. Forget the second fifty.'

'Run?'

'You're only alive because I am. They're

keeping you in reserve in case they need you again. Once they don't . . .'

'You mean when *you're* dead?'

'That. Or when the situation changes sufficiently to render me irrelevant. Either way, they'll kill you. It's not our fault but we're a collective liability.'

'You think I should go tonight?'

'If you want to. Personally, I'd get some rest and go tomorrow. But once Peltor's dead they're going to be looking for you because that's who the people at the Imperial's reception desk are going to see tomorrow evening.'

'Who's Peltor?'

'Ellroy. Stonehouse. Take your pick.'

'You're going to kill him?'

'Let's just say I'm going to talk to him. *Forcefully*.'

'How will you know when to go?'

'Because you'll call me when he calls you.'

'And when I run, where should I go?'

'Any place where nobody knows you. Not Moscow. Not Nizhny Novgorod.'

Julia put her head in her hands. 'Shit.'

'Look on the bright side. You wanted a new life in a new country.'

'Yeah, but . . .'

'Don't look for negatives, Julia. If I hadn't come here this evening, he'd have killed you. And from what you've told me . . . well, you can guess the way he would have done it better than I can.'

Julia surveyed her dismal apartment. 'I've been on the run since I was fifteen.'

'You'll be fine. Trust me.'

'You think so?'

'Sure. You've got what it takes. Just like me. We're the same, after all. Consider this a narrow escape when you're on a beach somewhere.'

'Who are you?'

Stephanie stood to leave. 'I'm the chance to begin again. Just like you wanted.'

Day Eleven

Five-to-two in the morning. They were both a little drunk after an evening apart. It felt good. She was lying diagonally across the bed, her head almost hanging off the edge. The room was upside down; through a crack in the curtains she saw rain slithering *up* the streetlamp-lit window.

When they made love Stephanie was happy to surrender to him in a way she could never have permitted with the men Petra took to bed. With them sex was athletic competition. With Newman that seemed utterly pointless.

She enjoyed the feel of his hands on her, moving her where he wanted, taking her how he wanted. It felt good to pretend to be taught. They didn't speak. She liked the feel of him, the tangible difference in age, the consequences of experience over enthusiasm. The more he gave, the lazier she grew, the better it felt. The alcohol was helping, no doubt about it.

When she closed her eyes she saw herself as

Julia, and Newman as Brand. They were in a suite at the George V. The distinction between what Newman was doing to her now and what she remembered from the film became blurred. She could almost feel Angeline with them. But it didn't seem to matter. It felt too good to protest against herself. So she went with it, opening herself totally to the passing physical pleasure.

He rolled her on to her front, took her hips in his hands and raised her buttocks from the mattress. She wrapped her arms around her giddy head, threading her fingers through damp hair. When she came crushed pillows swallowed her gasps and an involuntary giggle of happiness.

Later, she said, 'You're the first man I've really kissed in more than two years.'

'What does that mean?'

'For some people kissing is just a pit-stop on the way to sex.'

Newman considered this. 'I guess that's true.'

Stephanie said, 'I think kissing is the most intimate act there is.'

'I'm not sure I agree with that.'

Perhaps that was the difference between them. Petra had spent years using her body as a weapon of seduction or attrition. That was bound to erode mystery. She'd given her body to men she'd never contemplated kissing. She guessed Julia was the same but knew it was something Newman could never understand.

*   *   *

Daylight creeps into our room. I've been awake for half an hour. My head aches and my mouth is dry. I feel Robert on my skin but don't feel dirty. Quite the opposite; we've made love and I feel cleansed.

My thoughts turn to Julia. She's a girl who does what she has to do to survive. A girl who sees it through, no matter what. Ever since I mutated into Petra that has been my philosophy too. It's underpinned everything I've done. It's only now that I'm beginning to understand quite how corrosive it's been.

It corrupts the soul. I never noticed from day to day, or even year to year. It's taken Julia, the other me, to show me. In her late teens or early twenties, surviving the day-to-day fight on a diet of dreams. She tolerates a man like Peltor for the prospect of a future of her own choosing. I was like that at her age, tolerating Petra and the work I did for Magenta House. But for what, exactly? In the beginning, vengeance. Later, independence. Later still, nothing at all.

Perhaps it'll be easier for Julia. She may not know where she's heading but she knows with absolute certainty what she's running from. She's seen the kind of future Nizhny Novgorod is offering and doesn't want any of it. She still believes she'll find something better far away from there. She shouldn't be so sure. The chances are she's trading one future with no prospects for another. I should know. I've come across dozens of Julias in dozens of cities; they'll believe any lie as long as the dream survives.

We go out for breakfast. Most places are shut but we find a small dimly-lit café on Marzstrasse. We take the table by the door and order coffee. Outside, a stubborn wind blows ripples through the puddles on the pavement.

Robert tells me about his dinner with Abel Kessler; memories and alcohol, mostly. My attention drifts to Rudi the cockroach. That's what Julia called him. Rudi Littbarski. But there's another Rudi. It's coming back to me now. A name on a piece of paper. A place, a time: Rudi, Gare du Nord, 19:30. *Written on a scrap of paper that I found in the back pocket of a pair of jeans in the apartment at Stalingrad.*

While we wait I make the call from a payphone on the wall outside the toilet. There are two numbers at the top of the letter I took from Julia's apartment. I choose the second one, a mobile. A man answers.

'Herr Lander?' I enquire.

'Naturally. Who is this?'

'Marianne Bernard.'

It takes several seconds for the name to melt through the mental permafrost. 'Ah yes . . . Fräulein Bernard. How nice to hear from you. I trust you are well and that you had a relaxing Christmas and New Year.'

'Most relaxing.'

'What can I do for you?'

'I'm in Vienna and I'd like to see you.'

The pause tells me this is unexpected and unwelcome, even though the letter he wrote to Marianne Bernard was addressed to Julia's apartment.

'When would be convenient for you?' he asks.

'Today.'

472

'Ah, that's not so good. I have two meetings and then a lunch appointment. And this afternoon . . .'

'I'll be at your office at midday.'

There's a second informative silence. When he ends it by agreeing to my demand, I know something new: Petra is a client too important to be denied. What I don't know is why.

Back at our table, I tell Robert, 'We need to scrub up again.'

'For what?'

'A visit to the bank.'

'Why?'

I hold my cup with both hands and blow steam from the rich, oily surface of the coffee. 'It's rather like being a film star. Sometimes, when you meet your audience, you have to put on your face and live up to the ideal that exists in their minds. We have a meeting at midday where I will have to be the real Petra Reuter.'

'And me?'

My smile is a tease. 'You're going to be my new lawyer.'

Robert winces. 'Marvellous.'

They took the Rapid Transport train from Westbahnhof. It wasn't busy; most of the early commuters were travelling in the other direction. At Unter Purkersdorf they followed the directions that Julia had given Stephanie.

The siding tracks fanned out into an iron delta. Most of them were rusting, weeds growing up between black sleepers saturated with oil and

473

grease. There were half a dozen old carriages that had been converted for occupation. Most were clustered around a set of points that had been welded shut. Their wooden exteriors had been painted green, turquoise, red. There were curtains in the windows, hanging baskets beside carriage doors.

Rudi Littbarski's carriage was further along one stretch of abandoned rail, in the shadow of a derelict nineteenth-century factory. All that remained was a shell of red brick, broken windows and half an industrial chimney. Littbarski's carriage was Swiss; it still carried the faded insignia and letters of the SBB.

Stephanie looked at her watch. Five-to-nine. Don't go too early, Julia had said. A night-owl, Littbarski rarely went to bed before seven.

The handle had been sheared from the door and a lock had been inserted. Stephanie stood on the top step and pressed her face to the glass. The handle inside was intact. She walked over to the abandoned factory and returned with a red brick which she thrust through the window. The handle inside opened the door smoothly.

Littbarski was half out of bed when Stephanie and Newman found him. She pointed the Heckler & Koch at him and he froze.

'Who the hell are you? Get the fuck out of here.'

Stephanie shook her head. 'Don't try to play the hard case, Rudi. Not while you're standing there in your little black Y-fronts.'

His luminous white skin reminded Stephanie of a supermarket chicken. Tattoos peppered his arms and bony chest. Silver rings hung from both nipples.

'Get dressed, Rudi. Unless you want to see my breakfast on your floor.'

He reached for his clothes; black drainpipe trousers, black needlecord shirt, day-glo orange socks and a pair of Converse sneakers.

Stephanie peered down the open-plan carriage. 'Anyone with you?'

'No.'

A small gas stove sat beside a compact basin. There was a TV on the breakfast bar, a fridge beneath, a molasses leatherette sofa opposite. Drapes hung over the windows, tinting the dim light emerald, purple and rose. A thick chocolate carpet had been fitted throughout.

Stephanie said, 'I'm surprised you don't have more security.'

Littbarski tugged the zip on his trousers. 'Why would I need more security?'

'The things you do. The people you know.'

'I don't piss anybody off. I have a reputation in this city. You want something, I'll tell you whether I can get it for you and how much it'll cost. Then it's up to you. If you go for it, I'll deliver. On time, no extra charges. Why would anybody want to hurt me?'

'Is that how it was with John Peltor?'

'Who?'

'Paul Ellroy. Alan Stonehouse.'

Littbarski shrugged. 'Never heard of him.'

'Which one?'

'What?'

Stephanie smiled. 'Which one of them haven't you heard of?'

He glared at her and then began to look confused.

'Have we met?' he asked.

'In a way.'

Stephanie wondered how old he was. Not as old as he looked, she supposed. Too many years with too little sleep and no sunlight. Littbarski was one of the living dead; grey skin, grey teeth, red eyes. As he moved through the light a face of hollows became a face of shadows.

Gradually, he put some of it together. 'You're . . . *not* her. But the two of you . . . you're . . .'

'Yes.'

He opened a pack of Casablanca cigarettes. 'What's the story?'

'You tell me.'

'There's not much to tell. He approached me. Said he was looking for someone and that he'd heard I was the man to talk to. I already knew where to find Julia. But even if I hadn't, I'd have found her in twenty-four hours anyway.'

'Club Nitro?'

'Right. The owners are associates of mine. We do a lot of business out there.'

'I can imagine. Tell me about Peltor.'

'Ellroy. He's always been Paul Ellroy to me.'

She hadn't even threatened him and he'd surrendered his bravado without a whimper. Stephanie wasn't surprised. Everywhere Petra had ever been there had always been men like Rudi Littbarski. Small men trying to punch above their weight.

'He's in town,' Littbarski said. 'They're all in town.'

'All?'

'The oil conference. Some big thing out at the Austria Center. The whole city's jammed.'

'How would *you* know?'

'Are you serious? An event like this is a payday for me. OPEC, the UN, this thing, whatever. Right now, you can't find a room at any of the best hotels. The Americans are here, the Iraqis, the Saudis. You know what they do, the Saudis? They bring an entourage. They book six or seven rooms at a place like the Sacher or the Imperial. Just for the family and staff. Then they book two or three more rooms on a different floor for their whores. They have their favourites flown in specially from London or Paris or Los Angeles. But if they want something local, or something exotic, they send somebody to see me.'

'Something exotic?'

Littbarski looked pained. 'These days nobody is content with regular girls. They always want something special. Something . . . *baroque*. Under-age immigrants, amputees, dwarves. All kinds of shit. You know Clara Bazoli?'

Stephanie had heard the name but couldn't place it. 'Remind me.'

'The EU transport commissioner. Last week she ordered a Russian from me. For her husband!'

Stephanie shrugged. 'That does seem a strange present to give your husband. But what's so weird about a Russian?'

'Not a Russian. A *Russian*.'

'I don't understand.'

'A Russian is when a girl gives you a blow-job while a man fucks you in the ass. Signora Bazoli wanted to watch her husband having a Russian in their suite at the Inter-Continental. Can you believe it?'

'If I was Russian I think I'd find it rather offensive.'

Littbarski sniggered. 'It could be worse. You could be Algerian. Ever heard of *Algierfranzosich*? That's when a girl licks your asshole.'

Stephanie tried to control her fraying temper. 'And this is what you deal in, is it, Rudi?'

Littbarski mimicked offence. 'Don't take that tone with me, princess. I'm no different to a baker selling bread. I'm just providing a service.'

'Like the heroin dealer at the school-gate.'

'Fuck you.'

'Spare me the sweet talk, Rudi. Tell me why Paul Ellroy needed Julia.'

'For a home movie.'

'I know that. But why her? Why *me*?'

'I don't know.'

'Been to Paris recently?'

'What?'

'By train, perhaps? Gare du Nord?'

He looked truly perplexed. 'I don't know what you're talking about.'

She decided to change direction. Based on what Julia had said Stephanie made an educated guess: 'You organized her surgery at the Verbinski clinic – right?'

Littbarski assumed the question was rhetorical. 'Right.'

'You saw the photos, then?'

'Of you with the tattooed freak-show? Sure. We all had a laugh.'

'Do you know where the photos came from?'

'Ellroy.'

'Do you know where he got them?'

'Sure. He was given them.'

'Given? Not sold?'

'He said was given them.'

'By?'

'You should know. You're in them.'

Stephanie's grip tightened on the gun. *'By?'*

'Someone you used to work for.'

The roof of her mouth felt dry. 'You're sure?'

'Of course I'm sure. That was why we were laughing. Ellroy was saying how you used to work for this old guy, and we could see the kind of work you do, so . . .'

'Wait. When was this?'

'Autumn, maybe. October or November.'

'Last year?'

Littbarski nodded.

Stephanie felt bewildered. He had to be talking about Alexander. But Alexander had been dead for more than two years.

'Did you meet him yourself?'

'Yes.'

'Where?'

'Here. In Vienna. He came specially from London.'

By the time Gordon Wiley walked into the Café Imperial for a late breakfast meeting he'd been awake for more than four hours. It was nine-twenty-five. John Peltor was already there. Sitting at a window banquette he was silhouetted by daylight and framed by heavy, gathered curtains. A waitress was placing a plate of fried eggs before him.

Wiley had always been impressed and intimidated by Peltor's physique. It wasn't just the volume of the man, it was his condition. As vast as he was, there was no fat on him. He looked as though he was made out of tanned marble.

The waitress poured coffee for both of them. When she'd gone, Wiley said, 'I spent an hour on the phone with John Cabrini earlier. He has no idea where she is. Alsace was a mess. All his leads have come to nothing. He's sitting there in that pod – that *multi-million-dollar* pod – listening to God-knows-what falling from the satellites and she's gone.'

The dining-room was quiet, the breakfast rush-hour in descent. Wiley liked the place. Large and airy, ochre and dark brown, traditional. In truth, it was a little worn but it had character. It felt as peaceful as a library. A woman in a sombre grey suit began tending the large vases of flowers.

Peltor nodded sympathetically. 'So where does that leave you, sir?'

'*Us*. Where does that leave *us*? In a hole. That's where.'

'There's still time.'

'No there isn't. I'm meeting Hussein Sayed and Azzam Fahad later today.'

'What time?'

'Midday.'

Peltor knew better than to try to turn two and a half hours into something it couldn't be. Instead, he said, 'Worst-case scenario?'

'They call the whole thing off.'

'Best case?'

'They agree to a postponement.'

'How long do you think they could wait?'

'Twenty-four hours. Maybe thirty-six.'

'Not longer?'

'I doubt it. And that's if they wait at all. What's on your mind?'

'There is another possibility. But it's a tough call.'

'Just tell me what it is.'

'You've seen the Brand disk, right?'

'No. But I know about it.'

'The girl.'

'What about her?'

Peltor looked around and then leaned towards him, dropping his voice to a murmur. 'She passed for Reuter once. She could pass for Reuter again.'

It took Wiley several moments to understand. 'I thought she vanished weeks ago. I thought that's why we paid her a hundred grand. To make sure she vanished.'

Retaining the second tranche of fifty thousand euros had been Peltor's decision. Made for entirely personal reasons, no one else knew.

He said, 'That's true. But I can find her.'

'How long would it take you?'

Peltor strung out the moment. 'It's not that simple.'

'Why not?'

'Once it's done, she'd need to be discovered. Then the news would need to leak out. It would have to look right.'

Wiley conceded the point. 'How long?'

'To make it convincing? Forty-eight hours.'

'What about the real Reuter?'

'We'd still need her. But this buys us some time.'

Wiley found one appetite enhanced, the other suppressed.

* * *

At ten, the time Kleist had suggested the previous day, Stephanie and Newman turned into Dorotheergasse. The shop was closed, the lights off. Stephanie rang the bell. They waited in the rain, then tried again. Eventually, she caught sight of him refracted through glass. They stepped inside and shook the wetness from their shoulders. Kleist locked the door and led them to the small kitchen at the rear of the premises where he began to prepare hot chocolate with cinnamon. This was a process Stephanie remembered. It was part of Kleist's professional calling-card; it came with the information.

He poured milk into a small, battered steel pan then held it over a gas flame. He made a play of concentrating on the task as he got straight to the point. 'Were you aware that Otto Heilmann was on the Amsterdam Group payroll?'

Stephanie felt winded, only managing a whisper. 'Heilmann.'

'You raised his name yesterday.'

That was true. But only in relation to Kleist himself; he and Heilmann had been colleagues in the Stasi. It had never occurred to Stephanie that Heilmann might be connected to Amsterdam.

Kleist seemed to read her mind. 'You asked about Butterfly. I made some enquiries. The Amsterdam Group was mentioned. I knew that Otto had worked for DeMille, one of their subsidiaries.'

Yet she *hadn't* known. Asking about Butterfly

and then mentioning Heilmann had been entirely coincidental.

'What did he do for them?'

'He was a consultant.'

'In what capacity?'

'Arms, mostly.'

Naturally; Stephanie thought of the Ukraine hypermarket.

Kleist said, 'Otto had strong contacts in the Middle East. When we worked together he spent much of his time in Syria, Iraq and Jordan. But particularly in Syria. He knew Assad personally.'

Stephanie was still reeling. Kleist spooned chocolate into the pan of warm milk, added cinnamon, then resumed the slow stir away from the flame. When it was ready, he poured into three enamel mugs. They moved through to his cramped office. A small square window looked on to a dark courtyard.

'Stern,' Kleist said, leaning against a desk under siege from paperwork. 'I think you should make contact.'

'Why?'

'Two reasons. Firstly, you were set up but so was Stern. At least, that's what he says.'

'Well he would, wouldn't he?'

'You have to admit it's a possibility.'

'Do *you* think it's a possibility?'

'Sadly, yes.'

'Sadly?'

'I'm not as retired as I might have led you to

believe yesterday. And with Stern out of the way, who knows where you might have turned to for your information.'

Stephanie shook her head in mock reproach. 'I have to say this: I keep thinking of you as some monstrous Cold War relic – I mean, poisoning Josef Kanek? – but every time we meet you do something to undermine the image.'

'I'm not going to apologize for that but I'll tell you something about Kanek, Petra. Everyone thinks of him as a dissident. A great scientific martyr of some sort. But that was never true. Josef Kanek never did anything to further scientific enquiry. He was a trader in stolen nuclear material. Now everybody does it. But he was among the first. That's the reason he was killed. Nothing else.'

'But poisoning? Wasn't that a little . . . *macabre*?'

'Radiation poisoning, Petra. He lived by it, so he died by it.'

'I had no idea the Stasi was so theatrical.'

'It was intended as a warning to others. And in that respect, it was effective.'

Kleist leaned over and picked up a rusty tin from beside the telephone. He flipped the lid and took out a Sobranie cigarette. Stephanie watched him light it and said, 'The whore's brand.'

Kleist inclined his head a little. 'Of course. What else would I smoke?'

'There's more to you than meets the eye, Bruno.'

'That should always be true for a good information broker. Stern, perhaps, takes it to extremes. Then again, he *is* Russian.'

Stephanie felt her heart stutter. 'Is he?'

Kleist looked amazed. 'You didn't know?'

Stephanie shook her head. 'What else?'

'That's all. Just that one thing.' He took a long blissful drag from the Sobranie. 'I can't tell you what a cheap thrill that was.'

'Does Stern know who set him up?'

'Probably. But he wasn't about to tell me. He wants you to make contact directly. I can't say I blame him. In his position, I would do the same.'

Stephanie drank some more hot chocolate then set her mug on the desk. 'One more thing. Grumann Bank – you're familiar with it?'

'Naturally. It's located here in Vienna. On Singerstrasse.'

'Do you know Gerhard Lander?'

Kleist's chuckle contained more menace than humour. 'I know Lander, yes. Not personally. But by reputation.'

'That sounds ominous.'

'It depends on the business you're in. Look at me. You might think a Stasi past would be a handicap in a post-GDR environment. Not true. I would say that my professional reputation has been enhanced by it.'

'What about Grumann?'

'Its clients value privacy over interest rates. In other words, it caters for people like you, Petra.'

486

'I'm already well catered for.'

'I don't doubt it. But if you ever feel the need for a change I'm sure they'd welcome you with open arms. Saddam used to have money there. I hear that Suharto was once a favoured account-holder. Others have included Yemen's Ali Abdallah Saleh, Vladislav Ardzinba, the president of Abkhazia, and my own personal favourite, Sudan's Omar al-Bashir.'

'Quite a list.'

'Forget Prague or Budapest,' Kleist said. 'Or even Istanbul. Vienna is where East meets West. I'm not talking about some cheap tourist slogan but an amoral reality. And Grumann Bank takes full advantage of that.'

'What do you know about Lander?'

'A senior director. In his mid-fifties, I would guess. As far as I know, he's been there all his working life. His grandfather, a fervent Nazi, was a co-founder. Needless to say the bank prospered through the Thirties and early Forties.'

'What about later? Were there no recriminations?'

'Fewer than you might imagine. A bank like Grumann will always adapt to the needs of its clientele and to the prevailing climate. Although, in truth, it hasn't had to do much.'

'No?'

Kleist shook his head. 'We're very polite in Vienna. We don't ask awkward questions. Especially if we're not sure that we want to hear the answers.'

'What about Butterfly?'

'That's the second reason for you to contact Stern.'

We're at the Künstlerhaus cinema on Akademiestrasse. There are computer terminals in the foyer. A couple of students are hunched over screens, stretching coffee from breakfast to lunch. Robert and I pick the most isolated terminal we can find. I leave a message on Hotmail.

> Hello Oscar. Let's talk.

Otto Heilmann. Is he the reason I'm here? I took him as a favour to Albert Eichner at Guderian Maier. A rather loaded favour, certainly, since Guderian Maier's interests govern my own to some extent, but a favour nonetheless. I had no idea that Heilmann was a consultant to DeMille. How could I? A week ago I'd never heard of DeMille. I didn't know what the Amsterdam Group was.

> Petra. Where have you been?

I look at my watch. It's taken less than five minutes.

> Take a wild guess, Oscar.

> All over the place?

> That's one way of putting it.

> How do I know it's you?

Robert sees the question. 'He's got some balls, I'll give him that.'

> Pick a contract and I'll give you the 1–2–3.

> Yusuf Aziz Khan.

> Peshawar, two rounds from a SIG-Sauer P226, US$1,250,000.

Robert's eyebrows rise. 'Something you did?'

I nod, still looking at the screen. 'About a year ago.'
'Who was he?'
'The Director-General of ISI – Inter Services
Intelligence – the Pakistani security service. ISI actively
supported the Taliban in Afghanistan. Yusuf Aziz Khan
was a promoter of that policy. Not something that was
greatly appreciated in the wider world.'
   'Is that how it works? Someone out there gets an itch,
calls are made, money gets paid, then you appear out
of nowhere to scratch it?'
   'More or less. It's a service industry, after all.'
   > I apologize, Petra. For the Lancaster. For everything.
   > That doesn't quite cut it. You *sent* me to the
Lancaster. I only just made it out, no thanks to you.
   > I'm not in the habit of betraying my most lucra-
tive clients.
   > Give me a name and we'll see who set us up.
   > John Peltor.
'Christ, not again,' I mutter. 'I should have guessed.'
   > How?
   > He used an alias.
   > Alan Stonehouse?
   > Paul Ellroy.
I try to put the sequence together. The Sentier bomb
goes off. I turn to Stern for help. Stern turns to a source.
Stern's source steers me towards the Lancaster knowing
full well what will happen because Stern's source is
John Peltor, operating under one of his known aliases,
Paul Ellroy.
   My head is spinning so I ask the only simple ques-
tion left.

> Why?

> Butterfly.

> What is Butterfly?

> It's a contract.

> Between?

> The Amsterdam Group and the governments of Israel, Iraq and Jordan. It's due to be signed today. The Israelis will not be present. All parties have agreed to this.

> Where will it be signed?

> Vienna. The Hotel Imperial. Gordon Wiley, CEO of the Amsterdam Group, is staying there. The signing will take place at six o'clock in his suite.

The Imperial. Where John Peltor was staying. Why not? Sometimes there was safety in numbers. Rudi Littbarski had told them that the hotel was full of Petrotech visitors. What could appear more natural?

> What kind of contract is it?

> Two-tiered. Construction and security. The contract is for an oil pipeline running from Mosul, in the north of Iraq, to the Israeli port of Haifa via Jordan. Allowing for some detours, the proposed route covers a distance, more or less, of 1050 kilometres.

Robert reads Stern's outline and says, 'There used to be a line between Mosul and Haifa. It fell into disuse and was then cannibalized for parts. The idea of a new pipeline has been discussed from time to time but it's always been rejected.'

'Why?'

'Too expensive. Economically and politically.'

> The proposed construction budget is thought to be $4 billion. The contract will also include additional elements such as the construction of a new oil terminal at Haifa and state-of-the-art installations at Mosul.

> And the second tier?

> That covers maintenance and security for the pipeline during its construction and for the first ten years of operation.

Robert whistles softly.

'What?' I ask him.

'You got any idea of the kind of money this is going to involve?'

'None.'

'Okay, just to give you an idea. Let's take security and break it down. Given that this is starting in Iraq and ending in Israel, we can assume this would be an attractive terrorist target. That means security needs to be high. Normally high security averages out at one man per kilometre. A lot of work is now done by drones but they're not cheap – say $12,000 each for a camera with instant transmission, but a lot more if they're armed – and you still require a physical response.'

'How do they work out the ratio?'

'They ask how long it would take someone to lay a charge on the line. Probably fifteen minutes. Which means any given stretch needs to be patrolled more frequently than that. So why don't we round it down and say one thousand men.'

'Okay.'

'The next thing to remember is that a pipeline is like the plumbing in your apartment. If the pipe blows that's

491

very inconvenient but you can deal with it. You stop the flow, repair the damage, then turn on the tap again. But if your boiler goes, then you're in trouble. Same here. Blow up a pumping station and it really starts to get messy. For a line of this length call it another thousand men. That makes two thousand in total. The running cost of each of those men will come to around $1,000 a day. In other words, this is a contract worth $2 million a day, every day, for the next ten years. That's more than $7 billion but with a tail-off over the duration of the contract . . . let's call it five billion. Just for security.'

'On top of the four billion for construction.'

'Right.'

'And all the other stuff. I mean, how much will a new oil terminal at Haifa cost to build and protect? Or the infrastructure proposed for Mosul?'

'Plenty. The total value of this contract has to be $12 billion. It could be as high as fifteen billion.'

'What kind of profit margins could Amsterdam expect?'

'Probably somewhere between twenty and thirty percent.'

I turn back to Stern.

> What else, Oscar?

> Brand was proposing to go public with his objections to Butterfly.

> Which were what?

> I don't know. He never got the chance to say.

> But Brand's objections would be listened to, wouldn't they?

> More than that. They'd be acted upon. He may have been known as The Whisperer, but he was heard everywhere. The problem is this: trust isn't transferable. The alliances he helped to build, the truces he brokered, the assurances he extracted – they're fragile. Almost without exception. Now that he's gone – who knows?

> Supposing it was proved that he wasn't the man everyone thought he was – that would change things, wouldn't it?

> Dramatically.

> One more thing. What can you tell me about Otto Heilmann in relation to the Amsterdam Group?

Stern replies immediately; in other words, no need to hunt for the information. Otto Heilmann advised the DeMille Corporation on Warsaw Pact military capabilities in the aftermath of the collapse of Communism. That's the official version but the subtext is clear: Heilmann was a provider of cheap men and cheap weapons. Anything from an AK-47 to nuclear material. Not only valuable to DeMille, he was also close to some of the senior figures at the Amsterdam Group. From Stasi agent to prosperous capitalist entrepreneur, he built a reputation as a man who could always deliver. Until he ran into Krista Jaspersen and over-reached himself.

Five minutes later I bring our dialogue to a conclusion by asking Stern how much this information will cost.

> There's no charge, Petra.

> You waived your fee last time, Oscar. Look what

happened. Let's keep this strictly business. I like to have my consumer rights intact.

> No. I insist. I owe you. And before you go, are you aware that the price on your head has gone up to $10 million?

Singerstrasse, a narrow street favoured by antiquarian booksellers, interior designers and Grumann Bank. A small brass plaque beside a nondescript door marked a modest entrance. Inside, a plain staircase led directly to the first floor. Gerhard Lander's office was large and comfortable. Just like Lander, who sat behind a desk of polished walnut; fat, balding, his piggy eyes were partly concealed by small oval glasses. He wore a large gold signet ring engraved with the bank's emblem, a double-headed eagle. He stood to greet them.

Stephanie ignored the proffered hand. 'Do you know who I am?'

Lander shifted from one foot to the other.

'Have you ever seen me before?'

'I think so. *Thought* so. Once. But now I'm not so sure.'

'My name is Petra Reuter.'

Lander nodded grimly.

'And I don't take kindly to people using my name in vain.'

'Who would?'

'That's what I'm here to find out. Who was she? And what has she been doing in my name?'

The squirm was predictable. 'Ah . . . that will not be so easy . . . questions of confidentiality, you understand.'

Stephanie pictured Rudi Littbarski peddling the same threadbare defence.

'What about my confidentiality, Herr Lander? I'd say that's been breached rather spectacularly, wouldn't you?'

'Perhaps. Perhaps not. There is, after all, the issue of verification. The one who was here before said *she* was Petra Reuter. Now you say *you* are Petra Reuter. Who am I to believe? Perhaps neither of you are Petra Reuter.'

Stephanie held him in her gaze. Very quietly, she said, 'Tell me honestly: do you think the woman – the *girl* – you saw before was Petra Reuter?'

'Well, at the time . . .'

'Not then. Right now.'

He was aching to look away. But didn't. Or couldn't. 'You're putting me in a very awkward situation.'

Stephanie smiled coldly. 'I hope so, Herr Lander. But not as awkward as the situation I'm in, I'm sure you'll agree. Do you know who Bruno Kleist is?'

'I know the name. Yes.'

'You know what he does?'

'I've heard.'

'And that his reputation speaks for itself?'

'I've heard that too.'

'Kleist will vouch for me. Call him now.'

Lander sat down in a leather chair as plumply padded as he was and touched a button on the intercom. He asked his secretary to call Kleist and put him through. Beside the console were four photographs in plain silver frames featuring a slender ash-blonde woman in her forties and three teenage children.

'The one who was here before,' Stephanie said, 'she came with a lawyer, right?'

'Yes. An American.'

'*This* is my lawyer. Another American, as it happens. Please believe me when I tell you that the difference between the two of them is far greater than the difference between me and my imitator.'

Newman said nothing but played his part perfectly, standing motionless, looking directly at Lander, eyes as blank as he could make them.

There was a buzz. Lander picked up the handset and introduced himself to Kleist. Faint electronic twittering leaked from the earpiece. Lander put his hand over the mouthpiece and asked, 'Do you have any distinguishing marks?'

'I have a scar on my left shoulder.'

Lander relayed the information, got the response, then said, 'How did you get it?'

'A car crash.'

Another pause, then: 'Where?'

'Sri Lanka.'

'Herr Kleist says you're a fraud.'

'Tell him he should know.'

Lander did and Stephanie heard the laughed endorsement. Lander replaced the handset and looked pale. Stephanie and Newman sat down opposite him. She said she wanted a complete record of the account. Lander asked his secretary to produce one immediately.

'How long has it been in existence?'

'Since late last year. I don't know the exact date. I can check it for you.'

'Was it established before the two of them came to see you?'

'Yes. About a month earlier. The meeting occurred because we needed some means of visual identification. It's not a requirement for all our accounts but it was a condition specified by Herr Ellroy.'

Stephanie understood why. So that there could be photographic evidence, if required, of Petra going in and out of Grumann Bank.

The account details were brought in by a pencil-thin secretary with pinched features and dyed black hair. She handed over a burgundy leather folder that Lander passed to Stephanie. The account had been opened with a two hundred thousand euro cash deposit. Since then there had been five deposits and three transfers out, leaving a current balance of just under three hundred thousand euros. All the activity had been conducted electronically.

Stephanie gave the folder to Newman who

examined it in detail. Lander's forehead began to shine. Stephanie gazed out of the window behind him and saw pigeons circling the spire of the church on Franziskaner Platz.

Lander cleared his throat and said, 'If I may say so, there's nothing illegal about the account.'

'Just the account-holder,' said Stephanie sharply. 'I trust that Grumann Bank values discretion above all things.'

'Naturally.'

'Good. Because we were never here today. No matter what happens to the account. Or to Mr Ellroy.'

'I understand.'

'I hope so. I can't imagine I'd find it difficult to discover where you live, Herr Lander. Or where your wife has lunch. Or even where your children go to school.'

Newman set it out for her over lunch. The bank account was the same as the apartment at Stalingrad, the film shot at the George V or Julia's apartment overlooking Mexikoplatz; an individual component of a larger mechanism to discredit Anders Brand. He drew attention to the depositors to her account at Grumann Bank.

'The names are listed,' he said.

'So?'

'There's no need. A number would have been fine. These companies are listed because they're *supposed* to be identified.'

Which made sense. There was no point in laying a trail so obscure that it couldn't be followed. The trick was in finding the balance.

They were in a café on Operngasse. A pretty girl with blond highlights brought their food. For Stephanie, *leberknödelsuppe*, a clear beef broth with dumplings. Newman had opted for something more substantial; *tafelspitz* with fried grated potatoes and horseradish.

For a while, they ate in silence. Stephanie thought about what Rudi Littbarski had said. A man had come from London to provide Peltor with photographs of her and Komarov so that her scars could be replicated on Julia at the Verbinski clinic. Photographs that were the property of Magenta House. Perhaps they had found their way into the open. That was the easiest and least unpleasant option. Yet even as she considered it, she knew the truth: a statistical possibility, yes, but nothing more. The man had belonged to Magenta House. But she couldn't think of anyone who that might be. Except for Alexander, who was dead.

She turned her thoughts to Otto Heilmann. Kleist's revelation and Stern's information made perfect sense when one factored in John Peltor. She'd eliminated an Amsterdam asset in Russia and had been identified by Peltor after their chance meeting in Munich. When someone had decided upon a strategy to discredit Brand she must have been the ideal choice. Petra Reuter, a woman guaranteed to contaminate by association. The opportunity to exact retribution for Otto Heilmann's death must have been an appealing bonus.

Somehow Peltor had discovered that Stern was Reuter's favoured source. After that, setting her up for Golitsyn must have been simple. Peltor would have known that she'd turn to Stern after Sentier. The question was this: how had he found out about Stern in the first place? Stern hadn't been able to provide an answer to that and Stephanie couldn't think of one herself.

When Newman had finished his food he opened the Petrotech information pack he'd collected the previous day.

'What time did you say it was?'

'Three-thirty,' Stephanie said. 'Hall D, Blue Level.'

'Here it is. Discussion forum, the second of six debates spread over three days. American Power Exported: the Axis of Capital.' Newman chuckled. 'I like that. The Axis of Capital.'

'Makes a change from the Axis of Evil, I suppose.'

'That depends.'

'On what?'

'Your viewpoint. I mean, as a general rule democratic governments are determined by the requirements of business, not by the wishes of liberal humanists, let alone the public.'

'So?'

'Well it's not exactly a secret that the world is run by corporations and markets. In that sense, corporations have outgrown nations. They've slipped the bonds of national boundaries. They have their own laws, their own security interests, their own intelligence networks. For some people this is a truth so ugly they'd sooner accept any alternative. For them, the Axis of Capital *is* the Axis of Evil.'

'Very neat.'

'Thank you.'

They took the U-Bahn out to the Austria Center.

Sleeping with Newman had been a mistake. A mistake Stephanie knew she'd repeat as frequently as she could. The problem was that she felt genuinely attracted to him which was not how it was supposed to be. Relationships born under fire died in the aftermath. Adrenaline was the aphrodisiac and then the oxygen. Starved of it in tranquillity, the passion died, suffocated by the mundane. Usually that was a blessing, not a curse.

As the train pulled out of Schwedenplatz, she said, 'Ever wondered what kind of father you'd make?'

'Sure.'

'And?'

'I don't think I'm made of the right stuff.'

'Why not?'

'I'm never in one place.'

'A cheap excuse, Robert.'

'I agree. Also, I don't have the time.'

'That makes two of the lamest reasons I've ever heard.'

'I know. But they *are* the reasons.'

'I doubt either of them needs to be true.'

'You don't know me well enough to know.'

'I know that any man who can remain faithful to a woman who's been dead for twenty years has a head-start on most potential fathers.'

Newman held up his hand to halt her. 'Two things. One: I'm not a potential father. Two: I wasn't faithful over twenty years because Rachel was dead and because . . . well – how can I put this? – I got my share.'

Stephanie giggled. 'Oh, that's nice. That's really nice.'

'You know what I'm saying.'

'I know this: all those women – your *share* – they're an irrelevance. In your heart, you were faithful.'

'Suddenly you're an analyst?'

'Trust me, Robert. I recognize the symptoms. Over twenty years I'll bet you haven't changed at all. You're just wearing a better suit.'

The Austria Center. Stephanie and Newman picked up their McGinley Crawford guest passes from the information desk. The name on Stephanie's pass was Marina Schrader. The ground floor, Yellow Level, was swamped by exhibitor stands. They made their way through them, trying to get a feel for the place. The public address system echoed eerily over the din of the crowd.

Although Petrotech focused on the oil services industry, the first two stands they saw belonged to Qatar Petroleum and the Kuwait Oil Company. They'd barely reached them before Newman ran into his first acquaintance, a lawyer from Baker Botts of Houston. Stephanie was happy to play the shadow, speaking only when spoken to, smiling blandly when necessary.

Newman knew plenty of people; Hong Kong financiers, Saudi vinyl producers, Iraqi oil reservoir engineers, Siberian gas barons, Nigerian geologists. By the time Stephanie had him to herself again, they'd reached a stand belonging to a company named Provisia, just by the escalators rising to the Green Level. Newman tapped the display board to the right of the stand. At the bottom of it, printed in small red capitals, it read: A KPM FAMILY MEMBER.

'The KPM Family,' he said. 'A strange way to describe a network of companies dedicated to the design and manufacture of military hardware, don't you think?'

Energy giant ConocoPhilips had a stand to showcase some recent technical innovations for the forthcoming development of oil and gas fields in Kazakhstan, the Caspian and Venezuela. Remington Industries had erected a vast billboard announcing a new contract for equipment sales to Chevron-Texaco's liquefied gas facilities close to their fields in Australia and West Africa.

By the escalators Stephanie came across Mirasia. She recognized the name immediately. The Russo-French firm's brochure had been in Leonid Golitsyn's attaché case. Their display focused on the new Mir-3 pipeline drone. The list of advance orders included Exxon Mobil for new projects in the Middle East and Russia, Apache Corporation for their existing facilities in the North Sea and the Gulf of Mexico, and Burlington Resources for expanded operations in the North Dutch Sea and Canada.

'Robert! I don't believe it. Is it really you?'

The man coming over to them from the next-door stand spoke English with a thick accent. Stephanie knew where he was from before Newman uttered his name.

'Sergei. My God.'

'I know. How long has it been?'

'Too long. This is Marina Schrader. A colleague of mine. Marina, Sergei Volkov.'

They shook hands as Stephanie took another look at the name on the board behind the man. Vostok-Energo.

'Still in Moscow?' Newman asked.

'No. I'm out in Khabarovsk. Been there three years. I love it out there.'

'Really?'

'Really.'

Newman explained for Stephanie's benefit. 'Vostok-Energo is the Far Eastern export arm of Unified Energy System, which is Russia's elec-

tricity monopoly.' He turned back to Volkov. 'Let
me guess. China?'

'That's right. And both Koreas. We're looking
to sell seven billion kilowatt-hours a year by 2010.
Longer term we're hoping to ramp up to fifty
billion. Still living in Paris?'

'Yes. But I don't get to spend as much time
there as I'd like.'

'You never did. What about Scheherazade?'

As they walked away from the Vostok-Energo
stand, Stephanie said, 'That's twice.'

'What is?'

'That someone's brought up her name. Kessler
asked after her last night.'

'So?'

'Exactly. So?'

'So nothing.'

They entered Hall D on the Blue Level. There were
several hundred people in the audience. At the
front a moderator sat between two groups of three.
To his right, Stephanie saw Richard Rhinehart,
Elizabeth Weil and a third man. She didn't recognize the three to the left but Newman pointed out
two of them; Ron Walsh of *The New Yorker* and
Maria Montero, a political academic from
Princeton. There was a large screen behind them:

AMERICAN POWER EXPORTED:
THE AXIS OF CAPITAL

A question came from the floor. *Has the current US administration been hijacked?* The moderator looked to Weil. 'Elizabeth, as a member of the Potomac Institute, I think this one might be for you.'

She nodded graciously. 'I thought so.' She peered into the audience in the general direction of the enquiry. 'The simple answer is: of course not. The fact is, the president of the United States does reflect some of our thoughts. That much is true. But that doesn't mean that we're feeding them to him. It doesn't even mean that he arrives at his conclusions the way we arrive at ours. Contrary to what a lot of people would like to believe, no one has hijacked this presidency. Or the last presidency. Or even the presidency before that. No one's been brainwashed. There's no conspiracy. I'm sorry to disappoint you.'

Newman prodded Stephanie in the ribs. 'See the guy down there. Third from the front, just off centre, with two spare seats to his right.'

She couldn't see him clearly because of the distance and the people in between but she saw who Newman meant. 'Yes?'

'Kenneth Kincaid of Kincaid Pearson Merriweather.'

'The KPM Family.'

Newman nodded. 'Owned by Amsterdam. Owners of DeMille.'

Ron Walsh was saying. 'The point is, every time America gets into trouble overseas, the administration in Washington tends to reduce the problem to a single dimension. Usually, good versus tyranny. The reality is – and *always* is – much more complex.'

'That's not necessarily true,' insisted Richard Rhinehart. 'Look at Bosnia. Nobody did anything until we did. The rest of the world looked the other way. We don't do that and people don't like it. We were right to intervene in Bosnia and history will prove that we were right to intervene in Iraq. What's more, if we intervene again, you can be sure that history will prove us right again.'

There was mild astonishment on every face Stephanie could see.

Walsh smelt an opportunity. 'Like where, Richard?'

Rhinehart, Stephanie realized, hadn't made a mistake. No matter how provocative, he'd meant to say it. 'Let's wait and see.'

'Syria?' Walsh prompted.

Rhinehart shrugged. 'Who knows?'

'Iran? Saudi Arabia, perhaps?'

'Time will tell.'

Stephanie remembered something Newman had said of Kenneth Kincaid in Paris. *A friend of this president, the last president, every president.* She leaned forward to get a better look at him. A small, compact man in a dark brown suit, with grey hair razored to a fuzz and an eagle's beak nose. He radiated ferocity.

Stephanie scanned the auditorium and

wondered why Leonid Golitsyn had intended to be present. To meet with Kincaid, perhaps. Or Rhinehart. Except that Golitsyn was a man who could meet anybody anywhere at any time. So why here?

The next question came from the audience. 'Your views, Mr Rhinehart, are backed by wealthy corporations, large media companies, billionaire entrepreneurs. How can you defend yourself against the central accusation of this debate, which is that you're not exporting democracy but capitalism?'

'I hadn't realized it was an accusation. I was under the impression that it was a topic for open discussion.'

Laughter rippled through the auditorium.

'Very clever, Mr Rhinehart. But why don't you try answering the question?'

'Okay. It's not true.'

More laughter.

But the man stayed standing, determined to have satisfaction. 'I'm glad you find it so funny. But to me, and to many others here, that only serves to underline the arrogance we've come to associate with people like you.'

That seemed to hit a nerve. Rhinehart sat up straight in his chair. 'Look, most of the people you want to put in this bracket have historical roots on the left. They were democrats. *Are* democrats. Not the traditional breeding ground of capitalism I'm sure even you would agree.'

Elizabeth Weil took up the issue when

508

Rhinehart had finished. She pre-empted her answer with the same dazzling smile she'd employed so effectively at the Hotel Bristol. 'We don't want to rule the world. We're not trying to force everyone to live the way we live. All we do is think about the way things are and then try to come up with ideas to make them better. Now if those ideas end up as government policy, that's great. That's why we're here.'

'Even if those policies make other governments nervous?' Maria Montero asked.

'Well, there does come a point where we have to stand by our beliefs.'

'No matter what?'

Weil was still smiling but the warmth had gone. 'Look, Maria, let me say this: we'll behave in the way we know to be right. And we'll explain our ideas in a way that is open and honest. And if people don't get it, we'll try again. We don't want anyone to misunderstand us. But if they still don't get it – or *won't* get it – then that's too bad. And if that means there are some people in certain parts of the world who have to live in a state of anxiety . . . well, I guess they're just going to have to get used to that.'

Out of the corner of her eye Stephanie saw Kincaid moving. A younger man had appeared and they were murmuring to one another. She couldn't see clearly because his body was half-turned from her but there was something about him that looked familiar.

'Kincaid's getting up,' she whispered to Newman.

The men headed for their nearest exit which was on the far side of the hall. Instinctively, Stephanie found herself rising to her feet.

'Where are you going?'

'I'm not sure . . . there's just something I need to . . .'

She could only see their backs now. But the harder she looked the more persuaded she was. She left the hall and searched for the stairs up to the ground floor. At the top of the steps Yellow Level was as busy as when they'd entered. She stood at the centre of it and cast her gaze in a circle.

Newman appeared at her side. 'What is it?'

'Can you see them? Where are they?'

With the advantage of height it didn't take him long. 'Over there. Outside. Kincaid's talking to . . . hang on . . . it's Wiley.'

'Gordon Wiley?'

'Yes. And there's another guy . . .'

Stephanie cut through the crowd, skirting the huge Areva stand. Through the throng she caught dappled glimpses of the heads of KPM and the Amsterdam Group standing beside two limousines, a stretch black Mercedes and a silver Lexus. She moved into the foyer, Newman close behind.

She didn't go out into the drizzle. Instead, she watched them through glass; Gordon Wiley and

Kenneth Kincaid in animated conversation. It didn't last long. Thirty seconds, perhaps. Then Wiley turned his back on Kincaid as the third man held open the back door of the Mercedes for him. Wiley climbed in. Kincaid headed for the Lexus. The third man closed the Mercedes door and opened the front passenger door. He took a last look around before getting in, which was when Stephanie saw him clearly.

The Mercedes crossed the Brigittenauer Bridge and joined Handelskai. Gordon Wiley sat alone on the back seat, partitioned from the two men in front by a glass screen. He made two calls. The first was to a mobile phone in Vienna, the second to a landline in Paris.

Half an hour later, the Mercedes drew to a halt outside the main entrance to the Central Cemetery on Simmeringer Hauptstrasse. Wiley got out of the car, wrapped a navy cashmere scarf around his throat and pulled on a dark grey overcoat. The sky was a swirling mix of cloud and dusk, the icy drizzle almost sleet. All in all, conditions to match his mood. And not just his.

They met at the impressive Fritz Wotruba cube marking Arnold Schönberg's grave. Azzam Fahad of the Iraqi oil ministry was wearing a sable hat. A gift from Moscow, Wiley guessed. Azzam had been a regular visitor for thirty years.

'You gave us assurances, Gordon.'

'I know. And they were given in good faith.'

'You promised us this matter would be concluded by today. Perhaps you don't appreciate the pressure we're under in Baghdad.'

'That isn't true.'

'It's a delicate time. And a delicate idea.'

'No one is more aware of that than I am, Azzam.'

'Then why are we meeting? It's over.'

'I'm freezing. Let's walk a little.'

They circled the Presidential Vault containing the remains of Dr Karl Renner and then strolled around Dr Karl-Lueger-Kirche. The cemetery was quiet and they were almost alone.

Wiley said, 'Everything *is* going to be okay.'

'It's too late.'

'I'm asking for an extension.'

'What's the point?'

'The matter is being concluded as we speak.'

'She's dead?'

'Not yet. But she'll be on the news tomorrow morning.'

'It was supposed to be on the news the morning after Paris. She was supposed to be with Brand. That was the whole point, wasn't it?'

Wiley winced. 'I know it's late in the day but we're going to pull through. You have my word on it, Azzam. Which is why I want to reschedule.'

'For tomorrow?'

'The day after.'

'Why the delay?'

'So that you can see the evidence for yourself. So that you can be sure.'

'I thought you said it would be on the news in the morning.'

'It will be – the fact that she's dead. But I'm also talking about her and Brand.'

Azzam Fahad stopped walking to consider it. Eventually, he said, 'Where?'

'Paris.'

Azzam said, 'You should know that we've kept all our options open. At every stage of our negotiation with you, we've actively considered alternatives.'

'I wouldn't have expected anything else.'

'We have people lined up to replace you, Gordon.'

Wiley resisted the instinct to ask for names. 'There's nobody out there who can put this together the way we can. We both know that.'

'Not as a single entity, perhaps. But broken into pieces – it can be done. Quite easily, as a matter of fact.'

Wiley tried to manufacture a smile. 'In that case, I guess it's up to us to make sure it never gets to that.'

Azzam nodded. 'Paris, then. Where and when?'

They parted at the arcades, close to the memorial for the miner August Zang.

I'm alone in the drizzle on Bruno-Kreisky-Platz, outside the Austria Center, trying to put the pieces

513

together. The man holding open the Mercedes door for Gordon Wiley was Roland, my part-time lover in Brussels. Can it really be only ten days since I woke up in his apartment overlooking avenue Louise? It seems much longer.

Mentally, I rewind and play. Roland entered Hall D and spoke to Kenneth Kincaid. They left together. Outside the Austria Center, Roland gravitated to Gordon Wiley, leaving in the same car as him. I'm guessing that Wiley sent Roland into the convention hall to bring Kincaid out. What does that make him – a messenger boy? Why not? That would explain a lot. The blown cover of Marianne Bernard would make sense. Even though I allowed him almost no access to my life, Roland knew enough to form a starting point. After that I presume it was easy. Perhaps it wasn't even him. Perhaps he just pointed others in the right direction. Perhaps he was left to get on with what he did best: nourishing my sexual appetite. Knickers down, defences down.

I feel like crying. At my own stupidity. My arrogance. What was I thinking? But there's more to it than that. Despite the cold, cavalier nature of our arrangement, I feel betrayed. Almost violated. There's not much justification for this feeling; after all, it's not as though I invested any trust in Roland.

Perhaps it's because I thought he cared. And now it appears that he cared even less than I did. For me, it was simply a matter of cheap pleasure. And some of that pleasure was to be found in the idea that Roland actually felt something for me. For her, for Marianne.

Now, however, it seems I was just a work detail, a shift on the factory floor.

I remember the last time I spoke to Roland. It was shortly before I left his apartment the morning after my return from Turkmenistan. I was dressed, he was still in bed. He was looking at me in a curious way so I asked him what he was thinking. He replied, 'That I went to bed with one person and woke up with another.'

And I said, 'I know the feeling.'

Robert appears at my side. He doesn't ask what's wrong. He just puts his arm around my shoulder and says, 'Let's get out of here.'

They didn't talk much on the U-Bahn. At Stephansplatz, Newman phoned the Imperial and tried to get through to Gordon Wiley's suite. Stephanie stood close by, trying to clear her head.

'It's over,' he told her.

'What do you mean?'

'Wiley's gone.'

The Butterfly signing had been scheduled for six in Wiley's hotel suite.

Newman said, 'He checked out. Wherever he was heading in the Merc, it wasn't back to the Imperial. Maybe Stern got it wrong.'

'Or Wiley changed his plans.'

'Could be.'

'So what now?'

'I don't know. Maybe we should go and check.'

Stephanie felt drained. 'You go. I'm going back to the hotel.'

'You okay?'

'I'll be fine. I just need to be alone. I've got to think.'

She took the U-Bahn as far as Zieglergasse and walked the rest. The spectre of Roland lingered. His participation explained how many subsequent events had occurred but not why.

She checked for messages at the Lübeck's front desk but there were none. Still no word from Julia. She took the stairs to the second floor. In their room, she kicked the door shut with her heel, shrugged off her jacket and stepped out of her shoes.

'Don't make me do anything we'd both regret.'

She recognized the voice. Iain Boyd.

She said, 'I'm guessing it's a little late for that.'

'Turn round. Slowly.'

The familiar features came into view; ruddy, weather-beaten skin, thick blonde hair cut short, square shoulders. He wore a black jacket by The North Face, a pair of jeans and scuffed walking boots. She looked at the gun.

'A Glock 17. When in Austria . . . ?'

'Don't bother. I'm not in the mood, Stephanie.'

'How are you, Iain?'

His eyes were flint. 'Surprised. Angry. Disappointed.'

'Sorry to hear that.'

'Where's your friend?'

'He'll be back soon.'

There was a pause while Boyd decided whether

she was lying. 'I never thought it would come to this. Not after all I did for you.'

'How'd you find me?'

'You mean, apart from following the trail of corpses you've been leaving all over Europe? We've had Kleist under surveillance for three days.'

'We haven't been here for three days.'

'Christ, Stephanie, wake up. They're ahead of you. When you dropped the decoy at Lyon they looked the other way. After Obernai they knew you were heading for the border into Germany. That you were going east.'

'*They?* Aren't you one of them?'

'Don't get lippy with me. Sit down.'

'Where?'

'End of the bed.'

He'd cleared a space. When she and Newman had left the room the bag had been on the bed. Now it was in the corner by the table, its contents in a pile on the carpet. As she sat down he crossed the floor to the window, drew the curtains, then stood with his back to the wall. The invisible thread from the Glock's tip to the centre of her chest never faltered as he moved.

'They guessed you'd head for Vienna so they checked to see who you knew here. Kleist.'

'*How* did they guess? I could have kept going. Romania, Russia. Anywhere between here and the Bering Straits.'

'I've no idea. I'm just the bullet. But they knew.

And as usual they were right. Unlike your usual trick – Stern – Kleist is still an easy man to find.'

'Very funny.'

'I wish it was.'

'How many Magenta House people are here?'

'Four. Including the boss.'

'Rosie?'

'To you, perhaps.'

'I thought you'd retired, Iain.'

'They brought me back for you. Against my will. She thinks I'm the only one who can talk you down. The alternative is less complicated.'

'Then I suppose I should be grateful to you.'

'I nearly said no. Sorry, can't be arsed, send someone else. You'd be dead by now.'

'Not necessarily. You trained me.'

'Drop it, will you? This isn't a joke, Stephanie.'

'I was set up.'

'I don't care.'

'I don't believe that.'

'*They* don't care.'

'But what about you?'

'It doesn't matter what I think.'

'So why are you here?'

'You've got to come in.'

'To Magenta House?'

Boyd nodded. 'For debriefing.'

'I don't work for them any more.'

'Grow up, Stephanie.'

'They'll kill me.'

'They'll kill you if you don't. That's for sure.'

'You mean *you'll* kill me.'

He looked at her. Pained and resolved in equal measure. They'd had something once. But that wouldn't matter to Boyd. He'd take no pleasure from it at the moment of execution but, in years to come, he'd be able to rationalize it; the culling of a sick specimen to protect the overall health of the population.

Stephanie thought of Julia and the prints she'd seen at the Verbinski clinic.

'I can't come in, Iain.'

'Then you'll make a dead man happy.'

Alexander. Always a good card to play.

She said, 'I don't trust you.'

'You're going to have to do better than that.'

'Think for yourself. You know me.'

'Not any more.'

In a corner of her mind an idea had lingered: that Boyd would always be there for her somehow. More than anyone, he'd created Petra but he'd also been the man who'd resurrected Stephanie. A far greater achievement, in both their eyes.

'I need time, Iain.'

'If it was up to me . . .'

'Not days. Hours.'

He shook his head. 'You know the way it works.'

'Do they know you've found me yet?'

'They know where I am.'

'But you haven't contacted them since I walked in here.'

'Don't bother asking.'

'Okay. I'll ask something else. How is it that Lance Grotius had my old Magenta House clearance code on his laptop?'

'No idea.'

'You haven't thought about it. I can tell from your expression.'

The accusation was only partly true. A thought had occurred to him. Not concerned directly with Grotius and a laptop, but related. Five days earlier, in Paris, he'd confronted Pierre Damiani in his apartment overlooking Parc Monceau. That lead had been fed to him by Magenta House. *Every* lead had been fed to him by Magenta House.

The identity that Stephanie had kept in the safe-deposit box at Banque Damiani had not been issued by Magenta House. It had been an independent creation. He wondered how the organization had learned of it. And then he wondered why he'd been selected to find Stephanie. Because she trusted him? That was the reason Rosie Chaudhuri had given him. She'd also implied that because Boyd knew Stephanie better than anyone else, he'd be better equipped to locate her. But he'd turned up nothing. He'd had to rely on them. In other words, they could have sent anyone.

'My code was on his laptop, Iain. I need you to believe that.'

'Whatever.'

'Let me explain something to you. Magenta

House was split into two assassination sections. All the information relating to those two sections was stored in a computer in the basement of the building. That computer was hermetically sealed. Information was brought in and taken out on modified disks that could only be used on other computers, providing they met the security criteria.'

'Fascinating. And irrelevant.'

'Didn't you hear what I said? Grotius had my clearance code on his laptop. That could not have been retrieved – or stolen – electronically.'

'I don't know why I'm listening to this.'

'I've been sold out.'

'And you think it's Magenta House?'

'It looks like it but I don't know. Just like you don't know how they figured out I was heading for Vienna, not Vladivostok.'

'Forget it.'

Stephanie felt her temper fraying. 'There's a woman in this city masquerading as me. Same name, same look. She's even got the same scars. Know why? Because she *is* me. Know how she got the scars? Cosmetically. Again, like me. The surgeon who did it took her cue from a series of stills from film footage of me and Komarov in an apartment in London. Magenta House film footage. How do I know that? Because they used it as leverage on me. What I don't know is this: how stills from that footage found their way to the Verbinski clinic here in Vienna.'

'If it's not going to make any difference what's the point?'

'The point is this: maybe it's Magenta House but maybe it's not. In which case, they're being set up too. And that's more serious than having me on the run. That means they're no longer quite the invisible organization they thought they were.'

Boyd wanted to maintain the rhythm of refusal but found he couldn't. He replayed her argument in his mind.

Stephanie looked at the contents of her bag and said, 'There are two DVDs over there. One of them has footage of my clone in bed with Anders Brand and a hooker. You can see the scars on her quite clearly. They appear genuine. Take the disk, have a look. *You* should be able to tell.'

The clock ticks. I'm sitting on the bed, Robert's on the chair by the window. We're waiting for Julia to call. There's nothing else we can do.

'Why do you think he backed down?' he asks.

'I'm still not sure.'

'Something you said?'

'I guess so.'

Boyd looked at me for a long while before asking me how long I needed. Twelve hours, I told him. He seemed pained and pitying in equal measure, then nodded his assent. That was just after six. Robert returned here at seven. Since then, we've been killing time. The longer we wait, the slower each hour passes.

'Tell me about you and Scheherazade, Robert.'

'What about her?'

'The first time I saw the two of you in the Lancaster, you didn't look like lovers. But you didn't look like just-good-friends, either.'

He takes his time. 'We go back a long way. Originally I met Scheherazade through her husband, Omar. And I met Omar when I was working for my uncle.'

'This was after Lebanon?'

'Yes. Several years later. Most teenage rebellions occur during the teenage years. Mine happened during my twenties. Most teenage rebellions kick against conservatism. Mine kicked against liberalism.'

'As personified by your father?'

'And by the life I'd been living with Rachel. It was broken. It couldn't be fixed. I just wanted to get as far away from it as possible. My uncle got me a job at the New York offices of Mackenzie Resources. I started at the bottom and worked my way up and that's how I met Omar. In Riyadh, on business. Soon after, he asked me to work for him.'

'Did he know about Lebanon?'

'Yes. Which makes his attitude towards me even more unusual. I was tainted by that experience. Very few people in that world would have hired me. But he was an unconventional man in some ways. He always took people as he found them. So I went with him. And through him, I met Scheherazade.'

I raise an eyebrow. 'That's appreciation for you. A man offers you a job and you take his wife as well.'

'Nothing happened between us while Omar was

523

alive. There was never any possibility of that. Even after his death, there could never have been anything overt. Scheherazade wouldn't have allowed it.'

'Why not?'

'Her background. Her devotion to her husband. Discretion was more than a choice. It was an obligation.'

'So you waited until the dust had settled?'

'The dust never really settles for a widow like Scheherazade when her husband was a man like Omar.'

I remember the little I knew of her before that night in the Lancaster, most of it gleaned from the French press. Much of the coverage had ignored her business acumen and had focused on her love-life instead. Nearly all of it had been idle speculation. There had been a few romantic rumours but only of the vaguest kind. There had never been a hint of scandal.

'Your relationship was a secret?'

'An open secret. When someone like Abel Kessler brings it up, or Sergei Volkov, it's because they knew we were close but have never been sure quite how close. They suspect but they can never confirm.'

'How complicated.'

'That was one of the reasons it ended.'

'What were the others?'

Robert smiles. 'They're private, Stephanie. But they're not startling. They're the usual things.'

Privacy's fine by me. Where would I be without it? I say, 'It's nice that you've stayed close.'

'It is.'

'She has a great reputation as an investor, doesn't she?'

'Yes.'

'How much of that is down to you?'

'Scheherazade has a brilliant mind. I helped where I could but the reality is she didn't need me that much. People tend to forget how smart she is. They say that she married Omar because he was rich and old. The truth is, Omar had the sharpest mind I've ever encountered. Scheherazade was attracted to that. Genuinely. She knew their time together would be limited but she was determined to make the most of it. That's the kind of woman she is. She married Omar because the other men she knew didn't match up. Simple as that.'

'Except you.'

'Only after he was dead.'

The phone rings. I answer it.

'Petra? It's Julia.'

Kärntnerstrasse, ten-forty-five. The café was half-empty, warm and smoky, Chopin playing softly over poor speakers. Julia was already there, drinking coffee with a glass of cheap armagnac. Stephanie ordered a cappuccino at the bar then sat opposite her at a table by the window.

'You sure about this?' Julia asked.

Stephanie nodded. 'Midnight?'

'Yes. He doesn't like it if I'm late.'

'What about you?'

'I'm ready to run.'

'Don't go back to your apartment. Just in case.'

'I wasn't going to. When I leave here, I'll collect my money and vanish.' She picked up a small cloth shoulder-bag and pushed it across the rough wooden table. 'Look inside. I've taken precautions. Anybody tries to screw with me, they're going to regret it.'

Stephanie peered inside the bag. The gun was a Russian PSM, a weapon developed for the old Soviet security services. After the collapse of the Soviet Union they had started to crop up across central and eastern Europe. The silencer, Stephanie noticed, was custom-made.

'Do you know how to use this?'

Julia looked contemptuous. 'Alexei taught me. He was an expert.'

'This belonged to him?'

She shook her head. 'I got it from Club Nitro. There's a guy there. Kurt . . .'

'You know that I know Kurt, don't you?'

Julia managed a fragile smile. 'Well, he wouldn't do it for me at first. But when I said I was going to use it on you he wouldn't even let me pay for it.'

'It's an unusual gun.'

'Kurt has unusual friends. Anyway, this is Vienna. Everything is available.'

'So I've heard.'

Julia gazed into curls of cigarette smoke. 'As soon as I had it in my hand, I wanted to go straight over to the hotel and do it myself. When I think of all the lies I tolerated. Girls like me – it doesn't matter where we are, there's always some bastard waiting for us.'

'I wish I could disagree with you. Where will you go?'

'I don't know yet. I have a friend in Amsterdam. It would be nice to see her again maybe. What about you?'

'I'd like to run. But I'm not sure I can.'

'Which is why *I* have to run?'

'I'm afraid so. There can be only one Petra.'

'But I thought she was supposed to be dead.'

'She is.'

Julia poured the rest of her armagnac into her coffee. 'Seems like we have a connection; whatever one of us does affects the other. We're almost the same woman.'

Stephanie nodded. 'How can I contact you?'

'Why would you want to?'

'To tell you when it's safe to stop running.'

Julia grinned mischievously. 'Maybe I'll get a taste for it. Like you.'

'If you're like me, you'll want to stop. Better to have the option, at least. Do you have an e-mail address?'

'Sure. Several.'

'Me too.'

'See?'

Julia ordered another couple of cappuccinos and they talked. At eleven-forty-five they settled the bill. Which was when Julia said, 'We're about the same size, wouldn't you say?'

'More or less.'

'Perhaps we should swap clothes. You should

wear what Julia wears when she's being Petra. Especially the glasses.' She took them off to show Stephanie. 'He'll be expecting this beautiful bruise.'

They changed in the cloakroom. Julia had a slightly fuller figure than Stephanie. As they stepped on to Kärntnerstrasse and exchanged kisses, she said, 'I guess I'm going to have to lose weight if I'm ever really going to be you.'

Stephanie shook her head. 'No. The real me is exactly the way you are now.'

'So what does that make you?'

'Exactly what *I'm* supposed to be right now. An impostor.'

Day Twelve

'**You are here to** see Herr Stonehouse?'

The man at Reception was utterly inscrutable yet Stephanie saw straight through his politeness. *You're a tramp and if Herr Stonehouse wasn't such a valued guest I'd toss you straight back into the gutter.* He picked up the phone, pressed a three-digit number and spoke softly. It was ten past midnight in the opulent lobby of the Hotel Imperial on Kärntner Ring.

'Room 510.'

Up to the fifth floor, down a long, quiet corridor, one turn to the left, then as far as the room at the end. She looked left and right, took out the Heckler & Koch, held it at her side and rang the bell. She heard the approach on the other side of the door. He was talking. A phone conversation? Or was there someone in the room with him?

The door opened. John Peltor, in the middle of a call, snatched a glimpse of the clothes and sunglasses, then slapped a hand over the mouth-piece and hissed, 'You're late. It's after midnight. What have you done to your hair? I told you never to change anything unless I . . .'

He didn't see the gun. Not until Stephanie pointed the weapon at his teeth. He stared into the black hole at the centre of the silencer. And then at the face behind.

'I'll get back to you,' he murmured, before finishing his call.

He reversed into the suite. Stephanie closed the door behind her and followed him in.

'Take it easy, Petra. Okay? Don't do anything we'll both regret.'

'Unlikely.'

The room was huge. Cream walls with inlaid panels of pale pink-and-cream striped wallpaper, thick gold curtains, a candle-bulb chandelier, antiques, oils on canvas set in generous gilt frames. Peltor put his phone on the coffee table. There was an open attaché case on the sofa beside a small olive canvas knapsack.

'Nice room,' Stephanie said. 'I should have listened to you in Munich. Corporate slaughter clearly pays.'

'Don't play the nun, Petra. It doesn't suit you.'

'Are you picking up the tab? Or is it on an Amsterdam expense account?'

He was wearing some unpleasant beige slacks and a lime polo-shirt, tightly tucked in to emphasize the narrowness of his waist in comparison to the broad sweep of his shoulders.

'What are you doing here, Petra?'

It was the first time she'd ever seen him nervous.

'I'm the one with the gun, I'll ask the questions.'

'I got people all over Europe looking for you.'

'I know. I've run into a few of them.'

'I heard you made a real mess of Grotius.'

'It was no more than he deserved.'

'Maybe. Not like Gavras, though.'

'Who?'

'Rafael Gavras. Obernai. The guy who stuck a kilo of Semtex under that shit-heap you were driving. For a while there I felt sorry for the poor bastard. Then I found out he was Cuban.'

'I heard on the radio that he was arrested.'

'That's the best thing that's happened to him lately.'

'Dead?'

'Deader than Nixon's nuts. Can you believe it? The guy gets bailed, six hours later he's history. A tragic domestic accident. Broke his neck while combing his hair. Something like that.'

Anxiety dressed as bravado. Typical Peltor. Stephanie told him to drag the chair by the desk to the centre of the floor.

'Gotta hand it to you, Petra. That's not a bad impression of Julia.'

'Doing an impression of me?'

'Right. What did you do to her?'

'Nothing. Sit down.'

He lowered himself on to the chair. 'You didn't kill her?'

Stephanie stared at him. 'Why would I kill her?'

'Where is she?'

'By now? She's gone. Vanished.'

'No way. Not without her money. She's not the type.'

'I told her to forget the money. I told her who you really are. *What* you are. After that, she wasn't too concerned with the money. How'd you find her?'

The chair creaked, barely taking his vast frame. 'Internet.'

'Is that the way you meet most of your women?'

'Fuck you.'

Stephanie took off the glasses so that he could see her eyes. 'I've been on the run for ten days, no thanks to you. I'm tired and I'm upset and I'm a woman with a gun. You'd do well to remember that the next time you open your mouth.'

Peltor knew better than to doubt her. 'I needed someone who could pass for you. Took me a few days but I narrowed it down to about a dozen. All in Europe, two of them here in Vienna. I swear this city oozes cooze. You can smell it on the street . . .'

'Please. Less local colour.'

'So I contacted this ratty little asshole . . .'

'Rudi Littbarski?'

'You know him?'

'Not socially.'

'Littbarski knows every creep under every rock in this town. He found out she was a regular at this sleaze-pit out by UNO City. Club Nitro. So I went out there with him and it went from there. I saw her a few times, then made her an offer. How did *you* find her?'

'I'm a big fan of Parisian art-house movies.'

Peltor raised an eyebrow. 'I guess that means you met my pal Étienne Lorenz.'

'In a manner of speaking. I'm curious. Munich and our chance meeting at Café Roma – all planned?'

'No. I was as surprised as you.'

'You have no idea how surprised I was.'

'It happens. It happened to *us*. Remember? JFK?'

Stephanie tightened her grip on the gun. 'You're lying.'

Peltor tensed. 'I swear, Munich was a coincidence.'

'Last chance.'

Peltor's eyes widened. '*Munich* was a coincidence.'

'But?'

He was shaking. Stephanie had never imagined she would see such a thing. She'd assumed a man like Peltor would face the bullet with a tirade of defiance spat through gnashing teeth.

'*But?*' she prompted him for the final time.

'*After* Munich . . . was not a coincidence.'

'What was it? Amsterdam? I know Heilmann worked as a consultant for DeMille.'

Peltor looked amazed. 'Was that why you killed him?'

'No.'

'Why, then?'

'None of your business. Tell me what happened *after* Munich.'

'Well . . . you killed Otto. That's what happened.'

'And?'

'And it didn't take a genius to figure out who did it. Not after I ran into you. That was how your name came up. We were looking for someone to discredit Brand. I doubt you'd have been a natural candidate. But after Otto you seemed ideal. Nobody could've discredited an honourable man better than you *and* we'd get payback for one of ours.'

'Let me get this straight: if I hadn't killed Heilmann, Paris would never have happened.'

'It would have happened. But not with you. And maybe not in Paris. But Brand was always going to get it. One way or another.'

Stephanie thought briefly of Jacob and Miriam Furst. She took three slow, deep breaths to calm herself.

'What about what you said to me during our breakfast at the Mandarin Oriental? All that advice you gave me about retirement?'

For a moment Peltor looked genuinely upset. 'Whatever you think of me, Petra, I never wanted you to go the way of Juha Suomalainen.'

'You told me he died up a tree in a chainsaw accident.'

'Dead before his time, Petra. That's the point.'

'Since you've raised the subject of premature death, let's talk about you.'

Stephanie raised the gun a little. When he managed to speak, his voice was a low tremble. 'You don't have to kill me, Petra.'

'Technically, that's true. And generally, I don't kill for my own amusement. But in your case, I'm going to make an exception.'

He asked her what she wanted. To kill him in cold blood. That was the truth. Instead, she said, 'Answers.'

Relief flooded through him.

'But let me explain something to you. If I think you're lying, I'll shoot you. If I think you're being evasive, I'll shoot you. Now talk me through Passage du Caire.'

'You still pissed about that? Come on, Petra, we've been in situations . . .'

'Don't play the solidarity card. We're not the same. Never have been. Why Anders Brand?'

'People listened to Brand. He was tight with the Arabs.'

'Could you possibly be any less specific? If I wanted vague generalizations I'd be watching CNN.'

'There was this deal . . .'

'Butterfly.'

'You know about that?'

'Broadly.'

'Brand was vital.'

'Why?'

'He was the honest broker. The virgin in the whorehouse. You know where this line goes?'

'Mosul to Haifa.'

'Via Jordan. But close to the border with Syria. Jordan has agreed transit rights. Israel has agreed to the new terminal at Haifa. All that remained was for Iraq to sign up.'

'I can think of a number of sticking points. Israel in particular. Why hasn't Iraq signed up?'

'There are too many internal objections to the project. They're being organized by a number of leading Shia clerics. It started out as one or two dissenting voices. Now it's gathering momentum.'

'Frankly, I'm not surprised.'

'Frankly, neither are we.'

Stephanie looked puzzled. 'I don't understand.'

Peltor shrugged dismissively. 'It doesn't matter. That's the point. As long as the contract is implemented. That's the beauty of it.'

'Explain that to me.'

'Look, Brand was in a unique position. He could have delivered the Shia for us. He spoke to the Shia leadership, including al-Sistani. We know they could've been persuaded by him. Washington was banking on that. That he'd do the right thing. But he wouldn't.'

'Wouldn't or couldn't?'

'Your guess is as good as mine.'

'My guess is wouldn't.'

'Mine too. Anyway, when he didn't deliver Washington began to apply pressure. But it back-fired. So now they had a situation where not only was Brand not going to deliver but it started to look like he was going to turn round and actively campaign *against* the deal.'

'Taking the Shia leadership with him.'

'Most of it. And bringing on board some of those who were against him before. All in all, a situation the new Iraqi government couldn't be seen to be going against.'

'Leaving Amsterdam with a giant problem.'

'Again.'

'Again?'

'This is the second time they've been here. They signed a contract in December 2002 for this pipeline.'

'*Before* the war?'

'That's right. You remember the scandal. Bush was handing out contracts for the reconstruction of Iraq before the invasion. In fact, while he was still telling everyone that he hoped a peace-ful conclusion could be reached. Anyway, Amsterdam's name never entered the public arena but . . .'

'How typical. What happened?'

'They were told to drop it.'

'Was the agreement signed?'

'Sure. But they chose not to commit commercial suicide by pursuing it.'

'Because they knew they'd get another chance?'

Peltor nodded. 'They were guaranteed it. Which is where we are now. They're not going to let this go, Petra. They've invested too much. Politically and financially.'

'Which brings us back to Brand.'

'Exactly. The first priority was to make sure Brand's mouth stayed shut. Permanently. The second priority was to discredit him. To give the Shia leadership a reason to distance themselves from Brand and to give the Iraqi administration an exit.'

'Which is where I come in.'

'That's right. Brand dies. Then it turns out he's not the saint everyone thought he was. Turns out he likes fucking hookers and terrorists. Turns out he consorts with Zionist extremists.'

Stephanie frowned. 'I'm sorry?'

Peltor's smile was sly. 'Two of the Sentier dead were Zionist extremists.'

'I didn't hear that.'

'We held it back when things went wrong.'

'How did you organize it?'

'The same way we organized you. We took someone they trusted and got them to make the call. Same place, same time.'

'Same outcome?'

'Obviously. No loose ends.'

'How imaginative.'

'I like to think of it as . . . *garnish*.'

'More like overkill. So, with Brand gone and his reputation in tatters, what was supposed to happen next?'

'We expected people to distance themselves from him. We wanted old alliances to break down, new alliances to be made. Meanwhile the new Iraqi administration would get to promote the pipeline as a great project to fund regeneration. With the added sweetener of being financed by foreign aid.'

'And for Amsterdam that means the thick end of $15 billion. Right?'

Peltor said, 'I'm impressed. But you're way off the mark.'

'How come?'

'Amsterdam's negotiating other deals that are dependent on the success of Butterfly. Saudi Arabia, Kuwait, Oman, Bahrain, Qatar. If you'll pardon the phrase, they're all in the pipeline. It's kinda like the Domino effect. Once Butterfly happens, so do the others. Fifteen billion? In the long run, it could be fifty plus.'

Stephanie shook her head. 'You people . . .'

Peltor smiled a little. 'You should know, Petra. Amsterdam learned its lesson from the Saudis. They're conducting themselves the Arab way, not the American way. There's no policy. No guiding philosophy. Just a series of lucrative commercial marriages.'

'Corporate polygamy.'

'Damn right.'

'I assume Amsterdam's relationship with the Israeli government would fall into this category.'

'Very much so.'

'And they're happy with this?'

'Who, the Israelis? Sure. They're getting a protected oil supply. And that's not all; they don't even have to pay for the new oil terminal at Haifa. Don't tell the US taxpayer but they're the ones who are going to pick up the tab.'

'And if there's violence?'

'Come on, Petra. This is the Middle East. Who gives a fuck about violence? They deserve each other, all of them. As far as I'm concerned they can carry on killing each other until it's last man standing. And then I'll volunteer to take care of *that* motherfucker personally and the whole goddamned Middle East problem will be over.'

'Where were you when Rwanda needed you?'

'You know as well as I do that violence has an upside. The more there is, the greater the need for security. You know what violence is? It's a big fat number in DeMille's profit margin. That's what it is.'

'And bonus share options for you?'

Peltor nodded. 'And you. If you want them.'

'First you try to kill me, now you try to recruit me. What next? Marmalade lessons?'

'It's called a changeable business climate. I meant what I said in Munich, Petra. You're wasted on the small stuff. You'd be great in this environment.'

'I hadn't realized it was a firm offer.'

'It wasn't. It was a feeler. But it could be.'

'I'm not sure I'd deal with the politics.'

Peltor's mood began to brighten. He patted his stomach and surveyed the grandeur of his hotel room. 'Fuck the politics, feel the money.'

'Is that the official motto of the Amsterdam Group?'

'Should be.'

'So Sentier was nothing more than a diversion?'

'I wouldn't say that. It got rid of Brand.'

'You could have done that anywhere.'

Peltor considered this, then conceded. 'Sure. But kill a few Frenchmen in Paris and who's gonna care? Nobody outside France, that's for sure. Kill a few Jews and it's all over the news. If you and Brand had died together it would've been perfect.'

Stephanie paused to marvel and seethe, one visibly, the other invisibly. 'I'll give you this much, at least: it's been an education.'

'Come on, Petra. Level with me. You don't really want to be running around dodging bullets for the rest of your life, do you?'

'No.'

'Then let's talk. Put away the gun. We'll forget all this.'

'We?'

'You forget the last ten days. We forget what happened to Otto Heilmann.'

'How do I know you're in a position to make such an offer?'

'I give you my word.'

'Not good enough.'

'Whose word would be good enough?'

'Gordon Wiley,' she said.

'So we'll call him.'

Stephanie thought about it for a while. 'How did you find out about me?'

Peltor frowned. 'What do you mean?'

'Brussels.'

He grew cautious but when she grew tense, he chose the truth. 'We had someone on the inside.'

'I know. Roland. I saw him yesterday at Petrotech.'

'Jesus – you were there?'

'Sure. With Wiley and Kincaid. And cuddly Richard Rhinehart. But how did you find out about Brussels in the first place? How did you know where to place Roland?'

Peltor opened his mouth, then hesitated.

'I hope you're not being evasive.'

The pause elongated.

She steadied her hand. 'Speak now.'

'Hammond.'

'Who?'

'Maurice Hammond.'

'Who the hell's Maurice Hammond? I've never heard of him.'

'He's a Brit.'

Stephanie felt the hairs rise on the back of her neck. 'Go on.'

'He's an intelligence consultant for Amsterdam Europe.'

'With a background *in* intelligence, I'm assuming.'

Peltor nodded. 'Ex-SIS.'

'Ex?'

'He's retired.'

'Let me guess. He was the one who came here from London with the photos of me. The photos that were used for Julia's scars at the Verbinski clinic.'

'That's right.'

A former SIS officer. That didn't quite make sense. Magenta House had no relationship with any established security service. That was the point of it. Yet there had to be a connection. It was too close for coincidence.

She didn't say anything for a while and was aware of Peltor watching her in constant analysis. There were so many questions but she didn't *need* anything else; she had enough to run from.

Nevertheless, she said, 'Who killed Leonid Golitsyn and Fyodor Medvedev?'

Peltor looked her straight in the eye. 'I did.'

No apology, no remorse.

'Why?'

'Golitsyn was the link between Brand and Amsterdam. Wiley trusted Golitsyn where he wouldn't trust his own people. Golitsyn operated on a higher level. Then it turned out that he was leaking classified information to Brand. Golitsyn betrayed Wiley.'

'Why was Golitsyn helping Brand?'

'He had the same feeling for Butterfly that Brand did.'

'They both saw through it?'

'There's nothing to see through, Petra. They were wrong.'

What was it Stern had said? *Golitsyn floats above the world.*

'One more thing: Jacob Furst.'

'Who?'

'The man who called me in Brussels to get me to come to Paris. He and his wife were killed. Who did it?'

'Grotius.'

Peltor's eyes betrayed him and the last of Stephanie's doubt evaporated. She took care not to let it show.

'You've got Wiley's personal number?' she asked.

'Sure. Want to call him now? Why don't we call him, Petra? We can make a deal. We're all professionals. Deals are what we do.'

'Where's the number?'

'In my cell.' He started to rise from the chair. 'I'll call him for you.'

'Sit down!'

Peltor froze. 'Okay. I'm sitting. Take it easy.'

She picked up his phone from the coffee table

and tried to access the address book. The phone didn't respond.

Peltor said, 'It's locked.'

'How do I unlock it?'

'Star 23.'

She looked at him and then at the phone. An unpleasant memory surfaced. Singapore. The Fullerton Hotel. An exploding mobile phone, the handset containing a small disk of Semtex impregnated with mercury droplets. She'd activated the device from Hong Kong. It had blown apart a lawyer's head.

She doubted Peltor would be fool enough to have such a device in a phone he used regularly. But why take the risk? Perhaps there were other modifications.

She tossed him the handset. 'You do it.'

'You want me to call him?'

She shook her head, then threw him a small message pad from beside the phone on the desk. 'Write down the number.'

Slowly, so that she wouldn't misinterpret his movement, he reached into the open attaché case on the sofa and extracted a Mont Blanc pen. He looked at the phone's screen and scribbled the number on the top sheet, which he tore off and offered to her.

'Here you go, Petra.'

I want to throw up but know that I can't. There's already something in my mouth. A gag of some sort, tied tightly, tugging at the corners. My eyes are still shut. I don't open them in case he sprays me again.

I know that I passed out but have no idea how much time has elapsed. My blood seems to have been substituted by wet sand. I can barely move. Nothing's responding.

I'm on the bed; I can feel the mattress and the bedspread beneath me. My hands are above my head, bound at the wrists and tied to something solid.

I try to piece it together. I took the paper. I looked at the number. Then there was a sharp snap and a piercing pain in the back of my right hand. I saw a tiny sliver of metal protruding from a puncture point. And even as I saw it, I felt the prickly heat spread through my fingers.

I fired the gun into the space he'd occupied but Peltor was already moving. The bullet ploughed harmlessly into the bed. I tried to fire a second shot but my fingers wouldn't respond. The gun slipped from my grasp.

That was when he piled into me like a linebacker, his bulk crushing the air from my lungs as we hit the floor. After that, my memory is a collection of scattered moments; a fistful of hair being grabbed, an assortment of brutal blows to the body, a heavy thud to the temple, a blast of spray to the face.

The effect was instant. A cloying sensation at the back of the throat, eyes stinging, skin burning. The first automatic intake of breath – a natural reaction to shock – did the damage, sucking the mist deep into my lungs, accelerating its passage into the bloodstream.

After that, I'm not sure.

He's removed the black jeans I was wearing. Eyes still closed, I run a clothing inventory by feel; as far as I can tell, my T-shirt, knickers and socks are all that's left.

Only when I hear him walking away from the bed do I open my eyes. The room moves, compounding my nausea. My head throbs. There's wetness just above the hairline over the left temple. My nose, mouth and throat feel raw while my eyes are dry; every blink is a scratch.

Peltor sees me and smiles. He kicks off his loafers and peels off cream socks.

'Avrolax, in case you were wondering. First the dart. Then the can.'

The Mont Blanc pen. Of course. In Russia, these days, modified gun-pens are a fashion accessory. Like wearing a Rolex.

'Lance was a big fan. Got him a lot of dates.'

Now I know how Robert felt when Grotius attacked him in Paris. Peltor sits on the bed beside me without fear of reprisal. I'm finding out what Avrolax can do but he already knows. He puts his hand on my left thigh and squeezes gently.

'I'm gonna take off the gag, Petra. Whimper if you want to. But no screaming. Not unless you want me to give you something to scream about.'

Not an idle threat. He'd be thrilled to do it. But at the moment I'd be more likely to vomit. He leans over me and unties the knot.

'I gotta admit this is a real bonus. I was expecting Julia. But this is so much better.'

He stands up and pulls the polo-shirt over his head,

revealing the monumental physique last seen on a freezing rooftop in Munich. I use my clumsy fingers to investigate the bindings around my wrists but I can't find a weak point.

'Lance told me about the two of you,' he says, as he unfastens his belt. 'How you met in this bar in Larnaca. The Mistral. See? I even remember the name.'

He drops his trousers and steps out of them. He's wearing nothing underneath. Not even pubic hair. He has a tattoo. It's not like Kostya's; this etching is no more significant than a statement of contemporary fashion. And there's nothing less significant than that. Across his lower abdomen, in black Gothic script, is a tediously predictable phrase: *Born to Kill.*

I try to remember those lessons from long ago. Partition of body and soul; keep one part of the mind to oneself and reduce the body to a vehicle. That's the theory but I'm out of practice. Naked now, he starts to stroke himself.

'He told me everything. How he picked you up. How he took you back to his hotel. How you couldn't get enough of him, no matter what he did to you. I can believe that, Petra. I've seen it in your eyes. You're a wild cat.'

How typical of Grotius to manufacture triumph out of rejection. And how typical of Peltor to accept it, suspending all critical faculties in order to nourish a pathetic fantasy. I'd love to say something spiteful but that's only going to encourage him.

He climbs on to the bed and removes my knickers. I don't kick out because I'm not sure I can. And because

I know he wants me to. Then he puts his palm flat on my stomach.

'There's no one like you.' He gently runs the hand under my T-shirt from stomach to sternum and back. 'Not in our world. Not anywhere.'

He withdraws the hand and then tears the T-shirt slowly and effortlessly, the sinews ebbing and flowing along forearms as thick as my thighs. Up the front, through the collar, along either sleeve, a meticulous process. His eyes never stray from mine. He's waiting for the first glimmer of fear which, paradoxically, strengthens my resolve.

Once I'm naked – apart from my socks, which he chooses to leave on – he sits back and examines me. He prods the sutures in my side, then picks at one with a nail. The flesh snags when he pulls it out.

'That looks kinda tender,' he says, aggravating the delicate wound.

I can't quite suppress the flinch. Excitement flares in his eyes. His other hand maintains a gross erection.

'I know you never liked me, Petra.'

He leans over me so that his huge body casts me into shadow. Then he dips his head towards my shoulder. He's so close I can feel the heat he radiates. He presses his mouth to my scar and begins to work his tongue around it.

'You always thought I was some hick asshole,' he whispers.

How true.

When I don't react he sits up. 'In Munich, when we were on the roof, I saw you looking at my body. I could tell you wanted it so bad. You just didn't want me.'

Under different circumstances, I'd laugh. The ones with the muscles always assume that women find them attractive. The truth is, of course, that mostly it's other muscle-bound men who find them appealing.

He rises from the bed and goes into the bathroom. I hear water running from a tap. I twist my body to see if there's anything within reach of my fingers. Nothing. I lift my head. Is there something one of my feet could drag towards me? No.

Peltor returns and sits on the bed beside me. 'You're going to talk to me, Petra. I swear to God you're going to talk to me.'

He trails fingertips over my face, around my throat, across my breasts, never looking anywhere other than into my eyes. He squeezes a nipple. I bite my tongue. The squeeze becomes a pinch.

When he finally sees pain he sighs, almost sorrowfully. 'Petra, Petra, Petra.'

The mantra. Just as Julia described it.

Time to change strategy.

'What do you want, John?'

'John, is it? Not asshole?'

'What do you want?'

He bends down and kisses me, finding my reluctant tongue with his, before whispering into my ear, 'You, Petra. I want you. Nothing else.'

In my world, assassins are colleagues or adversaries. They're clinical or useless. But he's psychopathic. He's like a religious fanatic; there's no possibility of negotiation. There's no logic that can appeal to him. There's nothing he needs. There's nothing I can sell him or promise him. At this moment, with the most primitive chemicals saturating his brain, he has everything he wants spread before him.

I try to ignore the fingers that are creeping between my thighs. The prospect of sex disgusts me but I know I can survive it, no matter what he does, no matter how long it takes. It's what follows that scares me. He looks at me with eyes that have glazed over fully. They have no depth. Every restraining instinct is suspended.

'Petra,' he murmurs thickly. 'Petra, Petra, Petra.'

His huge hands move on to my thighs and press them apart. When he looks down between them his jaw slackens with pleasure.

'Say you want me, Petra.'

He leans over me, his weight pinning me to the mattress. I can smell his breath.

'Go on. Say it.'

But I can't. I won't.

I hear a soft click.

'Come on, Petra. Say you want me inside you. Say you need me.'

A tentative female voice calls out. 'Room service.'

We freeze, our widening eyes asking the same question for different reasons.

For a big man he moves amazingly swiftly. He's off me and standing at the foot of the bed in a second, a blur of shiny muscle. I hear the door close.

'What the fuck is going on?' he bellows into the corridor.

You can't expect to be taken seriously when you look

*like he does; skin slippery with sweat, an erection like
an enormous coat-peg, that stupid goatee beard.*

*A single muted shot rings out and Peltor is punched
backwards. He hits the coffee table and falls.*

Now that's what I call room service.

Stephanie watched herself emerge from the
corridor holding a Russian PSM with a silencer.
That was how it appeared to her; Julia was still
wearing the clothes they'd swapped in the café.

Julia saw Stephanie on the bed – prostrate, naked,
confused – and put her hand to her mouth. Peltor
was gasping, his right hand covering the bullet
wound just below the rib-cage, blood leaking freely
over his granite torso. Julia put her gun down on
the bed and severed Stephanie's wrist bindings.
Then she went over to Peltor.

'You were never going to pay the second fifty
thousand, were you?'

'I was . . . I swear I was . . . I . . .'

'So how come you stole the first fifty thousand?'

'Take it easy . . . let's talk . . .'

'No more talk. Where's my money, you
bastard?'

His reply came between halting breaths. 'There
. . . over there . . .'

He pointed to the sofa. Julia looked across and
saw the canvas knapsack beside the open attaché
case.

Stephanie was still on the bed, barely able to

move. Her hands were swollen and numb, her muscles as dead as lead, the room spinning. She couldn't see Peltor on the floor. But she heard him hissing to Julia through clenched teeth.

'More . . . I can get you . . . more. Another fifty . . . another . . . hundred . . .'

Julia shook her head in contempt. He coughed an offer of two hundred thousand at her. She spat on him then collected the knapsack from the sofa and peered inside. Her initial payment of fifty thousand was still there; the chance to begin again.

There was a second shot.

Julia hit the wall face first. The exit wound in her throat left a scarlet rose on the wallpaper. She disintegrated over the sofa, the knapsack tumbling to the ground.

Peltor was clutching the coffee table for support with one hand. The Heckler & Koch had been underneath Stephanie's jeans which were on the floor beside him. As soon as he'd been shot – even as he fell – he'd been aware of that. Always the operator.

It took Stephanie several seconds to realize what had happened. To understand that the second shot had not been Julia finishing off Peltor.

Stephanie heard him moving and forced herself up on to one elbow. The room swam. She glimpsed Peltor hauling himself to the kneeling position. She heard the hard click of her gun clattering on the coffee table. And then remembered where Julia's gun was. On the bed. She'd put it there when she'd severed Stephanie's bindings.

Sweating almost as furiously as he was bleeding, John Peltor steadied himself to point the Heckler & Koch. Petra cast off Stephanie's remains and forced herself down the bed, retching as she moved, to retrieve Julia's PSM.

The door was shut but the Housekeeping pass key was still in the slot. Iain Boyd pressed his ear to the door. Nothing. He slipped inside quietly and moved into the suite.

The man he knew as Paul Ellroy was dead. He could see two wounds, one to the torso, one to the head. Stephanie was on the bed in a foetal curl, not moving. A second woman, who looked very much like her, was dead on the sofa. A large pool of blood had formed on the carpet beneath her head. He checked the bathroom then returned to the bedroom.

Apart from the pair of socks that she was wearing, Ellroy and Stephanie were both naked. Boyd looked around; clothes everywhere, two guns, a torn T-shirt, a small aerosol, an open attaché case and a canvas knapsack spilling euro notes.

'Stephanie.'

He could see she was breathing.

'Stephanie,' he repeated. 'It's me. Iain.'

Still nothing. Gently, he laid a hand on a cold shoulder.

'You okay?'

He began to uncurl her. She was bleeding lightly from the wound in her side and from a temple graze. She'd retched over herself. There was residue around her mouth, on her breasts, in her hair. Her eyes were red. Not just from tears, Boyd thought, there'd also been something else. He looked at the aerosol. She was very pale.

'Can you hear me?' he whispered.

She wasn't registering at all.

He picked her up and carried her to the bathroom. He filled a basin with warm water and held her over it. He made her rinse out her mouth, then cleaned her face and wiped the blood from her hairline. She was trembling.

Back in the bedroom, he sat her on the bed while he scavenged for clothes. Her knickers were covered in Peltor's blood. So were Julia's shirt and jacket. He manoeuvred her back into her black jeans. In the wardrobe was a laundered shirt on a hanger wrapped in plastic. A buttercup button-down Ralph Lauren, the calling card of the preppie executive. Just the image Ellroy had coveted. Boyd helped her into it. It was enormous.

Stephanie flinched. She wasn't sure whether it was the feel of it or the smell of it. No amount of hotel starch could put enough distance between the cotton and its owner.

Boyd took off his jacket and put it around her shoulders. Then he crouched in front of her and raised her head so that they were looking at one another. 'You're going to have to walk, Stephanie. I can't carry you out of here.'

'I told him,' she murmured.

'Told him what?'

'In Munich. I told him.'

'What did you tell him?'

'You don't retire from this life. *It* retires you.'

Taborstrasse, one-twenty-five in the morning, a meagre apartment on the second floor, above an optician. There were people there. She wasn't sure how many. Three or four, maybe. They moved quietly between rooms, their voices soft. She heard English but was left in the hands of a woman called Fatima who spoke to her in faltering German. She helped Stephanie into a warm bath and brought her clean clothes; underwear, thick socks, two long-sleeved T-shirts, black cotton trousers, a dark blue sweater.

Back in the bedroom, Boyd said to her, 'Get some rest.'

'Where's Robert?'

'Safe.'

'Is he here?'

Boyd shook his head. 'He's still in Vienna. We moved him.'

'Where?'

'Somewhere more comfortable than this. You'll see him later. Now try to get some sleep. If you need anything, I'll be outside the door.'

'There's no time. There's so much to . . .'

'No there isn't. It's over.'

He shut the door. Stephanie drew the curtains. The room overlooked Taborstrasse. A cable supporting two lamps ran from beneath her window to the other side of the street, crossing the power-lines for the trams. The thought evaporated the moment it formed; she lacked the energy. Or was it the will?

She lay on the bed. There had been pictures on the wall once. Dark squares and rectangles marked out their positions on wallpaper with a floral print. She stared at the ceiling and thought of Julia. Her death seemed particularly cruel. She'd earned the right to a new life and Stephanie felt sure she'd have made something good out of it.

Julia had died because of Peltor's greed. So had he. Stephanie didn't understand why he'd felt the need to steal back the first fifty thousand. Because he could? Perhaps. Just to prove to Julia – moments before he killed her, Stephanie supposed – that he'd known all along where she'd hidden it. To emphasize his control over her. To prove to her how worthless she was. That was the kind of man Peltor was.

Julia had saved her life. Without her intervention, Stephanie knew that she would have died a protracted and vicious death. And that once it was over, Peltor would have taken credit for the corpse of Petra Reuter. Stephanie recognized the irony: Peltor's greed had prevented him from achieving all he had wanted. But there was no pleasure in that.

Not with Julia dead. Not with Petra Reuter dead.

Eventually she slept. It was after six when Boyd woke her. They went into the tiny kitchen. The apartment was quiet; Stephanie couldn't hear anyone else. Boyd prepared coffee.

'How did you know where I was?' she asked.

'How do you think? I had you followed.'

'What?'

'Wake up. Why did you think I agreed to give you more time?'

The answer compounded her despondency. 'To see what I'd do?'

Boyd nodded.

She dropped her head and muttered, 'Bastard.'

'If you'd been half the woman I used to know I wouldn't have taken the risk.'

'I'm glad I'm not.'

He caught her eye. 'So am I.'

'What about Robert?'

'We had him under surveillance as well. He didn't go anywhere. But we moved him after you and I left the Imperial.'

'I should have guessed.'

'For what it's worth, they weren't happy about it. They wanted me to bring you in there and then.'

'So why didn't you?'

Boyd allowed himself the faintest hint of a smile. 'You know why not. I wanted to see what you'd do.' He paused for a moment, then added:

'Besides, I've always trusted you more than I trusted them.'

Stephanie moved over to the window. A passing tram grumbled; she felt the faint reverberation rising from Taborstrasse. Boyd took three chipped enamel mugs from the wooden pegs nailed to the wall.

Stephanie said, 'I'm sorry you had to see me like that.'

He was still facing away from her. 'Me too.'

'Who's the other mug for?'

On cue, the door opened.

Rosie Chaudhuri was a conundrum; the only good memory Stephanie had of Magenta House. However, now that she ran the organization Stephanie found it hard to see her as the woman she'd once known. The position she currently occupied was synonymous with the worst of all Stephanie's memories. Rosie was a new head on an old body.

'Hello, Steph. How are you?'

She didn't say anything at first. Instead, she thought of the photographs that had reached the Verbinski clinic. Magenta House photographs. Originally, they'd been leverage. Now they were evidence.

Rosie had grown her black hair long. Stephanie had forgotten quite how attractive she was; dark brown eyes, beautiful clear skin, high cheekbones, complemented by an elegant, conservative dress sense. Bombs might detonate but standards never slipped.

Boyd poured coffee for all of them. Rosie sat at the diminutive table that occupied most of the floor space, leaving Stephanie standing. Reverse psychology. To be recognized then ignored.

'It's a hell of a mess out there,' Rosie said.

'I want to see Robert.'

'In good time.'

'Now.'

'In good time.'

Stephanie stayed beside the window, her arms folded. 'Who's Maurice Hammond?'

They both stiffened. Stephanie was surprised; she'd anticipated a reaction from Rosie – that was why she'd tossed her the question nice and early, to try to catch her off-guard – but she hadn't expected anything from Boyd.

Rosie said, 'Maurice is a former director of 850.'

'How well do you know him?'

'We've met. Why?'

'Late last year he came to Vienna with a set of photographs of me. Of me and Komarov, to be precise. Stills taken from some film footage. You know the film. You were the one who showed it to me in Zurich.'

'Are you sure about this?'

Stephanie nodded. 'Do you know who Lance Grotius is?'

'I do now.'

'Grotius had my Magenta House clearance code on his laptop.'

'Stephanie . . .'

'I was set up right from the start.'

'And you think we had something to do with that?'

'I know you did. As an organization.'

'I can assure you . . .'

'No you can't.'

Avenue Kléber, Paris, 08:15.

Wiley closed the double-doors so that he was alone in the boardroom at Amsterdam Europe's head office. He sat at one end of a long table, a slim plasma screen in front of him. At its centre was the Amsterdam logo. Beneath were two words: Tomorrow Today. Under current circumstances, the very antithesis of prophecy.

The INTELSAT link came to life. John Cabrini had lost his sheen. He was still wearing a Clive Ishiguro silk polo-neck yet he looked anything but dapper. Eight days based in the New York mobile control suite had aged him. Artificial light, artificial air. And, as it had turned out, artificial optimism.

Wiley said, 'Talk me through Vienna.'

'Peltor's dead.'

Wiley had heard the news an hour earlier. 'What about Reuter?'

'We have a body.'

'Is it her?'

'No. It's the substitute.'

'What about the location?'

'It's been secured. The bodies have been

extracted. Everything's under control. We're relocating them.'

'Together?'

'Separately. She'll be planted, he'll disappear.'

'How soon can we leak the news?'

'Around eighteen hundred your time.'

'What about Reuter?'

'We know she was there. We don't know what happened. We're assuming she killed both of them.'

'How come?'

'The substitute was scheduled to visit Peltor at midnight. We don't know how he tracked her but the sweep team found cash in the room. Looks like it was hers.'

'Maybe she was carrying it.'

'Maybe. Or maybe he had it and that's why she went there. She'd want it back.'

Wiley considered Peltor. He'd told Wiley on more than one occasion that Julia, the Reuter clone, had been paid off and had disappeared. Wiley wasn't entirely surprised to discover that this probably wasn't true. There had always been something of the cowboy about Peltor. A confidence that strayed into arrogance, a casual disregard for authority, an unjustified tendency to assume superiority.

Cabrini said, 'The Reuter clone was shot with a Heckler & Koch USP. The same kind of gun that Reuter herself used in the barn in Alsace. We'll run tests for an exact match but I think you can assume it was the same weapon.'

'So Reuter shot her clone.'

'Looks like it. Peltor was shot with a Russian PSM. There's no previous on that.'

'Wasn't the clone a Russian?'

'She was. But I'd still put my money on Reuter.'

'What chance of finding her now?'

'Ultimately, it's assured. There are two ways it can happen. Either she pops up to dispute the identity of the clone. That's the easy, quick way. The moment she does, we take her out. The only way she can dispute the identity is by proving her own identity.'

'Why would she do that?'

'Precisely. She wouldn't. Which leaves us with the alternative.'

'She does nothing and stays hidden?'

'That's right. So if you're asking me about today, tomorrow or the day after, I can't promise you anything. All I can say is this: as long as the ten million is on the table, we'll get her. Sooner or later. The money is your guarantee. She'll be in an airport somewhere. Or a hotel. Or reading a newspaper in a café. Or just walking down a street, anywhere in the world. And someone will recognize her.'

There had been no inquisition. No accusations. Rosie had asked for her account of the last ten days and Stephanie had given her an edited version that had been essentially honest. When she'd finished, Rosie had left the room. There'd been no requests for clarification. Stephanie looked at her watch. That had been more than two hours ago.

Boyd had been with her for some of the time. She'd tried some small talk but he'd been mono-syllabic. She remembered that; he was the man who'd taught her to be comfortable with silence. *If you've got nothing to say, say nothing at all.* On that score, no one had ever had cause to accuse Boyd of hypocrisy.

First Grotius, then Peltor. She didn't regret killing either of them. For the first time, there was no remorse. None at all. Especially when she thought of Julia. Both men had abused her in their own way. For Julia's sake more than her own, Stephanie took some pleasure from their deaths, which was a truth she found simultane-ously alarming and disgusting. But a truth never-theless.

Rosie entered the kitchen alone. Stephanie was sitting at the table. She didn't get up. Rosie sat down opposite her and said, 'Nice to see you haven't lost your mental edge, Steph. Hammond was the right card to play.'

'It was a guess.'

'I realize that.'

'Who is he?'

'A former director of SIS. A consultant for the Amsterdam Group. And a Magenta House trustee.'

Stephanie frowned. 'A *trustee*?'

'It's a nickname. Magenta House was originally established by four senior intelligence officers. Two from SIS, two from MI5. Collectively, they were known as the Edgware Trust, hence *trustees*. It was their job to oversee Magenta House. To ensure that it stuck to its mandate, to ensure that it had sufficient finance. Only one person within the organization is permitted to know the identities of the trustees. These days, that means me. The original four were Elizabeth Manning, Sir Richard Clere, Maurice Hammond and Alastair Smith. Hammond is the only one left. The other three have been replaced. The original set of trustees set the parameters for Magenta House and then pooled their collective clout to turn it into an operational reality. Of course it was a tiny outfit back then. But no less effective. In some senses, rather more effective. Smaller, leaner, less . . . *cluttered*. They set up illegal funding streams and they appointed the first chief.'

'Alexander.'

'Exactly. Everyone's personal favourite. He and Hammond were friends. *Good* friends, going way back. Alexander's background was military intelligence.'

'So Hammond knew about Berlin?'

Rosie shifted awkwardly. 'Trustees aren't made aware of operational details for security reasons. The element of distance is a barrier of mutual protection. But Berlin was different. The entire organization was at risk.'

'Does he know that I killed Alexander?'

'Yes. He was fully briefed. They were all fully briefed.'

'What's his position regarding Amsterdam?'

'He sits on the board of Amsterdam Europe.'

Stephanie raised an eyebrow. 'You knew this?'

'Yes.'

'And that didn't ring an alarm?'

'In case you've forgotten, the Amsterdam Group is a highly respected financial institution.'

Rosie was right. She *had* forgotten. Until now, why would Hammond's appointment have been a reason for concern? If Amsterdam was good enough for former presidents and prime ministers, surely it was good enough for former intelligence mandarins. In the real world that was what Hammond was; a retired SIS director, nothing more.

'There aren't rules against this?'

'C would be prohibited from such an appointment but SIS directors are allowed to accept positions in the commercial sector. Hammond has never attempted to make a secret of it.'

'So that makes this . . . *personal*?'

'I'm afraid it looks that way. On one level, at least. Alexander was a friend of his. It's that simple. That *stupid*.'

'But does he know who I really am?'

'He shouldn't. As a trustee, he's not supposed to have the clearance. But he does.'

'How's that possible?'

'It seems Alexander and he were closer than anyone knew. He was able to access Magenta House records right from the start. Hammond was the man who originally nominated Alexander. Now we know why.'

Stephanie wondered how far the penetration went. 'So you knew about my safe-deposit box at Banque Damiani?'

'Yes. Even while you were still with us. Alexander spent a lot of time and effort trying to trace your independent identities.'

'How much do you know?'

'We've identified the location of six or seven. But we never discovered who created them. That was a source of some irritation to Alexander.'

Stephanie felt a pulse of relief. That was why Cyril Bradfield had stayed safe. His name hadn't appeared on any of the computer files that she'd found on Grotius's laptop. Files that had originated at Magenta House. There was only one other missing name.

'Did you ever find out about my money?'

Rosie smiled. 'No. That was the other thing that used to drive him insane.'

That explained how Albert Eichner had also remained safe, *despite* being the man who had steered Stephanie towards Otto Heilmann. Neither Bradfield nor Eichner had made it into a Magenta House file so they'd been beyond Hammond.

'Hammond sold you out, Stephanie.'

'And you. Or rather, Magenta House.'

'Yes. But we can take care of that. What we *can't* do is get involved with *you*. It's not our business. You're not one of us any more.'

There was a Passat waiting for them on Taborstrasse. Boyd sat in the front next to the driver. Stephanie sat in the back with Rosie.

'Where are we going?'

'That depends on you.'

'Where's Robert?'

'Waiting for us.'

The car pulled away from the kerb.

Stephanie said, 'You came after me because of Heilmann, didn't you? It wasn't Brand or Golitsyn, was it?'

Rosie said, 'We came after you because of DeMille. Because of Amsterdam.'

'I don't understand.'

'It's one thing to kill drug-dealers, terrorists, arms-traders or even other intelligence operatives but . . .'

'Heilmann was an arms-dealer.'

'Heilmann was tied to Amsterdam. They're the threat, Stephanie. They're the ones who come after you because they can afford to. We needed to know where you stood in relation to them. Boundaries are disintegrating. National security agencies operate according to a narrowly defined agenda. Corporate giants have a broader perspective, a greater reach and an increased willingness to do whatever is necessary. We had to be sure of two things: first, in order to protect ourselves, that they wouldn't find out who you really are.'

'And second?'

'That you weren't working for them.'

'I killed Heilmann. Remember?'

'Stranger things have happened. All we knew for certain was that you were operating on the open market. Who pays the most? The people with the most money. It was an unavoidable suspicion. We knew that you'd worked by proxy for the Russian government and that on that occasion you were paid by a Russian oil company – Vyukneft. You see? You'd already set a precedent.'

They took the A4 Ostautobahn out of Vienna. Stephanie saw signs to the airport and guessed that was their destination.

Rosie said, 'Hammond is in Paris. He'll be in London next week, as scheduled. He has several meetings there. These days he's something of a grandee and he rather enjoys it. He likes the lunches, the premières. Covent Garden, English Heritage, the National Gallery.'

'A regular pillar of society.'

'If he arrives in one piece, we'll be taking care of him.'

'Stroke, heart attack or accident?'

Rosie's reply was deadpan. 'He's at an age where either of the first two wouldn't be a total surprise. But I thought you might want to speak to him first.'

'In Paris?'

She nodded. 'He'll be there until the day after tomorrow.'

'And if I don't?'

'You left us after Berlin, Stephanie. We haven't seen you since. Petra's retired. Remember?'

'How could I forget?'

'We can put down in Paris on the way to London. You could be there in two hours. Think about it. No documents, no questions. It's just a phone call away.'

'What about the last week?'

'It never happened. We just needed to be sure about you.'

'And *are* you sure?'

'Yes.'

'You wouldn't lie to me, would you? I don't want to spend the rest of my life looking over my shoulder.'

'You *will* have to look over your shoulder, Stephanie. But not for us. You have my word on that.'

Vienna-Schwechat airport. The Falcon 2000 was parked a discreet distance from the commercial aircraft, its engines already running. As they climbed the aircraft steps, the pitch of the engines rose. Newman was sitting towards the rear. Before Stephanie had reached him, the door had closed and the wheels were rolling. Rosie and Boyd took seats at the front.

She held Newman tightly.

'You okay?' he whispered into her ear.

'Not really, no.'

The aircraft taxied to the runway and was cleared for instant take-off. Almost immediately they were in dense pewter cloud. For five minutes the aircraft rolled with the punches, then punctured the gloom and rose into an aquamarine sky.

'Are *you* okay?' she asked him.

'I'm fine. I'm just worried about you.'

'Don't be. I'll get over it. I always do.'

'What happens now?'

'That depends.'

'On?'

'Whether you come with me.'

'Do you want me to?' he asked her.

'It would be a lot easier if I didn't.'

'Or if I didn't want to?'

'Yes.'

'Trust us to make it difficult.'

She smiled. 'I know.'

'Look, Stephanie. I was dying before we met. Slowly but surely.'

'In luxury, though.'

'Luxury's an anaesthetic. One way or another, I'd like to spend some time fully conscious.'

They were over Germany when Rosie made her way to the back of the aircraft and asked to speak to Stephanie. Newman made way for her. As she settled into the tan leather seat she said, 'I can't believe you didn't retire after Berlin, Steph.'

'Nor can I. Not now.'

'Why didn't you?'

'Let's just say it was a mistake I'm not going to repeat.'

'Because of Newman?'

'Partly.'

Rosie grew serious. 'When you step out of this aircraft you're going to be on your own.'

'I know.'

'I meant what I said in Vienna. We can't do anything for you.'

'I realize that.'

'Is he the running type?'

'I hope so.'

'They won't stop, you know. There's too much riding on it.'

'I know.'

Rosie looked up the aisle towards Newman. 'You should be alone. For his sake, for your sake. You can't afford the baggage. He'll slow you down.'

'I know he will.'

'He doesn't have to get off the plane.'

'He knows the score. Besides, he's a survivor.'

'Well, it's up to you. Before you go, there is one more thing.'

'What?'

'I know it always bugged you not knowing Alexander's first name.'

Stephanie nodded. 'It just seemed so pretentious.'

'Not when you know what it was.'

'Go on.'

'Alexander.'

'Alexander Alexander?'

Rosie nodded.

Stephanie said, 'Did he have a middle name?'

There's a car to meet us at a distant corner of Charles de Gaulle beside an Air France service hangar. An old blue Citroën. By the time I'm next to Robert on the back seat, the aircraft is already moving; there will be no record of it on French soil.

Five minutes later, we're clear of the airport and heading for the centre of Paris. The driver picks a plastic bag off the front seat and hands it to me. I look inside. A SIG-Sauer P226. Petra Reuter's gun of choice. There's also a small rectangular card with two Parisian addresses on it, both in the 7ème arrondissement, and a photograph of Maurice Hammond. She may be a friend but Rosie is still definitely Magenta House.

I get the driver to drop us at Gare du Nord. We find an internet café nearby where I post a message to Stern requesting a meeting in the ether at five o'clock. From Gare du Nord we take the Métro to Bastille.

At five o'clock we enter Web 46 on rue du Roi de Sicilie, which is an internet café I used a few days ago, though it seems far longer.

> Hello, Oscar.

> Petra. Even in death you're full of surprises.

> I'm sorry?

> You're dead. Didn't you know?

> Nobody told me.

> The news will break in about an hour. You were killed late last night in Vienna. The notorious terrorist Petra Reuter – dead at last.

> What a relief for everyone.

> Butterfly will be signed tomorrow.

I stare at the screen; Stern usually has to be prompted.

> I thought it had been cancelled.

> Rescheduled.

> Where and when?

> 14:00 at the offices of Balthazar Karyo, out at La Défense.

> Who on earth is

That's as much as I type before Robert says, 'Scheherazade's lawyer.'

I delete the half-finished enquiry and stare at him. He waits for the questions that I struggle to contain. One thing at a time, though. I return to Stern.

> Why's he relevant?

> He represents the Amsterdam Group's largest private investor.

Robert says, 'I never knew that.'

'That she was an Amsterdam investor?'

'That she was the largest investor.'

'You never thought to mention this at all?'

'Scheherazade has investments everywhere.'

> Scheherazade Zahani?

> Very good, Petra. If you ever tire of your current line of work, perhaps you'd consider coming to work for me.

> What am I missing, Oscar?

> Leonid Golitsyn knew about you.

I've almost forgotten that the first time I heard that name, it came from Stern.

> Knew what about me?

> Who you are. What you are. And why you were being used. Golitsyn knew Zahani. He introduced her to the top people at Amsterdam. Now that you're dead, Butterfly is safe.

> Unless I turn up.

> True. But why would you do that? To clear your name? To be frank, I can't think of anything that's likely to enhance your reputation more assuredly than your death. Petra Reuter – you can kill her but you can't stop her.

They ducked into a café and took a table away from the door. Newman ordered two glasses of red wine.

'She's the key, Robert. She's Amsterdam's largest investor. She knew Golitsyn and Wiley. She knows you. The basis of her wealth is oil. Butterfly is due to be signed tomorrow under the watchful eye of her lawyer.'

'I know how it looks.'

'It's not how it looks. It's how it is. But there's something I still don't understand.'

'What?'

'With hindsight, she must have known who I was when I went to see her. Or, at the very least, she must have had a good idea. She could have nailed me and protected her investment; she stands to make a lot of money out of Butterfly. But she chose not to. That doesn't make sense.'

'I agree. But only if you follow that narrow line of logic.'

'Meaning?'

'If she made the choice to let you go, she will have done it for a reason.'

'Any idea what that might be?'

'No. But I will say this: Scheherazade conducts her business the way Omar conducted his. You can't assume that just because she's a major investor with Amsterdam that she wouldn't act in a way that might be detrimental to Amsterdam. That's not how she operates. Her relationships are unilateral. And her relationship with Amsterdam – no matter how much money is involved – may be less important than other relationships she maintains.'

'A woman of infinite options.'

'Exactly.'

The waiter brought their wine and a small carafe of water. Stephanie thought about what Newman had said and tried to tie it to what she already knew.

'I have an idea,' she said, 'but I'm going to need your help.'

There was a payphone beside the toilets. Newman dialled the number. Stephanie stood close enough to the receiver to allow her to hear. The call was answered at the fourth ring.

Newman said, 'It's me.'

'Robert?'

Instant recognition.

'Yes.'

'Where are you?'

'Paris.'

There was a long pause; not what Scheherazade Zahani expected, clearly. She said, 'I've been trying to get hold of you.'

'I've been out of contact. Look, I need you to do something for me.'

'Of course. Anything.'

'Tomorrow morning. A meeting at your apartment. Ten o'clock.'

'Well . . . sure. I mean, if you want to come now, we could . . .'

'No. Tomorrow at ten. And I want you to invite someone else.'

Another pause. 'Who?'

'Gordon Wiley.'

Her tone changed from concerned to terse. 'What's going on, Robert?'

'I know he's in Paris. I know about Karyo tomorrow afternoon.'

Stephanie could almost feel the question that wasn't articulated at the other end of the line: *how*?

Newman said, 'Listen to me carefully, Scheherazade. I need you to tell Wiley what I'm going to tell you. Petra Reuter wants to make a deal. She doesn't want to run and she doesn't want to die again.'

'Robert, come over and we can talk about it.'

'I can't.'

'Please, darling . . .'

'Trust me. I know what I'm doing.'

'Those were the exact words Leonid used when I spoke to him the night before he died.'

'I've got insurance.'

'Her?'

'This is the only way.'

'Look, there's not enough time. Wiley won't agree to it and . . .'

'You're the largest single private investor in Amsterdam, Scheherazade. You can get him to do whatever you want. That's why the signing is happening out at La Défense. Karyo's your lawyer, not one of theirs.'

Zahani dropped the pretence for icy silence.

'Ten o'clock tomorrow,' Newman repeated.

'What if they won't . . .'

'Make them. And tell them that she won't be coming with me. I'll be alone but if anything happens to me . . . well, you can guess the rest.'

'How did you get involved with her, Robert?'

'You wouldn't believe me.'

'I'd believe anything of you.'

'Some other time. I'll see you tomorrow morning.'

'Okay. For you.'

They stepped on to the street into the jaws of a worsening wind.

'So what now?' he asked.

'We need to disappear. Until you make the deal they'll be looking harder than ever for us.'

'Any ideas?'

She nodded. 'I know the perfect place.'

They walked to rue Vieille du Temple, less than five minutes away. The red and gold sign above the shop was illuminated by three small lamps: Adler, *boulangerie – patisserie*.

Stephanie peered through the window. Claude Adler was carrying two empty wicker baskets towards the rear of the shop. She knocked on the window.

'*Fermé!*' he roared, without bothering to look.

Stephanie tapped again and he turned round to see who it was.

As he opened the door for them, he said, 'Petra. I'm sorry, I didn't . . .'

'Forget it, Claude. I know what a nuisance customers can be.'

'Very funny. Come in, come in.'

Stephanie introduced Robert then said, 'The last time I was here you asked if there was something you could do to help. Well, there is.'

Day Thirteen

Half-past-midnight and the guttering candle was almost dead. Sylvie Adler produced a replacement from the wooden cupboard over Stephanie's shoulder, dipped the wick into the oily flame, then crushed the new candle into the soft remains of the old. Stephanie saw red and gold reflected in Sylvie's tears.

There were three bottles on the table, two from the Languedoc and a half-drunk bottle of Calvados. Between them was the last of dinner; cassoulet, bread, cheese, cups of espresso and an ashtray full of dead Gauloises.

Stephanie hadn't meant to drink. She needed a clear head now. But she'd succumbed anyway. Just as she had with Julia in Vienna. In fact, because of Julia.

Claude Adler lit his last cigarette of the night. 'Did you ever see Jacob draw?'

Stephanie shook her head.

'Even with the arthritis, it was something to

watch. These horribly disfigured fingers, they could barely hold a pencil.' He curled his own fingers into a claw. 'And then the tip would touch the paper and something beautiful would appear. Quickly or slowly, rough or polished. He used to say that forgery was craft. I think he was too modest. He was a forger, yes, but an artist also. He didn't just copy. He created. He injected life. *Everywhere*.'

When Adler had asked Stephanie why the Fursts had died she hadn't been able to give him an adequate answer. Because the world isn't fair, she'd said. He'd nodded and drained his glass; a grudging toast to an unpleasant, universal truth.

Shortly after one, Claude and Sylvie went to bed, leaving Stephanie and Newman in the kitchen. The flickering candlelight lent his face colour and deepened the lines. She looked at him and for a brief moment imagined they were together under the moon in Mauritius. Exactly where she should have been at that instant. Where she could still be in thirty-six hours. Where *they* could still be.

'What are you thinking?' he asked her.

'Nothing,' she said. 'Nothing at all.'

She could hear Claude Adler moving upstairs. That was how she knew it was four-thirty. That was when his day started, seven days a week, hangover or no hangover. Cyril Bradfield had told her that.

Stephanie and Newman were in the small living-room overlooking rue Vieille du Temple. Newman was asleep on the sofa, Stephanie was on an old armchair, her legs folded beneath her. A car passed by on the street below, the exhaust in need of a new silencer.

She'd tried to sleep but her mind wouldn't let her. She'd given up at three and had made herself coffee. Sitting alone at the kitchen table, she'd thought about Julia. The first time she saw the film, Stephanie had realized she was watching a dead woman. Filming Petra Reuter with Anders Brand only made sense if she died. Seen from that perspective, there seemed something predetermined about the different paths that had taken Stephanie and Julia to Room 510 of the Imperial Hotel.

Now there was the possibility of a definitive exit. Or, as Julia had put it, the chance to begin again.

She went through to the kitchen where Adler, dishevelled, was making coffee.

He said, 'You made the papers.'

There was an early edition of *Le Monde* on the counter, opened at the appropriate place. It was a brief report. There'd been a shooting in an industrial compound off Haidestrasse in the Simmering district of Vienna. The police had been called to the scene after an anonymous tip-off and had discovered a single female body. Although they had yet to confirm it the victim was now widely believed to be the notorious terrorist-turned-assassin, Petra Reuter. There was no mention of Peltor. Stephanie wondered what had happened to his body. Dumped in the Danube? Why not?

'Is it true?' Adler asked.

'Is what true?'

'The description of you. Terrorist. Assassin.'

'Who did you think I was, Claude?'

Hunched over the sink, his back to her, he shrugged. 'I don't know. No one ever said. Not exactly. I mean, it was obvious you were *different* but . . .'

'It's true, Claude. At least, it was.'

He turned round. 'So Jacob and Miriam . . .'

'They were never involved. They were innocent. But they died because of me. Because they knew me.'

Stony-faced but devoid of obvious judgement, he nodded, then looked down at the papers. 'So . . . is it good news?'

'In a way.'

'It must be liberating to be dead.'

'Not yet. But it could be.'

Five-fifteen. Adler was downstairs in the bakery, Sylvie was in the bathroom, the radio on, music muffled by the clatter of running water. Newman was standing by the kitchen window, arms crossed, tired. They went through the plan for a third time. When Stephanie had finished, Newman said, 'What if Wiley won't cut a deal?'

'He has to.'

'But what if he won't?'

'Tell him I'll kill him. Not today or tomorrow. But soon. Grotius is dead. Peltor's dead. He knows there's no protection from me. He'll make a deal. There's no reason for him not to. Amsterdam have what they want: a body. A dead Petra Reuter. I don't care if she's discredited. I don't want her back. So as long as they leave me in peace, I'm happy to stay silent. Everybody wins.'

'So you do your thing, I do mine, then we meet.'

'That's right.'

'Then what?'

'Then it's up to us.'

She walked from rue Vieille du Temple to boulevard de Sébastopol. It was a bitter morning, puddles frozen, car windscreens frosted, breath iced. Sylvie Adler had given Stephanie a thick coat and a scarf but neither could protect her fully from the temperature.

She'd remembered from her previous visit that the easyInternetCafé was open twenty-four hours a day. She took a terminal, sent a message and waited.

Parting from Newman had been strangely muted. Neither of them had been quite sure what to do, what to say. They'd hugged, kissed, hugged again. He'd whispered into her ear, 'Be careful.'

'You too,' she'd whispered back.

Then they'd looked into each other's eyes, both anticipating something more. But there wasn't anything. Not yet. Not until they were together again.

The screen flickered.

> Petra. No sleep for the dead? How strange.

Stern. Stephanie looked at her watch. Twelve minutes. She shook her head, the theory gathering momentum and forcing a smile through the fatigue. She started to type.

By the time she left the easyInternetCafé it was six-thirty-five. She made the call from a France Télécom phonebooth, dialling the memorized mobile number. She wasn't confident of getting through but was eventually answered on the thirteenth pulse.

'Madame Zahani?'

'Thank you for agreeing to see me.'

'Under the circumstances, how could I refuse? Robert gave you my private number?'

'Not knowingly.'

'Then I must remember to change it.'

Scheherazade Zahani wore a large, white towelling dressing-gown, nothing on her feet, no make-up. Stephanie was surprised, then suspicious. It seemed consistent, though; the calculated choice of a chess player. They were in the kitchen; stainless-steel, ceramic and glass, vast and gleaming. Zahani had dismissed the apologetic cook the moment he'd appeared and was now making tea for them. Again, a deliberate choice, Stephanie felt.

Zahani said, 'You took a risk calling me, then coming here.'

'Robert described you as a woman of infinite options. I didn't think you'd want to overlook some of them. Not until you knew what they involved.'

'We'll see. What do you want?'

'I want to know about Butterfly. Specifically, what it would mean to you if the deal were to collapse.'

'It won't. It'll be signed at two this afternoon.'

'Hypothetically.'

Zahani considered it briefly then shrugged. 'I have plenty of other interests.'

'It wouldn't matter to you?'

'I'd lose some money. But it wouldn't matter, no.'

'Why not?'

'One can never underestimate the extent to which America will fail to understand the world beyond its borders. Bearing this in mind, one can always position oneself to take long-term advantage of a short-term setback.'

'You have another position?'

'I have several. I *always* have several. Not to do so would be foolish in the extreme. There are many possible outcomes for Iraq and its neighbours. The regional situation is as it's always been: *liquid*. But I suspect this isn't really why you're here.'

'No. It's Robert.'

Zahani smiled a little. 'I imagined it would be.'

They talked for half an hour. They started with Robert then diversified. Zahani gave Stephanie the assurance she'd come for, while Stephanie gave Zahani the answers she'd needed. Above all, the confirmation of the coincidence; Stephanie running into Newman on the car-park ramp with all its consequences. She appeared to find it reassuring, the missing component dropped into a complex equation, allowing her to come to the conclusion she knew to be true.

As Stephanie was preparing to leave, she said, 'The last time I was here you suspected who I was, didn't you?'

'That would be over-stating it. But I had an instinct about you.'

'Yet you helped me anyway and, in doing so, jeopardized Butterfly.'

She took her time. 'It kept my options open. My *long-term* options.'

Stephanie wondered what those might be.

Zahani said, 'My husband was Yemeni. Did you know that?'

'I thought he was Saudi.'

'A common misconception. He emigrated to Saudi Arabia to make his fortune. Being Yemeni helped him. It automatically removed him from the court politics of the royal household. My husband grew up poor yet even when he was rich he clung to the principles that had helped

587

him when he was young. These were things he passed on to me. He taught me that the most valuable commodity of all is time. And that patience is control. The reason time is so valuable, he used to say, is that it's the one resource the poor have in abundance and that the rich can't buy. In business, for instance, Western companies – including, I'm afraid to say, the Amsterdam Group – worry about the next financial quarter, or the next financial year. In Iraq or Bangladesh or Afghanistan, wherever there are many poor – that's not a pressing concern. So, when it comes to dealing with the West, this is what they understand: that if they wait long enough they will prevail by default.'

Stephanie smiled. '*Always* the chess player.'

'Always. For me – for *us* – it's like this: a Muslim tribesman meets an American in a remote mountain pass. The American asks for directions. The tribesman insists they share some tea first in a gesture of friendship. The American accepts. The tribesman gathers some sticks, lights a fire, boils the water and brews the tea. Before long, the American grows restless. He tries to remain courteous but wants to be on his way and, eventually, his impatience gets the better of him. He glances at his watch. The tribesman sees this so the American apologizes. To which the tribesman says, "You've got the watches but we've got the time."'

* * *

588

Café Bleu on rue Cler was very small. In the summer, Stephanie supposed, tables spilled on to the pavement and tripled capacity. Today, on a morning in January, the space beneath the canopy was empty. The interior was predictable; rough wooden tables, a bar of battered zinc, walls stained sepia by decades of tobacco.

She sat by the window and peered through the peeling paint on the dirty glass. She checked her watch. Five-to-nine. Any time now. She ordered some coffee.

Maurice Hammond was three minutes late, according to the schedule that Rosie had given her on the flight from Austria. Each morning he walked from Pension Sylbert, just off avenue Bosquet, to the same café on rue Cler for breakfast, entering at exactly nine o'clock. Stephanie had asked Rosie how she knew this.

'He told me once. Every time he's in Paris, it's the same ritual. Same place to stay, same place for breakfast.'

He looked older than in the photograph. Shorter, too, with a patrician nose over a full moustache. He was hampered by a limp – the right knee, perhaps, or even the hip – and was wearing a suit that was too big for him. Chalk-stripe, double-breasted and slightly shabby, Stephanie guessed it had fitted neatly before age had reduced him.

He took a table on the far side of the café and spoke to the waiter in fluent, elegant French.

Stephanie hadn't decided where to kill him. Her initial inclination had been to shoot him in his room at the Pension Sylbert. Then she realized that she wanted to see him first. To see exactly what a friend of Alexander's might look like. During the atrophied years of Magenta House, there had never been so much as a whisper concerning Alexander's personal life. The idea that he might have had friends, or enjoyed books, or opera, or a glass of wine – anything, in fact, that humanized him – had seemed scorchingly perverse.

So she'd settled for Café Bleu. Her curiosity satisfied, there would be plenty of easy opportunities. Perhaps even in the café itself. Or out on the street. She wasn't worried about witnesses. She knew how to melt into the fabric of a city better than anyone. Within an hour, a physical description would be out of date.

She went through the two papers she'd brought with her, *Le Figaro* and *Libération*, and found her death reported in both. The article in *Libération* mentioned a possible recent sighting: *There are unconfirmed reports that Reuter was in Paris late last year. An unnamed witness claims to have seen her leaving the Four Seasons George V with another woman.*

And so it begins, Stephanie thought. The unconfirmed report would, in time, be confirmed. Soon after, the film footage would seep into the public domain and Anders Brand's posthumous disgrace would be complete.

* * *

Slowly, I realize that I'm not going to kill him. Or even question him. Through the early hours of this morning I went over all the things I thought I might say to him before I pulled the trigger. There would have been outrage, naturally. And accusations of betrayal, bloodied hands, ethical bankruptcy. All the tools of Petra's trade, in fact. But now the moment is here, I find I really can't bring myself to do it.

For one thing, killing Maurice Hammond would drag me back into the realm of Magenta House and that's something I'm not going to allow. They can do their own dirty work. Much as I like Rosie, she tossed Hammond to me as cheaply as a waiter's tip.

I don't take any comfort from the fact that he'll die in London next week. I can't even feel particularly hostile towards him despite what he's caused me. It doesn't even bother me that this man was a friend of Alexander's. I simply don't care any more. Not about him. Not about them.

The newspapers are right. Petra Reuter really is dead. I've seen it in print. Now I know it's true. I'm Stephanie Patrick. Whatever I do now, I do in my own name.

At her apartment on avenue Foch, Scheherazade Zahani took Newman by the arm and steered him towards the armchair next to hers, leaving Gordon Wiley to occupy a nineteenth-century sofa upholstered in cream and gold silk. Newman remembered the salon. The only changes he could see were on the walls; the two Jan van Eyck canvases that had hung opposite the French windows had been replaced by a religious portrait by Bernard van Orley and a painted panel depicting the crucifixion by Gerard David.

There were four other men in the room. The one standing beside Zahani's chair was Balthazar Karyo, her lawyer. In New York he'd been known as the Brute in the Suit; short silver hair, a thirty-year-old stud scar running from forehead to jawbone, a thick nose that carried three obvious breaks, but impeccably dressed. Newman and Karyo had always got on but neither betrayed this to the room. Newman looked at the three men behind Gordon Wiley. One of them would be a lawyer, perhaps even two. But he was certain that at least one would be security. Looking at the trio, it was impossible to separate them.

Wiley said, 'I still don't understand how you got involved in all this.'

Newman said, 'It's like that old blues line: if it wasn't for bad luck I'd have no luck at all.'

'I guess you probably think you know her pretty well by now.'

'I'm here to make a deal. Nothing else.'

'Come on. What do you think's going to happen? You cut the deal for her, then what? The two of you ride off into the sunset? You both live happily ever after?'

'I'm only here to make sure there *is* an after.'

'She'll cut you loose.'

'Doesn't matter.'

'She could kill you.'

'I doubt it. She's already had a lot of chances.'

'You were useful to her. But once she has her deal, what more can you offer her?'

'That's not really your business, is it?'

'No. It's yours. And you should be thinking about that.'

'And you should be thinking about protecting what you have,' Newman said. 'You gambled and lost. But she's offering you a way out. You should be grateful that it's come to this.'

'Don't be naïve.'

'You're the one being naïve.'

'Have you any idea who you're dealing with, Newman? Do you know what she's done? I've seen her record. Dead bodies on four continents. Terrorism, contract killing, it's a hell of a picture.'

'You've got what you want. She's in no mood to take this further. She wants a new life. A quiet life. There's no reason for her to cause you trouble. As long as you don't cause her any.'

'What is this? Stockholm Syndrome? Suddenly you're Patti Hearst?'

'I don't understand your reluctance, Mr Wiley.'

'Then I'll explain it to you: she's loose.'

'I'm sorry?'

'A loose end and a loose cannon. And that's not a good combination.'

'You're wrong. But she could be both, if you press her hard enough.'

'Where the hell is she?'

593

'Out there. Waiting.'

'You don't owe her anything, Newman. She kidnapped you. Or have you forgotten that already?'

'I'm under no illusions.'

'Then be smart. Do the right thing. I don't care if the two of you have something going on but she's a terrorist, for God's sake. An assassin.'

'She's in business, Mr Wiley. Just like you. Give her what she wants. You'll regret it if you don't.'

Wiley looked across at Zahani. 'Sherry, talk to him, will you? Tell him.'

She looked at Newman first, then shook her head. 'No, Gordon. Robert's right. You gambled and lost. With other people's money. *My* money.'

'*Lost?* What are you talking about?'

Newman said, 'You don't get it, do you? If she wants to, she'll destroy you. All of you. One by one.'

'Oh, come on. *Please*. I don't have to listen to this melodramatic bullshit.'

'I'm afraid you do,' Scheherazade Zahani insisted. 'This has gone on far too long. Let's end it here, Gordon. All she wants is to be left alone. She's happy for the world to know that Petra Reuter is dead. She just doesn't want to be dead herself. That's not so unreasonable, is it? Let's make a deal with her. We can't afford not to.'

Avenue Kléber, 11:42.

Gordon Wiley let himself into the corporate apartment, a penthouse above Amsterdam Europe's

594

head office. He entered the study. Sensors triggered the lights, casting amber pools on to a vast Bokhara silk carpet.

He sat at his desk and called his secretary, two floors below, to tell her that he would remain in the apartment until one-thirty, when he was due to depart for La Défense. After the Butterfly signing he intended to take the Gulfstream back to Washington. She said she'd make the necessary arrangements. Wiley thanked her and replaced the handset. Agitated, he took a deep breath and tilted back in the chair. Which was when he realized that he was not alone.

Silhouetted against the net curtains covering the French windows was a solitary figure with a gun. The curtains billowed on the breeze. One of the windows on to the balcony was ajar.

He didn't even raise his voice when he said, 'How'd you get in here?'

'Your security's average from the street up. From the roof down, it's a joke.'

Wiley looked incredulous. 'You climbed?'

'I've been a climber all my life. I'll bet that isn't in any file you've seen.'

'How did you know I'd come back here?'

'You have to collect the disk.'

'How did you know *that*?'

Stern had known.

Stephanie said, 'You don't know anything about me, do you?'

'Frankly, I feel I know too much.'

'You know nothing. Everything you've heard is a lie.'

His eyes were drawn to the tip of the silencer. 'What do you want? You already have your deal. Or haven't you heard?'

'That's not why I'm here.'

'Anything happens to me, you can kiss it goodbye.'

'I'm not here to kill you,' she said. 'But if I have to, I will.'

He nodded, one part reassured, the other curious. 'So why *are* you here?'

'First things first. I want the film from the George V.'

She detected the slight change in his expression, the subtle shift in body-language. 'Right,' he said, drawing the word into a phrase, playing for time.

'The *original* disk,' she added.

'I'm sure we can come to an arrangement and . . .'

'I'm sure we can. Give it to me and I won't kill you.'

'It's not here.'

Stephanie raised the SIG-Sauer P226. 'Give me the disk.'

'I can get it for you later.'

'It's in the safe. The safe that's governed by a biometric security system that requires an iris scan. The safe that's behind the plasma screen in the wall.'

Wiley stared at her blankly.

Stephanie said, 'I'm not leaving empty-handed. It's up to you.'

'Okay. But before we do this can I say something?'

'If you keep it short.'

'We can still make a deal. A *solid* deal.'

'I don't want your money. I want the disk. That's all.'

He didn't say anything but she saw signs of the internal struggle. The film on the disk was the key to the confidence of his co-signatories. Without the disk, Brand remained a fine man. A man whose legacy would still command influence. Nothing hardened a good reputation better than a tragic death.

She headed off Wiley's calculations at the pass. 'You only have one choice if you want to live: to give it to me. If it's really worth dying for just say so and we'll move swiftly along.'

'You don't honestly think you can sabotage this deal once you have it, do you?'

'I don't care. Either it fails or it doesn't. Makes no difference to me.'

'What would make a difference?'

'Give me the disk, Wiley.'

The plasma screen was built into the wall on the opposite side of the room to the desk. The glass surface ran flush to the paint. There'd been no give when she pressed it and no way of drawing it forward. She'd checked earlier but only out of curiosity; Stern had provided her with the information she needed.

She said. 'Go ahead. Enter the code on the desktop.'

Wiley tapped a sequence on the keyboard. Stephanie watched the plasma screen retract two centimetres into the wall then vanish upwards in total silence. A rectangle came forward to take its place, settling in perfect position. At its centre was the safe door. Above and below it, and on either side, were the matt black panels of the biometric security system.

Stephanie said, 'You know it really doesn't bother me that people like you are so obsessed with money. I don't care what you're worth. It's not what you've got that matters, it's what you do. You were already rich, you and your organization. You never *needed* this deal. Take it from someone who knows something about killing for money, Mr Wiley, I recognize you.'

'You don't honestly believe that, do you? That Iraq was some kind of commercial venture.'

'Iraq was a *joint* venture. Commercial *and* political. Both interests dovetailing, both interests so inextricably interwoven that it's probably impossible to separate them.'

'Bullshit.'

'Really? Who are your investors, Mr Wiley? What proportion of your private equity comes from Saudi Arabia? What proportion from the Arab peninsula or the Middle East in general?'

'What *is* your point?'

'That it's a wonderful deal for those on the inside. Profits from increased oil revenues subsidized by the US taxpayer. Or else profits from increased arms sales, also subsidized by the US taxpayer. How do you suppose they'll feel – the autoplant worker in Detroit, the farmer in Kansas – when they learn that chunks of their tax bill are going directly into the pockets of billionaire Saudi princes?'

Wiley chuckled unconvincingly. 'I've got to hand it to you. You sure know how to tell a story. Very imaginative. Very *entertaining*. And everyone loves a good conspiracy theory. Of course, it's not true. But what's the point in denying it? You've already made up your mind, I can see that.'

'Open the safe.'

Wiley rose from his chair and crossed the carpet. He stood in front of the safe, half a metre from the wall. There were no vox instructions, no lights, no keypad. The safe door had no handle. But behind the black panel above the door an iris scan was taking place. When it was complete, there was a whisper as the seals retracted. The safe door withdrew five millimetres then slid down, disappearing into the gleaming steel housing. Tiny internal lights illuminated the contents; documents, three rolls of undeveloped film, photographic negatives, bearer bonds. The DVD was in a dark blue plastic case. Beyond it was a small gun. A Polish P-64.

Wiley knew that she couldn't see the gun. He reached inside. His fingers hovered over the disk – he closed his eyes for a moment, almost in prayer – then touched the P-64. *Don't be an idiot. It's not worth it.* Breathing hard, he picked up the disk instead and turned around slowly.

Stephanie took the disk. 'Just out of interest, how much profit has to be at stake before it's worth killing someone? And does it matter who that person is? I mean, Brand was famous. Well respected. What was he worth? Three nobodies? Ten? A hundred?'

'Very clever.'

'I'm serious. There has to be a dollar amount. I don't think you'd have anybody killed for ten dollars of profit. But for ten billion? Recent history shows you'll kill for a lot less. So where does it start? What's the figure that makes the first body worthwhile?'

'You should know. You're the expert.'

'Okay. If that's the way you want to play it. Yusuf Aziz Khan, former director of Pakistan's ISI: one million two hundred and fifty thousand dollars. They offered one, I asked for one point five, we settled in between. Eddie Sullivan, founder of ProActive Solutions, killed this month in Turkmenistan on behalf of the Russian government, three-quarters of a million. Your turn.'

Wiley was dumbstruck.

'*Your turn*,' Stephanie insisted.

But he couldn't bring himself to. Instead, he

fumbled for an alternative. 'How much would it cost me to buy back that disk from you?'

Despite herself, Stephanie smiled. How typical of him; money, the only language a man like Wiley truly understood.

'You tell me,' she said. 'What's it worth? And before you answer, bear this in mind: if you try to take me for an idiot, it'll hurt.'

Wiley took his time over a deep breath. 'Ten.'

'Ten what?'

'Ten million US. Cash. Or any way you want it.'

'The same as the contract on me? I can see the symmetry but we're a little beyond that, don't you think? What about the three or four billion of pure profit you're going to make from Butterfly? What about the knock-on contracts? All with a protected profit margin built in. How much are we talking about? Ten billion? Fifteen?'

'You're way wide of the mark.'

'You won't be in the queue for food vouchers.'

'Twenty million.'

She shook her head in contempt. 'Not even close.'

Wiley tried to muster some defiance. 'Okay. You pick a number.'

'Five-three-one-four-two.'

'*What?*'

'That's the number. Five-three-one-four-two.'

'What are you talking about?'

'Do you know who Jacob Furst was?'

'No. Never heard of him.'

'He died here in Paris eleven days ago. The same day as the Sentier bomb. Peltor killed him. And his wife, Miriam. Peltor used them to lure me to Paris, then murdered them. Jacob was in his late eighties. He survived Auschwitz; 53142 was the number tattooed on his wrist. That's why I'm here.'

Wiley felt the remains of his hope evaporate like dew in the desert.

'If you kill me, they'll come after you.'

Stephanie felt nothing at all and it showed. 'I know.'

He panicked and did the first thing to come to mind. The *only* thing to come to mind. He spun round and reached inside the safe for the P-64. But he didn't even manage to touch it.

The bullet entered through the right shoulder-blade and punched him against the wall. Then he pitched backwards and fell, hitting the carpet with a grunt.

Stephanie stood over him. Entirely predictable, she thought. A man whose element of surprise was confined to his choice of tie. She raised the gun again.

'*Wait!*' he gasped. 'You said . . .'

'I know what I said. But it's a woman's prerogative to change her mind. That was for me. This one's for Jacob.'

She fired again.

'And this one's for Miriam.'

After the third shot, she dropped the gun beside the body. The SIG-Sauer P226, the weapon of choice for the assassin Petra Reuter.

Five-past-one. Stephanie waited among the ground-floor arcades beneath the beautiful seventeenth-century houses that formed place des Vosges. A brisk breeze blew through the square's perfectly pruned linden trees.

'Hey you.'

He was still wearing the same suit and shirt he'd worn to Grumann Bank on Singerstrasse in Vienna but he'd showered and shaved at the Adlers'.

Stephanie said, 'You scrub up okay.'

'I thought I better make the effort.'

'For Scheherazade?'

'For Wiley.'

They smiled at the lie, then kissed. She held on to him.

'Did you get the disk?' he asked.

'Yes. I got it.'

'How did he take it?'

'Poorly. How did it go with you?'

'There was a lot of noise. But he agreed to the deal. We're in the clear.'

It didn't feel right. Not now. But she knew that in the days to come her head and heart would reconcile. She squeezed him tighter and said, '*You're* in the clear.'

He tensed. 'What do you mean?'

'Wiley's dead.'

He took a step back so that he could look at her. 'How?'

'He went for a gun.'

Newman looked amazed. 'Wiley? A gun? You're kidding.'

She shook her head. 'I told him I wasn't there to kill him. But now I'm not sure that's true. I don't know.'

'Shit. We're screwed.'

'You're not.'

'What are you talking about?'

'You're not going to like this, Robert.'

'Then make it quick.'

'I saw Scheherazade this morning. Before you did. We struck a different deal.'

He frowned at her. 'What deal?'

'You're safe, no matter what.'

'Wait. You went behind my back and . . .'

'Don't be angry. It was the only way.'

But he *was* angry. Justifiably, Stephanie felt. But she knew she'd been right to do it anyway. She threaded her arm through his.

'Come on,' she said. 'It's freezing. Let's walk.'

They strolled along one arcade, then another, past expensive boutiques and chic art galleries. Neither of them said anything for a while.

Stephanie thought of Gordon Wiley and wondered whether she would have shot him had he not gone for the gun. She wasn't sure. She suspected she might have. Which would have made him Stephanie's first victim. As it was, he *had* gone for the gun, so he was Petra's last. In any event, she felt no remorse. It wasn't justice but it was the best she could do for Jacob and Miriam. And the others like them.

'She never mentioned it,' Newman said.

'Of course not. She's a woman of infinite options. That's what you said. Butterfly was only one of them. And not the most attractive, either.'

'What did she tell you?'

'There's another project. No America, no Israel, just as lucrative. It's a new deal, politically and financially. As usual, she's ahead. Butterfly was one step back, this is two steps forward.'

He thought about it for a while, then said, 'Syria?'

Stephanie shook her head. 'China.'

'China?'

'And Saudi Arabia. A different axis altogether. But not a new one.'

'No.'

'I saw the stamps in your passport at your apartment. Shanghai. Beijing.'

He nodded slowly. 'But I never knew *she* was close to Beijing. Do you know what the deal is?'

'She didn't say. But she told me that a Sino-Saudi deal was always going to be more lucrative. She always considered Butterfly expendable.'

'The two deals couldn't coexist?'

'Apparently not.'

His dismay dissolved into a tired smile. 'I don't

know why I'm surprised. After all the years I've known her, I should've guessed.'

'I'm sorry I had to go behind your back. I thought you'd be difficult.'

'I would have been.'

'She still cares for you, Robert.'

'I know. But it's just too complicated.'

'Rather like us, then.'

His nod looked reluctant. 'I guess so.'

'You know it makes sense.'

'Sure. It just doesn't feel like it.'

'Wiley's death actually makes it easier. It takes away the element of choice.'

'Easier for me. Not for you.'

Stephanie shook her head. 'Easier for me too, Robert. I'm a mess. I don't know who I am any more. Or who I'm going to be. I need a clean break.'

'From me?'

'From Petra. From the present, from the past.'

'What will you do?'

'What I always do. Run.'

They walked diagonally across the square past mothers and children, past lovers, past a blind man with a tin cup. Despite the bitter cold an artist was painting a watercolour; steep slate roofs, ornate brickwork, tall dormer-windows.

Newman said, 'I often wonder whether Rachel and I would have made it in the real world. In some ways, it was easy for us. The normal rules never applied.'

Stephanie understood. 'You'd have made it. Don't compare us, Robert. I'm not worth it. She was special.'

'But you're . . .'

'No, I'm not. Whatever it was you were going to say, I'm just not.'

They stopped and turned to one another.

'Are you okay?'

He nodded. 'I'm a whole lot better than I was when I walked into the bar at the Lancaster.'

'What will you do now?'

'The same as you. A clean break from the past.'

She smiled a little sadly. 'I should go.'

'If you ever need anything from me, don't hesitate. Not for a second.'

'I won't. I promise.'

'Look after yourself, Stephanie.'

She kissed him. 'You too.'

'When you find out who you really are, give me a call if you ever pass through Paris. I'd be interested to meet her.'

Early February

When she woke up the aircraft was somewhere over the Andaman Sea. She watched twenty minutes of *The Third Man* on one of the movie channels. A member of the cabin crew brought her a cup of coffee.

She read again Maurice Hammond's obituary from a recent edition of *The Times*. All the right ticks in all the right boxes; the right school, the right university, the intelligence service. A witty raconteur, a keen Anglican, a man of integrity. It didn't say how he'd died. That had been reported in the deaths column of a previous edition; at home, peacefully in his sleep.

Pure Magenta House: no trace, the calling-card of the Ether Division.

British Airways flight BA015 began its descent for Singapore. Stephanie peered out of the window. Early evening dropped a deep gold haze over the oil tankers clogging the Strait of Malacca.

She'd destroyed the disk in Paris. Anders Brand

remained the man he'd always appeared to be. Julia remained anonymous, as she deserved to be. As for Petra Reuter, there was only confusion. There'd been a body in Vienna yet twenty-four hours later, in Paris, the killing of Gordon Wiley had appeared to bear her signature.

She thought of Leonid Golitsyn. *Golitsyn floats above the world.* That was what Stern had said of him. And Stern was the one who'd provided Stephanie with the knowledge she'd needed. In Vienna, and then again in Paris, hours before the end, Stern had come through for her.

The flight touched down just before six. She had two hours on the ground before the second leg for Sydney. Yet again, she was a woman in transit. From one place to another. From one identity to another. From a congested past to an empty future. In that sense, Australia seemed a perfect starting point. Later, who could say? Perhaps even the house in the South of France that Albert Eichner had offered to buy for her.

Inside the cool, cavernous terminal at Changi airport she settled in front of a computer terminal, checked for messages – there were none – then sent one of her own to Stern.

> Thank you for Paris. Thank you for everything. I have only one more thing to ask. Diamonds or bread?

She cruised the terminal for an hour and a half, drank some tea, browsed the shops, stretched her legs. Everything had revolved around Golitsyn, she now realized. But Golitsyn wasn't the answer.

He was the missing link to the answer.

Why shouldn't Stern be a woman? And why not an old woman? In the information business there was no substitute for experience. That had been true for Golitsyn; his access had been legendary. Natalya Ginzburg had said so herself. A courier between Washington and Moscow in the old days. A man who'd continued to float above the world, no matter what the prevailing political climate. Just as she and her husband had, until his untimely death. But Natalya Ginzburg and Golitsyn had been friends long before that. Ever since childhood.

Golitsyn was connected to everyone. And she was Golitsyn's closest confidante. The one he whispered to the morning he died. The one who knew where the film was. Who knew the location of the safe in the penthouse on avenue Kléber. Who knew which security features protected the safe and who knew the security features protecting the building. Stern had suggested a rooftop entry. Stern had known it would be okay. Because Golitsyn had known.

A soft female voice echoed in the terminal. The final call for BA015 to Sydney. Stephanie checked her watch. Seven-forty, fifteen minutes until departure. She returned to the computer terminal and accessed her messages again.

Still nothing.

Perhaps she'd made a mistake. Yet in her heart she knew she hadn't. Golitsyn and Brand had not been an alliance of two; they'd been two parts of an alliance of three. Natalya Ginzburg had known exactly what was going on. Which was why, as Stern, she'd directed Stephanie to Golitsyn. She'd wanted to save her friend and had hoped that her favourite client would do it.

Another final call. Less than ten minutes to go.

Stephanie thought about place Vendôme. Ginzburg's curiosity made sense now. *I never thought I would actually meet you.* That was what she'd said. Stephanie had asked her if she knew who she was. *Who you are and what you are.*

Two days later, when she'd returned to place Vendôme to see Ginzburg again, the conversation had concluded in the Zil limousine that Brezhnev had given to her husband. And it had been during that ride that Ginzburg had revealed to Stephanie the details of Butterfly that Golitsyn had disclosed to her. She'd also mentioned the contract on her – five million dollars, soon to rise to ten – and had urged Stephanie to run. It made sense now. Ginzburg had tried to protect her. Or, seen from a parallax view, Stern had tried to protect Petra Reuter.

Four words appeared to fill in the blank spaces.

> Only we know which.

Stephanie nodded. The secret joke that Natalya Ginzburg had shared with Leonid Golitsyn was the confirmation Stephanie had wanted. Natalya Ginzburg was Stern.

Stephanie was the last to board the aircraft. She

settled back into seat 3K. The aircraft doors closed. The 747 rolled back from the stand.

She felt truly liberated and immediately thought of Julia. This was her future, not Stephanie's. The one-way ticket, the promise of a future cleansed of the past, the intoxicating possibilities ahead.

The chance to begin again.

ACKNOWLEDGEMENTS

I'd like to thank the following people for their help: in Paris, Carmela Uranga; in Brussels, Gérard de la Vallée Poussin; in London, Dominic Armstrong.

I'd also like to thank my agent, Toby Eady, and those who work with him, as well as Susan Watt, my editor, and those who work with her.

Finally, I'd like to thank my wife, Isabelle, for her continued love, support and patience.